ENEMY WITHIN THE GATES

RICHARD DRUMMER

For Shirley

For my parents, Buzz and Marilyn, who always offered their support and the freedom to find my own direction. There are no greater gifts you could have given.

Miss you.

1

35°47'35"N 115°37'35"W

Vindication. Redemption. The interview of a lifetime. The thoughts echoed in Derek Waltstein's mind as he drove through the dead calm of an arid Nevada desert night, the headlamps illuminating a narrow path of asphalt that lay out before him like a winding gray snake. Cruising through the pre-dawn darkness, he lit another cigarette off the short stub of the last, which he casually flicked out the open window.

He watched through the side mirror as the glowing embers of the discarded butt flared and danced in the turbulent wake. The inrush of nicotine that usually helped calm his frayed nerves was having no effect. Waltstein was wired to the bone, and chain-smoking an entire carton of Marlboros would do nothing to knock this edge off. His fingers fidgeted nervously on the steering wheel as he accepted the limitation. He would proceed the best he could.

The GPS had long ago indicated an empty gap between the last point of civilization and his destination, which was now coming into view on the center display. Sky Ranch Estates was considered a public airport but constructed to be a private community with a runway through its center as the main selling point and theme of interest. It performed the intended function, but only at a minimum. The expected steady stream of wealthy investors with private aircraft and ties to Las Vegas never materialized. Sometimes, even a sure thing could fizzle. Waltstein thought again about the information he had downloaded about the small airport, remembering the line, 'Occasional livestock on and in the vicinity of aircraft movement areas.' Great, he thought, make a perfect landing in the middle of the desert and run into a fucking bull.

He continued watching the screen as the void between his car and the destination narrowed. Up ahead, he could now make out the dim glow of street lamps illuminating the outline of an old diner. He smiled nervously, thinking again of the potential prize of this late-night rendezvous; vindication, redemption, the interview of a lifetime—a meeting with the man that speaks for the most deadly terrorist in the world.

A flurry of emotions erupted, from confidence to elation, to fear, then back around again. Waltstein fought harder to rein in control. There was so much riding on this chance meeting that it excited him to extremes yet scared him shitless. This one encounter would either lift him back within the ranks of the best of his fellow journalists or leave him trampled in the dust, no better off than where he had been just a few short months ago. In a flash of uncertainty, he asked himself again whether professional salvation was worth the cost of his life. Could he take the man he was coming to meet at his word? He recalled the stories about the thousands of bodies buried and silent in this organization's wake and admitted the answer was an emphatic no.

He was well aware that he was putting himself in harm's way, but logic suggested you would not lure one washed-up, overfed reporter into the deep, dark desert simply to kill him. Common sense may be screaming to stay the hell away, but the law of averages told him it was worth the risk.

Waltstein recalled how this impromptu meeting with the mysterious Mr. Smith had dropped in his lap the night before when an anonymous call had come into the news center. He was lucky enough to be within earshot of the receptionist who fielded the call and requested she transfer it to his line. After a short moment of listening, however, he was ready to dismiss the caller as just another radial extremist espousing empty threats. That all changed when the man revealed he represented the leader of the Islamic group, OASIS. This fearsome organization posed the largest threat to peace for the Middle East in all of its violent history.

OASIS had formed from the unprecedented alignment of three previously disjointed, warring factions. Little was known about the group so far. The caller claimed to have a video of their leader announcing his intentions to the world. Sure, it could still be bullshit, but Waltstein's instincts willed him forward like a psychic magnetism. His inner senses were uncannily accurate when he trusted them, and he'd learned the hard way of the consequences for ignoring that internal compass.

Six years earlier, Waltstein was following a bombshell story involving a young college coed who accused members of the basketball team of rape. According to her statement, she accompanied friends to a frat house party and suspected the drink she was nursing all evening was drugged. She awoke hours later in an upstairs bedroom, naked and bruised. Her identity was withheld pending toxicology results and arraignment of the accused. But Waltstein had seen the police report and leaked her name to his network. By that evening, her face was displayed on almost every lead story. Waltstein was riding high as the one reporter bold enough to publish the truth about the girl who cried wolf. The girl, however, could not cope with the shame and accusatory slurs. She climbed into a bathtub and slit her wrists.

Days after her body was discovered, the results of her blood tests revealed high levels of Rohypnol, a crude and dangerous date rape drug, thereby validating her initial assertions. DNA testing also confirmed the identity of her assailants.

The networks that had refused to reveal the young woman's identity were the first to point to Waltstein as the heartless reporter who had shamed an innocent girl into taking her own life.

Waltstein lost his job, then spent years freelancing for grocery store tabloids hoping for an opportunity to redeem himself, praying for a night like tonight. Everyone should be allowed to make a mistake, he thought. But every bell and whistle in the back of his brain had screamed alarms that night as he passed on the girl's identity. He chose to ignore his gut instincts, and for that, he paid a steep price. He assured himself that would never happen again as he pulled into the parking lot of the old silver-skinned Skyway Diner. Smack dab in the middle of nowhere.

He went through the mental checklist he had prepared for the meeting. Cover your back, watch for anyone or anything out of the ordinary, follow your gut, and use your head. Heeding his own warning, he circled the diner, scoping out the shadowy backlot for potential threats. Satisfied, he drove back around and parked in front. An ancient neon OPEN sign above the front door buzzed as it flashed only three of the letters. The combined light from the sign and an overhead street lamp bathed his car in a sickly greenish-red hue.

There was only one other vehicle in the potholed dirt lot, an old sun-bleached VW beetle. He assumed it belonged to the cook or the waitress, or both, and concluded that Smith had not yet arrived. He decided to use the time to review his notes once again, slipping them from his satchel. The top page was a bullet list marked in blue highlighter. At the bottom, he had scribbled; no story is worth your life. He nodded silently, understanding that with every cutting-edge news story comes a risk with telling it. He would rely on every journalistic skill he'd developed over his fifteen-year career. Gather all the facts, document the findings, then present them in a compelling bulletproof format. There could be no loose ends to come back and bite him in the ass. Nothing to leave the reader wondering if the facts had been investigated thoroughly or at all.

Although he was more of a messenger than a reporter tonight, there would be a story to tell. When the details of this hastily arranged rendezvous were revealed, people would clamor to hear more. What could he tell them about the mysterious and elusive Mr. Smith? And what was his connection to the man now perceived to be the most dangerous person in the world? Only Waltstein could answer these questions. He was already formulating how and when to release the information. If played right, he could share detail after detail and still have enough in reserve to write an in-depth book documenting this mysterious meeting. He smiled, envisioning television interviews and a lengthy book tour. He straightened in his seat and flattened the wrinkles in his navy blazer, brushing away a sprinkling of donut crumbs. A better diet and a few trips to the gym would be needed to knock off the extra weight he now carried.

A cold wave of reality cut through his thoughts. "Getting a little ahead of myself," he mumbled aloud. He still had to interview the spokesman for a terrorist—a man who may well be versed at ending lives himself.

He sat back and silently read off the rest of his pregame strategy; I have to be the one controlling the interview. I have a list of questions needing answers. He called me, not the other way around. This man has something to say, but he needs me to express it and share the story with the world.

Waltstein struggled to pump up his courage but could still hear this man speaking *at* him, speaking *down* to him. The truth was, his brief conversation with the mystery messenger had rattled him to the core. Even worse, his role had been reduced to that of listener and documenter only. At one point, he had asked the caller a question and was admonished for interrupting. Although Smith never raised his voice, he articulated himself with a condescending overtone. His smooth, caustic words belittled this reporter into feeling like a dog being scolded for piddling on a new carpet. If he didn't control this interview from the onset, then his role would be further reduced to nothing more than a useful idiot.

"The biggest story of my life is on the other side of that door," Waltstein said aloud. He gathered his papers and slid them back into the weathered brown satchel. The same one he had carried since beginning his journalism career. He hoped it brought him luck tonight. In the field, luck was always a welcome wingman, but he would rely more on his well-honed skill set while making the most of this chance encounter.

Chance encounters, he mused. Tonight's meeting was the second of two such fortuitous events. The first had led to his rescue from The National Chronicle, a grocery store rag tabloid where he had labored for three years. He thought back to that attractive brunette in a Starbucks line. Women like that never gave Waltstein a second glance. But this one happened to be a head hunter for a fledgling network that, at the time, was rumbling just under the radar. She casually glanced his way and recognized him from his Chronicle ID badge and lit up like he was Brad Pitt. A cup of coffee and an exchange of business cards led to an interview with business mogul Malcolm LeClair. He explained to Waltstein that, despite past missteps, his investigative skill set was precisely what the new network needed. He left LeClair's office that day with a new job at Global Access Media and a new lease on life.

Waltstein was still ten minutes early when he pulled open the weathered diner door. He scanned his surroundings and selected the optimum seat to observe the road outside for Mr. Smith's arrival. He chose the worn red vinyl booth furthest from the door and sat with his back to the wall. A lone, sleep-deprived waitress made her way over with a cup and a coffee pot, which he gladly accepted. He sipped the strong brew while watching the road through a large, grease-streaked window. A streetlamp over the nearby intersection cut a conical tube of illumination on the old blacktop's worn white stripes. He was counting the bullet holes in a stop sign when a muted voice called out from behind.

"Mr. Waltstein."

Waltstein convulsed in his seat and spun to confront the source of the surprise greeting. Standing in the doorway of the restroom stood a very plain-looking man in a generic brown leather jacket. A black beret covered much of his dark hair. Sinister brown eyes stared at him, displaying no emotion. Before Waltstein could respond, the man slid into the opposite side of the booth and folded his hands on the table. Waltstein cursed to himself. He had assumed that no other cars outside meant that Smith had not yet arrived. How the hell had he gotten here? That might have been why the man had insisted on a desolate location near an airstrip. He must have flown in.

Working to shake off the effects of the uncomfortable introduction, Waltstein said, "Mr. Smith, I presume?"

The man nodded acknowledgment with an expression as blank as he imagined a human was capable of. All his facial muscles appeared to be disconnected, non-functional, off-line.

"That is correct," he said. "I am known in many places, by many names. For our purposes, Mr. Smith will suffice. Do you understand why you are here?"

Waltstein tried to place the accent but couldn't. It sounded as much Middle Eastern as European. A strange mix, he thought. Almost as though someone had thrown the accents of six countries in a blender, then served them on an unsalted cracker. There was little inflection. The timbre of his voice was indistinguishable from thousands of others. This man could likely roam the earth without ever being noticed for any outstanding characteristics. He was the perfect agent to deliver this message, a nearly invisible man.

"You have something you wish to share with me?" Waltstein asked, apprehension clawing within him like a deep-seated itch.

The man blinked in slow motion, his eyes narrowing, the first show that those muscles even worked. "You flatter yourself. I wish to share a message with the world, and you are nothing more than the chosen courier."

The statement further deflated Waltstein's ego, but he'd expected as much. He would endure more of the same before he got what he had come for tonight.

"I bring you the words of our supreme leader, Sirhan Abbas," he continued. "In return, you will assure me that his message will be broadcast by your station at 10:00 pm eastern time on February tenth."

Smith reached into his pocket and retrieved a small device, then held it up for Waltstein to see. It took the reporter a moment to realize it was a memory stick, but unlike any he had ever seen. It was a large, thick rectangle, colored a deep crimson, and housed in a clear case with no markings.

Smith set the device on the table and slid it toward Waltstein, who reached for it.

"I can get this played," Waltstein said. "That won't be a problem. I can't guarantee it will be at exactly the time you're asking."

A fist slammed down onto Waltstein's fingers and held with the pressure of a steel press.

Smith leaned forward until his face was inches away from Waltstein's. He lowered his head. Dark eyes glared up from beneath thick brows, only now revealing a hint of the fire simmering beneath the surface. In a hushed but commanding voice, he said, "I did not ask you to share this when it was convenient." His laser-like glare felt as though it could bore holes through Waltstein's skull. His fist pressed even harder into Waltstein's hand. "You agreed to come here knowing exactly who I am. You assured me that you had the connections and power at your network to broadcast our message." He looked down at the USB stick, then back to Waltstein, his eyes narrowed with a menacing scowl. "Now take this device and do as you have been instructed. Do not test my patience, little man."

Waltstein dared not move, concentrating all his might on masking his fear. His fight or flight reflex was overloading, demanding action, willing him to bolt out of his seat and run, never looking back. He fought the urge and held himself in place, knowing he was losing the upper hand of the situation.

Christ, who was he fooling? He never had control, never stood a chance against this man. So this was it, then? Take a fucking memory stick and leave with his tail between his legs? No! Hell, no!

He wrestled his fear into a wave of boiling anger. No, goddamn it, a voice screamed from deep inside, I'm not done here. Now it's my turn!

"What is your connection to Sirhan Abbas?"

Smith released Waltstein's hand and settled back in his seat. He folded his arms with a contemptuous grin as though amused by this senseless American who dared to question him further. He looked away a moment before returning his gaze on Waltstein, his expression once again a blank slate. "I live to serve Abbas," he answered with a discomforting calmness. "I do as commanded for the glory of this holiest of celebrations."

"What celebration is that?"

"The dawn that approaches when everything the sun touches will belong to the true followers of Allah."

Waltstein mulled his words over, searching for the right follow-up question to keep the information coming. "Can you tell me where this celebration will be taking place? Is there a specific country in the Middle East that—"

"Ignorant little man," Smith scoffed, "Allah will take from those deemed unworthy and give to those who fight in his name."

"Yeah, I get that. There's going to be a fight. But against who? And what exactly will belong to the true followers?"

Smith now understood an earlier observation made by a brother in arms who had spent considerable time in this country. He had concluded it was possible to attend some of the finest universities the United States had to offer and still come out stupid. He smiled at the irony of his old friend's statement.

"To quote some of your own vernacular, Mr. Waltstein, what part of 'everything the sun touches,' did you not understand?"

Waltstein felt a lump form in his throat and nearly gagged. Smith could not be serious. He wasn't talking about a few disputed territories or border skirmishes in the Middle East. This was about world conquest! He had heard extremist threats before, but this one? No way! Off the charts. All the same, he could not bring such an unsubstantiated boast like that back to the newsroom without more information. He needed details about this man's armies, locations, maybe even a filmed interview with the leader himself. So far, he didn't have enough to write more than a quarter page, even if he stretched the hell out of it. He had to keep it together and get more out of Smith, or this was all for nothing. Just keep it rolling, he thought.

"Tell me…um, tell me about Sirhan Abbas."

"All you need to know is on that device. There is nothing further to be said."

Waltstein sensed the man's agitation as his thin veil of calm demeanor shrank. He had no choice but to push on. There would be no bright tomorrow without this story. He recalled some of the sketchy details he had heard about the mysterious leader, then drummed up every remaining ounce of confidence. He blurted out, "Sirhan Abbas has called for mass beheadings of Christians in Afghanistan. What man of peace would approve such despicable acts as—"

"We are not men of peace," Smith shot back. "We are men of action! We are the soldiers of Allah! We stand on the mountain top, looking down at a world that we will soon control. We will be your lords. You will accept our law, our God, and our way of life."

The waitress looked up lazily from the other end of the diner, then returned her attention to a crossword puzzle book.

Smith regained his composure and added, "This should be very simple, even for you. You will accept our demands, or you will meet your death at our hands."

Waltstein's face turned ashen, but his mental motor remained in overdrive. He pushed forward, aware only that he feared going back to LA empty-handed even more than he feared this crazy son of a bitch.

"The president recently stated he would not consider relations with OASIS until its human rights violations are addressed. Do you believe Sirhan Abbas will comply?"

Smith's left hand shot across the booth and grabbed Waltstein by the throat. His fingers wrapped around Waltstein's windpipe and pulled him forward. The right hand moved down into his jacket and slid out a pistol with a short silencer. He jammed the barrel into the center of the shocked reporter's chest. "You just do not know when to shut that big mouth of yours, Mr. Waltstein. Someday it may cost you your life." He paused, then asked, "Is this the day?"

Waltstein struggled for breath through the vice-like grip on his throat. A twinkling blackness appeared in the corners of his vision. He was within seconds of losing consciousness. His heart boomed in his chest like a cannon as adrenalin flooded into his bloodstream. His entire body convulsed and trembled. His bladder loosened. He realized now the terrible mistake in coming here. He was utterly at Smith's mercy, and the man was not the merciful type. He had failed. He now understood the futility, the folly in expecting a positive outcome from meeting with such an evil man. All hope of pursuing the epic story was now lost. It no longer mattered. Surviving this ordeal was all that did.

Smith pushed the pistol silencer harder into Waltstein's chest. "I need your undivided attention. Do I have it?" His nails dug into the skin of Waltstein's throat. "Do I have it?"

Waltstein managed a nod.

"Good. You will announce to the world that you have this video and will broadcast it in its entirety on the date I have given. Until then, no one is to have access. No one. You will not plug this in or reveal its contents before the broadcast. Do not even remove it from its case until it is time. We will know, Mr. Waltstein. We will know if you do. Nod if you understand and accept what I have told you. Because that is the only way that you walk out of here with it in your possession. In fact," Smith brought his face even closer and whispered, "that is the only way you walk out of here at all."

2

Guantanamo Bay, Cuba

Only six inmates remained at the military prison at Guantanamo Bay since its official closure. The facility had become less functional as a penitentiary for combatants of the United States and more of a symbol of imperialistic injustice. Although much of the valuable intel gleaned from its occupants had saved the country from further catastrophic attacks, it was the abuse of power and the deplorable reputation on human rights that had finally ended the way *business* was conducted. That reputation was not undeserved.

Some of the most evil beasts on the planet had been held here, alongside many who were innocent of any crimes. The courts made no distinction and ruled that no one should be imprisoned without due process of the law. The point had been argued unsuccessfully that military combatants from outside the US were not entitled to access the American legal system. The last two presidents had sided with the courts, pushing to forever open its gates and release the remaining prisoners. Upon its closure and transfer of operations, over 700 prisoners were released. It was now an antiquated behemoth with minimal staffing and multiple layers of oversight.

The six that still remained were here only because of their direct involvement in terrorist acts worldwide. A small coalition of victims and anti-terrorism enforcement fought tenaciously to keep them locked away for their crimes. In the end, however, their battle was being lost. These mass murderers would all eventually walk out of this place and pick up their causes where they had left off.

FREEDOM WAS mere days away for prisoner 4135, one of the most notorious this institution had ever detained. His reputation was legendary. And his list of crimes stood as a stark reminder that the man should never again be allowed to see the light of day. Many of the offenses he was suspected of being involved in lacked hard evidence to tie him directly. Much of the Intel proving his guilt had been obtained by less than conventional means. It was therefore inadmissible in court. Military interrogations, abhorred by the world's peace activists, had supplied the links that tied this man to some of the most heinous atrocities ever inflicted against other human beings. For every case that could be proven legally, there were two others where he had been implicated. Prisoner 4135 was complicit in the deaths of thousands of innocent people.

Before being captured, he had orchestrated the destruction of a school in Ghazni, Afghanistan. Two hundred children attending classes that day were blasted into oblivion. He posed as a janitor and set off a series of bombs that leveled the building. Wiping out the seed of your enemy was considered acceptable military tactics. It was also intensely satisfying. Few who opposed his extreme view of victory ever came forward. They were either too afraid to speak against him or already dead.

Prisoner 4135 was accustomed to the daily regimen of this place and his jailers. He found it amusing. They were forced to make his life comfortable while being detained and interrogated. His prayer time was reverently adhered to, as well as the types of food he was fed in accordance with his religious beliefs. He smiled as he finished his breakfast. The people who now controlled this facility made it their cause to ensure he was treated as more of a guest than a military combatant. When the day came, they would be the easiest to defeat and the first to die. Their good intentions would be their undoing.

His handlers approached to escort him to the interrogation room. He rose and walked toward them, leaving his tray behind. Someone else would clean up after him.

"I see you have more time to waste with your pointless questions," he said with sarcastic defiance.

"Oh, I wouldn't say pointless, would you, sergeant? I would call it quality time with our favorite guest." Corporal Bolinski winked as he handcuffed the prisoner's outstretched wrists.

Sergeant Dobbin nodded. "Yes, that special time of day when we reflect on our life experiences."

"Succinctly stated," Bolinski said as he took hold of the prisoner's right arm. Dobbin wrapped a gloved hand around his left. They guided him toward a room in the old facility the prisoner knew all too well.

"You have learned nothing from me in the past and will not learn anything today. Your superiors forbid you from injuring me to obtain information. I will walk away from this place very soon. Then maybe someday, you will be *my* prisoner."

The irony of the statement was not lost on Sergeant Dobbin. He knew how he would be treated if he had the misfortune of being captured by this man's forces. He decided to prod him a bit further. "Tell me, Abu, exactly how would you welcome us if we became your house guests?"

The prisoner's facial expression remained blank. "You would be tortured until you told us everything we wanted to know. Then you would be beheaded. Your bodies would be dragged through the streets to celebrate the death of two infidels."

Dobbin offered a mocking smile. "You're going to have to try a little harder than that if you ever want your country to be a travel destination. I'm already thinking Cairo, even Paris, would be much more favorable."

Bolinski smirked at the sergeant's goading of the assassin. The man deserved a horrific death. Instead, he would walk out of this compound in four days and board a plane supplied by a group of human rights sympathizers. Then he would be flown to an unknown destination in the Middle East. At least, that was how the news storyline would read.

The actual events about to unfold were part of a classified operation to exploit prisoner 4135 and his inevitable freedom. If all went according to plan, he would be an unwitting participant in the elimination of his superiors. The next twenty-four hours would determine whether the mission could proceed as planned.

The guards directed their prisoner to a gray steel door. The sergeant knocked twice and the electronic lock released with a buzz and a sharp clunk. He pulled it open as Bolinski held tight to the prisoner's forearm and guided him in. The door latched loudly behind as they directed the prisoner into a brightly lit cubicle, furnished only with a stainless steel table and two metal chairs. Dobbin walked to the opposite side of the table and directed the prisoner to sit while he kept a hand on his club. Bolinski locked the prisoner's wrists into a pair of chained shackles attached to the table and removed the handcuffs.

"You cannot harm me. I will not answer your questions," the prisoner declared with smug self-assurance.

The guards shared a sideways glance, then exited through a door that led to the observation room. Both took their places behind a large two-way mirror. The three other occupants looked up and nodded in silent acknowledgment.

Private Jerry Frazier sat at a bank of recording equipment. He cued up the system to capture any information the prisoner might give up during the interrogation. He didn't expect any more today than they had ever gotten from this man. But protocol had to be followed and documented. He checked the microphone and video signals coming in from the adjacent room and slid his headphones off. "Everything is ready here," he said.

"Showtime," announced Marcus Gante, the intelligence officer. He stepped away from the mirrored glass where he had been watching the prisoner and walked toward the door leading to the interrogation room. He glanced back at Dr. Karl Maxwell, the third man in the room. "At least he's consistent," he added, "a total prick till the end." He pushed through the door and closed it behind him, then took a seat at the steel table across from the prisoner.

"Comfortable, Abu?" he asked.

"Does it bother you that your country does not allow you to harm me to extract information?"

"Does it bother *you* that so many lives have been ended because you misinterpret your holy book?"

"Allah speaks to me. He directs my hands to do his bidding. The day comes when you shall fall by his sword."

"Not today, Abu. Tell me again how you got your hands on twenty pounds of C-4 and blew up a police station."

"I never said these things. You are a lying infidel."

"And you are a brainless meat puppet that kills everything that doesn't agree with you. Now that we've gotten our greetings out of the way let's move onto something more productive. Tell me about your mother. Is she still charging a Rupee for a roll in the dirt?"

Prisoner 4135 smiled, savoring the moment. Freedom was but hours away, and yet this man still attempted to taunt him.

"You show anger with your words. You cannot harm me, and I will tell you nothing. I walk away from you and this place very, very soon, and you will have gained nothing."

"I prefer to compare your release with flushing a toilet. Somewhere in this world, a large turd named Abu Dahl is going to splat down and stink up everything around. You are a total piece of shit, and millions of people would cheer if you would just stop breathing and die."

"You waste your time with these insults."

Gante nodded. "We both know you're not going to answer my questions. But since I have to sit here anyway, I figured I would just enjoy myself for a change." Gante relaxed, sliding down into his chair. "Let me share a thought I've had for all the time we've spent in this room together. There is not a god in the universe that would condone the slaughter of innocent people. Hell, the whole point of religion was to inject some fear into soulless creatures like you. To make you believe there would be consequences for your actions in the afterlife. But you made up new rules that say your god wants you to kill, so now it's okay. You even think you'll be rewarded for your actions with seventy-two virgins. My question is, have you ever stopped to think about those virgins? Because spending their eternity as your concubines must surely be their punishment for having committed more terrible sins than you. Being with you must be their hell. Yup, pull down that veil, and I'll bet you see a face like a dish of worms, with the sweet demeanor of an ax murderer." Gante chuckled. "Now that's what I call paradise." He paused again, noting the prisoner's tensing face, hands balling into fists. Finally, he thought, something that gets a reaction out of this emotionless dirt clump. Wouldn't you figure it had to do with getting laid? He enjoyed the moment, smiling broadly at the man's steely glare. "Be sure and pack about a million condoms in your overnight bag when you cross over, buddy. I wouldn't want to get any of that on me."

The prisoner bolted forward in his chair, then thought better of it and composed himself. "You cannot speak to me this way," he stated flatly, "your Geneva Convention forbids it"

"Yes, and that same document forbids acts of genocide as well. But that didn't stop you from killing innocent people." Gante straightened in his seat and added, "Abu, you are a disappointing waste of oxygen and carbon. The sooner you die, the sooner people can rejoice and spit on your dead stinking corpse."

The prisoner considered the taunts being thrown at him from this filthy, self-absorbed American. How he would love to climb over this table, bite through the man's windpipe and spit the piece of flesh at him, then watch as he gurgled and drowned in blood. This man's job was to maintain his composure and extract information. Yet, here he was, no longer attempting to restrain his anger and frustration. This would be the last time they faced off in this room, and the man had failed. It gave the prisoner a deep satisfaction. Never before had Gante hurled such insults. It was clear how frustrated this agent of Satan was that he had never gained any useful intelligence during his twelve years of imprisonment. He now admitted his failure with this unusual show of emotion.

Abu Dahl smiled. America, once the most powerful nation on earth, had lost this battle. Defeated by its internal bureaucracy. Elected officials had stripped the country of its power, turning it into a pathetic collection of whiny weaklings who could agree on nothing. Diplomacy, rather than the blade of a sword, was now the only tool available to end wars. Their nation would stand for a few more years at most. But it had already begun to crumble from the inside. Abu thought of a future where the great buildings and monuments of Washington, DC, would someday resemble the decaying ruins of Rome, another civilization that imploded from its internal fight. The thought of the capital city in flames calmed him.

He felt a brief pang of pity for this interrogator. Should he offer some small scrap of information? Something that would give false hope and send them all running in circles? He thought better of it and decided to leave as he had come, in control and unbreakable. He sat up taller in the metal seat and awaited the next question or insult, defiant to the end.

DR. KARL MAXWELL stood behind the large observation mirror with his arms folded, watching the prisoner's body language. The relaxed posture and defiant smirk broadcast the message that he believed himself impervious to this place—the victor. Maxwell was pleased with the display of confidence. It was critical that Abu Dahl believed he was in complete control. Using his ego against him would be the assassin's undoing that would help carry this mission forward.

"Are they ready for us next door?" Maxwell asked.

Sergeant Dobbin picked up a wall phone, keyed in four digits, and waited. There was a click, then a soft female voice responded, "Department twelve."

Dobbin said, "Department twenty-two, we are a go."

"Department twenty-two stand by." There was a short silence before the voice answered, "Department twenty-two confirm status. We are a go."

Dobbin hung up the phone and nodded to the doctor.

A moment later, there was a rap on the outer door. Bolinski pulled it open, allowing two technicians clad in green scrubs to push a gurney into the room. On top of the stretcher were patient restraints, monitoring equipment, a face mask connected to a small green cylinder, and gas masks. One of the techs grabbed two of the masks and wordlessly handed them to the guards. Bolinski and Dobbin both pulled them on and adjusted them down over their faces. The techs each grabbed one of the remaining masks and put them on.

Dr. Maxwell pushed a button mounted beneath the observation window. A red light flashed in the interrogation room, signaling the intelligence officer that it was time.

Gante noticed the light. Without breaking eye contact with the prisoner, he gave a slight nod toward the mirrored glass. He rose, still staring down into the eyes of the evilest man he had ever encountered. He imagined the blood from thousands of innocent victims dripping from those cuffed hands. This bastard would walk free, and the killing would begin again. The irony was that Gante knew he could end Abu's violent rampage right here and now by simply sending a forty-five slug into the man's brain. Bang, splat, done.

He paused as he pictured the scenario. He could feel the pressure on his finger as he slowly squeezed the trigger, the temporary elation from blowing this piece of shit to kingdom come. The euphoria would be short-lived, however. He would pay the price for his actions behind bars for the rest of his life—another demented twist in today's lopsided version of justice.

Still, he thought, his life in exchange for the thousands that he would probably be saving? It seemed like an easy choice. Scores of would-be victims would never know they owed their next breath to a man who sat languishing in prison for blowing the head off their would-be executioner. Tempting.

He smiled down at the face of evil, imagining the man's brains spraying onto the white concrete walls in a butterfly pattern of blood, bone, and gray matter. The vision had a surprisingly calming effect.

Gante had imagined many phrases or catchy comments he wanted to say to this beast on their last day of interrogation. They had all drifted through his mind at one time or another, begging to be the line used to close this dark chapter of his duties at Guantanamo. But now that the moment had finally arrived, none seemed appropriate. He drew a blank. Rather than feeling flustered at the loss of words, he took it as a positive sign that his conscience was clear. Who else could have sat with this man day after day as he recited his atrocities against humanity? The prisoner had smugly acknowledged each as more of an achievement than the maniacal theft of life. For Gante, maybe it meant that his own life had hope of returning to near normalcy after so much time in the belly of the beast. He had failed to ascertain any meaningful intel from the man. That was not his fault, but that of his own system working against him. It had denied him the proper tools to extract the information needed. In another place and time it would have seemed incomprehensible not to use any means necessary to probe the mind of an enemy bent on your destruction. He knew such passivity would never be considered in this man's war camp where the punishment for even the most menial crime was death. Still in all, Abu Dahl's release marked the end of a terrible chapter in his own life. He had given his best effort and now accepted the outcome. He leaned in close to the prisoner, smiled again, and said the first words that came to mind.

"Fuck you."

He turned and walked toward the control room, leaving Abu Dahl for once suffering from a lack of words. The door latched behind him as he watched the prisoner through the two-way mirror, still imagining the top of his head blown off. He had a strong premonition that someone else would do it for him. That this man would lay buried in a shallow grave sometime very soon. The thought brought a satisfied grin and closure.

Maxwell shot a glance at Private Frazier and said, "Do it."

Frazier nodded, then hit a switch killing the audio and video feeds. He rolled his chair over to a tall white cabinet covered with large gauges and mushroom switches. It was connected to the interrogation room wall by a pair of clear hoses. He pushed one of the buttons, and the needle on the largest gauge sprang to life. There was a slight hissing sound from the cabinet as gas began to flow into the adjoining room. Dr. Maxwell checked his watch as he observed the prisoner, waiting for the desired response. It didn't take long for the man's eyelids to begin drooping and then close. The prisoner's head dropped to the table with a soft clunk, out cold.

"Cut it," Maxwell called out.

The private hit the other two switches on the cabinet, stopping the flow and tripping an exhaust fan. He watched as the needle on the gauge monitoring the level of gas in the room slowly descended. When it neared the safe region, he turned to the techs and gave a thumbs up.

Everyone in the room had drilled for what came next. The gurney was rolled into the detainment cell by the two techs, with Bolinski and Dobbin following behind. The prisoner was lifted on, strapped down, and fitted with a face mask that supplied a steady flow of the general anesthetic. Dr. Maxwell, the anesthesiologist for this operation, checked the gauges for the proper oxygen to gas mixture, then stepped back to follow the gurney.

The small caravan pushed the unconscious patient out of the room and down a long corridor. A wide door opened, and they entered a surgical suite where they were met by an awaiting medical team. The group surrounded the patient and slid him onto an operating table, preparing him for the quick procedure.

An ear, nose, and throat specialist walked over to his right side while a general surgeon stood to his left. Maxwell stepped forward, removed the face mask, and then worked a thin tube into the patient's mouth. A mobile C-arm X-ray was rolled into place to image the patient's head as the three doctors donned lead aprons. The resulting images were immediately displayed on two large overhead monitors.

The ENT specialist reviewed the images, tracing the sinus cavities of the patient with his finger. "It's a little tighter than anticipated," he said, "but still within range to proceed."

The general surgeon nodded his agreement. "May I have the device, please?" he asked.

A physician assistant rolled over a tray covered with various tools and a small gray box. The doctor opened it and extracted a tiny chrome device, and examined it closely. It looked similar to a pharmaceutical cold capsule but less than half the size. He carefully twisted the body of the device and felt it click, activating the on-board electronics. There were no lights to indicate the gadget was functional. Instead, he glanced over to another tech who was watching a display similar to a radar screen. Within seconds, a small blip appeared on the monitor. A low level, five-millisecond microwave pulse, generated every eight minutes, was now being transmitting. The signal was detectable from up to two miles away by specially equipped drones.

The tech turned, gave a thumbs-up, and announced, "The device is active.

The surgeon nodded, then inserted the tiny beacon into a receptacle at the end of a stainless steel rod. On the other end was a trigger assembly. He looked to the ENT and announced, "Going for the full six-point five-centimeter insertion." The surgeon gently worked the rod with the device attached up into the right sinus of the sedated prisoner. Once he reached the desired position, he stepped back. "Can we get an image of this, please?"

The mobile X-ray technician pushed a button on his console. Another view of the man's head appeared, this one showing the long rod protruding from his right nostril.

Both doctors studied the image for a moment before the ENT said, "I think another three to five millimeters would lodge it a bit more securely."

The surgeon noted the incremental markings on the insertion rod and slowly pushed the device further into the man's sinus cavity.

"That was four millimeters. Can I get a picture of that, please?"

Another X-ray was taken, and the results pleased both doctors. "He will never feel a thing," the ENT offered. "Nicely done, doctor."

The surgeon nodded and squeezed the trigger on the insertion tool, releasing the device. He carefully slid the tool out and asked for one more image. The results were as desired. The device was firmly in place and functional.

Both doctors moved away as the physician assistant stepped up and laid ice packs over the man's nose. This was just one more step in the process. It was critical to reduce any sign of swelling or discomfort before the man was allowed to come out of the anesthetic. He could suspect nothing, or the entire mission would fail.

The prisoner was rolled into a recovery room with his guards walking alongside. Once there, he was fitted with a wrist strap device that monitored oxygen levels, blood pressure, and heart rate. A digital wall clock had been set and now counted down the time from twenty-two hours.

The entire plan hinged on making one full day in this man's life vanish. He had been kept in his cell away from other prisoners and had not seen daylight in weeks. Over the last thirty-two days, his timetable had been gradually adjusted to drop forty-five minutes from each day. With no timekeeping devices visible and no reference of day and night from the sky, his body clock accepted the alteration in time with little protest. Up until this day, he had been kept in interrogation for longer and longer periods and always allowed to fall asleep in his chair. He would be awakened and told that he had been sleeping longer than he actually had. The end effect had worked as the psychiatrist had predicted. The prisoner was oblivious to the minute changes that had taken place each day. He now believed that his release was three days away, when in fact, it was actually four.

PRIVATE JERRY FRAZIER sat at a control console in a soundproof room. A pair of video monitors displayed the recordings made over the last six weeks during interrogations of prisoner 4135.

Frazier selected portions of each session, then copied and pasted them onto a new track. He ensured the data streams never appeared broken, reviewing each change before moving on to the next. The prisoner's own smugness had helped make this job easier. He'd sat in the bolted-down seat in nearly the same position day after day, slightly slumped, hands folded defiantly on the table. The camera remained zoomed in on the prisoner, so there were no worries about synchronizing the movements of the interrogator.

Frazier worked through the night, sipping coffee as he reviewed the newly completed twelve-hour video. He completed the major portion of his task ahead of schedule, then moved on to the last step. He used a cut tool to carefully crop around the clock that always appeared in the upper right corner of the videos. This was the only place where one could see any trace of the edits as the clock jumped from different times of different days. He ran a subroutine that deleted the clock, then selected an image that had been created with the desired date and time. With expert skill, he pasted the new continuously running clock over the void. Another few mouse clicks later, and the entire video repopulated. The new clock now appeared in precisely the right position on each frame.

The final product showed prisoner 4135 as he had been on every other day of interrogation. All evidence of his being drugged and rolled out of the room unconscious was now deleted and would pass the tightest scrutiny.

With the task complete, Frazier copied the video onto a blank DVD and labeled it as the interrogation that had started the day earlier. He then cleaned house, erasing all signs of his work. He reformatted the archive and ran another program that erased the hard drives multiple times. It would be impossible to retrieve any of the old information.

Frazier carried the new DVD back to the observation room. He loaded it into the video storage system that held all the backup data from the central computer. He did not alert anyone that his task was complete. That call was to be made only if something had gone wrong and the results were less than perfect. He then headed back to his quarters for some well-deserved shut-eye, content with the outcome and quite proud of the handiwork that could never be shared with anyone.

3

Stuttgart Army Airfield, Germany

Disciplinary hearings were something base commander George Phillips endeavored to avoid. Every soldier under his command, no matter how seemingly cocksure or combatant, sometimes broke the rules. Phillips believed that an otherwise untarnished military career should not be destroyed due to one careless night of over-imbibing or an argument that digressed into a fistfight. These were soldiers, after all, trained to kill for their country. Sometimes it was difficult to channel that rage, and he believed in second chances. Most of them deserved it…most of them.

The personnel file that lay open on his desk told the story of a soldier who did not. A West Point honors graduate who, by all rights, should be enjoying an ascending career in the military. But the lieutenant would likely never reach the rank of captain. You could only lead a man onto the path, Phillips reminded himself. The rest was up to the one doing the walking.

The lieutenant in question had earned average ratings and

remarks from his first commander and now Phillips. He had also exhausted a charitable number of second chances. Yet, he retained the habit of turning minor scraps into significant problems rather than taking his lumps and moving on.

Phillips recalled some of the issues between the lieutenant and other base personnel and shook his head. The man had obviously set out to prove his mental superiority. Instead, he alienated himself, earning a reputation as a hot-headed, egotistic loner. The damage was irreversible. His fellow officers and most of the enlisted men detested him. Even among those who had attended the academy alongside him, there was no connection. This man had managed to graduate from the centuries-old military institution of Patton, Eisenhower, and McArthur, earning high academic achievement and little else. He had not learned to lead, or for that matter, how to follow a leader. He had proven himself incapable of either, even though he was brilliant by most standards.

Phillips now believed his problem came down to misguided motivation. The brash lieutenant had entered the military looking for what it could do for him, not the other way around. He imagined the rude awakening when this man found himself in a school full of what he had referred to as 'gung ho, easily led Dudley Do Rights.' Commander Phillips acknowledged it was time to rid himself of the young lieutenant and the aggravation that accompanied him.

He still chose not to wade through the piles of paperwork that came with writing up a negative rating. Let someone else figure it out, he thought. It won't take long.

He thought back again to the well-oiled machine his base had been before the arrival of the troublesome officer. Months of turmoil had followed. And yet, the man was as brash and uncontrollable today as he had been on that first trouble-plagued day.

Phillips had never transferred a man off his base for insubordination and first dismissed the idea out of principle. No man is beyond reproach and repair. No man is disposable. He now admitted that, in all the years spent adhering to that philosophy, he had been wrong. There were exceptions, even to this rule. He conceded his failure. He had not made a better soldier from the one who had walked through the door. He may even encounter a few more before he reached retirement. But he would not allow the defective internal mis-wiring of one man to destroy an otherwise sound code of ethics. He would continue the tradition instilled in him by his father. "Leave no man behind." There was now one caveat to be added to that noble goal; you can only save those who seek to be saved.

Phillips closed the file and held it another moment, waiting for his conscience to tell him this was the wrong thing to do. It didn't. He nodded, exhaling a breath of finality, then stamped the file cover with his transfer authorization. The problem was someone else's now. Good riddance and God help the next commander of Lieutenant Dennis LaMonk!

4

Los Angeles, California

"Mr. President, you have turned a blind eye and a deaf ear on the American people. For years, they have begged for help from a system that rewards the rich and punishes the poor. Well, now they have turned to me, sir. They have told me what they need, and by God, I am the one that can and will deliver it to them! I have solutions. I am the solution!"

"Senator Karlson," the president retorted calmly, "you, madam, are a brilliant orator. When you speak, even I want to believe you. But there is no substance to your words. The promises you make are impossible to keep. You have a convenient habit of glossing over the details and skipping right to the happy ending. You also suggest that change in itself is the answer. It is not. Being president requires making difficult decisions for the good of the entire country. Not just those who yell the loudest at your paid protests. I wonder if you are even capable of listening—"

"How dare you, sir!" Karlson struck back like a coiled

viper. "How dare you suggest I'm not capable of listening. It is you who ignores the pleas of the hungry while offering tax breaks to your wealthy friends. You and your party spend billions on an unpopular war on foreign soil while your nation begs for help. Oh, I'm listening, all right. I'm listening to the muted voices you refuse to hear with an instinct you don't possess. It is called compassion. I hear their cries, and I say enough is enough. Now we do things my way!"

"Senator, I'm sorry, but your time is up." Grayson Taylor, the moderator for the evening's debate, cut the senator off, then felt the scornful glare of a woman interrupted. "President Tenor," he continued, "the next question goes to you."

"I'm sorry too, Grayson, but I need to finish my point about the president's lack of—"

"Senator, if you please! You agreed to the terms of this debate. You need to wait your turn."

"I think we've all waited long enough, don't you?" She looked directly into the camera. "Don't you? The country belongs to us, people. Let me…let us take it back!"

The studio audience erupted, rising to their feet with loud cheers, yells, and thunderous applause. It drowned out the moderator's attempt at asking the next question. For those keeping score, this was the winning play of the game. Karlson smiled with smug confidence. She was no longer the welterweight contender fighting against an incumbent president. This night had given rise to a new Goliath.

"YOU HANDLED HIM BRILLIANTLY!" Gene Lawton, Karlson's campaign manager, congratulated her. He pressed the pause button on the remote, halting the replay of the presidential debate from the night earlier. "Listen to those cheers! You had him against the ropes right from the beginning. Of course, it helped that we seeded the crowd a little bit."

"A little bit?" she chuckled. "May I remind you, Gene, that seventy percent of that audience were our people! Tenor stood there, staring like a deer in the headlights. He never knew what hit him."

Karlson swiveled her stool around and reached for her drink. She took a long, satisfying swallow, crunching on ice chips. She smiled, remembering the blank expression on the popular incumbent president's face.

This was the first of three scheduled presidential debates for the first-term California senator. More than that, it was the first long stride toward taking the White House. Karlson turned back toward the television. Her likeness was frozen in a defiant grin. For a moment, she saw a woman from a different time. Her chestnut brown hair required coloring and highlights more often these days. Her face revealed the creeping lines of age despite the Botox injections and skin tighteners. But the high cheekbones and mesmerizing green eyes were as stunning today as when she had been a Hollywood heartthrob.

When she'd first met her husband, Clifford West, Karlson was a popular actress. He was the California Attorney General. Her most recent movie, "Undertow," was the top box office draw, and he was the rising star in politics. Their torrid love affair kept the tabloid photographers busy chasing after that elusive and steamy photo of the couple caught in a compromising position.

By the time West was elected governor, Karlson's acting career had begun a slow downward spiral. Taking a backseat to her husband's success was painful. She spent years nursing her ego with Johnny, Jack, and Jim. Some old friends persuaded her to indulge in her political passions, and she jumped in with both feet, taking up every cause that came her way. Save the Whales and Seals, PETA, Earth First, and Greenpeace. The birth of their daughter, Jordan, kept her home just long enough to realize how much she still craved the spotlight, whether it was on the big screen or in politics.

She spent the next fifteen years speaking on varied subjects. Ban the internal combustion engine. Eliminate red meat consumption for all Americans. Piping the water from the Great Lakes to irrigate drought-ridden Iowa farms. It all came so naturally that she decided acting had been a mere stepping stone in preparation for her political calling.

With the support of her well-connected Hollywood friends and her husband, Karlson ran for the California senate. She took the office in a near landslide. Now, two years later, she was dead even in the polls with Davis Tenor, the current POTUS.

Tenor enjoyed broad support among business leaders and foreign governments, relationships he'd forged while in the private sector. He was well respected, accomplished, and loved by millions. And he was in the way.

Gene Lawton sat near the television with a yellow legal pad, analyzing the replayed debate while making a list of issues requiring attention. Lawton's prowess at creating political giants while tearing down opponents was legendary. He was considered one of the greatest in the business.

"Katherine," he said, "we need to adjust our position on a few points." He tapped his pen on the notepad. "Tenor claimed that tax revenues increased last year when the small business credit went into effect. We can play this as a tax break for business on the backs of the middle class. You can drum up support to overturn it once you're in office."

Karlson turned from her frozen image on the screen. "That's an easy one," she nodded. "Get Jenny and David to write some sample spins on it. We'll pick the best one for a new ad."

Jennifer Griffon and David Marsden were the brilliant writers of the hottest drama on television, Capitol Beat. Their passion was politics, and their candidate was Ms. Karlson. They had the literary prowess to turn a mouthwatering slice of cherry pie into a writhing plate of maggots. With a few skillfully crafted lines, they could make this tax credit look and feel like the black plague.

Karlson swirled the ice cubes in her near-empty drink and added, "Tell them it only helps the wealthiest three percent. A little shot of class envy should knock that piece of shit back down the sewer."

Lawton smiled and continued. "Tenor was also correct when he spoke of the military seeking a more high-tech approach to the war. On his last trip to Camp David, he was briefed on some new battlefield innovations. It gave him a moment of being on top in the debate while making you appear out of the loop. You need to pick some brains in the military oversight committee. Find out how far along these new war toys have progressed. I hate to say it, but progress and victory in this war do not bode well for your campaign platform."

In a mocking southern accent, Karlson said, "I'll have lunch with the distinguished old fart from Louisiana. A couple of shots of bourbon, and he can't take his eyes off my cleavage. He's pathetic but amusing. I'm sure we'll get what we need. Any other issues?"

Lawton ambled over and kissed the back of her neck. "The last issue is how much time do we have left tonight?"

The Senator turned and looked up into his hazel eyes. "Enough...let me freshen my drink. I'll meet you in the bedroom."

5

At precisely 9:45 pm on February tenth, a large safe was opened in the executive office of Malcolm LeClair. A controversial memory stick that had helped further divide an already polarized nation was removed and placed in a brief-case. This was handed to one of the corporation's attorneys, a rugged-looking courtroom warrior who wore his $1600 Armani suit like a coat of armor. Escorted by four armed guards and a second attorney, the case was carried through the reception area to the main elevator and down to the third floor.

The procession threaded its way through the building. All motion and sound ceased throughout the cubicle labyrinths as its occupants stood peering over their enclosures to witness the progress.

They exited the elevator at the Global Access television studio entrance and were routed to the control room.

The lead attorney entered and was directed to a USB patch bay mounted above a rack of computers. As per his instructions, the attorney removed the odd-shaped red memory stick, slid it out of its clear plastic cover, and plugged it into the slot marked USB-two. He stepped back as a studio technician visually inspected the connection, then took a seat at the massive audio-visual console. His fingers danced on a computer keyboard as he opened the device file and verified its contents. When he had located the video file, he hit play and then pause. The system was now ready to reveal its message to the world.

Two of the guards took up posts outside the control room. The remaining pair covered the entrance of the studio, barring access to anyone without special clearance.

The attorneys were shown to seats they would occupy until the video had been played and recorded. The original was to be hand-delivered to FBI agents waiting less than patiently in the main lobby. The government had been informed of the existence of the device and threatened to lock down the network and confiscate the drive. The argument was made that revealing its contents posed a potential risk to national security. In a stunning defeat, a federal judge blocked the government's action. He ruled in favor of LeClair, stating that freedom of speech took precedence over their claim. They would be allowed access to the memory stick only after its broadcast.

The studio technician switched two of the eight monitors to display the controversial file. He pushed play again, and the first image flashed on the screens. "We're all set here, Mort," he said to the man seated to his left.

Mort Hastings, network news director, responded with a nod as he scanned the monitors and control settings. He sipped cold coffee, memorizing every displayed image. He noted the time on a digital clock above the large window that looked out over the television studio. He watched the newscaster below, listening to his dialogue through headphones while matching it with the teleprompter monitor.

"He's going off script again," he complained to anyone listening. "Six minutes to go, and the famous Burt Ledger still won't follow his lines." He glanced to his left and said, "Mandy, bump him back on track, please."

Mandy Geraldo, the dialogue editor, nodded and waited for the news anchor to take a breath. She then queued up her microphone. "Time is tight, Burt. Stay on script."

Without so much as a blink of acknowledgment, Burt Ledger redirected his discussion back to what was being displayed on the scrolling prompter. Say what you would about his attitude; the man was smooth, professional, and always an asset on the airways.

Ledger would soon deliver the blockbuster story that every other network anchor would die for. It was history in the making that the American public would forever remember, like the first walk on the moon or the assassination of John Kennedy. For better or worse, it would be the face and voice of Burt Ledger that would be recalled whenever this story was discussed.

"THE IMAGES and sounds about to be played have not been viewed by anyone before this moment as per the explicit demands made upon its receipt," Ledger began. "We do know that it is a message from the reclusive leader of OASIS, the radical Islamic terror organization behind most of the suicide bombings and attacks throughout the Middle East and the rest of the world. We have never seen this man's face and don't know whether he will expose himself now. We do anticipate the possibility of graphic images and language. Therefore, we strongly advise viewer discretion, at least for this first viewing. Again, we remind you this is a dangerous extremist organization with thousands of deaths attributed to their fight.

"Their violence knows no bounds, and we here at Global Access Media mourn the loss of one of our own. Derek Waltstein disappeared shortly after delivering the message you are about to see. Derek spoke of his chilling encounter with a mysterious courier. He would say only that he feared for his life if he revealed details about that meeting. To our knowledge, he never did, but his home was found ransacked with signs of a violent struggle. Derek has not been heard from since. We fear the worst and ask for your prayers for our missing comrade."

"And now, please join us in viewing for the first time the personal message to the world from the leader of OASIS. Ladies and gentlemen, Sirhan Abbas…"

"SWITCH TO COMPUTER ONE," Hastings directed, his eyes locked on the monitors and clock. "USB input two, and cue playback in three, two, one…"

The flag of OASIS, a blood-red fist over a bright yellow sun on a black background, was displayed against an eerie melody played by a Middle Eastern Ensemble. Nothing changed. Nothing moved for what felt like an eternity.

He stepped into view. His appearance itself was like a shock to the senses. He stood, glaring into the camera. Not moving, not speaking. His entire demeanor screamed defiance, as though daring the viewer to look away.

No one did. No one could.

He had chosen not to mask his face. His dark, chiseled features and short facial hair appeared divergent from every other Middle Eastern leader preceding him. His eyes appeared completely black beneath his thick eyebrows and bright blue turban. He was dressed in desert military camos with a splattering of color across the left of his chest, presumably medals of rank and distinction. He appeared young for such a position of power. But the youthful face was in stark contrast to those dark orbs that projected the image of a nomadic warrior. It was easy to imagine this man crossing the threshold of time and riding from a thousand years past to once again repel the invaders. His sinister expression left no doubt as to his intentions. He stared forward, his long, sculpted nose pointing downward. Lips pursed in what appeared to be a permanent scowl.

He began speaking in refined English. Slowly at first, his voice flowing along with the accompaniment of a strange flute melody. He spoke in rhythm with the music in a way that seemed to grip the listener and pull them in. His volume increased with the intensity of the instruments, and his tone became sharper as the words came faster. The overall effect was strangely hypnotic and most powerful.

"Citizens of the Great Satan, hear me. Your moment of power on this earth has come to an end. There will be no sanctuary. There will be no quarter. You shall burn in the eternal fire as we, the true believers, take what is rightfully ours. And what is rightfully ours is all that you see. It is the very ground you stand upon and the air you breathe. It is the world, and we are here to claim it all in the name of Allah.

"You shall watch helplessly as we begin our attacks. And how shall the battle start? With warships? With bombers? No! You are already defeated. For your enemy is not at the door. He is already within the gates. We stand among you! And it was you who let us in. You watched, you even helped us, and now your foolish good nature will be your undoing. We are your neighbors, we are your co-workers, we are your friends, and we are your executioners! Do not waste your time searching for a way to defeat us. Use the days you have remaining to prepare to meet your fate."

He paused and stared straight ahead. The background music changed to a trilling violin that mimicked the human voice. An up-tempo rhythm played as he continued. The second verse to a captivating yet terrifying song that listeners were powerless to ignore.

"The path to life within the new empire is straight and true. Every boy and man among you must accept our teachings without exception. When you have found favor in our eyes, then and only then shall you be allowed to live among us. Your daughters and your wives shall bear our children so that our numbers grow even greater. This world will be united under one power, under the only true religion. Until that day, the blood will flow like a river.

"The time of the great holy war is upon you. The true followers shall soon return this world to paradise. You will know this to be so when the attacks begin. The first four fires shall burn like torches for the world to see that the Great Satan can and will be defeated. It will be destroyed by stopping the mighty gears of your economy. Once the machine is broken, the walls of your kingdom will come crashing down. We will open the gates from within, and our freedom fighters will flood through and finish what we have begun today. The smoke shall rise above the rubble of your automobiles, computers, jet planes, and oil fields.

"I have a warning for the Muslims among you that have accepted the western lifestyle of the infidel and do not stand with us now; you shall be the first to die. You have turned your back on your brothers and have chosen only those sections of the Koran that are convenient for you to follow. Foolish, ignorant people! An urn does not hold water if there are pieces of it missing. Your crimes are far greater than those of the infidels. For you have been shown the truth and have chosen to ignore our teachings. For this, there is no mercy. Your heads shall be severed from your bodies with dull swords. You will feel every chop of the blade and beg for death.

"People of America, your day of judgment is upon you. Make your choice, or it will be made for you."

The message ended as it had started.

BURT LEDGER SAT at the news desk staring at the playback monitors. The man whose mouth was always in motion sat in stunned silence, a tear streaking down his cheek. The words and imagery of the video were still impacting him like a head-on crash. He struggled to find the words to calm and reassure the American public that what they had just witnessed could not come to pass here. But he couldn't. It would be a lie. Dark days lay ahead. He could sense it now.

Mandy Geraldo blinked herself back to the moment and began typing messages into the teleprompter. Ledger took no notice, still staring ahead blankly. She clicked her microphone and spoke into his earpiece, "Burt, start reading. Just start reading."

Ledger broke his gaze and looked up to the control room window with an expression of a lost child. It took another moment before his mind rebooted. He began speaking, though not yet reading the scripted words. "That was, ah, oh my God, that was the most frightening speech I've heard, ever." His eyes wandered as though deep in his own thoughts and memories. He shook his head, squeezed the bridge of his nose, then blinked. He focused on the teleprompter, and the professional within clicked back online. He began reading fluidly, relaxing with each sentence. Good old Burt Ledger was back in stride.

THE LEAD TECH was the first to notice. "What is that weird smell?" he asked, scanning the control room for a burning cable or an overheating transformer. The air quickly filled with the nauseating odor of sizzling electronic components. The other tech jumped up and began ripping through the bundles of cables that connected the racks of audio and video equipment, searching frantically for the cause of the pungent stench. Others in the room glanced about uncomfortably, coughing as the fumes grew stronger. The lead tech came upon it, not comprehending what he was witnessing. He had never seen anything like it before. The odd memory stick protruding from USB port two was increasing in size, as though someone had connected it to a compressor and was inflating it with air. It had grown twice its original size and was still swelling.

"Hey, something is seriously wrong with this thing," he yelled. "I think we should all get the hell out of here!"

Chaos ensued as Mandy and Mort bolted from their seats and rushed for the door just ahead of the two technicians.

The attorneys glanced at each other, assessing the situation, seeking verification that a serious threat existed. Their sole function was to verify the safe transport and viewing of that memory stick. There would be severe consequences if they simply ran out of the room and left it unattended. In the end, self-preservation prevailed. They both charged for the entrance, right behind the guards who had reached the same conclusion.

Shouts mixed with screams. The eight occupants clustered and jockeyed for position to get through the entrance. All pushed against each other and the door. Mort frantically pulled at the handle. Mandy pushed back against one of the techs just enough for Mort to force the door open, and she dove through. Mort wedged his foot into the door, then worked himself through the gap. It slammed shut behind him as he fell into the hallway. Mandy kneeled to help him up as those still in the room realized they were working against each other. They all backed away from the door, just as the chain reaction within the memory stick reached its zenith. The most technologically advanced explosive ever created detonated with an unearthly fury.

The blast shook the entire building. A focused beam of destructive energy, a thin blade of death, shot out from the device at the speed of sound. Everything it touched was decimated.

The remaining six people standing at the doorway were hit by the full ferocity of the weapon. With a precision near that of a laser, they were cut in two. The narrow band of flesh and bone hit by the blast was instantly reduced to fragments and vapor. Their disconnected torsos dropped upon their still standing legs and remained upright for a moment before crumpling lifelessly to the floor.

The destructive wave continued out nearly unimpeded. A narrow swath was ripped through the door. There was enough energy remaining to hurl the two security guards posted outside the room like rag dolls through the air. Their rumpled bodies slammed into the elevators at the end of the hall and dropped into motionless heaps.

Exposed wires sparked in the smoky air. Pieces of debris and misted blood floated down to the crimson-soaked floor. The building fire alarm sounded, and sprinklers began spraying down upon the gruesome scene. No one in the control room survived.

Mandy Geraldo regained consciousness in the surreal aftermath. Blood droplets and pieces of flesh dotted her face. From the main studio, she could make out the approach of footsteps and muffled voices. She tried to speak but found words would not come. Mandy worked herself up against the wall to where she could peer through the sliced open section of the control room door. Her mouth gaped as she stared at the pile of body parts just inside. Her mind could not, would not register the images against any memory it held. She had seen so many photos and live videos of the after-effects of explosions, but never anything like this. This was impossible.

The carnage was gruesome yet bewildering. Only a narrow stripe around the room had been affected, but within it, the devastation was complete. Everything above or below that mysterious area was nearly pristine or minimally damaged. Within the narrow blast zone, however, nothing remained.

Mandy looked to Mort and saw the empty expression of a man in shock. He slowly turned his head with a blank stare, and she was horrified to see a splintered section of human bone jutting out of his skull just above the ear. She screamed, but no sound came. She moved away and struggled to stand but fell back to her knees. A jagged piece of steel had shot like a spear through the door and lodged deeply into her right thigh. She winced at the searing hot pain, almost welcoming the sensation as an acknowledgment that she was still part of this world. She glanced behind as a fireman came running her way. Help had arrived, too late for most. Maybe too late for Mort, who had likely suffered severe brain injuries. Surviving such a cataclysmic event, even unscathed, could leave a person broken inside, never able or willing to come to terms with the horrific scenes they had witnessed. Time would tell, she thought. But the emptiness she saw in Mort's eyes told her that he would not be capable of confronting these demons anytime soon.

BURT LEDGER HAD HEARD the shouts and screams from the control room. His years as a war correspondent kicked in, and instinctively he ducked behind the news console. His timing spared him from the wave of glass that blew into the studio like glimmering buckshot. Both cameramen also reacted to the warnings and dropped to the floor. Their injuries were minor compared to what they would have suffered had they been standing in direct line with the blast.

Smoke rolled out the empty window of the control room as Ledger picked himself up. He used his arm to brush away the glass fragments and debris from his chair and desk. He sat down, took a breath, then looked toward the camera.

"Ladies and gentlemen, the control room of our studio has just been rocked by a massive explosion. We have no information about the source or the number of survivors. My God, there were some wonderful people operating the controls tonight, and I don't, I can't, oh, oh lord help us."

A large flood lamp crashed to the floor. Ledger wiped the wetness from his eye and continued on, oblivious to anything but the camera and the story he felt compelled to tell. It would have been a monumental broadcasting moment remembered by the world, only no one would ever hear. The few remaining functional monitors all displayed a test pattern. Global Access Media had been blown off the air. Broadcasting the message of Sirhan Abbas had come with terrible and unimagined consequences.

The new war had begun.

6

Fort McNair, Washington, DC

The intercom on Lieutenant Dennis LaMonk's desk energized with the brash voice of his superior. "I need you in here."

General Horace Lattimer was a man of few words and expected immediate and proper responses from anyone. He also demanded unquestioned loyalty from the small circle of personnel under his command. LaMonk struggled with that part of his assignment. Loyalty was not an ingrained attribute. He grabbed a notepad and headed into the general's office.

"Lieutenant, the shit is hitting the fan from multiple directions," the general announced before LaMonk had settled into a chair. "I need you to compile a presentation for me to share with the army chief of staff. He will present it to the president this evening. Here is what we're dealing with."

He placed three photos on the desk like a card dealer laying out a hand.

LaMonk fought to conceal his shock. The first image showed some type of control room with what appeared to be a focused stripe of pure destruction. If this was the aftermath of a bomb blast, it was unlike any he had ever seen. The second photo showed a tangled pile of body parts lying on blood-soaked carpeting. He willed himself to examine the image closer and noticed they all appeared to have been cleanly sliced through the midsection. He tried to envision the type of device that could cause such carnage. His first thought was a high-intensity laser beam, but such technology was still years away. Wasn't it?

"What you see here is the terrorist bombing at the Global Access Network studio in Los Angeles. The weapon utilized is far beyond our own current technology. The details we have so far are in a PDF file that I will give you."

LaMonk was speechless with informational overload. He had heard of the bombing in only the broadest terms. The government controlled all details released to the public about the weapon and the nature of the attack. Only a handful of people had witnessed these images. Already, he wanted to unsee it all.

The general set down another photograph, this one of a man wearing an orange prison jumpsuit. A contemptuous scowl was frozen on his face. "This is Abu Dahl," he said, pointing.

The name registered with LaMonk, but he couldn't place it.

"This is the face of the enemy, Lieutenant. He is being released from Guantanamo Bay in the next few days and then flown to parts unknown. The military, in conjunction with the CIA, has undertaken a mission to track him. The expectation is he will lead us to Sirhan Abbas, commander of OASIS."

Lattimer added one last image, a tiny, chrome-plated device lying in the palm of an outstretched hand. "This little gadget," he explained, "will enable us to follow Abu Dahl to the enemy's headquarters. A surgical strike will then be deployed to cut off the head of this serpent. Lieutenant, I know you have extensive experience in creating these presentations. This one will be the most important of your life. The president will be using this information to determine the proper courses of action." He pulled a thumb drive from his computer and slid it across the desk. "This has everything you need. The project must be complete and ready for my review by seventeen hundred hours. You are new to us here, but we have rules for handling sensitive information. I'm only going to say this once." The general leaned forward and lowered his voice. "Do not, I repeat, do not copy any of this information. All new files must be backed up to this device alone and not your own hard drive. Is that understood?"

"Yes, sir, understood, sir."

"Very well. You have your orders. Get to it."

LaMonk rose and took the device. He was still rattled by the gruesome images he had seen but was now more concerned about the tight timeline given to work within. As he walked the short distance back to his desk, he began envisioning his presentation and the proper order of displaying key details. The last thing he needed was for the general to reject his finished product and demand significant changes with minutes to prepare instead of hours. It had to be done right the first time. He inserted the thumb drive into his computer and opened the first PDF file, reading about the weapon used in the LA bombing. His jaw muscles went slack as he stared transfixed in disbelieving silence. It seemed that modern warfare had leaped ahead decades overnight.

7

Guantanamo Bay, Cuba

He awoke with a start, jerking his head up from the metal table, rattling the handcuffs that confined him. He felt a wetness on his arm from drooling in his sleep.

His thoughts still wandered through images from a vivid dream of his home. The simple joys of peaceful existence among the people of his village. Memories of the girl he had loved as a young man. She had married another. He imagined wandering the long, steep foothills through the mountains. Inhaling the scent of wild blooms along the winding trail. Their fragrant beauty was so fresh in his mind that he could smell them right here, right now, even in this sterile concrete cubicle. He would soon re-live it all again. Feel the morning sun on his face, the warmth of a night fire, and a simple meal among friends. He was going home.

His eyes fluttered open again, having dozed off once more, still in the embrace of his most carefree and happy memories. His head ached, and his mind floated in a fog. He waited for the disorientation to fade, taking in the details of the all too familiar interrogation room. Slowly, he began to reconstruct the disjointed segments of time. They must have kept him here all night, futilely attempting one last time to break him, to extract so much as a crumb of useful information.

Even without remembering everything of the previous day, he knew they had failed. No one could break him, and certainly not an enemy that had grown so weak and passive.

This once powerful nation stumbled over itself. Its spineless leaders meekly cowered as they offered up an olive branch to the very men sworn to murder its sons and daughters. He savored the irony, knowing he could never strike at a better time against an opponent so content with defeat. He envisioned the day when he and his brothers would stand on the capitol building steps in Washington, DC, as they raised the flag of OASIS for the world to see. The image energized him. He sat up straight in the metal chair, his eyes narrowing as a satisfied grin spread across his face.

"You have failed again," he announced to the empty room. "You do not deserve the power that you hold over the world. Your moment of judgment is coming. Your empire will crumble before your eyes. Then, you will bow at our feet and beg for your lives."

He crossed his hands on the steel table and waited. They would come for him shortly. He would be returned to his cell, fed, and then he would wait some more. Freedom was but a few hours away now. His grin curled further upward. Soon, very soon, the infidels would come to fear the sound of his name.

8

Fort McNair, Washington, DC

Lieutenant LaMonk sat at his desk, skimming through spam emails and news stories on the web. He paid little attention, lazily killing time until the designated hour that he could go into action. His entire military career was at risk by enacting this plan. But then, it was a life he was more than ready to leave behind. His re-enlistment date was fast approaching, and he had failed to reach the anticipated rank of captain. Without it, his hopes of promotion had been crushed. Now, however, he believed the gods had smiled down and granted a golden opportunity. All he had to do was be wise enough to capitalize on it correctly. He was.

His most recent relocation and third field assignment had so far proven to be nothing more than an extended stay in hell. No better than the previous two. He had been sent as a replacement for General Lattimer's last assistant, who was promoted and reassigned. LaMonk's selection had little to do with earned respect, trust, or even confidence. Instead, he was chosen from a nearly empty talent pool because he was the only qualified candidate available.

He was desperate for an exit strategy. Weeks earlier, a chance encounter with a congressional aide led to a conversation with a senator looking to make a name for herself. While visiting the base, she had offered her business card and a sly wink in exchange for any information he had to share. It was her way, she explained, of having multiple sources of Intel to help her contribute more effectively to the committees that she sat on. That card, he decided, would be the key to unlock his new life. He'd already had a belly full of General Lattimer and field assignment number three. Now all he needed was the magic bullet. Something so valuable that it would prove his worth to the senator and launch him into a new career. There were likely dozens of positions she could assist him into. He imagined a new life with a complete wardrobe change that did not include a uniform. Thankfully, he did not have to wait long.

Until now, LaMonk's lower security clearance prohibited him from viewing any sensitive or otherwise valuable information. Then, because of his new position, his security level was upgraded from confidential to top secret. A day later, he had seen the file on this covert military mission. Here was the key to unlocking his future! Well, it was time to share. He expected a fitting reward for the treasure trove he was about to offer.

LaMonk chose this morning to send his notes on the general's meeting at the White House to the senator. This military base would come to life at 5:00 am, so he decided to send the message at 3:30. He selected a few critical pages and photographed them with his phone, adding a cover letter of re-introduction as a teaser. Just enough to grab their attention and motivate them to arrange a meeting.

He opened the middle drawer of his desk, reached under, and pulled down the business card taped to the bottom. Sending his message via fax, he reasoned, still provided the least chance of tracing. All Electronic traffic was closely monitored by the base. The analog phone landline, he'd discovered, was not. He connected his phone to his laptop and chose the images to print. The next hour was the most dangerous. It was the only time he ran the risk of being discovered with the classified documents. The printer came to life and shot out the three selected images. He shuffled them into the fax machine's feed tray and added the introduction page he had typed earlier. Holding the business card in his left hand, he keyed in the number listed. LaMonk hit the send button and waited anxiously for the machine to connect. It didn't.

Shit!

He listened as the number rang, heard the non-melodic tones of the machine attempting a handshake connection, and then a recorded message announcing he had reached a non-working number. He fumbled the card in his trembling hands. What the hell was wrong? Had the number been changed?

His mind was racing for answers when he heard activity outside the office door. No! Nobody was due to come in until 7:00 this morning. He had verified it on the duty roster. That's when he heard a vacuum switching on. It was the cleaning staff. No one could see him sitting here at this time of night, especially in possession of confidential documents. He had no alibi to explain his actions.

A bead of sweat worked its way down his forehead and dripped onto the business card. The salty liquid soaked into a corner, turning it a shade of gray behind the printed phone number. That's when he noticed it. He glanced from the fax machine's display, then back to the number on the card. He had misdialed a single digit!

He took a deep breath. Then as controlled as possible, he re-entered the number, pausing when he finished to verify no mistakes. Once again, he pressed the send key. This time he heard a rewarding ring tone, followed by the familiar bip-buzzing of the fax machine as it made a successful connection. A moment later, the sheets began to feed into the device. As the last document cleared the machine, LaMonk grabbed the papers and fed them into a shredder. The receptacle was empty, and he gathered the short, thin strips in a small paper bag, which he then crumpled up and stuffed down his pants. He quickly disconnected his phone and laptop. Next, he slipped out the fax machine's memory backup battery before powering it down, erasing all record of his transmission.

He treaded lightly to the door, opened it a crack, and peered into the hallway. Halfway down was a custodian vacuuming the floor. He danced as he worked, plugged into earbuds and oblivious to anything around him. LaMonk slipped into the hall and silently closed the door behind him, then walked the other direction to the nearest exit. Stepping out into the darkness, he inhaled a deep, relieved breath of crisp early morning air. It was the first breath of his new life.

9

Washington DC

Katherine Karlson tossed a fresh teabag into a second cup of hot water. Her angry eyes glared transfixed on the newspaper editorial page. Her lips pursed as she glowered over the column she had read. Her disgust peaked, and she tossed the paper across the table as Gene Lawton stepped into the room.

"Damn that man," she exclaimed, "he talks out both sides of his mouth at once!" She pointed to the crumpled paper. "This is the same ungrateful little peon that begged us for exclusive interviews and promised positive press. Now he treats President Tenor like he walks on water! I think Mr. Gestin needs some reminding how this system works; when you bet at the races, you pick your pony and stick with it."

Lawton grabbed a coffee and sat in the chair opposite Karlson. "I think you read too much into that piece, Katherine," he said calmly. "Gestin was admonishing the governors that didn't balance their state budgets. Tenor gets mentioned because he's one of the few that reduced spending while he was a governor."

Karlson gave him a disapproving glare. "And if he's balancing a budget, then he's cutting funds from some other vital program. That's what this paper should be concentrating on."

"Kat, if I'm getting sixty percent of the press to go our way, I'm ecstatic. We are at eighty across the board! Think about that. When was the last time a paper voiced direct opposition to you or any of your proposals? We need to choose our battles. This issue isn't even worthy of a phone call."

Karlson pondered his point as she poured milk into her tea. "Still, Gestin may need reminding to write about the issues that will help his candidate get elected. That's how Washington works, and he knows it."

Lawton opened his notebook and added it to the long list of entries. "All right then," he said, "I'll mention it at the press dinner."

"And while you're at it," she added, "we need something new and negative about Tenor every week. What about sending a team with cell phone scanners to pick up his calls?" Lawton winced painfully. "You saw the mess that came about when a group got caught doing the same thing years ago. I'm not crazy about that one."

Karlson wasn't about to allow her suggestion to be dismissed so easily. "Nobody ever went to court. Nobody went to jail. Nobody ever pointed their finger at the guy that set up the operation. And it worked! The information they recorded destroyed the man's political career. I'd call that a damn good plan! I want the same setup; civilian vehicles following and tapping his calls every time he's mobile. Better yet, make it two teams. There's less chance of being noticed if they alternate."

Lawton scribbled more notes and paused as a thought came to him. "You're not going to get within range of the presidential motorcade to pull that off. His chief of staff, though. . ."

Karlson smiled and gave him a mock slug in the arm. "That's why you're the big dog."

"Good morning, mom. Hello, Gene." Jordan West descended the stairs with an infectious smile and a copy of the paper. "Did you guys read the editorial about the governors and their overspending?"

Karlson smiled and winked at Lawton, then turned to her daughter. "We were just discussing it, dear. I felt the reporter was using it to grandstand for Davis Tenor."

"Really?" Jordan said. "I thought it was amazing how many states operate in the red. Tenor must have done something right if Indiana was one of only twelve not writing bad checks while he was in office there."

Karlson loved seeing her only child so engrossed in assisting her election campaign. Moments like these, however, were when she hoped the kid would hurry up and see the world of politics for what it was.

Jordan's father, Clifford West, had been an exception to many of the rules. Taking a middle-of-the-road approach to his governing style had proven itself effective, earning him support from both parties. Although not on the list of states in the black, he had kept California solvent through some very lean times.

Jordan related more to her father's approach. And despite the differences in philosophy, she truly believed that Katherine Karlson would make a fine president. She supported her mother's campaign in every way she could—

stuffing envelopes, handling the phones, walking door to door to meet voters. From time to time, she even made public appearances on behalf of Karlson.

She had cut the number of classes she was enrolled in by half to be available when needed by the campaign. Her course load was the bare minimum required to remain listed as a full-time student. Her time was split between her home in Los Angeles and Washington, DC. That forced her to take many of the lessons online. Jordan wanted to be helpful but dreaded the thought of losing an entire year of school. After the election, she reasoned, she could add extra classes and still graduate on time.

"Mom, I'm doing that meet and greet at the Essex later this afternoon," Jordan reminded her mother as she poured herself a coffee. "Did you have anything else you needed me for?"

"I don't think so, honey. Gene and I were finishing up here and prepping for an interview on the debate."

Lawton looked up from his laptop. "You're going to want to review this information on Tenor's first marriage and divorce. There are some messy details we can throw out there when the time is right."

Before Karlson could respond, Jordan said, "I hope you're not going to sink to that level. You don't need to go there, mom. Let your message come through, and you'll win because you deserve to win."

Karlson, who was unaccustomed to anyone correcting her, felt the claws coming out. She quickly regained her composure, stood, and put an arm around her daughter. "You're right, of course. This information is good to be aware of but otherwise completely worthless. We'll probably just file it away. Now you, young lady, need to get on your way and get some schoolwork done!" She walked Jordan to the door and saw her out.

Her smile vanished as she turned back to Lawton. "What the hell were you thinking? You know damn well you can't talk about shit like that in front of her!"

Lawton closed his laptop. "Fine, we won't use the divorce info."

Karlson threw up her hand to stop him before he could say another word. "I didn't say don't use it. I said we don't talk about it in front of my daughter, or anyone else for that matter. Just give it to the third-party supporters and let them post it."

Lawton showed no outward reaction but stowed his laptop into a briefcase and got to his feet. "I'll be over at my office," he said with an icy edge as he headed for the door. "Call me when you're ready to continue."

Karlson let him leave, then opened her laptop to read some emails. She did not like him having the last word but was in no mood to continue this conversation just to proclaim herself the victor. Gene was fun, but he was an employee. She might have to remind him of that again soon, but not before the interview. His head needed to be clear and on topic. She also made a mental note not to piss him off again until after she'd been satisfied tonight.

10

Arlington, Virginia

"Look, Vince, your support puts you in the catbird seat for guaranteed approval of your program. Senate bill 8837 is on the inside track right now. What's that? Yes, you have Senator Karlson's word that she votes with you on this. In return, you bring New York, including your esteemed colleague who seems to enjoy straddling the party line. . . Perfect, we knew we could count on you. As always, you have our continued support. Thanks, Vince, we'll talk soon."

Gene Lawton hung up the office phone and cracked his neck as he glanced over the list of names yet to call today. He was making progress but would be at this for another few hours. It was time for a break. He walked past the fax machine as it churned out another document, reminding him to look over its stack of contents soon.

The coffee was still fresh, and Lawton was pouring himself a cup when his assistant walked in with a FedEx packet. "Mr. Lawton, the files from Washington are here."

"Thanks, Marcy," he said, not looking up. "Leave them

on the desk, please."

She walked behind his workspace and set the package down, noticing the stack of faxes in the incoming tray. The phone rang before she could grab them. She answered with her usual salutation. After a moment, she smiled. "Hi Carol, hold on, please." She held out the receiver. "Mr. Lawton, Mrs. Lawton, on line four."

He returned with a steaming cup and took the handset. "Hi, Carol, is everything all right?" Lawton settled into his chair and gave Marcy a look that said he would be tied up a while. She took the opportunity to pull the faxes from the machine and stacked them on his desk, noticing the line in bold print on the top sheet. 'Classified Military Mission.'

She tapped Lawton on the shoulder to get his attention, then pointed at the heading. He turned in his chair and casually glanced over in mid-sentence. The top line caught his eye, and he scrambled to pick it up. "Honey, sorry to cut you off," he said to his wife, "but something big just came up. Let me call you back."

Lawton fumbled to replace the receiver as he read through the message, then flipped back to the cover page. Who was this LaMonk, and how did a man of such dubious loyalty end up in the pipeline that handled critical classified information? He made a mental note to never turn his back on the guy as he re-read the message.

This was astounding. The president had authorized a covert mission using a militant detainee as a homing pigeon to lead them to Sirhan Abbas. This was arguably the most dangerous man in the Middle East, if not the entire world. Take him out, and you stop OASIS cold. He nodded in agreement with the plan, thinking that for once, President Tenor had gotten it right. It was brilliant in its simplicity, and as the details of the mission attested, easy to implement. "Kill

Abbas and stop OASIS," he said with admiration, pushing the fax aside and reaching for his yellow pad.

His pen had barely made contact with the paper when the grin disappeared. He stared forward, his head shaking in disbelief. "Oh, my God!" He pushed back from the desk as all color drained from his face. "Kill Abbas and stop OASIS," he repeated. "Kill Sirhan Abbas, and you end the war. . .and the election!"

He chastised himself for not seeing it sooner. This information wasn't a golden egg to be used against his opponents. It was a neutron bomb that could win the war for the incumbent president. With only months before the election, Karlson's lead would be irreversibly shredded.

"We're going to lose! We're going to fucking lose!" he yelled, slamming his fists on the desk and springing out of his chair. He paced the office as sweat soaked through his shirt and beaded on his forehead.

This election was over, just like that. The best campaign Lawton had ever run would never pull into the station. Derailed by a clandestine hail Mary. How do you counter something like that? How do you compete with the guy bringing peace to a place in the world where peace has never existed? You don't, he conceded. If this mission is successful, then history was about to be rewritten. Katherine Karlson would be nothing more than an interesting political footnote. And he would fail to put his candidate in the White House. He covered his face with his hands, envisioning the conversation he would have with the senator. 'Sorry, I did my best, but you're going to lose.' A brilliant campaign is ended, all because of this fucking military mission. "Damn it all, damn it all!" He punched at the desk. "If this mission succeeds. . ." Lawton stopped mid-sentence, realizing he had spoken both the problem and the solution. "IF!"

11

Washington, DC

Jordan West left her mother's condo and walked the three blocks to a local coffee shop. The brief moments of solitude were becoming less frequent as the election neared. This place had become her secret refuge. They also made excellent coffee.

She ordered up a large dark roast and a muffin and settled in at a high top near the back wall. Checking her watch, she confirmed there was plenty of time to kill before heading to the Essex. She cracked open her laptop, pulled up the web page for the company hosting the event, and read about their product, a multi-purpose electric vehicle platform. The execs were in town drumming up support and funding while ensuring their project remained the darling of Karlson and her party. Although Jordan had little influence, she nevertheless insisted on understanding the topics of discussion. She paged through the product details with genuine interest.

She closed the website and worked through a lesson on one of her online classes. Her mind kept going back to the earlier conversation she'd overheard between her mother and Gene. Did they intend to use that divorce information about the president and start a mudslinging campaign? So far, Karlson had kept her message focused on the issues. Still, it concerned her that Gene had even brought the story up.

Jordan was quite proud that the campaign centered on the positive changes Karlson would bring when elected. There were a few slips here and there, and Jordan was quick to point them out. Her mother usually feigned ignorance of such details, explaining that she could not possibly control every piece of information being stated and reported. Even so, there was more than one instance where her mother had made contradictory statements. Like the time she was speaking to a group of auto union representatives. She made promises that came out of nowhere, as though making them up as she went. Or when, during a speech about the third national health care overhaul, she promised an end to high deductibles for all families. Jordan knew her mother's plan never mentioned that issue.

The prickly truth was she had seen this disconnect between her mother's words and deeds multiple times before. Sometimes it seemed the woman would say whatever it took to appease every single person in a room. This was an impossible feat for anyone. Unless, of course, the goal was to win their support with no intention of actually delivering on the promises made. Not an uplifting thought. Especially for a young woman who believed her mother could drop all of this double-talking crap and still win the election on a firm platform of honesty, integrity, and common sense.

There was one other revelation that kept swirling up, the worst of them all. A repulsive image permanently etched like white phosphorus in the darkness when she closed her eyes—the kiss.

She cringed at the thought as her hands fidgeted, remembering the day she had walked in on her mother and Gene sharing what appeared to be a passionate kiss. Karlson had pushed away from the embrace, feigning the victim. She admonished Gene for his inappropriate actions, then glanced at Jordan standing in the doorway. At the time, Jordan accepted her mother's explanation, desperately wanting to believe it. Now, as it played back again, she remembered her mother's eyes being closed and her arms wrapped around him. These were hardly the actions of a victim. And Jordan was sure the woman had heard her come through the door. She had seen a subtle tell of acknowledgment before she pushed away from Gene.

It was acting, the well-honed skill of Katherine Karlson. That meant Jordan had likely interrupted a passionate moment between the two that may otherwise have ended in the bedroom. She cringed at the thought of her mother having an affair with that man.

Jordan had never told her father what she'd witnessed. In retrospect, she felt he sensed it anyway.

A crack had developed between her parents when her mother announced her bid for the presidency. The gap grew substantially wider when Gene came on the scene. She knew her father loved his wife, but the air between them had become noticeably cold and negative charged. It was as if her mother had moved on from their marriage. Clifford West had been reduced to a stepping stone, powerless to do anything but accept the newly imposed reality.

Jordan struggled to direct her thoughts back into the school lesson as she became aware of a conversation between two guys sitting nearby. The topic had gone from another U2 band comeback to covert government activity.

"Bush led us right into the Iraq war with no proof of

anything. The whole yellow cake thing? What a bunch of bullshit. And we're still there because he wanted to be a 'Wartime President.'"

She listened as a lanky guy with shoulder-length blonde hair and multiple piercings espoused the views shared by many. His companion, a guy with a hairstyle right off a sixties British Invasion album cover, set his cup down and focused thoughtfully on his friend.

"They had enough Intel to know what was going on," he said, "but they jumped before proving the existence of WMDs. No aerial views, no monitoring of the shipments from neighboring countries. Nothing, except the CIA director himself calling it a slam dunk. Bush acted on it anyway. Enough evidence has come to light since proving Saddam did have uranium and poison gas stockpiles at one time. But it didn't matter anymore. Everyone had already made up their minds." He settled back into the worn couch. "I think the history lesson here is that the best Intel in the world means nothing. Not unless you're smart enough to properly analyze it and keep emotions out of any decisions."

Jordan was intrigued. If she closed her eyes, she could imagine a well-informed political consultant making this argument. But here was a guy that looked more like he loaded cargo ships than worked in government. She smiled with interest, tuning more into their conversation.

The pierced guy looked down thoughtfully at his chain-wrapped biker boots for a moment, then added, "Now look at the trouble with this triple alliance in the Middle East. Three tribes of people, three slices of a big ass pie coming together as one. Scary, man. The new Persia has arisen. Now is the time we should cut our losses and run. We've been fighting and giving back pieces of that sand trap for twenty years, and for what? It's still about the oil and our government trying to control the world."

Without thinking, Jordan blurted out, "Nearly every war ever fought has been over the control of resources."

They both turned to her as if in rehearsed unison.

"Oh crap," she said, covering her mouth. "I'm sorry, you guys. I guess I was thinking out loud." Jordan felt their eyes upon her and immediately regretted her outburst. But the subject was one on which she had strong opinions.

"No, no, that's cool," said the one with the sixties haircut. "Finish the thought." He grinned at her as though she was already part of the discussion.

"Forgive me for crashing in, but why do you think things are so different now? The Japanese attacked Pearl Harbor to cripple us in the Pacific so they would have unfettered access to oil. Germany invaded Africa and Russia for the same reason. Israel was conquered and re-conquered throughout history because it was the natural land path between Africa and Europe. And there was fresh water to fight over. Honestly, it's stupid that we're still dependent on foreign oil when we've achieved energy independence here. But could you imagine the economic chaos if suddenly we had no access to oil? Global manufacturing stops, commerce quits, all the money dries up, and the military is crippled. Then we're invaded, and we learn to speak Chinese, or Farsi, the end."

Jordan finished her quick summary of the history of war and looked from one guy to the other. They both grinned back. The one with the sixties hair held his hand out and said, "My name's Ethan, and this is Cody."

Jordan introduced herself and stepped over to shake their hands. They both still grinned back mischievously. "What?" she asked.

Cody, the multiple pierced blonde one, said, “It’s not very often someone finds our debates interesting enough to join in.”

“And never by someone who uses facts in their arguments instead of pure emotion,” added Ethan, the Buffalo Springfield look-alike.

“Yes, well, I’m surrounded by this stuff every day, so I hear some pretty compelling points of view.”

Ethan smiled again. “Tis the town to argue politics. Do you work on the hill?”

“I guess you could say that.” Jordan enjoyed the conversation but knew the potential danger of revealing too much information about herself. She was not required to have a secret service escort and didn’t look forward to dealing with such a boat anchor in her life. She had been careful to ensure she remained incognito enough to lead a nearly ordinary life. The day would come soon enough when a small security force would become mandatory. Certain people would always be eager to exploit her, even harm her if they knew who she was. She decided this was not the time to let her guard down. “I’m an assistant on the Karlson campaign,” she offered, thinking that should be enough information for now.

“Well, she’s on the right side,” said Cody, elbowing Ethan. “I was hoping for Michael Lacrosse to get the nomination, but Karlson got it, so she gets my support.”

Jordan wasn’t thrilled with the lackluster endorsement for her mother. Still, it was better than the alternative. She was careful not to show emotion to such statements. She bit her tongue and kept silent.

Ethan wasn’t so kind. “This is part of the great divide between Cody and me,” he said. “Let’s face it, one party thinks with its head and the other with its heart. I have a few friends running businesses, and I watch the government take more and more of what they earn. People in this country have been convinced that businesses are evil things. They are treated as though they've done something terrible because they work harder to earn more and want to keep it."

"We're just saying everyone should pay their fair share," Cody said.

"And what is fair?" Ethan asked. "How much more than fifty percent of all that I earn should a government be entitled to take unquestioned? Didn't we already have a revolution because of taxation without representation?"

That was her cue. Jordan knew American history, and no amount of self-control would hold her from commenting on her favorite subject. "The funny thing is," she said, "it's your representatives that keep pushing for more taxes. Alexander Hamilton would have taken up arms against his new government if this had happened in his lifetime. And he's the one that created the American tax system in the first place, modeled after the British structure of all places. Well, not income taxes, of course. That came much later. But government and military to be funded by the people was his doing. What we have now, this tax and spend nightmare, is not at all what he had in mind."

"Wow," exclaimed Ethan, nodding and eyeing her like he'd discovered a hidden jewel. "Senator Karlson must not require her staffers to share her opinions on spending policy."

"Oh, believe me, she does!" Jordan laughed. "So she and I just don't have these conversations. I think that's why I jumped in when you two were talking. Sometimes I just need to vent. And I did, and I'm good to go." With that, Jordan stepped back to her table and packed up her laptop.

"Hey, wait," called Ethan. He jumped up from his seat to

catch her as she headed toward the door. “Cody and I play tonight at Nancy Whiskey. Can I put you on the guest list?”

“Seriously, you two political talk show hosts are in a band?” After listening to twenty minutes of point-counter-point, Jordan was having trouble imagining these guys rocking out. But now that she thought about it, they definitely looked the part. Even if they turned out to be a mundane DC garage band, it would be a nice change of pace, and she was happy for the invitation.

“That might be rough, but I’ll see what I can do, thanks.”

Ethan reached for her hand, shook it, and slipped her a band business card. “There’s a Facebook page for the group on the back. We go on at eleven. It would be nice to talk with you again.”

As he released her hand, Jordan slowly stepped back, their gazes remaining fixed. She smiled and began thinking that this had been the most enjoyable moment she’d had in weeks.

12

Arlington, Virginia

Gene Lawton washed down a stale sandwich with cold coffee as he paced past his desk. He eyed the pages of ideas he'd scribbled so far. The answer wasn't among them. This was beginning to feel like the quest for the holy grail. There had to be a way to make this work. Every instinct told him so. Still, the elusive perfect plan danced beyond the periphery of his imagination. He was exhausted but would not, could not consider quitting. Nothing else mattered until he figured this out.

He had spent the last twenty-two hours brainstorming. Scribbling down every thought that came into mind. He'd even called on a small group of trusted advisors for additional input. It was a fine line to tread as he sought their ideas without giving away too many details. Most of what he'd learned could not be shared with anyone. That made the task all the more challenging. He glanced over at the remaining day-old sandwiches as he got a whiff of his own odor. All thoughts of hunger quickly dissipated. At least he could take time out to brew a fresh pot of coffee. An infusion of caffeine might spark some life into his numbed brain. He headed for the reception area to get one going.

The implications of what he was attempting rattled him, and rightfully so. Interfering with a clandestine military mission to save this campaign could be considered treason. What if his actions cost the lives of the people involved. He would be forced to live with that grief behind bars. But did the reward equal the risk? Was getting his candidate into the White House still the best and most logical plan of action? Lawton was not the type to accept failure in any form. The answer then was an emphatic yes.

So, on to question number two, how to go about scuttling a military mission? He would also have to guarantee it could not boomerang back on himself or his candidate. God, she would owe him big for this one. Who else could she find that would even ponder these questions before turning tail and heading for the hills.

He poured himself a fresh cup and decided to take a short break. He found the remote and clicked on the TV, then dropped into the couch.

The television was tuned to a news network with a short clip from Afghanistan looping over and over. It was a common practice used when the story's length was longer than the accompanying video footage. He watched as the same four Marines kept climbing out of a Humvee to take up defensive positions. The image then switched to a group of Afghanis burning an American flag. Same old same old, he thought as he stood up and began pacing the room.

His head throbbed as though it were filled with gears out of synch, grinding and squealing like metal on metal. His mind was exhausted, incapable of any new thoughts. He fumbled with the remote, flipping mindlessly through channels, paying little attention to anything displayed. Two-hundred stations, he thought, and nothing worth watching.

A blip of a news story on an unfamiliar station caught his attention. He stared at the images, feeling a connection being made deep in the folds of his brain. He thought of the documents and photos laid out on his desk and then looked back at the news network. Neural synapses suddenly sparked and returned online, pulsing and firing. His head hummed like a rebooting dynamo. The new thought came to him like a vibrant dream. An incomplete framework of a massive idea revealed itself. He immediately began constructing the missing segments to complete the plan. Brainstorms such as these were the reason he was so valuable to his clients. But this one took even him by surprise. This was incredible! And assuming the demeanor and tenacity of the people it would involve, he could all but guarantee the results would be exactly what he needed.

He rushed back to his desk, grabbed his notepad, and began scribbling the steps necessary for his plan. He had filled three pages and was halfway through a fourth when the phone chirped on his desk.

"Where have you been?" Karlson demanded, sounding as much concerned as annoyed. "I've been trying to reach you all day!"

"Katherine, there's been a rather significant development. I think it best that we meet in private to discuss the details."

"Well, aren't you the voice of doom and gloom! What's happened?"

"I received a bit of a bombshell from a new inside source. It's going to change everything one way or another. I'm still developing a strategy so we can use it to our advantage." Lawton looked over his notes like a general studying field maps and battle lines.

“What could possibly hurt us now?” she asked. “We lead in every poll, and we’re still gaining ground.”

“If we play this right, it may amount to nothing more than a speed bump. But it’s big, and there’s much to discuss. We have major decisions to make that can’t be done over the phone.”

“You’re scaring me, Gene,” she said. “Stay there. I’m on my way.”

13

Washington, DC

Jordan was pleased that the business meeting had taken less time than anticipated. The company executives made an appearance and took some photos with her. Brief statements were made to the press expressing their gratitude and loyalty to the Karlson camp. She'd seen it all before. This was a typical dog and pony show. Jordan was polite and engaging during their conversations, which she found vague and short on specifics. It was clear they didn't expect her to know much about their product. They would have been surprised. She didn't take it personally, though. It was the way things were done in this town. Another hoop to jump through for the team.

A chauffeured town car awaited at the Essex Hotel's main entrance. Jordan's stomach grumbled as she climbed in. She rarely ate while on the clock and had shied away from the impressive spread of sandwiches and appetizers. Jordan had seen candid photos of others caught with a mouthful of food or sipping a drink and was not about to offer up such an embarrassing photo op. The campaign didn't need that kind of negative press right now.

Needless to say, she was starved. She asked the driver to swing past her favorite Chinese takeout joint, phoning the order ahead to save time. She would eat and relax back at the condo for a few hours before heading out to see her new friends play. Hopefully, she could talk her best friend, Amy Pierson, into joining her.

Jordan sat back, took in a deep breath, and caught herself thinking about Ethan again. It was surprising how much she looked forward to seeing him. This was such an awkward feeling. She didn't typically warm up to guys that hit on her. Then again, he really hadn't, had he? She was the one who forced herself into a private conversation. They could have easily blown her off. But here was this nice-looking guy cut from the rough, yet so out of the ordinary, so unpretentious and sincere.

She had tried dating in DC and found herself paired up with young stuffed suited wannabes. They were typically so transparent, saying or doing anything to latch on to their next ride up to Capitol Hill. A few had shown interest in her. She found their actions, their demeanor, and for that matter, their lack of normal human traits not worthy of her time. They were perfect, with the whitest teeth, the brightest smiles. Hair arranged painstakingly to frame their handsome faces. They said all the right things, and they were painfully polite. Maybe that was the biggest turnoff. They were like talking Ken dolls. So polished, starched, and probably prettier than most of the women they dated.

She chuckled to herself, thinking she preferred a guy with a little dirt under his fingernails. Someone creative that didn't always say the right thing or try to live life scripted. She wondered if she was describing Ethan or maybe hoping he was as genuine as he seemed. This wasn't like her, and she thought about pushing the whole thing out of her mind. Then again, what harm was there in pursuing a relationship if it offered a temporary escape from the anything-but-honest world she worked in?

She pulled out her phone to call Amy, but it began vibrating before she could dial. She read the incoming caller ID and smiled as she pressed the answer button. "Hi, Daddy! How are you?"

"I should ask you the same, kiddo. Are you so busy that you don't have time to check in with your dad once in a while?"

Jordan realized it had been over a week since she had talked to her father. Not a terribly long time, but unusual for them. She had an endearing relationship with Clifford West, and they conversed regularly. The subject matter of their discussions covered most anything, but rarely politics. She was grateful for that, especially now.

"You know mom," she said. "She always has something for me to do. I just did a meet and greet with some local business bigwigs."

"Ah," he answered in a knowing tone. "Sending her lieutenant to muster support with the if-then delegation."

"Exactly," Jordan chuckled at her father's quick and accurate assessment of the meeting. If Senator Karlson addressed their lobbying concerns, then they would continue to offer their support. That was how it worked, pure and simple.

"Keeping up with your classes?"

"Yeah," she responded in a less confident tone. "Even with the reduced credits I'm carrying, a couple of these subjects are tough. And getting support online can be a bear."

"You can always come home for a few weeks and do it the old-fashioned way sitting in a classroom."

"Nice thought." She paused, thinking how great it would be to go home and be nothing more than a student again. "Things are heating up here, but I would love to make that happen soon. I can't recharge my battery as fast out here as I can at home."

"That makes perfect sense. DC is a very demanding place. Some people live for that environment, but it hits you like it hits me. It takes away more than it gives back."

"That's exactly how it feels," she exclaimed, glad to know they both saw the land of superficial for what it was. But then, they always had that connection. A simple conversation with her dad could always bring her back from dark places."Meeting any normal people out there?"

"Funny you should put it that way, but yes. I've had a few nice conversations with some locals. I'm looking forward to more."

"Very good. Did your mom meet them?"

"No, not yet, we only met this week."

"She will soon enough then. I think doing background checks on everyone you meet is your mother showing she loves you."

Jordan laughed out loud. She had entertained that same thought on more than one occasion. "I do cut her some slack on that one. She's in go mode, and you know how she gets when she's hell-bent on a goal."

"Yes," the governor agreed, "and you've always known not to stand in the path of oncoming heavy machinery." He chuckled at his own line. "She has her moments of lucidity here and there. Hopefully, you can get some plain old mom time soon."

"True."

"Speaking of having no time, I gotta run myself. Just wanted to check-in and make sure you're holding up okay."

"I am, and thanks. Hope to see you soon."

"Same here. Love you, kid."

"Love you, dad."

She started putting the phone away, then remembered about calling Amy. The conversation with her father had topped off her tank. She smiled, noticing the sunlight that streamed through the side window now felt a little warmer and brighter.

14

Two straight days of non-stop activity, and Gene Lawton never felt more engaged and on target. The formidable list of contacts to call had steadily dwindled as he worked non-stop, downing pot after pot of coffee while pacing the room and talking incessantly into the ever-present phone earpiece. The plan was now in place, with most of the heavy lifting complete. The last piece of the puzzle would be to call in every favor and promise owed him or the senator. That could come later. For now, he concentrated on the multiple roles he would play in this twisted reality theater. He switched seamlessly from producer to screenplay writer, and finally, director.

He paused a moment between calls, listening as the two speechwriters in the next room prepped the senator for the performance of her life. The one that could carry her to victory. Tonight, Katherine Karlson would broadcast an offering of hope and compromise. Her audience was at the epicenter of the violence—the people of Iran, Iraq, and Afghanistan.

Lawton grinned at the seeming simplicity of his intricate

stroke of genius. In the next few days, Karlson would stand alone as the sole candidate who understood the strained emotions and intricate details of the Middle East conflict. But as crucial as the message appeared, it was not the primary objective. The plan's true brilliance was not in the message itself but in what lay concealed. This entire choreographed show was Gene Lawton's Trojan Horse.

This would be the defining moment in the senator's campaign. It also eliminated a potentially insurmountable obstacle that could have destroyed her. Lawton had used that information and accomplished the impossible, proving once again that he had no equal among his peers. He would be seen as the brains and power behind Katherine Karlson, the man who won her the presidency. Once he accomplished that, he could write his own ticket. There was no limit to his opportunities as White House Chief of Staff. Political favors and the tide of contributions and gifts would roll in behind him like a tsunami.

Months from now, Gene Lawton would be one of the most powerful men in DC and well on his way to amassing his personal fortune. He envisioned an enormous wave again but this time saw himself riding its crest on a surfboard that bore the likeness of Karlson. True enough, he wouldn't be in this position today without the good senator. She had risen from a fading glimmer town actress to become a mighty political force to be reckoned with. Without his guidance, though, she would never have made it this far, this fast. Instead, she would have been flipped and tossed aimlessly with no direction, like a rudderless rowboat at the mercy of an angry sea.

Katherine owed him more than she would ever acknowledge. For now, at least, knowing that her success also guaranteed his own would be enough. He enjoyed their affair and understood it would never amount to anything more than the occasional interlude between the sheets. She would not leave her husband. Lawton himself had fallen out of love with his own wife long ago but would not leave her, either.

The intimate moments with Karlson would soon be ending. The relationship would return to that of two professionals. He made a mental note to bed her at least a few more times before the election. After that, memories of their love-making would have to suffice. And they were abundant and intense. He thought of her warm skin as he kissed her neck. Feeling her firm breasts in his hands. Her tongue meeting his, her body responding to every move as he slid deeper inside her. He closed his eyes and could feel her tense and quiver beneath him as she climaxed. Her soft and gentle moans keeping rhythm to his body thrusts.

The image shattered as the senator's voice, shrill and agitated, cut through the silence. She entered the room with one of her speechwriters in tow.

"I told you how many times already? There is nothing memorable in any of this! Honestly, Jenn, you write better lines for actors than for the people they're supposed to portray!"

"Senator, I've written some excellent points that will make people take notice. Look on page…"

"Let me stop you there. I don't see any JFK zingers, and that's what we're talking about here, hon. I need that big line that the voters will be repeating years after this election. And I need more than one. I need greatness. That's why you're here, isn't it? Please, go write something historical, for God's sake. We're up against the clock, and you haven't given me shit!"

Karlson marched over to a liquor cabinet and pulled out a

tumbler and bottle of Scotch. Her hand shook as she poured out four fingers of liquid courage.

Lawton observed from a distance, reading Karlson's body language. Waiting to be sure she had exhausted her thoughts. He knew from experience that she was not open to input if she still had something to say. Her mannerisms told him she was nervous and testy, balancing on the brink of something much worse. This had all the earmarkings of previous episodes where she had completely lost control and required hours of consolation. He did not have that kind of time and needed to douse the flames before they burned out of control. It's what he did, and he did it better than anyone.

The first step was getting the senator back into her comfort zone. Next to her beauty, confidence was her most powerful attribute. She needed to believe that the words she spoke would be historic. Lawton recalled one of JFK's most notable quotes, 'Ask not what your country can do for you, ask what you can do for your country.' Even these memorable words were not original and rumored to have been borrowed from Kennedy's former headmaster.

The primary function of a modern-day statesman was to read someone else's words convincingly from a teleprompter. It was the speech writer's responsibility to create those phrases and slogans that would be remembered long after the public had forgotten that few of the promises ever came to fruition.

Lawton jumped into action. "Jennifer, this is one of those moments when you shouldn't be so concerned with plagiarizing other speeches. You know all of the great ones by heart. Just do a little cut and paste. Stick a few good lines together and connect them with your own words. I really need you to pen two memorable quotes before the end of the day. Can you do that?"

Jennifer was accustomed to writing under pressure. She also prided herself on originality. It's what made her so valuable when writing scripts for the Capitol Beat show. She paused to consider the irony of the situation. She exercised more discretion when creating dialogue for fictitious characters than this. Although troubled by the thought, she also saw a twisted humor. She nodded to Lawton. "I'll see what I can do." She grabbed her laptop and headed for a secluded corner. "Some of the things I hear," she muttered, shaking her head. "Who would believe I didn't make that up?"

15

Jordan was impressed, but Amy was absolutely flipping out over this band. 'Protocol 4' was far better than Jordan had anticipated. Then again, she had seen enough of other dismal, screaming, head-banging bands in the past that her expectations were low. This was a pleasant surprise. There was melody, there was great rhythm, and they were tight!

Jordan didn't know much about drums. Even so, she could tell that Ethan's driving beat was a big part of them sounding like a band rather than just four individuals. She watched them watching him and could tell where the music was going by the subtle acknowledgments between them. They moved and played as one. Something you rarely saw in any band, let alone a 'B' band in a 'B' bar. She watched, felt, listened, and enjoyed what she knew was a rare moment.

Upon finishing their last song, the stage crew began hauling amplifiers and drums away to make room for the headline act. Jordan watched as Ethan oversaw the dismantling of his drum kit before he disappeared backstage. She had looked forward to talking with him again but figured

Ethan and Cody were probably amongst the throes of adoring groupies by now.

She leaned over to Amy and shouted over the pulsing intermission music. "I don't think they're coming back out."

Amy started to respond, then grinned. "Look behind you," she said.

Ethan was ordering a drink at the bar. He looked over to Jordan and motioned for her to wait. Grabbing his drink, he came over and slid into the chair beside her. "You made it! I didn't know if your mother would let you come to this club without a military escort."

Jordan looked perplexed. Did he know more about her identity than he had let on?

Ethan gave a sly smile. "You know, you looked so familiar to me that I did a quick lookup online and found a picture of you and your family. I guess I'm that much more impressed that your opinions are still your own. Your mother is a very persuasive woman."

Jordan's smile faded as an internal alarm sounded. Her eyes instinctively scanned the room for threats.

"I liked your band a lot," she said, "but we were just getting ready to go. Thanks for the invitation. It was fun."

Ethan picked up on her apprehension. "Hey, I didn't tell anyone, not even Cody. Please, stay awhile." He reached over to take her hand. "I didn't tell you I knew who you were to frighten you or blow your cover." He leaned in closer, his lips touching her ear. "I told you because I wanted to be truthful."

The admission didn't help.

"Ethan, I had a nice time talking with you, but I've been in situations where people wanted to get next to me because of who I am."

Ethan looked at her a moment, then chuckled. "I'd like to get next to you *despite* who you are. I can't tell you the last time I had a stimulating conversation with a woman. It's just weird that it happens with someone who should be at the opposite end of the political spectrum. We found more common ground in a half-hour than, than. . .look, if you'd rather go somewhere else, we can do that, but I'm asking you, please, spend some time with me..."

The look in his eyes and tone of voice told Jordan that either he was a brilliant liar, or she had stumbled upon someone truly sincere and worth getting to know. This wasn't the way she had envisioned meeting Mr. Right but decided it was worth pursuing.

"I know of a little speakeasy not far from here," she said. "Now that you know my little secret, you'll understand that I have to watch where I go. I don't know how safe it is for me to be here much longer."

Ethan nodded with a mischievous grin. "That sounds great," he said, "and we can leave whenever you want. But I think you're safer here than you realize. I counted three of your guardians already."

Jordan watched as Ethan pointed toward two agents. One stood near the stage, and another was sitting not far from them at the bar. Even though they were in plain clothes, she could tell by their mannerisms that they didn't belong here. Surprised, a little embarrassed, and downright impressed with Ethan's observational skills, Jordan said, "They're not with me, you know. I had no idea. So, where is the third? I don't. . .wait, okay, that was too easy. And I didn't see that before? "

The last secret service agent was the most obvious, dressed in a suit and talking into his shirt cuff. You wouldn't notice him standing to the side of the main entrance unless you walked in and turned around. Standing in plain sight, he had become near invisible.

"So," asked Ethan, "would you like to go?"

"You know, I'd kind of like to hear a bit of the next band first. We're already here, and mother sent the marines to guard me. I think we should relax, have another drink and catch their set." She smiled and nestled into her chair. For once, the sight of her security detail was putting her at ease instead of pissing her off.

Ethan pulled his chair closer to hers and said, "That sounds like a well-thought-out, logical plan of action." He clinked his bottle against hers and flagged a waitress.

16

At 3:00 pm on the dot, Gene Lawton heard the outer office door opening, followed by footsteps and muffled voices. He entered the reception area and made introductions with the three visitors. They walked together to the senator's office. Karlson would be joining them shortly, he explained, and they should feel free to set up their equipment.

Lawton sensed their excitement as they unpacked and assembled tripods, cameras, microphones, and lights. He imagined how much more energized they would be when they took the bait. He offered refreshments, which they all politely declined. The plan relied on this group dropping their inhibitions and letting curiosity dictate their actions. He excused himself to allow them time to get comfortable and examine their surroundings.

Karlson stood in the adjoining room as he walked in and pulled the door behind him. She smiled giddily. "Are we ready?"

"Give them a few more minutes, then we'll make a noisy entrance. Matthew, is everything good for you?"

Matt Grunberg, Senator Karlson's chief of security, poked

his head out from the closet-sized networking room. "Yes, sir, we're ready to go here."

Karlson's eyes twinkled with admiration. "I'm still amazed you were able to make all of this happen so quickly, Gene. I wouldn't know where to begin to bring all of this together."

Lawton smiled back. "It was no cakewalk. I'll admit to being dumbfounded when this landed in our lap. The biggest task was figuring how to turn a detriment into an asset. Speaking of which, Ms. Karlson, you are on!"

He pushed open the connecting door into the senator's office, then held up a finger for Karlson to wait as he went through. She took a moment to smooth out her flattering gray Ann Klein business suit.

"Lady and gentlemen," Lawton announced, "may I present the senator from the great state of California, Katherine Karlson."

He moved aside to allow Karlson to seize the attention of the three people gathered around her desk. A tall, stunning woman with waist-length jet black hair stood, smiled, and held out her hand. Hers was a face sculpted by the masters. Her eyes were deep, bottomless black pools, her makeup highlighting her natural beauty. She was dressed in a simple yet stunning navy pantsuit with a beige button-down blouse that accentuated her lean, shapely form.

Lawton stepped forward and began introducing the visitors. "Senator Karlson, may I present Deeba Gohar, from Al Jazeera television. The sound and lighting equipment tech is Maaz Nubeer to your left, and the camera operator is Kasheef Sahir."

Deeba took Karlson's hand and gave it a firm shake. "I am grateful you have agreed to an interview with us, Madam Senator."

"The pleasure is all mine, Deeba," Karlson exclaimed. "Our countries have so much in common, yet such monumental misunderstandings. I hope we can shed some light on a few of them today."

"That is my wish as well," the beautiful reporter replied. Her voice was silky smooth with only the slightest hint of an accent. "The best way to inform the people of the region that you do not support this terrible war is by explaining it directly to them yourself. I believe that after this interview is broadcast, millions of Muslims across the world will stand beside you in your quest for the American presidency."

Karlson fought to maintain her composure. Yes, this was going to work, and yes, this would bring her three steps closer to a lock on the highest office in the land. "I feel exactly the same way," she replied. "Now, if you are ready, we can begin. I thought I would sit at my desk during the interview. Will that work for you and the crew?"

"Yes, of course," answered Deeba. "Kasheef will film from over my shoulder. We will edit in some additional second camera shots of me asking the questions after we finish. Maaz, would you set the lights, please?"

The engineer nodded and switched on a pair of flood lamps mounted to large silver umbrella-shaped reflectors. The room lit brightly. He adjusted the reflectors until the senator and reporter were both bathed in a warm glow of soft, bounced light.

"Very good," nodded Deeba, "now let us begin." She looked to Kaseef to see that he had the cameras rolling. He nodded and gave a thumbs up.

"In four, three, two. . .this is Deeba Gohar with Al Jazeera television, the voice of the Middle East. Today, I have the honor of speaking with the distinguished Senator of California, Katherine Karlson. Ms. Karlson is a candidate for the

United States' presidency and a strong supporter of the Muslim people. Good afternoon, senator, and thank you for taking the time to address some of the issues that are critically important to our people."

Karlson straightened in her chair, feeling the magnitude of the moment, presidential and powerful, but at the same time like a little girl who had finally gotten a pony. She suppressed the urge to beam from ear to ear, keeping her emotions in check, channeling them appropriately for the part she portrayed. She was the brilliant actress once again. Her rehearsed smile was the picture of sincerity.

"Thank you, Deeba, and thanks to your film crew for joining us this afternoon. I believe in the unity of our people. My promise to you and everyone watching is that when I become president of this great nation, I will always remember that the price of greatness is responsibility."

Jennifer Griffon smiled as she listened from the conference room. "Didn't waste any time throwing that one out there," she said quietly, referring to the Winston Churchill quote she had pilfered for the senator.

Karlson felt the entire interview going her way. The questions being asked, although not reviewed beforehand as was the custom, were being tossed like slow-pitch softballs. No surprises, nothing to catch her off guard or make her look bad. It was clear that Deeba and her crew were pleased to have a new ally in the United States Senate. They were presenting Karlson to their audience as the new hope of Islam.

She finished answering a question concerning a bill she co-sponsored that would give full government benefits to all immigrants when Lawton came from the next room and whispered something in her ear. The expression on her face changed to one of concern, and she turned to Deeba. "The

President has asked to speak with me immediately. I'm sorry, but you will have to excuse me for a few moments."

Deeba nodded her understanding as the senator rose and walked with Lawton back the way he had come. They passed through the outer door and pulled it shut.

Karlson hurried over to the security room where Matt Grunburg sat. "Have they seen the documents yet?" she asked, not attempting to mask her excitement.

"They haven't made a move for them yet, but I think the cameraman noticed them as soon as you left the room."

Grunberg eyed the three video monitors displaying Karlson's desk and office from hidden cameras. "Now look," he pointed, "he's telling the other two about what he's seen."

They watched as Deeba stood and peered over the desk at a manilla envelope on the credenza. In large red letters was stamped a single word; CLASSIFIED. She whispered something to the sound tech who stood to keep watch for the senator's return. Deeba hurried behind the desk with the cameraman. He filmed while she expertly extracted the documents from the folder and flipped through the pages. In less than a minute, they had scanned them all without stopping to examine any of the pages. She slid the documents back into the envelope and placed them exactly where she found them. All three then took their places in front of the desk.

"Christ, she's good!" Karlson exclaimed. "Tell me she hasn't pulled that one before."

"I think we have what we need," Lawton added. "Let's finish this up. Matt, is this security video being stored anywhere else in the system?"

Grunberg broke his attention from the monitors and glanced back. "It records through the central surveillance system of the building, then the data is burned to a DVD.

Other than that, the hard drives re-record over themselves, and there are no duplicates."

Lawton's brow furrowed as he leaned in closer. "This is absolutely critical," he said in a near whisper. "There cannot be any record of this event. Are we clear?"

"As we discussed earlier," Grunberg huffed with annoyance at being questioned. "I am the only one with access to these files. I will personally go down and erase the hard drive and destroy the DVD within a couple of hours."

Lawton nodded, patting him on the back. He turned to Karlson and gave her a wink. "Intermission is over, senator, and time for act two."

"Well, then," she said, "let's not keep our guests waiting any longer." She walked back to the door leading to the office, then turned and gave Lawton a thumb's up.

"I'm terribly sorry about that," Karlson announced louder than necessary as she pushed through the door. "The president does not call often, and when he does, he expects an immediate response." She walked back behind her desk, careful not to acknowledge the documents on the credenza. She settled back into her chair, flashed her most charming smile, and said, "Now, where were we?"

DEEBA GOHAR STRUGGLED to keep her thoughts on the remainder of the interview. She had recognized a few of the names written in the documents pirated from the good senator. Abu Dahl was an insurgent who had been imprisoned for what, eight years? Everyone knew Sirhan Abbas was the leader of all united freedom fighters throughout the Middle East. So why would their names come up now in a classified US military document? What was the connection between the two? She wanted to read it in its entirety and decided to view the footage in the van as they drove back to the studio.

In another day or two, it would no longer be a secret. The world would know every detail. She worked to subdue the smile that kept curling her lips. Just a little longer with this self-inflated windbag, she told herself. Then, the fireworks would begin.

This interview itself was a plus for her career, but the secret document's discovery would launch her to new, unimagined levels. If this didn't get her the position as network anchor, nothing would. She had been close to locking it down once before, but at the last moment, it had been rescinded. She knew why immediately. Girosh Mohammad oversaw and controlled everything at Al Jazeera back at the main studio in Doha, Qatar. He had denied the promotion. The reason was supposed to be a secret, which meant that everyone knew. He was sleeping with the woman who became the new anchor. This bombshell story would change everything. He would have to promote her this time. But just in case, she had a little ammunition of her own, namely some video footage from a hidden camera showing Mr. Mohammad having his way with the current anchor in her dressing room. Mohammad would be forced to offer Deeba the anchor slot, or the steamy porno starring himself being serviced by the lovely Talla Marwesh would find its way into the hands of his wife. An anonymous email would do the job quite nicely. She contemplated sending the video anyway, even after accepting the new position. After all, the pig should pay.

17

Guantanamo Bay, Cuba

The new Airbus A319 CEO class jet descended gracefully from the azure Caribbean sky. It kissed the hot concrete runway with a chirp and huff of blue smoke. The pilot taxied to a secluded corner of the US Air Force Base and shut down the engines.

The owner of the wide-bodied craft had arranged this controversial visit months earlier. With the help from a long list of special interest groups and curried political favors, the television mogul had made the otherwise impossible flight a reality. Inside, twelve excited passengers unbuckled their seatbelts and mingled about, congratulating themselves on their contributions to the noble cause.

Marissa Danforth was an outsider to the tight-knit group. The young freshman congresswoman from Minnesota strolled among the throes of Hollywood and Washington, DC elite as they laughed and conversed about movie roles, pending legislation, and the day's upcoming activities. She sipped gourmet coffee from bone china and nibbled on a freshly baked croissant, listening intently. Marissa smiled with nervous excitement and thanked her good fortune for being added to the guest list. Now all she needed was to be welcomed into their fold.

Her attendance was a last-minute addition, and she had only been casually introduced to the other passengers. To be fair, it wasn't her reputation or deeds that earned her passage. She owed that distinction to her older sister, Glenda Danforth, a rising actress who took up the cause of the lead organizer. Glenda was currently on location in Madrid, shooting her next movie, and unable to attend. She sent Marissa in her place.

Marissa's stance on issues such as this current crusade had caused an uproar in her home state. She was elected by a slim margin, then proceeded to ignore her own campaign pledges, adopting an alternative agenda as soon as her black pumps touched down in DC. She now faced a recall petition less than a year into her first term. It was doubtful she would hold the seat for another.

Although she strongly believed in the cause that brought these people here today, her direct involvement had a more selfish motive. She was looking for them to take up her cause and help propel her into a senate seat. So far, the plan was not working. She walked among these VIPs remaining hopeful but feeling invisible. Without their support, she was destined to return home to scrutiny, censure, and obscurity.

There was a sudden flurry of activity, and Marissa caught a glimpse of their hostess. Erin Laurent emerged from her aft bedroom suite wearing a subtle but flattering Claiborne outfit in vibrant blue. The other passengers gathered around, heaping praise. Thanking her for including them on this momentous journey.

Laurent was an actress first and foremost, but her

activism played a strong second. She had sworn a personal oath to fight for the freedom of the infamous prisoner of Guantanamo Bay. Now, after a year of staging worldwide rallies and protests and building a loyal and very vocal following, the day had finally arrived.

Laurent's last two films were box office flops despite the hype and sizable personal investments spent on promotion. They were decent movies. But audiences dwindled since she became a vocal opponent of her own country. Most of Hollywood stood beside her, blaming her dwindling success on the political backlash. Behind the scenes, however, the big production companies subtly began distancing themselves. Her name was poison to a good script. Erin Laurent had destroyed her own marketing potential. People could no longer imagine her in any of the roles she played. Not when they remembered her screaming into a bullhorn at police, calling them the real enemy.

These days, when she wasn't marching for her latest protest endeavor, she was seen out on the town with the owner of Global Access Media. Rumors that the two were romantically involved circulated in the tabloids and gossip shows. The fact that this entourage was traveling on Ethan LeClair's personal jet had not gone unnoticed. Every major paper would be covering this story of the prisoner's release as it unfolded. Of course, GAM would be the only network with the inside scoop. One reporter and cameraman were allowed on the plane. It was no secret who wrote their paychecks.

Erin Laurent worked her way through the length of the jet, talking animatedly to friends and supporters. When she reached the cockpit, she unclipped the microphone from its cradle, turned to face her guests, and squeezed the talk button. Her voice came through the premium audio system clear and bright.

"Friends… we've done it!"

Instant applause and joyful cheers went up as they all shared the moment of self-congratulation and closure to an enduring year-long process. They were still hugging and shaking hands when Laurent continued.

"I am about to walk into the bowels of this notorious prison to free a man whom justice has ignored. He will be given a second chance at life because of what we here have accomplished. I can't thank you all enough for your unwavering support through this ordeal. Senator Dunwade, you stood with us from the beginning and brought our cause to the forefront with your speech at the capitol. Valerie Tynes and Victor Manly, two fine actors and my good friends, your contributions helped carried us forward when we needed you most. Congresswoman Marissa Danforth, you went against your own party base to rally for our cause. That took balls, lady! I know your sister, Glenda, is very proud of you." Laurent pointed to Danforth, giving her a wink.

"It's been a long, hard road," she continued. "The costs have been high, both personally and professionally. But at the end of this day, each of us can proudly proclaim, 'I share in the deeds and actions of Abu Dahl from this day forward.'"

There was another warm round of applause, and Laurent basked in the glorious moment. She then gave the sharply dressed young flight attendant a nod. The man stepped forward, turned the release bar, and pushed open the cabin door.

The bright tropical morning sun flooded into the plane, instantly raising the temperature and humidity. A stairway was rolled into place, and Laurent walked down the steps toward an awaiting green army sedan. A uniformed officer stepped forward and greeted her.

"Good morning, Ms. Laurent. I am Lieutenant Hodges, and I will be escorting you to meet with Major Geddings."

Laurent put on a smile as Hodges opened the back door of the sedan. Turning to the rest of her group, she shouted, "Wish me luck," giving a thumb's up, then sliding into the no-frills vehicle. She found the interior even more understated than the outside. Thankfully, the drive would be a short one.

The sedan pulled away and crossed the military airport, arriving at the security gate of the prison entrance minutes later. A tall gate of chain link and barbed wire began to open. The sedan proceeded through to a small guard shack at an inner gate manned by two sentries. Hodges pulled up and displayed his credentials to a bar code reader. The device beeped, and the guard nodded, waving them through the second gate as the first closed behind. Hodges drove to a parking area and pulled in near the entrance, then came around and opened the passenger door. "Follow me, please," he said.

They entered the building, walked past two armed guards, then came to a long, high stainless steel counter. Hodges grabbed a clipboard, passed it to Laurent, and asked her to sign in and show her identification. She scribbled her name and slid her passport to the duty officer behind the counter. The officer, a middle-aged hulk of a man in desert camos with a severe buzz cut, scanned her ID. He handed it back, along with an identification card on a lanyard.

"As you know, Ms. Laurent," he said in a deep southern drawl, "this is a secure military installation. You are required to wear this identification while on the base. Stay close to the lieutenant here, and do not seek entry into any areas other than where he directs you. Is that clear?"

Laurent had been briefed on what she saw as pretentious

military protocols that were to be followed to the letter. "Yes," she said, nodding, "I understand."

The duty officer pushed a button under the counter and a security door unlocked with a loud metallic clank. Hodges directed her in and down a wide, cream-colored hallway to an orange door with a small wire mesh window. He opened it and ushered her inside.

Laurent found herself in a sparsely furnished meeting room where two other officers sat conversing. As she entered, the officers rose to greet her.

"Good morning, Ms. Laurent, I am Major Geddings, and this is Colonel Bradley."

Laurent offered a smile and shook their hands.

"As you're no doubt aware," he continued, "the man you are here to collect is extremely dangerous, and—"

She put up her hand and stopped him mid-sentence. "You have never found him guilty of a crime in court, Major. That makes him a political prisoner." Her eyes narrowed with a defiant glare.

Both Bradley and Geddings had seen Laurent in action before. They knew there would be no reasoning with her. That battle was lost long ago, and it was not their job to change the outcome.

"Ms. Laurent," Geddings said when he was sure she was done making her point. "I serve at this base as the chief psychiatrist for all patients and soldiers."

The actress began speaking again, but Geddings held up a finger.

"It is not my intention to stop you from carrying through with your plan. But I would be remiss if I did not at least attempt to warn you about the man you have come to free."

Laurent rolled her eyes and turned away.

"Hear me out," he insisted. "This is for your own good. I

have done a thorough psychological profile of this man. You need to understand that Abu Dahl *is* evil incarnate. He is personally responsible for the deaths of hundreds, if not thousands, of innocent people. As well as being a murderer, he has brutally raped girls as young as eleven years old. He personally coordinated attacks that decimated entire villages. You say he was not found guilty of these crimes, and that's true. That is only because the people who would testify against him live in fear. The price, you see, for speaking out against him is death."

Geddings looked away, searching for words that might be heard by a woman who had already decided not to listen. Words that might save her life.

"I don't agree with what you're doing," he continued. "Having said that, I don't wish to see you harmed in this misdirected endeavor. For your own sake, do not leave this man unattended. Do not allow him access to a weapon, or you will die at his hands. He may act otherwise, but know that he detests you because you are a woman that speaks your mind. Do not believe for a moment that he views you as anything more than a useful tool that he would strike down the moment he deems you unnecessary. Do what you must but get as far away from this man as soon as you possibly can."

Before Laurent could formulate a rebuttal, the outer door opened. In stepped two large guards escorting a thin, dark man in an orange jumpsuit. He was manacled at the wrists and ankles, the chains jingling as he shuffled in. His deep-set eyes swept from left to right, studying everyone in the room. His gaze fell upon Laurent, locking there as if he were breathing in her image, scanning her from top to bottom. He caught the scent of her perfume the moment he entered. It lingered like a strong sweet taste on his tongue. He glared hungrily at her red lips and exposed cleavage, feeling equal amounts of disgust and lust. His pulse quickened, and he felt a throbbing in his groin. His eyes gave away nothing.

Laurent stepped toward the prisoner with arms extended. "Mr. Dahl, I have been looking forward to this moment for so long!"

Ignoring the towering guards on either side, she wrapped her arms around him and kissed his cheek. The backs of his shackled hands were squeezed against her firm thighs in the embrace. He slid them up, feeling the outline of her panties through her slacks. Recalling the role he needed to play, he stopped moving before she realized he was groping her. He switched from predator to victim, leaned forward, and whispered, "Please, take me from this terrible place!"

Stunned, Laurent broke away from the embrace, incensed that this poor, tortured soul was begging for his freedom. She turned to address Geddings and Bradley and boldly commanded, "Remove this man's restraints. He is free now."

Sergeant Dobbins spoke up. "Technically, he is not free until he is aboard your aircraft and off this base." His statement was met with an icy glare from the actress.

Before she could launch a retort, Geddings said, "The only one here that can make that decision is Colonel Bradley."

Bradley eyed Laurent a moment before responding. "No."

"Colonel, if you please! I've come a long way to free this man who has been unjustly—"

"Young lady, the security of this entire facility is my responsibility. This man will remain shackled until he no longer represents a threat to my personnel." He looked to Dobbins. "Sergeant, please escort this prisoner and this civilian off my base."

Laurent huffed indignantly and turned away.

Major Geddings caught her by the arm and squeezed softly. “Please remember what we’ve told you here today,” he whispered. “The advice offered was for your own personal protection.”

Laurent’s eyes narrowed as though she were thinking about saying more. The expression cooled as she turned away, falling in step behind the guards and the prisoner as they filed out of the room.

The colonel looked to Lieutenant Hodges. “Unshackle him when you arrive at the aircraft. Offer the restraints to the pilot. I would expect him to have some common sense. Especially if he’s ex-military.”

Hodges nodded wordlessly and followed after the entourage.

Erin Laurent’s glow returned as they loaded into the sedan for the short trip back to the airport. She and her group of activists had gone up against the most powerful military in the world and won! She reminded herself to contain the enthusiasm until safely aboard the plane. Then they could finally celebrate their incredible accomplishment.

She turned around from the front seat and looked back to Abu Dahl, who sat between the two guards. She smiled and said, “So much has changed in the world since you were brought to this terrible place. I hope you don’t have too much trouble adapting to the newest technology.”

“Technology is not important to me,” he answered. “I only wish to return to my homeland and embrace my freedom.”

Laurent nodded with a sympathy bordering on pain, imagining all the great pleasures of life this tortured soul had been deprived. Stolen time and memories, never to be retrieved. She started to speak again and stopped, alerted by something in his eyes that she’d not seen earlier. Something disturbing.

He stared back at her with a look that made her feel naked, self-conscious, vulnerable. Laurent was never made to feel so uncomfortable by a man's gaze. She turned back around and stared out the windshield, wondering what just happened. She attempted to reconcile the sinister expression as the actions of a typical man who hadn't seen a woman in many years. But it went beyond that. There was nothing suggestive or even sexually hungry in those eyes. His glare felt dark, unclean, condescending, and violent. She imagined that given the opportunity, he would not just have his way with her. He would consume her. Defile her. Ravage her.

Laurent was dismayed and disappointed by her own vivid imagination. Had she really gleaned all that from a single glance? She squeezed her eyes tightly shut in an attempt to force the thoughts out of her mind. Her reaction was sophomoric and over-reactive. Yet, she still felt his eyes upon her, even now. Through the back of her skull, right through the car seat, she felt him. Felt him penetrating her.

She forced a smile, but it wasn't working. She realized now that the man unnerved her. She would make it a point to put some distance between them on the plane. She would also warn her other guests to keep their guard up, just in case. Second thought, saying so could make her appear the fool after everything she did to gain his freedom. She would ask the flight attendant to keep an eye on him instead.

The sedan pulled up to the plane as the other guests emptied out and assembled on the tarmac.

Laurent dismissed her concerns and bounded from the car with renewed vigor. She threw her hands in the air and stepped victoriously into the group. "We've done it!" she cried. A cheer went up as everyone squeezed into a group hug. Laurent then pointed back at the car and directed them to make room for their guest of honor.

Lieutenant Hodges came around and opened the right passenger door. Out stepped Sergeant Dobbin, followed by Abu Dahl, and finally Corporal Bolinski. Bolinski took one step back from the prisoner. He put a hand on his club, watching as the sergeant removed the restraints. Dobbin moved to the prisoner's side to remove the ankle shackles, careful to avoid the possibility of being kicked in the process. He stood back up and unlocked the handcuffs.

Abu Dahl flexed and rubbed his wrists as the shackles came off, exaggerating his discomfort.

Hodges discreetly nudged Dobbin and said, "I'll take those."

Dobbin gathered the restraints and handed them to Hodges.

Laurent stepped toward the prisoner and announced, "Everyone, this is why we are here. May I present to you, Mr. Abu Dahl, a free man!"

They all held their places, smiling at the guest of honor but making no move toward him. Abu Dahl stood staring back at the group in his orange jumpsuit. His long, straggly hair and beard gently stroked by the soft Caribbean breeze. His expression was anything but welcoming.

No one moved for what seemed like an eternity.

Abu Dahl finally slipped into character, ready to play the part that was expected of him. "Thank you for fighting to win my freedom," he announced with a forced, humbled smile. "I pray that my deeds in life will make you remember this moment forever."

The ice was broken. The small group flocked around to shake his hand and offer congratulations on this new beginning.

Lieutenant Hodges used the moment to locate the pilot. He found him standing at the doorway, watching the activities below. Hodges climbed the steps and introduced himself. Tom Kellogg was an ex-navy fighter pilot. He ushered Hodges inside and introduced him to David Scott, his first officer and a former air force pilot.

"I assume that I don't need to explain to the two of you the type of man that is about to board your aircraft," Hodges said.

"We've done a little research on our own," Kellogg answered. "We'll be watching him."

"He is an active combatant who has pledged death to his enemies. That would be us. Tell me, and this is in the strictest confidence, do you travel armed?"

"You're asking us if we brought weapons on to a secure military installation?" the first officer asked. "I'm assuming there are no repercussions for revealing such information."

"Ordinarily, there would be, but there is nothing ordinary about this situation. I'm not asking to bust your balls."

Scott looked to the pilot, who gave a slight nod. "Yes, Lieutenant, we both travel armed. Force of habit. There's a stowed Kimber and H&K."

"Good," Lieutenant Hodges answered, "very good. I recommend you take these as well." He handed the first officer the handcuffs and leg irons along with a key. Scott accepted them and headed into the cockpit to stow them before they could be seen by the other passengers.

Hodges locked eyes with Kellogg. "If this man sees an opportunity, he will kill you. For the sake of yourselves and all of those clueless partygoers out there that we are sworn to protect, watch this man. Your lives may depend on it."

Laurent gave everyone time to greet Abu Dahl, then tapped her watch. "If we're going to stay on schedule, then we need to get aboard. Come on, everyone, let's go!" She directed the guests up the stairway as Lieutenant Hodges made his way back down.

She was about to follow the last of them up when Sergeant Dobbin approached. "Never let him out of your sight, Ms. Laurent," he said. "You are not safe until he is gone."

Laurent nodded hesitantly, her eyes staring downward. She gave an almost imperceptible nod, turned, and proceeded up the steps and into the aircraft.

ONCE THE CRAFT reached cruising altitude, Laurent unbuckled and came over to Abu Dahl, holding out a package. "These are fresh clothes and travel supplies: toothbrush, comb, shaving kit, things like that. Feel free to get freshened up in the restroom up front. We'll be serving dinner very soon. I hope you're hungry."

Abu Dahl smiled back, took the package, clicked out of his seatbelt, and headed for the lavatory.

Everyone sat in groups of four for dinner, which coincidentally featured Middle Eastern dishes. Laurent sat with Senator Dunwade and Valerie Tynes, leaving one seat open for Abu Dahl. He appeared a few moments later, donning a black jogging suit and sneakers. His expression hinted this would not become his favorite outfit. But it was clean, and it wasn't bright orange. Laurent waved him over to the open seat across from her. He sat down before a large platter of chicken shawarma and Kkshik—a porridge made from burghul fermented with yogurt, along with Kofta, spicy balls of minced lamb, and garnished with grape leaves.

Senator Dunwade puffed with pride for having suggested the menu items to make their guest feel welcome. "I assume it has been a while since you've enjoyed foods from your homeland."

Abu Dahl busied himself with scooping from each of the dishes with his fingers. "No, I ate Tabbouleh last night. It is required that we be fed with foods from our own culture." Abu took an entire stuffed grape leaf and crammed it into his mouth. He held up his finger as he chewed. When he had swallowed half, he added, "These are good, but the chef at Guantanamo makes the best grape leaves I have ever tasted. I will miss them, but nothing else."

The senator's face reddened, unaware that the prisoner had been so well fed. He made a mental note to check into the foods being served at the prison.

Valerie Tynes watched with equal parts of curiosity and repulsion. Abu Dahl used his fingers to sample all of the foods on the platters. He licked them after each taste, then dug in for more.

"So, Mr. Dahl," she asked, "do you have family that you will be returning to when you reach your home?"

The man stopped chewing and stared across the table. "No, my family is dead. My parents were killed before my eyes by a Soviet helicopter launching a missile into our home. My two brothers were both shot by American forces as we defended our land from attack."

Tynes felt a lump in her throat and swallowed hard, wishing she hadn't asked. "I'm sorry for your losses. I hope we have shown you that not all Americans support the war."

Dahl stuffed a Kofta ball in his mouth. This woman would be stoned to death for speaking such treason against her own country. "Yes, you have shown me much." Yes, he thought, you have shown me how easy it will be to defeat such weak-minded people.

The conversations continued and bounced from subject to

subject. Everyone anxiously awaited their turn to speak with Abu Dahl. Gradually his responses became shorter, often with only one or two-word replies. It seemed as though maintaining the thin veneer of feigned friendship was too demanding. He eventually ignored the questions altogether while continuing to sample every dish within his reach. The other passengers got the message and left him alone.

For her part, Laurent was drinking her way to numbness. She now was having serious misgivings about Abu Dahl. With every short, sometimes condescending reply he gave her guests, she became more convinced that she had erred in ignoring all the warnings. By her fourth glass of chardonnay, her thoughts shifted to a good night's sleep and getting him off this plane.

18

Washington, DC

The buzz on the street and social media was the Karlson/Al Jazeera interview. News anchors and teams of specialists analyzed its contents from every angle. Dagger-throwing debates raged, further dividing friends and electronic acquaintances. Supporters and opponents faced off and battled with keystrokes and emotionally lobbed emojis. Depending on the political persuasion of the network reporting the story, Karlson was portrayed as everything from the smartest woman in politics, single-handedly brokering world peace, to a poorly scripted, washed-up actress pandering to the enemy.

Karlson herself was savoring the moment because, good or bad, publicity was publicity. She basked in the spotlight and anticipated a large bump in the public opinion polls.

The interview was already proving itself a political godsend. It paved the way to upcoming appearances on the Tonight Show, The Gab, Meet The Press, and a cameo performance on Saturday Night Live. The first phase of Gene

Lawton's brilliant plan was a monumental success. Time would tell if the hidden viper inflicted its venom.

The sound of a television streamed in the background as Karlson finished the last of her salmon entrée in a private dining room of her favorite DC restaurant. The management treasured its powerful and elite customer base and sequestered them into this exclusive area. The general public was barred from entry. This was one of her secret ports of refuge where she enjoyed the solitude and ambiance as much as the splendid culinary offerings.

The server set down a cappuccino as her cell phone chirped. She read the caller ID before answering and sighed. It was Senate Majority Leader Linda Romulus. Karlson couldn't think of an excuse fast enough to ignore the call and answered.

"Good afternoon Madam Speaker," she announced with feigned politeness. "I was just thinking that you and I have not spoken in some time. How are you?"

"Very well, thank you, senator. Congratulations on your interview. You've done well in carrying forward our unified party message that we represent the best hope for peace in the Middle East."

"Well, thank you. That film crew was very excited to share our views with their audience. I have their contact information if anyone else wishes to use them." Fat chance of that, Karlson thought, even as she made the offer. She intended to keep a tight lid on access to Deeba Gohar.

"I have two reasons for the call, senator," Romulus said in her slow, nasally voice. "You are no doubt aware of the bill being voted on this afternoon?"

Karlson swallowed hard on a mouthful of hot cappuccino and burned her throat. "Yes, I was aware, madam speaker. I did not intend to vote on that issue."

There was an uncomfortable silence before Romulus responded. "I'm not sure we have all the votes necessary to defeat this proposal. I'm calling on you to help your party."

Her tone was soft yet reminded Karlson of being scolded by a high school teacher. She did not want her name on the voting rolls of this bill so close to the election. It was already dead at the door with little support. And although Karlson was against any tax decrease, this legislation had no chance of passage. Her participation, therefore, was not required. "My understanding was our opposition doesn't have the votes to carry this forward."

"Senator, my job is to make sure it has absolutely no chance. For that, I need you in your seat this afternoon. Can I count on your vote?"

She was caught. The shriveled old prune was using her position for everything it was worth. The day would come very soon when she could put this woman in her place. But until November, she needed her support. "Yes, madam speaker," she managed to say in a near convincing tone. "I will be there." *Can I finish my damn coffee now?*

Romulus wasn't finished. "I noticed during your interview with Al Jazeera that you referred to yourself as a co-sponsor on the low-income supplemental support bill. I remember how we fought for passage. Well, you can imagine my surprise when you stated this piece of legislation belonged to you. I don't think Reinstein or McCalvy would understand you taking credit for their hard work."

Jesus Christ, does this wench ever offer support? Incensed, Karlson's face flushed with anger. She struggled to control her tone. "I worked diligently with my fellow senators on both the drafting of the document and earning its passage. My name did not appear on it, but I did indeed earn the title of co-sponsor."

"It only counts if it's in ink. I look forward to seeing you this afternoon, senator."

Karlson ended the call and tossed the phone into her purse. Her cappuccino was lukewarm, and she'd lost all desire. She dabbed the corners of her mouth with a crisp linen napkin, reapplied lipstick to accentuate her academy award-ready smile, and headed for the exit. Her thoughts rolled through the appointments that needing rescheduling to make room for attending the senate vote. Despite the pleasant lunch, her brief conversation with Romulus left a sour taste in her mouth. "Your day is coming, bitch," she murmured as she climbed into the limousine for the short ride to the capitol. The hag would pay for not allying herself with Karlson when she had the chance.

19

39°43'40"N 43°49'80"E

With the last of the plates cleared, the flight attendant explained to Abu Dahl how to recline his seat for the overnight portion of the flight. Erin Laurent took this as her queue to head for the solitude of her cabin. She glanced back before closing the door to see Dahl being instructed on how to view a movie.

She stripped down to her panties and pulled on a T-shirt. As she walked back from the bathroom, she caught a glimpse of herself in the full-length mirror. She had aged gracefully and still maintained an exercise regimen to keep her body toned. The facelift flattened out time's creases and gave her a youthful glow. She stopped to admire her reflection, wondering if she should consider another round of liposuction.

Something moved in the corner. Laurent blinked twice to make sure it wasn't the dim light playing tricks. In a flash, he was on her, darting from the shadows and grabbing her from behind around the waist. She watched him envelop her in the mirror. As though she were witnessing it all happening to someone else. Her mind didn't yet register that she was being attacked. A fist came up, cocked back, and released with the force of a compressed piston, striking her in the right ear. The painful impact caused a bright flash behind her eyes. Her ears rang with a shrieking, high pitch as her vision filled with blackness. Her body went limp, and consciousness drifted away.

Laurent was vaguely aware of what was happening but incapable of stopping his advance. That same fist now pulled open her mouth and stuffed a linen napkin inside. Her head drooped uncontrollably as she struggled to focus on the reflection of his face in the mirror. She saw anger, rage, and lust in his terrifying expression as Abu Dahl gripped her jaw in one hand and pulled her hips tight against him with the other. She could feel the intruder pressing his loins against her, his erection nearly penetrating her from behind. She tried to work out a scream, but he dug his nails into her face and her abdomen, hard enough to draw blood. Small trickles of red worked their way down her cheek and belly. She willed her muscles to respond, but her body remained unmovable, like a machine that was offline, unable to offer any resistance. She was like a rag doll in his hands. He was in complete control, and it was the most dreadful, helpless moment she had ever experienced.

He released his hold on her hips, and she felt his rough hand sliding her panties down as he pinned her against the wall. Tears streamed down her face and onto the hand of her assailant. Her heart banged so hard and fast that she imagined it tearing out of her chest. It would be better, she thought, if she could escape to a safe corner deep in her mind until he was finished with her body. She tried to imagine another place, another time, anything but right here and now. Any thought that could distract her from this beast that she unwittingly unleashed.

His fetid breath on the back of her neck brought her back to the moment. She could tell that he was struggling to untie his new jogging pants. It would just be a matter of time now, and he would be done with her. Laurent prayed she would still be alive.

MARISSA DANFORTH DOZED off shortly after finishing dinner and awoke to a dimly lit cabin. Most of the other guests were either asleep or watching one of the many available movies. She felt a little dehydrated and headed to the attendant's station for a bottle of water.

Just beyond the refrigerator, she noticed Erin Laurent's private suite door ajar and a lamp still on inside. She decided now might be a good time to speak with her about support in the next election. She stepped toward the suite and pushed the door open. Every other thought vanished in a blink. Fear, panic, and anger all registered at once. Every neuro chemical in her brain flooded in tenfold. Every receptor, every muscle was seized and taken over by the most primitive areas of her mind and thrown into action. Marissa would later remember feeling like a passenger in her own body as she witnessed the unspeakable and became a weapon herself.

Abu Dahl held a firm grip on Laurent and was clumsily sliding his pants down with one hand while holding her steady with his other over her mouth. Marissa launched forward, thinking only of stopping this man.

Six steps from now, she would have to impede his actions and subdue him until help arrived.

Four steps away, she remembered a kata she composed

while working to earn her first black belt. Her sensei believed in both standard kata, a series of offensive maneuvers strung together like a dance and injecting personal creativity. "You cannot assume your enemy will attack in a fashion you have trained against," he would say. "Therefore, know the basics of form and function, but also be prepared to adapt what you know to the situation at hand."

Marissa ran forward, following a plan she had no knowledge of formulating.

TOM KELLOGG WAS ENJOYING a quiet moment as he stepped through the darkened cabin of the impressive Jetliner. He had been the pilot for Ethan LeClair for six months now and enjoyed nearly every moment so far. The aircraft was an absolute joy to fly, and the conditions flown under were near perfect. Of course, he catered to the whims of the Hollywood and Washington DC elite, who did indeed believe their feces was non-odorous. 'Self-absorbed bores,' he referred to them to his co-pilot. But he would not hesitate to climb into the cockpit of this glorious machine and fly them anywhere in the world. His contact with them was minimal. And he always had an excellent excuse for leaving a less than stellar conversation. He needed to get back up front and fly the plane.

Tonight, as they cut through the dark moonless skies toward their destination of Islama-who-the-fuck-cares, he left the cockpit to get fresh coffee and a snack for himself and his co-pilot. He passed the other passengers who were hunkered down for the evening after celebrating their successful and fearless conquest. They were wiped out and would feel the effects of their over-imbibing in the morning, just about the time the plane was making its fuel stop. For now, they slept off their hangovers with 'delusions of grandeur dancing in their heads.' Kellogg smiled as he pictured them in the morning, all looking for Motrin, Pepto, and breakfast at the same time.

He set out two cups, filled them from a fresh pot, then gathered up a few breakfast bars and other quick snacks. He was heading back to the cockpit when he heard a loud, out-of-place yell.

THE PLAN FELL into place quickly, naturally, as if some greater force programmed it into Marissa's head and she was following the script. Some of it she knew; other parts would be variations of moves she trained for. Some of it, she expected, was going to hurt like hell. It didn't matter. She was in motion.

Step one; distract the opponent. She ran up behind the five-foot-eight Abu Dahl and stretched both of her arms out. With lightning quickness, she brought both clenched fists together like weighted pendulums, directing the force into his ears. Marissa yelled out in a loud and piercing Kiai as her fists made hard simultaneous contact to both sides of his head. The concussive force knocked him nearly unconscious. Not quite, but enough to make him stagger back, breaking his hold on Laurent.

Marissa then launched into step two, disable the opponent. There was no way in hell she could stop this man other than to cut his oxygen, so that's what she did. She cocked her left fist back and launched it in a roundhouse punch into his groin, crushing his testicles. He reacted to the pain with a low guttural moan that emptied his lungs. That's when she made her next move. Her right forearm shot across his neck and pulled back hard against his windpipe. She locked that arm in place by gripping it with her left hand. She dragged him back toward her, causing a loss of balance as he gasped for air. She held him in an excruciating and effective chokehold that no one from her dojo had ever been able to break loose.

ALL THOUGHTS of sexual gratification vanished as Abu Dahl now found himself in a fight for survival. He thrashed over his shoulders, grabbing for his attacker's hair. She responded by squeezing her arm harder against his throat, nearly crushing his windpipe. Dahl fought against the pain, struggling for a precious breath of air. But her grip was tight and effective, showing no signs of weakening. He was at this little bitch's mercy.

ERIN LAURENT LAY CRUMPLED on the floor, eyes open, helpless to do anything but observe the struggle. She had nothing to offer in defense against this brute. She watched as he swung both arms out and around, trying to gain a grip on the skinny powerhouse that held him tight. Marissa continued walking him backward. He flailed, swinging his elbows back in an attempt to hit her in the kidneys. Her small but solid frame worked in her favor, and his blows barely made contact. Of all the unlikely rescuers, Laurent thought, her salvation depended on this meek young woman. And she was succeeding! She was beating him! Her lips moved silently as she prayed for Marissa to find the strength to finish the bastard.

ABU DAHL BELIEVED if he could regain firm footing, then he could flip her over him and beat the life out of her. He tried to stop the backward shuffle that she moved him in but could not get his balance. In all his years, it never occurred to him that a woman, any woman, could get the better of him in a fight. Yet here was this tiny little American, and she was winning. He wheezed as he fought to fill his lungs. The pressure of her bony forearm on his windpipe was excruciating and deadly in its effectiveness. He struggled against her with the last of his waning energy. But now, as consciousness began to slip away, he comprehended for the first time that she would be the victor.

WHAT THE HELL WAS THAT? Kellogg froze as the muffled but mighty yell reached him. Instinct told him exactly what it was, a karate Kiai. He looked around, unable at first to correlate the scream with his surroundings. Then it came to him; the prisoner they brought on board. He was attacking someone!

He dropped the snack tray and searched for the source of the alarming yell. It came from inside the bedroom suite of Erin Laurent. He reached up into a storage compartment above the coffee machine and pulled away a false panel, revealing a Kimber nine-millimeter with a fifteen-round magazine. He slid the weapon from its velcro holster, pulled the slide back and chambered a round, then brought the barrel up as he bolted through the open suite door. He dove to the floor, then rolled and aimed at the two people now embroiled in battle. He watched for a moment, unclear what he was witnessing. He nearly smiled when he comprehended the rare event. A petite brunette was taking this terrorist down. Kellogg felt a wave of pride in her courage and strength.

BLACK SPOTS BEGAN FILLING Abu Dahl's vision. He dug his unkempt nails into Marissa's arms, drawing blood instantly. She did not scream out, did not wince. Nor did she loosen her grip. In fact, the arm across his throat pressed in even tighter, restricting the blood flow to his brain as well as completely cutting off air. His arms dropped lifelessly, his legs buckling beneath him. It was over.

KELLOGG STOOD, keeping his pistol trained on Abu Dahl as the young woman dragged him, struggling across the room. The man had seventy pounds of muscle on her, yet she did not relent. Finally, he collapsed upon her, taking them both down. The woman never let loose of her hold on the terrorist's neck. After he lay unmoving another few moments, she released him, then rolled out from under his limp body.

Marissa sat for a moment, all of her senses still fixed on the man she just defeated.

She got up and hurried over to Laurent, who was now curled in a fetal position on the floor. Marissa brushed the hair out of Laurent's eyes. "It's over," she said, "you're going to be all right."

It took a moment longer for the actress to comprehend that she was now safe. She finally looked up into Marissa's piercing eyes with the bewildered look of a lost child. Her bottom lip quivered as she sat up and locked Marissa into a tight embrace as the tears began flowing.

"Thank you," she sobbed. She buried her head against her champion's chest. Finally feeling secure. Comprehending now that the threat was passed. This tiny woman had saved her. "Thank you."

ABU DAHL CONVULSED, reminding Kellogg that he was still a danger to everyone on board. He kept his pistol trained on the man's head and jammed his knee into his back.

The flight attendant entered the suite, shocked at what he saw.

"Marcus," the captain said in a composed but commanding tone, "we have a situation. Please go to the cockpit and tell David we need the restraints we got from Gitmo. And bring a few tie wraps back with you."

Marcus acknowledged with a nod and hurried to the front of the jet.

Kellogg kept his attention trained on the prisoner as the young woman got up off the floor. She grabbed a robe and wrapped it around Laurent, then helped her into bed. She straightened the covers, made sure Laurent was comfortable, then dropped into a chair. Kellogg could tell by her pained expression that she was reliving the moment. The adrenalin would be receding as she began realizing what she'd done. Her face registered disbelief, and he worried she might slip into shock. He needed to engage her in conversation to keep her focused and coherent.

"That was amazing, miss," he said. "One of the bravest and most selfless acts I have ever witnessed. You are a hero."

He glanced down at her arm, then added, “And, you are bleeding.”

Marissa stared into the steel blue eyes of the sandy-haired pilot, not yet connecting. She noticed her arm and the deep gouges.

“When did that happen?”

No sooner had she spoken when all sensation returned. She winced in pain.

“When our ungrateful guest here realized he was about to be defeated. Looks like he dug his nails in, hoping you would loosen your grip.” He looked down at Abu Dahl. “It didn’t work. That was a very effective chokehold.”

He watched as the color drained from her face. She was fading from him. He needed to get her talking more. “What degree black belt are you?”

Marissa shook her head as if pulling back from an all-consuming void. She stared with a puzzled expression. “Third, how did you know?”

“Miss, nobody pulls off moves like that without extensive training and discipline. What I saw you do would put many Marines in their place, and they’re the toughest sons of bitches I know, next to Navy SEALS.”

“Your Marines are weak and powerless against our —“

Marissa jumped in her seat at the sound of Abu Dahl’s voice, a look of fear and disgust spread across her face.

Kellogg rapped him hard on the back of the head with the barrel of his pistol, silencing the outburst. “Please don’t speak again,” he said quietly.

Marissa regained her composure and asked, “I heard you say you had his restraints from Guantanamo. How did you end up with them?”

“One of the guards explained how dangerous this guy was

and strongly suggested we bring them along. That was all I needed to hear."

Marissa's face flushed with embarrassment as she comprehended the folly of their actions over the past several months. This evil bastard took something from Erin Laurent that she would never get back. She was lucky to be alive. It hadn't entered their minds that he could be anything but the victim of a system that imprisoned innocent people. How could they have been so wrong?

Marcus returned to the suite, taking a full inventory of the situation before approaching the pilot. He eyed the former prisoner, face down on the floor with Kellogg's knee in his back and pistol pointed at his head. He pulled out the H&K that the co-pilot had given him and covered Abu Dahl while passing the restraints to the pilot. Kellogg tucked his weapon into his belt behind his back and secured the cuffs on Dahl, then clamped the manacles on his ankles.

"I was thinking of strapping him in the forward jump seat with those tie wraps. What do you think?" Kellogg asked.

"Best place to keep an eye on him, but there's nothing to tie him down to up there. It might be better to strap him into one of the rear-facing seats where the other passengers can keep watch."

"Even better," the pilot agreed. "On your feet, twinkle toes," he commanded the assailant, lifting him by his cuffed arms. Marcus took a position ahead, making sure no other passengers obstructed their path. He needn't have worried. All slept soundly through the entire ordeal. He walked past Senator Dunwade, thinking how oblivious the man was to events happening within yards from where he snored like a clogged vacuum. Typical politician.

20

Location unknown

Whenever possible, Sirhan Abbas began his day by meeting the sunrise in the saddle. While he believed in the importance of the morning call to prayer, it fell to him to ensure those millions of prayers stood for something. So he rode, ever vigilant, the enforcer of Allah's word.

His horse snorted as its hooves slipped, then regained footing on the uneven rocky trail. Abbas pulled back on the reins and waited. The first shards of daylight danced upon the crest of the eastern mountain top. It brightened and glowed as though the mountain itself fought to retain all of its power within. In an explosion of light, the sun burst over the edge, consuming the shadows as it rose. Abbas gave praise and thanks for the new day as his face was illuminated in the warm glow.

No one accompanied him on his morning rides. This was his moment to be alone with his thoughts. Yet today, he was burdened with more of them than usual. His confidential sources shared with him the American treachery surrounding the release of Abu Dahl. The information had proven reliable. What troubled him equally was that the data gleaned from his spies arrived so shortly before the same news was shared with the entire world on Al-Jazeera television. Improvements were necessary in his collection of intel. The message, however, would have been painful no matter how or when it was received.

Abu Dahl survived his protracted ordeal in the American prison only to be used as a tool by his captors. Abbas also learned that he was the intended target of the deception. He was looking forward to Abu Dahl's release and welcoming him back to the holy fight. Abbas seethed with anger at being forced into a compromised situation by his enemy. There would be a fitting price to pay, and he vowed his revenge against those responsible.

Now, what to do about the ill-fated homecoming? A message needed to be sent for all to see, one so powerful that none would ever again doubt the temerity of Sirhan Abbas.

Choosing the appropriate messenger would be as critical as the message itself. He thought of his faithful legions, the thousands of soldiers who would stop at nothing less than death before dishonor. Many could be relied upon to follow his word to the letter. Still, one name always came first to mind. A man who proved himself time and again. A man capable of blending in with the enemy and striking without ever being noticed. Crico Dreas. He nodded reluctantly to himself. His decision, although painful, was the most appropriate and decisive way to begin the retaliation. His greatest weapon was fear, and he would thrust it deep into the minds of the millions he would soon control. His jaw tightened with deep resolve as he prodded his horse forward. It was time to enact the plan.

As Abbas neared the cave's mouth that served as headquarters and home, a pair of horse handlers rushed out to meet him. He climbed down and handed them the reins, then walked to the entrance. He pulled off his gloves and marveled again at the near whisper silence of the massive diesel generator that supplied electricity to the mountainside fortress. His architects and engineers designed the secret headquarters so that it would never be discovered. Just inside the mouth of the cave, the rough-hewn rock gave way to poured concrete. A few more meters in, and he felt the cool breeze of the air conditioning system. His footfalls were silenced by the Persian rugs that decorated the floor and walls.

He walked past armed guards that stood outside the weapons arsenal, past the kitchen, where chefs bustled about preparing the morning meal and entered the communications room.

Two technicians worked at a table covered with computers, monitors, and radio equipment. He approached the one wearing headphones as the man tuned in radio signals picked up by a large antenna hidden in the mountain's top. Abbas tapped the technician on the shoulder. The man turned, caught sight of Abbas, ripped off his headphones, and stood at attention.

"My general," he said, then tapped the other technician, who gave him a wondering look before seeing their leader. He, too, jumped out of his seat and stood erect.

Abbas nodded and waved him down. "Go back to your duties." He looked to the first technician and said, "When can you send an encoded satellite phone message?"

"Within the hour, my general, we must wait for the American spy satellite to pass out of range."

"Good," Abbas responded. "I want you to make a call. Get word to the Ghost that I need his assistance. Come to my quarters when the call is connected."

21

31°37'43"N 65°43'69"E

The flight attendant came through the quiet cabin collecting the remaining cups and glasses and informing the passengers they would be landing soon. The giddy atmosphere of the previous evening was replaced with somber silence.

Erin Laurent had slept little since the ordeal despite the two sedatives she'd washed down with a half bottle of wine. She stared wide awake at the ceiling, trying to make decisions that would affect the rest of her life. The answers so far had proven elusive.

Though she desperately wanted to keep the details of her attack to herself, she knew that attempting to conceal any of this from Malcolm LeClair would be unwise. The truth of the ill-fated excursion and attempted rape were going to be public knowledge very soon. Despite everyone aboard being sworn to silence, none of them could keep a secret.

So how would LeClair react if he later discovered the truth from anyone other than herself? Would he understand how demeaning, how terrifying the entire ordeal had been? Of course, he would, but he would also be angry and disappointed that she didn't come to him first. He would likely think her foolish for going through with the prisoner's release in the first place. He'd already said as much. He'd been right, she admitted, and he would be much more sympathetic if she came right out and told him so. Done. She would tell him everything when she arrived home. At least there was more time to prepare before looking into his eyes and explaining that another man tried to. . .she still couldn't bring herself to say it. Not yet, anyway, but it would come. She knew that much. She had twenty-four hours to find the words.

Until then, Laurent could get a feel for the intentions of her fellow travelers. It was quite likely these *friends* of hers were thinking of nothing but distancing themselves from the fallout and laying all the blame at her feet. She also expected them to deflect any responsibility for their own actions. She envisioned each of them establishing their own new narratives of how they were misled. It was ironic, she thought, how laughably easy it was to get all these people to mindlessly follow her. Then again, she was no better.

Laurent cursed the day she'd been brought into this disaster, cringing as she recalled the memory, still wondering how she could have been so gullible.

The topic was broached by a friend sharing an op-ed piece in a restaurant over wine. As they'd conversed about the article, the idea of rescuing the prisoner became the main topic of their conversation. Laurent pushed back, suggesting there might well be more to the story, more facts to be considered. If only she'd stuck to her gut instincts. A pause before acting on impulse and a few hours of research would have saved her so much misery.

But as the wine flowed, the conversation became more

heated and emotional than logical. Any rational thought of cross-checking the details tumbled off the table. Looking back on it now, Laurent realized how she had been manipulated. Her friend believed adamantly in rescuing this man from prison, and with practiced skill, she guided the conversation to stay on topic. Laurent recalled that even before processing her own thoughts about it, she made calls from the restaurant, telling others and seeking their support.

She remembered the radiant smile and gleaming green eyes of her friend, another Hollywood icon whose acting career floundered. Then she'd discovered a new and fulfilling path in politics. Katherine Karlson had an answer for every question that Laurent could pose. Her argument was as powerful as the wine. Karlson wanted her to do this, Laurent could see that now, but she could not figure Karlson's motivation for such an endeavor. In the end, it didn't matter. Senator Karlson persuaded her to accept the challenge on behalf of all the oppressed prisoners suffering the world over. She left the restaurant that evening with a new agenda and a bold conviction in her heart. Now, she admitted, none of those thoughts were her own. She allowed herself to be manipulated, and there was no one else to blame.

That brutal bit of truth registered like a cog dropping into place, allowing the wheels of logic to re-engage. Laurent had turned a corner. There was no denying what happened, no question of fault. Just as ironic was how laughably easy it was to get all these other people to mindlessly follow on this ill-fated excursion. But it was done, a colossal blunder forever etched in stone. She wondered if this would be what she was remembered for. Had she created a new legacy that darkly eclipsed all of her other accomplishments in life? "No," she said defiantly, as a wave of determination took hold. She would deal with it, meet it head-on and make damned sure her existence stood for something greater than this debacle. It would be a long road ahead, but she was already taking the first step.

THE PLANE REFUELED IN LISBON. The passengers were offered a moment to deplane and walk off some anxiety. A few used the time to make calls to home, friends, and business contacts. Others just appreciated a moment away from the grimacing glare of Abu Dahl.

The pilot and co-pilot took turns guarding the prisoner during the brief break. Once the tanks were filled, they were back in the air, with five hours to go until the next destination.

22

Washington, DC

Jordan entered the kitchen to the welcoming aroma of fresh coffee and baking pastry. She took a seat at the table and poured herself a cup from a carafe as the housekeeper pulled a pan of fresh croissants from the oven. "Hola, Estrella," Jordan greeted her.

"Hola, Señorita West," the woman answered cheerily as she set her oven mitts aside and began cracking eggs for omelets.

Wednesday mornings were mother-daughter breakfast, a tradition Jordan still embraced. She smiled, reminiscing about past moments of the family ritual that was as old as she was. As a young girl, their mornings' subject matter bounced from fashion trends and boy bands to middle school crushes. The conversations these days pertained more to current campaign progress and world events. She clung to their exchanges like a warm blanket. Time was sometimes the most precious gift that one could give.

Today, however, those memories had the opposite effect.

They left her feeling even more guilty about coming to the table with a load to bear. She was hoping the subject could be broached without her appearing anxious or upset. That would demand an extra shot of self-control on her part.

Jordan tried to move beyond the issue, but so far, that wasn't working. She needed to voice her concern and needed to hear a reasonable explanation. She had her doubts that one existed. Her foot nervously tapped out an irregular rhythm as she waited for her mother.

"Well, aren't you the early riser!" Karlson greeted her, dressed, and made up for the day. Her fingers flipped through the multiple emails on her phone that accumulated overnight. She gave the housekeeper a smiling nod and sat down opposite her daughter. "I thought you would welcome the chance to sleep in a little."

Jordan feigned a smile and felt a wave of guilt for even thinking about ruining this moment. "Oh, you know me," she said uncomfortably, "trying to stay ahead of the classwork."

Karlson nodded without looking up, still very much preoccupied with her phone. She spent another moment reviewing which emails demanded immediate attention, then set aside the device. "Enough of that," she announced, pouring herself a cup. "This is supposed to be our time."

Jordan nodded her appreciation.

They exchanged pleasantries and made small talk as Jordan flipped through scenarios of how to bring up the subject. Often, their opinions differed, but this issue troubled her deeply and demanded resolution. The housekeeper served them breakfast as she waited for the right moment. Waiting was becoming more and more difficult.

She was close to letting loose when her mother said, "So tell me about your bar-hopping adventure the other night."

Jordan froze, a mouthful of hot brew catching in her

throat. This was a shot from left field that she never saw coming.

Karlson was a master at redirecting a conversation with seamless skill, and she looked on with a Cheshire cat grin. Jordan knew the look all too well. That self-satisfied, I know your every thought and secret before you even open your mouth expression. She realized there was nothing she could add that wasn't already known. This was nothing like playing twenty questions. It was a lie detector test, and it was the biggest downside of being the daughter of two politicians.

Jordan thought back with envy to some of her childhood friends whose moms were just moms. There was much to be said for that sort of relationship. It wasn't that she didn't appreciate her own mother's accomplishments. She just wished the woman could stay in character for an entire conversation. Be the mom for a while longer. Was that asking so much? She let out a sigh and faced the inconvenient reality.

"How about you tell me? I trust the memory of your security trio over my own anyway. I'll bet they took notes."

"Good eye, honey! I didn't expect you to spot all three. But you do understand it was for your own safety." Karlson smiled as though talking about having her daughter followed made it less intrusive. "Well," she queried, "is this band member a new love interest?"

Jordan noted the transition. Katherine Karlson, the politician, switching gears back to Kat Karlson, the mother. She sat her cup down and smiled. "I enjoy his company. We share a lot in common. He's a nice change of pace from the people I usually talk to. Is there anything in his background that I should be concerned about? I'm assuming you ran him through the standard checks."

"You do know me so well, don't you, dear? No, nothing

interesting came up. You do understand that I wouldn't bother being so thorough unless there was a reason. Anyway, you don't need a serious relationship in your life right now." She paused to let that last line sink in, then asked. "Did you like their music? You can never trust a secret service agent for their opinions of rock and roll. Sometimes I swear they wouldn't know the difference between—"

"Why did you do that interview with Al Jazeera?" Jordan blurted it out with an urgency and disappointment in her voice that was impossible to conceal.

Karlson sat upright, surprised at the outburst, her brows raising with an expression of annoyance. She exhaled hard, drumming her fingers on the table. "I have explained myself so many times already. Now I have to do it civilly, so I don't hurt your *feelings*." Her fingers mimed quote marks around the word. "I swear to God. . ." She threw her hands up in a resigned expression and sat back in her chair. "Fine," she started. "Jordan, there are some things I do that you may never understand. This one, however, should be easy enough to figure out." She looked away as though deciding how much to reveal to snuff this little fire out. "The Muslim population carries a lot of power and influence. With this one interview, I informed them all that I will strive to find common ground and make peace a priority." She paused, pleased with her choice of words. She grabbed her phone and tapped them in for later. "When I'm president, I will need their votes in this country as well as their support abroad." She leaned in and spoke in a hushed tone, "And we know that OASIS gets much of its information from that network."

"Then why did you risk an interview with them?"

"Hello. . . I sent an olive branch. Now everyone in that region knows that I want this war brought to an end by any means necessary."

"Their goal is to defeat our country, Mom, maybe you shouldn't have—"

"Let me stop you there, dear." Karlson's face flushed. "I won't get into a heated debate with you over campaign policies. I did the interview to show these people that the next administration, my administration, will not be their enemies."

"Come on, Mother, there wasn't another way to get that message out without pandering to the enemy?"

"Listen to me, Jordan! I don't have time for this shit with you!" Karlson's fingers curled up as though ready to claw through the tabletop, a vein throbbing on her forehead.

Jordan observed the reaction and pushed back from the table, surprised the comment had bumped her mother into full-bitch mode.

"That television station broadcasts to the entire Middle East," Karlson said, wagging her finger. "It is accepted as scripture. Those people carried my message back home with them, and the message was, 'we don't want this war any more than they do.' No, damn it, there wasn't a better way to do this. Time works against us every fucking day it goes on. We have to push to end it right now, or it blows everything!"

"I don't understand. You can make the changes once you're in office. You can bring the troops home and show everyone that you keep your promises."

Karlson closed her eyes, shaking her head. "Lord knows I love you, Jordan, and I appreciate your dedication to my campaign, so try not to take this the wrong way." She clasped her fingers together on the table and said, "Little girl, you don't have a clue how these things work. My campaign cannot survive a military victory for President Tenor. It would prove that his course of action had been correct and effective. That would make him unbeatable in November. If he doesn't bow to the pressure and end the war now, then it becomes my problem." Karlson stared into her cup as if a more perfect explanation might mystically appear like reading tea leaves. She clasped it tightly in trembling hands. "If we inherit this war," she continued," then we look foolish for not following our own demands. And a lost war during my presidency is a legacy that I cannot and will not accept."

Jordan considered her words, then asked, "You're still going to end it, though, right? That's what you promised."

Karlson blew out an exasperated breath. "You still want to ride that horse? Fine," her demeanor shifting again. "For years, we've been this big police force keeping the Sunni, the Shiites, the Kurds, and whoever the hell else from blowing each other apart. Now we have this Middle East unification, this, this monstrous machine that tramples and kills anything in its way. The deaths have tripled within the last few months alone, and we could be stuck there for decades unless Tenor ends it now."

"But you promised to pull the troops as soon as you were sworn in. You still can, right? What's changed?"

"Haven't you heard anything I've been saying? Everything has changed! In the last six months, every damn thing has flipped around. OASIS has become a brutal adversary. Believe me, we are not talking about some group of goat herders sitting around a laptop in a pup tent. They are organized, well-financed, well-armed, and they probably know more about us than we know about them. So no, I won't be able to end the war. I think escalation is our only option."

"Wait, you're saying you would reverse your entire stance if you get elected? That's terribly disingenuous, don't you think? I mean, if you're going to change your mind, then do it now and be honest with the people who support you."

"Jordan, if you could only hear yourself talking, you might grasp this better. I have run a campaign based on a pledge to end the war. Do you think for a moment these same people would stand behind me if I reversed myself now? It would be political suicide."

"So you hold off until you're elected and then say, what, that you were never informed of the true severity of the situation?"

Karlson nodded. "In essence, that's exactly what I would do. I wait until I'm briefed by the outgoing president and the joint chiefs. Then I throw them under the bus for withholding critical intel. That gives me a valid reason to extend our presence indefinitely."

"Mom! No!" Jordan cried in disbelief.

"That's plan B. We're hoping it doesn't come to that. It would be so much easier if Tenor just accepted defeat and pulled the goddamn troops."

"Then you lied," Jordan said, still not willing to accept her mother's deception. "You lied."

"Sorry dear," Karlson answered matter of factly, "but that's the soft white underbelly of politics. A campaign pledge is not a guaranteed political protocol."

The words hit like poison arrows. Jordan felt numb, as though the woman sitting across from her was a complete stranger. Worse, a stranger who just violated her. Was this actually the way it was done? Espouse empty promises to get elected with no intention of fulfilling any of them? Her stomach lurched, and her throat tightened. The entire year of life she devoted to this woman supporting her false message now felt as if it was all for nothing. The air became too thick to breathe. She rose to leave.

Karlson, still staring down at her cup, reacted as though the revelation held no more significance than informing a child that the imaginary characters of their youth were not real. “It may take a while,” she said coolly, “but once you realize that a lot of campaign promises are nothing but hype and bullshit, you can learn to work within the system.”

Jordan shook her head in denial. “I didn’t sign on for hype and bullshit,” she countered, avoiding eye contact as her voice cracked. “I did it to support a candidate and a message I believed in.”

Karlson looked up with a disingenuous half-smile. “Nothing has changed, not really. I’m still the best answer to the problems of this country.”

“Are you, mother? Like you said, everything has changed.”

23

Kandahar Airport

The jet made hard contact with the runway and did not slow until near the end of the concrete pad. The pilot reversed thrust and braked hard. He then turned toward a remote section of the airport where a small group of people awaited the arrival of Abu Dahl. The ground crew guided the plane into position, then signaled it to stop as a stairway was rolled into place.

Kellogg unbuckled from his seat and scrambled out of the cockpit. The flight attendant pulled the cabin door release lever as Kellogg stepped out and helped push it open. The still spinning engines whined loudly throughout the cabin as Kellogg hurried down the center aisle to retrieve the prisoner. He removed the shackles from Abu Dahl's ankles and then used a pair of wire cutters to remove the tie wraps that bound his legs to the seat. He drew his pistol and made sure the man knew it was pointed at his head. Kellogg tossed the hand cuff key into the prisoner's lap and stepped back. Abu Dahl stared at him with a menacing scowl as he unlocked the restraints and rubbed his wrists, then stood and walked toward the open entrance. Kellogg followed behind with his weapon trained on the center of Dahl's back.

Abu Dahl ducked his head as he stepped out onto the top rung of the stairway, squinting into the bright, hot Kandahar sun. He could not quite make out the faces of the men who had come to take him to his village, but it didn't matter. A smile lit his face. This moment was just as he envisioned throughout the long years in prison. The deafening whine of the engines faded as he heard a beautiful flute melody that called to him, welcoming him back to the land of his fathers. It was the same song that played as he sat beside a crackling fire the night before his capture so long ago. He felt the memory rekindle from that distant past and embraced it with all his senses. A warm, gentle breeze brushed his cheek, and he imagined it to be the breath of Allah standing beside him with welcoming arms.

He had returned! He defeated his captors by merely surviving his imprisonment and living for this day, ready to take up arms against them again. The price would be high for the years they kept him behind bars. Wasted years of life stolen with nothing to show for the time except the hatred that grew and festered. He would draw on that hate now as he brought them to their knees. Abu Dahl would exact his revenge on a world as it slept, unaware of the firestorm to come.

No longer a prisoner, he was now the unbreakable warrior. He started down toward the open arms of his brothers, more emboldened, more cocksure with each step.

He was halfway to the bottom when the stairway lurched forward beneath him. He staggered back and grabbed the handrail for balance, then turned and stared, disbelieving what he saw. The pilot and flight attendant were pushing the walkway clear of the plane. He watched in stunned disbelief as they scrambled back inside and pulled the cabin door shut. The jet engines began throttling up, and the giant rotors came closer, spinning ever faster. The ground crew rushed in to pull the walkway clear of the wing as the craft rolled forward. Abu Dahl regained his balance and jumped from the steps, glaring at the infidels that were making a mockery of his triumphant return. He screamed and punched at the air as the airliner rumbled past. The port engine blasted him with its jet wash, forcing him to retreat before being tossed like a leaf in a howling gale. Abu Dahl fell to his knees and watched as the craft rolled away, clenching his fists so tightly that his nails dug into flesh. It was not the homecoming he expected, but it was well deserved.

The co-pilot taxied the plane past the scattering group on the tarmac, then turned and headed for the runway as the cabin door was pulled shut and secured. The captain scrambled back into his seat as they traveled the short distance to the runway, then did a full throttle-up. The plane lifted off the ground to the sound of hand-clapping and jubilant cheers from the relieved passengers. They were finally free of the nightmare they helped create and rid of the refuse that had come to plague the airliner.

24

"Useless bitch! Useless, defiant bitch! I will rip out your heart with my bare hands!" Abu Dahl trembled with anger, a searing rage overtaking every last shred of self-control. He scratched and punched at the turbulent jet wash as the airliner rolled away and gained speed. "I will kill you! Every one of you will die by my hands!" His screams were mere whispers above the whining engines as the airliner lifted off and gained altitude, blending into the bright afternoon sky. He stood staring up, his defiance crumbling into humiliation. His jaw clenched tightly as he blinked back tears.

How could this have happened? He was a hero, a warrior, returning to his people after withstanding torture and imprisonment. All honor was stolen from his triumphant homecoming. He would pray for the death of everyone in that airplane who stared with disdain at him as he sat chained to a chair like an animal.

The thundering exhaust crackled and faded into the distance, and he became aware of voices from behind. He turned to see two men yelling and waving.

"Abu! You have returned!"

They hurried over to him with arms held out, their gray and black robes blowing in the dry wind.

"Abu, my brother, you have come back to us!" The taller of the two men embraced him in a tight bear hug, slapping him on the back. He moved away and made room for his companion to repeat the greeting, shaking him as he laughed.

"The Americans were no match for you, my friend! Now you can help us defeat them once and for all. There is so much to show you. We are becoming stronger in our fight with every new day."

Abu Dahl's anger receded as he recognized the two men sent to meet him. "Zaahir! Rifat! My brothers, how I have longed for this moment."

Thoughts of his ruined arrival gave way to happiness as he embraced his two oldest friends. They grew up together, battling side by side, first against the Russians and now the western infidels. War was all they knew for the better part of their lives, and they forged an unbreakable bond fighting together for the promise of paradise.

"Come, Abu, many others are awaiting your return." Zaahir slapped his shoulder and pointed to an old, rusting Chinese all-terrain vehicle.

"I must speak to Sirhan," Abu answered. "I must tell him all that I have learned of our enemy."

"He awaits you, my friend," Zaahir assured him. "We will take you there now."

Abu Dahl followed as the two soldiers of OASIS led the way to an old truck. He climbed onto the ripped brown canvas passenger seat and asked, "How long is the journey to meet with Sirhan?"

Rifat dropped into the driver's seat, pushed the ignition

button, and waited as the engine first did nothing, then spun, choked, and sputtered to life. He looked over with a grin, gripping the wheel with both hands as though grateful for the old machine's cooperation one more time.

"We will travel to a village up in the hills and spend the night. He will meet us there."

Rifat reached over and shook Abu's shoulder. "We will have time to share some news, and you can tell us of winning your freedom from the famous prison of the infidel. For tonight we celebrate! Our brother has returned!"

Abu Dahl smiled back and relaxed into the old seat, settling in for the long, rough drive. He was home now and would be received as a hero. The abrupt and terrible landing, the offensive exit from the plane would soon be forgotten. Only these two men and a handful of others were witnesses, and they were his brothers in arms. They could be trusted to keep this to themselves. They shared much darker secrets from the past, some of which still made his skin crawl.

These men were capable of terrifying acts of cruelty. He saw them at their worst. He remembered their sadistic expressions as they took the wives of men suspected of helping the enemy. They raped, tortured, and pummeled these women to death in front of their shackled husbands as they screamed and pleaded, helpless to do anything but bear witness. He then watched as Zaahir and Rifat slit the throats of these men and stood over them as they drowned in their own blood. They considered it equal retribution for their complicity in aiding the enemy.

Abu Dahl's mind raced from image to image. It seemed that the smell and sights of this familiar countryside were putting his brain into a fixed state of replay, all streaming before him, coming faster and faster. He was deluged with memories of running free through these mountains as a child, becoming a boy with a rifle, becoming a man with a vengeance.

And then she came back into his thoughts. That actress bitch who flew him to this place. He regretted being interrupted before he could defile her. He remembered the warmth of her flesh in his hands as he held her against him from behind. How she struggled so! It was the most pleasurable experience of his life. He would meet her again on his own terms. The next time, however, there would be no question who was in command. She would know to give herself to him, but she would die regardless. Abu would enjoy killing her as much as entering her. He imagined the tip of his knife blade breaking through the thin flesh of her throat, penetrating deeper, deeper, slicing through her windpipe as she looked at him with sorrowful, pleading eyes. Yes, you will plead, he thought, you will beg for death to take you before you have satisfied me.

The thought shifted, and he was back sitting in the jet next to that fat, egotistical senator as he fed his pig face while pretending to be important. His death was inconsequential. He would let someone else take that life. And that little bitch who attacked and choked him from behind? Few men ever bested him, and never a woman. It was clear to him that she was trained as an American assassin and was on that plane to guard against him. It would never happen again, and if they met in another place, he would take great pleasure in her slow, torturous death.

The sun was dancing low along the peaks of a distant mountain range before Abu Dahl realized he'd been daydreaming the entire trip. He looked over to Rifat, who was engrossed in piloting the ancient, clangy vehicle along the rough terrain. He was about to ask about their progress when a satellite phone chirped from behind inside Zaahir's backpack. Zaahir retrieved it, pushed the call button, and listened. After a moment, his gaze fell. He nodded his head. "It will be done," he said, then ended the call.

"I have received new instructions from Sirhan. We are to take you to the Angrat village ahead. There, you will be met by Crico Dreas. He will take you the rest of the way." Zaahir slipped the phone back into his pack and made eye contact with Rifat in the rearview mirror. Silent signals were exchanged. Rifat nodded his understanding and drove on toward the new destination.

Abu Dahl understood the need for secrecy to keep the whereabouts of Sirhan Abbas protected. There could be drone planes flying overhead right now, and they would only know by the nearly imperceptible sound of their small motors. He expected them to change vehicles soon and follow along a diversionary route to obscure their final destination.

The three rode the rest of the way in silence before arriving at a tiny cluster of rough stone structures encircling an ancient spring-fed well. Beside it lay an enormous flat-topped boulder. Rifat pulled up to the well, shut off the engine, and climbed out.

Further down the road sat an American Humvee. It had been left behind after the troops pulled out of Iraq years earlier and was now re-utilized.

The passenger door opened, and a man wearing a tan military uniform stepped out into the road. He paused, making careful observations of all he saw, then began walking toward them. Abu Dahl assumed this was the man who would take him to meet Sirhan Abbas. He climbed out of the vehicle to greet him.

The uniformed man held out his hands. "Abu Dahl, your

people welcome you back from the belly of the beast." He was a plain-looking man, with no single feature that could be noted or remembered. It was a face that could disappear into any crowd.

Abu took his hand and gripped it firmly. "The pleasure is mine. I am elated to be home in the land of my fathers and brothers." He smiled with joy, feeling one step closer to meeting with the supreme leader. His confidence returned in abundance. "Are you Crico Dreas?" he asked.

"I am known in many places, by many names. Crico Dreas is one of them. Come, let us sit and talk for a moment." He pointed to the huge flat rock. Both men walked to it and sat down side by side. Zaahir and Rifat came over and stood near them.

"My friend," Crico Dreas said, "you have done many things to show Sirhan Abbas and all of your people that you are indeed a great man."

Abu Dahl felt himself inflate with the flattery.

"Sirhan extends his apologies that he could not be here to meet you himself. He thanks you for your loyalty and your faith in our cause."

Abu Dahl looked down and smiled humbly. After all the years of imprisonment, he had not been forgotten. Abbas himself was guiding the plan to bring the two of them together, to fight side by side. It was a moment of total elation, the fitting reward for his steadfast loyalty. Eight years of life passed him by as he sat in the cell of the American prison. Eight years separated from those he loved, from the country of his birth, and from the fight he believed in so fiercely. Now he could taste this place, inhale its fragrance, behold the sounds and sights. He was home. And he would fight with every last drop of his blood to repel the enemy. This was his battle. It was his time to lead the charge to push all things western out of his country and into the sea.

He always expected to be elevated to a distinctive rank when he returned. He knew that moment was fast approaching. The once youthful and spirited foot soldier had returned, matured, driven, ready to lead his brothers in the noble fight. He stood prepared to take the battle to the doorstep of that cursed enemy with a rank worthy of his past deeds. Yes, he could see himself as a General within OASIS. He had proven himself time after time before being captured. He personally put to death every weak and unworthy soul he found supporting the invaders. These ungrateful, spineless creatures did not deserve to share this sacred place. The fire still blazed hot and deep within him. With every fiber of his being, he was ready to march to the death for their great and holy war. He looked into Crico's eyes and reaffirmed his conviction.

"I live only for the glory of Allah."

"Yes, I know this," Crico Dreas answered. "That is why my task today is so difficult."

Abu Dahl's expression changed from one of confidence to confusion. He searched the man's eyes for an explanation. Suddenly his hands were pulled from behind by Zaahir. A pair of handcuffs were ratcheted tightly around his wrists by Rifat. Zaahir stepped out in front and leveled a Makarov pistol at Abu Dahl's head.

"I am sorry, my friend," Crico said, "but you have been used by the very enemy that you escaped from."

"What? What is this, you say?"

"They have made you into a weapon, my friend. A weapon that leads them directly to our leader, Sirhan Abbas."

"This cannot be so! I have said nothing! In all my years being held in that evil place, I gave them nothing! Do you hear me? Nothing!"

"That is what troubles me most. It was not what you revealed, my friend. It is what you carried back with you. Or should I say, within you?"

Rifat held tight to the cuffs as Crico Dreas extracted a long bayonet from a sheath in his belt.

"I believe the only way for you to understand is to be shown." He held the knife in his right fist and brought the blade up to Abu's face. "I'm afraid this is going to hurt terribly." Crico Dreas stuck the sharp knife tip into the bridge of Abu Dahl's nose and pulled down, opening the entire left side. Abu Dahl screamed in agony as Crico Dreas sliced his face open, then dug around with the blade inside his left sinus. He did not find what he was looking for.

"Forgive me," he said, "wrong side." He moved the knife tip to the other side of Abu Dahl's nose.

"No, please, I beg you! I don't—"

Crico Dreas sliced deep into the right side now, cutting more aggressively. He split Abu Dahl's face in two, exposing the sinus flesh as the man let out a loud, high scream. The pain was excruciating, the worst Abu Dahl ever experienced. Blood pulsed and gushed and mixed with tears streaming down the open wounds. His nose now hung loose on his face, attached only by thin membranes of skin at the bridge and base. A small, shiny capsule glistened as it shifted from its hiding spot and slid downward in the massive tide of blood. Crico Dreas caught the tiny device on his knife blade and offered it up for Abu Dahl to see.

"I am quite sure this should not have been inside of you, my friend."

It took every bit of strength for Abu Dahl to hold himself up, let alone attempt to grasp what was happening. He looked down at the blood-covered capsule

"No!" he pleaded, choking back the hot, thick liquid as it

streamed down his throat. “This cannot be! I would never. . .allow this! With Allah. . .as my witness I swear. . . I do not know what this is!”

“No, I don’t suppose you do. Yet it seems everyone in the world knows there was a tracking device inside your head… everyone except you.”

The pain was coming in unendurable waves. Dark spots began obscuring his vision, growing larger and blotting out the sunlight. Consciousness was slipping away, but he clung to it despite the terrible reality.

“Zaahir, Rifat,” he sobbed through the dripping blood, “both of you know me!” His head rocked forward and back, eyelids flickering. “You know. . . I would never allow them. . .to put this inside of me. Please, you must. . .stop him!”

The reply from his childhood friend came cold and direct. “It is war, Abu. You have become a tool of the enemy. Now you must become an example.”

Crico Dreas extracted a long machete and said, “Sirhan Abbas sends this message. ‘Your people are grateful for your loyalty. We all give what is required of us. Now, you must offer one last sacrifice. Abu Dahl, Sirhan Abbas commands you to give your life.’”

The two other men stepped away as Crico Dreas swung the blade with all his might at the back of Abu Dahl’s neck. The weapon cut precisely and clean. The head toppled off, hitting the ground with a muffled thud and rolling over, coming to rest face down in the dirt. His lifeless body remained upright for a moment, spurting blood from the stump of his neck before dropping over and sliding off the giant stone.

“Leave his body where it lies,” Crico Dreas commanded. “Place his head with this device on the rock.”

"Should I destroy the device so the enemy cannot use it?" said Rifat.

"No, we want them to find it. Let them see there is nothing to show for their efforts but failure and death. Let them see that we will always know what they are plotting. There are no secrets anymore. There is only the word of Allah."

25

Washington, DC

Jordan awoke from a fitful sleep to the sound of unfamiliar voices. It took another moment to comprehend what she was hearing. The television audio, seldom heard in the condo, was blaring from the living room. She could make out her mother's voice as well, sounding like the color commentator for the television's narrative. She must be on the phone, Jordan surmised, talking to someone about what was being broadcast. She now recognized the newscaster's voice. Burt Ledger repeated the phrase, 'breaking news,' again and again as he talked animatedly. Jordan caught other keywords; Afghanistan, murder, Guantanamo Bay. She slid out of bed and headed downstairs.

Katherine Karlson noticed Jordan descending the stairs, turned, and waved.

"Hold that thought," she said into the phone and set it on the table. "Good morning, sunshine! Sleep well?"

Jordan's mood was still stormy from the last discussion

with her mother. She feigned a smile to avoid a clash so early in the morning.

"I made a pot of coffee," she offered, "nice and strong, the way you like it." She pointed to a carafe on the counter, then picked up her phone again. "Sorry, Jordan just came down. Like I said, I got a call from a friend at the embassy in England at four this morning. The first reports were sketchy, but more details came in when they began playing this video. What's that? Yes, I don't think there is any doubt it's him."

Jordan sipped the day's first cup as she watched the big screen.

'Breaking news from Al Jazeera television,' was the headline in large white letters. Karlson grabbed the remote and turned the volume louder, something she rarely did when watching the news. The video appeared to be shot in the mountains of Afghanistan with narration in both Farsi and English. The cameraman filmed while walking along a rugged, rocky path toward a group of armed men. They argued a moment but then parted, allowing him access to what they all gathered around. There, perched upon a blood-stained boulder, was a dirt-caked, grossly disfigured human head. The nose was butchered open from either side. The screen filled with the mutilated face, frozen in an expression of agony, suggesting the victim endured this torture while still alive. The dialog continued through the video while a name was repeated by the agitated tribal militiamen. Over and over now, they chanted, "Abu Dahl, Abu Dahl, Abu Dahl!"

The English narrator now added, "We have unconfirmed reports that the victim shown here is, in fact, Abu Dahl. The former detainee of Guantanamo Bay was recently released after years of imprisonment in connection with a series of European mass bombings that claimed the lives of hundreds."

"My God, how can somebody do that to another human being?" Jordan said, turning away from the graphic images.

Her mother, however, sat stone-faced, watching the entire report with keen interest.

"That's the man you helped Erin Laurent get released from Gitmo, right?"

Karlson's eyes remained fixed to the screen as she held the phone to her chest, nodding slowly.

"I don't understand," Jordan said, shaking her head in disgust, "why would they slice him up like that and then cut off his head? I thought they wanted him back. Instead, they torture and kill him? What is wrong with these people?

"They knew the CIA had him by the nose," Karlson blurted out, staring at the brutal images. "They were looking for the beacon."

"The what?" Jordan asked, completely puzzled.

Karlson broke her gaze from the television, realizing what she had revealed. "Oh honey, I don't know why I said that. I'm sickened by the brutality over there." "You should stick to your promise and get our troops out," Jordan said, releasing some of her pent-up frustration from the last heated conversation.

Karlson put the phone back to her ear. "I'll let you know when I'm on the way," she said, then ended the call. She turned to confront her daughter. "Are you going to start that again? Christ, kid, it's too damn early, and that is a very simplistic view of an extremely complicated issue." She glanced at her watch. "And it will have to be a subject for another day. I need to finish getting ready for a meeting. So how about you give it a rest for a while?"

She topped off her coffee in silence and headed for her bedroom, content to learn that the secret military mission was now exposed and foiled. She also hoped their plan served its intended purpose and forced the president to re-think his position on the war effort. She wasn't sure if the signal beacon transmitting from inside Abu Dahl's head was common knowledge yet, but it would be soon enough. For now, denial was the best course of action.

26

Jordan found herself walking down an unfamiliar street with no recollection of how much time had passed or how she'd come to be there. The gruesome images and conversation with her mother weighed so heavy on her mind that she felt faint, nauseous. The room was suddenly empty of oxygen, and she'd bolted for the door to catch her breath. Once outside, she kept moving with no thought of a destination.

She tasted a tear on her lips and realized she'd been crying. Great, she thought, I feel like hell, and now I probably look even worse. She paused a moment to view her reflection in a storefront window, surveying the damage and grinning back through mascara-streaked eyes. Good thing I don't wear much makeup, or I'd pass for Alice Cooper's ugly sister.

She regained her bearings and realized she wasn't far from her favorite coffee shop. Jordan stepped up the pace and headed for a pick-me-up.

She walked past the counter and straight into the Ladies' room, where she made some adjustments to her makeup and hair. The Alice Cooper analogy may have been a bit extreme after all, she mused. Then her mother's words came streaming back. "A campaign promise is not a political protocol." She looked into the mirror, still shocked, disappointed beyond words that the woman had uttered the line. She studied her own reflection, confirming she was not the one with the damaged philosophy. The ordeal left her feeling shaken and empty. All she wanted now was coffee, a snack, and time to think. She pushed through the restroom door and stepped into line to place an order.

With a hot drink and sugary treat in hand, she scanned the room for an open seat. She spied Cody and Ethan huddled over a laptop in the corner, and her mood brightened. She decided there would be plenty of time to brood later and grabbed an open seat beside them.

"Hey guys, what's new in the cyber world?" she asked.

Both of them looked up and smiled.

Ethan put his hand on hers. "Free time from the campaign?"

Jordan frowned. "Maybe a bit more to come. I'm thinking of going back home for a while."

Ethan returned the expression. "I'm sorry to hear that. Why would you leave now?"

Jordan looked around the room, thinking whether she wanted to discuss her situation. She decided against it.

"Being home with my dad always gets me back on target. I feel like I've already spent too much time in DC. The last thing I would ever want is to start thinking like the people here."

"Thanks a lot!" chuckled Cody, eyeing her over his shoulder.

Jordan patted him on the back. "You both know the types I'm talking about. I think I just need a break."

"I've always admired your dad," Ethan said. "He's one of

the rare ones that understand what's going on and doesn't sugar coat it."

"Unfortunately," countered Jordan, "campaigning is sugar coating." Hype and bullshit, to be more precise, she thought. "My dad doesn't have the stomach for this town. He's content with being a governor, and I'm glad."

"Now, hold on!" Cody turned and held up a finger. "Did you say your dad is a governor?"

"Great state of California," Jordan said, smiling.

Cody looked perplexed. "You gotta be kidding me. West, right? Cliff West, who's married to. . .wait, Senator Karlson is your…and nobody…holy shit!"

Jordan gave Ethan a puzzled look.

"I told you your identity was your business alone," he said. "I wouldn't repeat it."

"But Cody is your best friend. I assumed you would have told him who I was."

"I gave you my word. To some of us, that's still something of value."

Jordan smiled. "Thank you."

"I think I'm hurt by that," Cody smirked. "Way to keep a secret, best buddy. Oh, and by the way, that was sarcasm."

Ethan and Jordan drifted to the far end of the table, comparing their knowledge of history when Cody flagged them over, pointing to his laptop screen. "I've seen three blogs now that say the leak came may have come from Senator Karlson. Sorry, I meant your mom. This one even quotes a guy who says he was part of the Al Jazeera film crew and saw the documents in her office."

Jordan heard her mother's name and instinctively prepared to defend her, despite their current differences. "What leak are you talking about? And what documents?"

Ethan and Cody eyed each other uncomfortably. "Cody's

been tracking a story that came up this morning about that beheading in Afghanistan. Some insiders say that OASIS did this to their own guy because of a secret American military mission that went wrong. They're now threatening to retaliate. As usual, the whole thing is long on theories and short on details."

"I was watching this with my mother," Jordan said. "She didn't go into detail, but I got the feeling she knew more than she was letting on."

"It's weird they would execute this guy after waiting so long to get him out of Gitmo," Cody said.

Ethan shook his head. "He got all the way back home, then his own team whacks him. Definitely weird."

"A group of actors and politicians flew him from Guantanamo," Jordan added. "The organizer was a friend of my mother."

"So why would they help a murderer who has sworn to fight against us?" Cody asked.

Jordan shook her head. "I learned a long time ago not to argue with a bleeding heart. It's what they do." She thought a moment and added, "Something else my mother said that seemed a bit weird. She said the CIA had him by the nose. When I asked her what she meant, she backpedaled."

"Wait a second," interrupted Cody. "By the nose? That's rather ironic, considering they found this guy's head on a rock with his nose carved open."

Jordan nodded. "She said something else…something about a light, or signal… A beacon! She said they were looking for the beacon!"

Cody looked up with a bewildered expression that turned to excitement. He began typing rapidly. "Dudes, that's what the cameraman from Al Jazeera said. He'd caught a glance at the details of this mission but said it was about following a beacon signal to track down Sirhan Abbas." He pulled up another website that listed recent quotes by the cameraman. "Yeah, here he says there were secure documents left out in plain sight in the senator's office. All he did was film them."

"It's hard to believe my mother would be so careless with confidential files."

"But how else could he gain access?" said Ethan.

"Careful here," cautioned Cody, "we're still assuming this is valid information and that he's telling the truth in the first place."

Ethan pointed to the laptop. "There's enough information from other sources to make his story appear at least credible, don't you think? Play the video back again."

Cody restarted the clip from the beginning, and they all watched with renewed interest.

Ethan noticed it first, an odd glimmer off to the side. "Hey, pause this for a second, will ya?"

Cody froze the image as Ethan stared hard at the screen, then slid the computer over and began single-stepping through each frame. When the screen was filled with a full view of the severed head, he sat back and pointed. "There, you see that?"

"What are you looking at?" Cody squinted, searching for any anomaly he hadn't noticed earlier. He was rewarded with the faint reflection of sunlight from a small object. "Whoa!" he said, wresting back control of the laptop and zooming the image. With each enlargement, he re-centered and zoomed in again. Gradually, a tiny object began to reveal itself in greater detail.

"What is that?" Jordan asked, leaning in closer.

"Not sure yet, but it's definitely something man-made that doesn't belong there. Just another few steps in, and…"

There it was, nearly plain as day. Frozen in a pool of

congealed blood beside the lifeless head of Abu Dahl lay a small metallic device about half the size of a cold capsule.

"Could that be?…" Jordan wondered aloud.

"The beacon!" the three of them whispered in excited unison.

"Bloody hell! That tiny thing is a transmitter?" Cody stared dumbfounded.

"Oh God," Jordan shuddered as she realized the real implications of the discovery. "They dug that out of his face!"

There was a moment of silence as they all envisioned the gory scene that led up to this gruesome image. The sheer brutality of restraining a man while carving into his face in search of this device was beyond comprehension.

"That's what my mother must have meant by the CIA having him by the nose," Jordan said, revulsed at her own words. "What animals could do this to another human being?"

"The CIA must have been tracking him through that device, and these guys figured it out," Ethan said.

"Hoping he would lead them to their headquarters?" Jordan asked. Suddenly it made sense. Hell, it made perfect sense. "That was the secret mission!" she exclaimed. "Abu Dahl didn't know that thing was planted inside of him!"

"Only the bad guys found out and killed him for it." Cody was surprised at how simple it all sounded. The details fit so neatly into place that there had to be some truth to it.

Ethan's expression turned somber. "You realize what this means? The military was using Abu Dahl to get a bead on Sirhan Abbas, and now that door slammed shut." He looked from Cody to Jordan. "Every murder committed by OASIS from this point on could possibly have been prevented if this mission had not been compromised."

Jordan suddenly felt the weight of Ethan's words, and her

stomach twisted. If her mother was the source of the leak, then the woman had blood on her hands. She silently prayed that they were wrong, and Karlson had nothing to do with it.

Cody took pity on her, imagining what she must be feeling. "So, we might have a way to find out," he offered.

"Find out what?" Jordan asked.

"Find out if your mother gave away the secrets during her interview with Al Jazeera."

"You can do that?"

"Maybe," said Cody as he started tapping on his phone. He sent out two quick texts, and within a minute, he received a response. "My cousin, Murray, runs a little company that installs many of the surveillance systems in town." Cody tapped out another text as he spoke. "I know he did a lot of work on the Dirksen building because we talked about the testing process. They set that system up so that maintenance and diagnostics could be run remotely."

A response came back from the second text, and Cody read it with a satisfied grin. "Okay, this is too cool. So, he has the back door codes to access the surveillance system. It's not the kind of thing he does for fun, but he says he'll try to download the data from the memory drives if we can tell him the approximate time of that Al Jazeera interview. We can check it out tonight. Anybody up for a late-night video party?"

27

Baltimore, Maryland

Murray Falcone lived where he worked. That is to say, his address was in an industrial park, and his living room featured a parking area for his work van. With the high rent cost in the Baltimore area, it made more sense to combine his home and workspace. At least, he figured, until he got married. The arrangement worked well, and there were no simmering relationships on the horizon to threaten it anytime soon.

He sat before a massive cluster of computers and monitors. His fingers clacked on the keyboard in preparation for the night's featured event, logging in and viewing security footage from Senator Karlson's office in the Dirksen building. He opened a program for testing the system, ensuring his passcodes were still valid and capable of accessing the data within. While the computers connected, he reached for a beer and spun around to face his guests.

Murray's cousin, Cody, and his friends Ethan and Jordan sat at the kitchen table sipping beers, munching snacks, and following his actions as though watching a computer geek in motion was actually entertaining. Murray grinned at the thought but at the same time appreciated the company and the attention.

"I'm surprised it's this easy to access security information from a government building," Jordan remarked as she scooped a carrot stick into the artichoke dip she had brought along.

Murray shook his head, swallowing a mouthful of beer. "It's not as easy as it looks. I have access only because I do installations and final testing on these systems. Truth is, I'm bending quite a few rules tonight. And believe me, if you weren't related to the subject of our snooping, I would not have agreed to be involved." He leaned in closer and added, "I could lose my contracts and probably face some serious charges. I'm relying on your silence as much as you are mine. Whatever information we find tonight goes no further than this room. You have my word on that."

"Thank you," she said, "I appreciate that more than you know."

A beep from the computer caught Murray's attention. "We're in!" he exclaimed, turning back to the console.

Jordan scanned the impressive array of rack-mounted CPU's and numerous monitors, the most elaborate system she'd ever seen. There were so many lights flashing and cables running in every direction that she would have struggled to even locate the power button.

"Okay, now we see what's on those security server drives," Murray said as he set his beer down and began typing. "I have seven files from that time frame. Jordan, can you tell me the senator's suite number?"

"I believe it's 221."

"221 it is."

More typing, then he began scrolling the cursor across the screen. "I have two separate feeds from that suite with multiple camera channels multiplexed together." He turned to Jordan and explained, "That means the system stacks four cameras on each feed. It combines them together, so when viewed, you will be watching four different video streams. We'll start with feed one and see if that's our information." Murray opened the file, and immediately the images of the two entrances and waiting area were displayed on the large monitor.

"We have the right suite but the wrong rooms. Let's crack open the other file." He clicked on the file icon, and a message appeared. "Uh-oh," he said, "the file's been deleted."

"So we have nothing?" Cody asked.

"Not necessarily, but it does tell us that somebody had something to hide." Murray clicked a few files in other locations and then turned to them with a devious grin. "So let's find out how good the guy was that cleaned house."

He opened and examined the contents of the computer's recycle bin. "Well, they're not amateurs. They knew to clear the record of the file."

"Does that mean it's completely gone?" Ethan asked, taking Jordan's hand.

"Generally, yes, that would mean it's deleted. But I still have a few tools to play with. I'm now running a neat little program that scans the drive and searches for recoverable files. If our house cleaner was proficient, he would have erased the files and re-written over all of the data with ones and zeros. That would have been the end of it. We'll know if he did that in a minute."

They all sat in silence as the scanning software checked every sector of the hard drive.

"That could be it," Murray finally said, pointing to a group of green blocks in an otherwise blue section. "We may have gotten lucky. I can see they deleted the directory of the records but did not re-write over them. Let's see if we can restore and replay."

After a string of keystrokes, the manipulated data was saved to Murray's system. Moments later, the big center screen flashed to life with four separate images. It was apparent that not all the files were completely restored.

"Well, the good news is we have two angles of her office. The third looks like the reception area." Murray tapped on the lower right quadrant that flashed with static and shadows of indiscernible images. "The fourth is unreadable. There is also an audio file, but we don't need that right now."

"And that's Gene Lawton, the campaign manager, greeting the Al Jazeera film crew," observed Jordan.

As they watched the two upper images, the network crew exchanged pleasantries and set up their equipment. Karlson entered the room shortly after, and they began filming the interview.

"That all looks innocent enough," Ethan said with hopeful optimism. He glanced over to Jordan, sensing her apprehension. He wrapped his arm around her shoulder, felt the tightness of her rigid muscles, and began massaging her neck. For her sake, he hoped they would observe nothing incriminating tonight.

The network interview remained uneventful until the campaign manager entered the office.

"That's Gene again," Jordan explained.

They all watched as Lawton whispered something into Karlson's ear. She abruptly rose and followed him out a side door. Both disappeared off camera. The film crew sat alone and motionless in the office until. . .

"Did you see that?" Cody asked.

"I caught it too," Murray said

"What happened? What did you see?" Jordan stared at the image, searching for anything that had changed.

"There's something on the credenza behind her desk that they're pointing at. It looks like a folder or a booklet."

Cody walked to the screen as he spoke and pointed at the rectangular object. As he did, every member of the film crew sprang into action.

"What, what are they doing?" Jordan said.

"They're filming those documents page by page," Murray answered, alarmed. "This isn't good."

They watched in stunned silence as the female member of the crew came around the desk and flipped through the pages of the mystery document as the cameraman filmed each. It was over so fast that everyone watching felt as though they had observed the actions of professional spies merely portraying a news crew.

"What are they photographing?" Ethan asked, squinting, attempting to bring the image into better focus. "I can't see enough detail to make it out."

As they struggled to discern the document's contents, the missing fourth video image flashed and resolved itself into view. At first, it was a series of short bursts. Over time the picture remained on the screen longer and longer before turning back to snow. It showed an open door and the backs of multiple people standing around it, but nothing more.

"Jordan," Murray said, "do you know what that room is?"

She shook her head. "It's near the reception area, but I don't recall it ever being open."

Murray nodded. "Yup, I see it on this other feed now." He pointed to the video image of the reception room. The open door was visible from this angle, but the view of the occupants was blocked. Again and again, the signal from camera four teased with images of the people clustered about the mystery room before dropping out, revealing nothing more.

Murray busied himself manipulating the signal from camera two that showed Karlson's desk from a second angle. He isolated the image and zoomed in on the credenza and the mystery document.

"Wait, I know that symbol," Jordan exclaimed. "That's Military Intelligence. I've seen it on classified folders that my mother was reviewing."

"Holy shit!" Cody shouted. "Could that be the military mission everyone's talking about? If it is, we've just witnessed espionage!"

"But you can see my mother didn't intend to give it to them," Jordan said defensively. "They went through her papers when she left the room. It was awful questionable to leave those documents out like that, I'll give you that. But it looks like nothing more than a dumb mistake. Doesn't it?" She hoped something would prove them wrong about what they saw, but doubt was already gnawing away.

The video signal from camera four suddenly re-appeared with striking clarity. The outlines of three people stood huddled in the entry of the mystery door.

Murray studied the images from cameras three and four. Then, with the enthusiasm of a scientist making a miracle discovery, he announced, "I know what that room is! That's the security control closet. The video and alarm feeds are routed and displayed there before being output to the main security server in the basement. Look, you can make out the images on the video monitors they're watching." He stared another moment before realizing what he was witnessing. He pushed back from the console. "Oh my God," he said, nearly breathless, "they've been spying on that film crew the whole time!"

There was more activity in video four. The three people were moving about, talking animatedly. Two of the occupants turned and walked toward the senator's office. Their faces could now be seen on the feeds from both cameras three and four, filling the large screen. It was Katherine Karlson and Gene Lawton.

"Oh no," Jordan whimpered, "oh no."

"They were controlling the whole thing!" Cody exclaimed. "They set it up to make these people think they'd made the discovery of a lifetime, then waited until they took the bait! It was all…it was…"

"It was a ruse," Murray said solemnly. "Jordan, I'm so sorry you had to see this. Maybe it would have been better—"

Jordan shook her head. "No, I needed to," she replied shakily. Her shoulders slumped as a tear streamed down her cheek. "I had to see for myself. I needed to see the lie. It's all been a lie."

The video played on as Karlson resumed her role at her desk. She spoke animatedly as she concluded the interview. Jordan watched in pained silence as the images revealing her mother as a co-conspirator in treason were burned forever into her memory. Everything she held dear now seemed like nothing more than false figments of the role her mother portrayed on her way to the next plateau. Her entire life was an act. On-screen and off, she played a part. Jordan now felt like nothing more than a side note, a short cameo in the epic story of Kat Karlson, the actress, the senator, the president. She felt pain like none she'd ever experienced. A part of her soul was dying. Nothing would ever be the same. Her heart raced as her stomach churned acid. She hugged her gut to keep from doubling over, wishing to be a thousand miles away from it all.

"We've seen enough, Murray," Ethan said in a near whisper, wrapping both arms around Jordan as he led her away from the horrifying images.

28

Washington, DC

Jordan awoke early the next morning with eyes nearly swelled shut. She had never cried so much in her life. Even the death of her grandfather, a man who meant the world to her, could not compare to the loss she felt right now. Everything she had come to believe and fight for was a lie.

Jordan struggled to inhale against the weight of so many shattered hopes and dreams that bore down on her chest. Feeling violated and empty, her insides ached as she remembered the events and awful images of her mother's deception from the night before. Not even the presidency could be worth such a price.

Her cheeks flushed with shame and anger, recalling the fundraisers and social events she'd attended. The thousands of phone calls requesting money and votes for the campaign.

Her 'poor me' reaction soon vanished as she remembered that she was not the only one who was deceived. Karlson's followers believed she'd given up a life of Hollywood glitter to stand for the masses not being represented in Washington.

They trusted her and freely gave their time and offered support. They were deceived the same as she was.

Jordan remembered opening letters containing coins from kids living in poverty who sent in anything they could find, hoping that their lives would be improved by this woman. Sadly, she thought, empty promises were the only thing for sale here.

She rose from bed and walked down to the dark kitchen, loading a pod into the coffee machine. She offered a small prayer of thanks that her mother was sleeping in. It spared her a confrontation so early in the morning. She sat alone and sipped the day's first cup, smirking as she recalled an old commercial that referred to it as the think drink. She wished it would hurry up and help her brain generate a few new thoughts on what to do about last night.

She wondered how the country would react if the truth were revealed. There would always be supporters still standing behind Karlson, refusing to believe what she had done. There was never a shortage of those who were easily led. Jordan, however, felt the vast majority would be as appalled as she was. She owed it to them to stop this now. It would be hard enough living with this knowledge now etched permanently into her mind. It would be infinitely worse to allow the scenario to play out without at least attempting to force her mother to repair the damage. She realized her hands were tapping a nervous rhythm on the table as she sat rocking in her seat. Enough of this, she thought. She stood and opened the refrigerator, looking for an egg to fry. Jordan usually started her mornings with lighter fare, but today she craved an unhealthy dose of comfort food. She dug through the meat drawer and pulled out a package of bacon.

After breakfast and reading the internet news, Jordan decided to get out and walk off a few calories. A little fresh air might stimulate the neurons that the caffeine had failed to awaken. She slipped on her running shoes, plugged in a pair of earbuds, and headed out the door.

A few blocks down the road, she realized her thoughts were drowning out her music and decided to bounce a few of them off of Ethan. She sent a short text, hoping he would be up soon. He was, and instead of typing back a reply, he called. She answered, grateful that some people still preferred to communicate the old-fashioned way.

"You doing okay?" he asked.

"Better than expected, but no, not okay." She paused as the previous night's images flashed through her mind. "It's so hard to believe, even though I saw it all for myself. I'm just not sure of the next step."

"I would love to say you don't have to do anything, but we both know that's not an option."

So far, he was voicing her exact thoughts.

"I know," she conceded. "If my mother were a reasonable woman, she would recognize the terrible mistake she'd made and get her people working on damage control. But a reasonable woman would never have done this in the first place."

"Is there any point in trying to talk with her? I worry about what she would do if you told her what you know, what we all know."

Jordan's vision of confronting her mother was a screaming tirade with no end. She closed her eyes, shaking her head with sad resignation.

"I can't imagine a happy ending to this nightmare," she said, pacing the long, empty sidewalk and rubbing her temples, attempting to suppress a tension headache. "Mother won't take it well, but I have to give her the option of trying to fix this before I tell anyone else. Do you think Cody and his cousin can stay quiet until I meet with her?"

"I know they will. Murray is probably nervous as hell just having seen the video. He'll keep it to himself until you make the first move. But please, watch your back! This isn't some simple mistake that can be fixed by making a public apology. She's in some deep shit. You gotta figure she'll fight for survival, even if that means she has to challenge you."

"I don't think it will come to that," Jordan said, hoping she was right. "She's going to hate me for doing this, but we have to start with a face-to-face meeting. I owe her that much. We're supposed to have lunch today. I'll drop the bomb then."

"Please call me as soon as you leave. I have to know you're all right."

"I promise. I'm probably going to need a shoulder to cry on after I get ripped apart, along with a stiff drink."

29

Jordan returned to the condominium with a thousand pounds of guilt dragging behind. She paused to steady herself against the door frame. All of the mental coaching to psych herself up for this moment now seemed to shrivel away, leaving her defenseless and ashamed of what she'd come to do. She was not here to be the good daughter, but rather something barbarous. Something venomous and deadly, no better than some evil creature that clawed its way from the womb, only to turn and attack the one that had given it birth, given it life. Today she would deliver a message with the potential of destroying her mother. All the woman's years of meticulous planning, organizing, and campaigning were about to be nullified and made irrelevant by yours truly. Today, Jordan was an assassin.

Her mouth was desert dry, yet her palms slick with sweat. She couldn't actually do this, could she? No, damn it, that wasn't the question to be asking right now. Instead, she wondered how someone in this woman's position could have committed such abhorrent criminal acts and still be left standing. She grit her teeth and fended off another wave of guilt, reminding herself that she was not the one with the flawed morals.

How could her mother have been so stupid as to follow through with such a plan? She had destroyed herself. Her name would be poison. Every friend she ever made would abandon her, and only those with a death wish of their own would dare to venture near. Her own husband, Jordan's father, would be committing political suicide if he didn't make tracks for divorce court the moment word of this got out.

Jordan could not comprehend how the woman was living with herself. Why wasn't her conscience shaking her from the soundest sleep every night and beating her over the head with a splintered club formed from the words, 'you-fucked-up?'

But the woman was still her mother, and Jordan was about to destroy her run for the presidency. A near-certain victory would be ripped from her grip. And then what? Going on with life? Living tomorrow like none of this ever happened? Wake up, she chided herself. The days that would follow swinging this ax would be dark, painful, and lonely.

Jordan rounded the corner into the dining room and stopped dead in her tracks. Karlson was seated at the table with her back turned. She was chuckling lightheartedly into her phone in between sips of wine. She wasn't just holding up well under the enormous strain. She was suffering no effects at all. Like all of this was nothing more than another typical day on the campaign trail. Jordan slid back behind the wall, shaking her head in disbelief. How could this woman carry the lies and guilt with such ease when merely knowing what she had done was an unbearable burden for her daughter?

Karlson laughed again from the other side of the wall. Jordan's hands balled into fists, her sadness overtaken by anger.

A strange thought sparked deep in her mind, disconnected

and out of place at first. But the more she pondered it, the more it gained relevance and grew, interconnecting, weaving with other visions and memories. It evolved from that fleeting thought to a revealing observation with an undeniable conclusion. These terrible things were having no effect on Karlson because she was incapable of the proper emotional response. It was as though the very attributes that made her a successful actress were also detriments to normal feelings. Either she didn't possess them at all, or her internal wiring somehow bypassed the circuits responsible for fundamental human emotions. Jordan wasn't sure of the precise mechanism that was missing or damaged but could now see the results of its absence.

Her mother was always quite capable of showing coldness. In physics, cold was the absence of heat. Was it possible the same held true of emotions? Indifference or coldness could have been the natural state of someone with an inability to naturally convey their feelings. Jordan remembered her mother turning the affections on and off as though they were never heartfelt, but rather something more mechanical, regulated, controlled. As a child, she wondered if her mother actually felt these things at all or was just acting out which sentiment seemed the most appropriate. It sometimes reminded her of an old Bowery Boys movie, where the gang would have a numbered response for the mischief they had gotten themselves into. A fight with a rival gang, routine six, boys! Yeah, it was kind of like that. Acting proud of your daughter's accomplishments; emotional routine twelve. Receiving a beautiful gift from your husband, routine five.

Acting.

She could now summarize all of her mother's reactions into that one word. Rehearsed. Scripted and calculated. As if she'd been referencing from the pages of an instruction manual: 'Emotional Issues And Their Proper Responses.' This wasn't a revelation at all, she now conceded, but rather something she always knew. Her mother wore emotions like other people wore clothes, selecting the appropriate comeback with careful purpose, then slipping smoothly in and out of them at will.

Jordan listened to Karlson's gleeful exchange on the phone for a few more moments. Then, with a recaptured determination, she strode into the dining room. She came around the table and sat across from her mother, poured herself a glass of wine, and downed half in a gulp.

Karlson looked up and noticed her for the first time with a look of surprise that turned into a bright smile.

"Let me call you back," she said to the caller, "Jordan walked in, and we have so much to talk about." She slipped the phone into her pocket and folded her hands. "Well, hello to you too. I would offer you a glass of wine, but I see you've already got that covered."

Jordan stared back, swirling her glass.

Karlson's smile never faltered. She raised her own glass and clinked it against Jordan's.

"What was that for?" Jordan asked.

"A victory toast, or should I say a pre-victory celebration." She slid a printed page of data across the table.

Jordan studied it for a moment. "What is this I'm looking at?"

"That," Karlson replied proudly, "is the latest national polling information from three different agencies. They all say the same thing."

Jordan shifted uneasily in her seat, anticipating what she was about to hear. It wasn't going to make this any easier.

"With less than three months before the election, we're leading fifty-three to forty-one percent. Unless something completely unforeseen happens, I believe I can safely say that we're moving out of this condo in January. Jordan, we're going to the White House!"

Jordan's throat constricted as though being squeezed in a phantom chokehold. She struggled for breath, unable to speak.

"You were as much a part of this success as anyone, and I wanted to say thank you. All of our hard work has paid off, honey. Your mother is going to be president!"

The announcement tore at her insides. Jordan cursed her luck that this of all days was when her mother chose to share this information. *Nothing like shooting someone down at the pinnacle of their existence.* She briefly entertained the idea of retreating. Any one of a hundred other days would have been better than this. The thought made her feel like a coward. Postponing even a few hours gained nothing and would make it even more difficult the next time. She would have none of it.

"Can this get any harder?" she murmured.

Karlson gave her a curious glance.

Like it or not, the moment was upon her. "Mother, I know what you did in that interview with Al Jazeera. I saw the video."

"Oh Jordan, can't you give it a rest?" she said through a veil of thinning patience. "I know you were displeased that I did the interview, but there's no point in dwelling on it any longer. Can we please—"

"I saw the entire video, okay?" Jordan interrupted.

Karlson set her glass down and eyed her daughter. She struggled to remain upbeat but felt annoyance creeping up like a deep-seated itch. She replayed the mental images of the interview with Deeba Gohar. There was nothing incriminating that linked her with the Abu Dahl story being reported.

Still, was there any possibility that they overlooked some small, insignificant detail? She and her team watched that interview repeatedly. All were confident that it had gone as planned with no unseen issues. Then what the hell was this about?

"Jordan, we've been all over this subject. I don't believe anything else needs to be said. You're not pleased that I did the interview, and I still say it was a golden opportunity to reach out to the people of the region and tell them, show them, that we are not their enemy. You should be proud."

"Is that what I should be? Proud? Try this one on. Disgusted, angry, disappointed. No, disappointment doesn't even begin to cover it. Broken-hearted, Mother! Betrayed. The damage you've done may never be mended. You have to make this right, and you owe it to me and everyone else who trusted you."

"Stop! Jesus Christ, kid, stop already! It was a simple goddamned interview and nothing more. What the hell is this all about?"

"A simple interview? That's what you call handing over classified documents to the enemy? What the fuck, mom! I saw the security video from your office. You left classified information out in the open and allowed them to copy it. I watched you set the whole thing up. I watched you leave the room with that document in plain sight."

Her voice cracked as though she were reliving the moment. The hurt and disgust consumed her. Her eyes narrowed as she released the full measure of her anger.

"And then I watched you, Mother. I watched you watching them! It made me sick to my stomach to think you were even capable of such a terrible thing. How could you?" she yelled, "you've committed treason!" Her misty eyes wandered the room, searching and praying for a solution to make this all go away. "I don't know what you can do to fix this," she said with sad resignation, "but you need to start now. People will help you if you just ask."

The disclosure hit the senator right between the eyes with both barrels. She froze in place, her expression as neutral as a blank slate. Slowly, her facial muscles re-energized, and her mouth turned down as a tear welled up in her eye. She stared back at her daughter with an expression of indescribable pain and disbelief, the perfect portrait of an innocent victim who had been cheated on, abused, lied to, and left for dead. Every victimized character that Katherine Karlson ever portrayed in a movie now manifested itself simultaneously. The effect was powerful and moving. It was an Oscar-worthy moment that lasted all of ten-seconds before the dam broke, and she moved on to anger. The inner beast crawled out and took control. She rose from her seat and stared with cold, glaring eyes down at her daughter.

"You bitch!" she said, building from a low, slow growl. "You ungrateful, spoiled, ignorant bitch! Who the fuck are you to lecture me on anything? You have no idea the shit storms I've walked through to climb this mountain." Karlson swatted at her wine glass. It flew and shattered against the wall. "I'm about to win the most powerful position in the world. In the world, goddamn it! And you want me to step away and say, whoops, mommy made a mistake, terribly sorry, please forgive me. Is that what you have in mind? Hum? Because you know if this information got out, I would be ripped to shreds and forced to withdraw." She stopped to ponder the words she had spoken. Her brows raised as she made the connection. "But that's exactly what you have in mind, isn't it? That I admit to all of this and withdraw from the election."

A flash of the darkest doomsday flickered in Karlson's

mind. She imagined herself speaking in disgrace to the senate body while being drowned out by the boos from both sides of the aisle. Worse yet, she would face the wrath of that withered bitch of a majority leader, her and that condescending glare curled into a satisfying smirk. Karlson always suspected the woman was secretly more supportive of her rival, and she imagined the old prune would barely be able to control her glee.

"Who the hell comes up with a plan like that, Jordan?" She asked, nearly pleading for an answer.

And just like that, the storm passed.

Karlson's fists opened back up, the vein in her forehead stopped throbbing with every heartbeat, her eyelids closed tight. A sad, hurt frown replaced the storm of expressions.

"My God," she said, her throat tightening around the words. "I thought we were on the same side." She wore the look of a battered housewife again. But inside, the mental mechanics whirred and meshed. Her thoughts ground out scenario after scenario on how to adequately address this most catastrophic event.

The tirade left Jordan numb and shaking, as though she'd been picked up by a tornado and thrown into the next county. And now, having witnessed three massive mood swings in less time than it took to fry an egg, she had no idea whether she was talking to her mother, or Dr. Jekyll or Mr. Hyde.

"I supported you with everything I had to give, mother. But you've done something terrible. Now you have to try and fix it."

Karlson shook her head and pushed her hair back. "I doubt that's possible without destroying my campaign."

"Right now, you have to do whatever it takes."

"Really, Jordan? And how do you suggest we make everything right?"

"For starters, I believe you should admit what you've done. It might even help the military if they knew where the leak came from. I have to believe they would go easier on you for cooperating. You know you've committed treason, right?"

Karlson ignored the question. "So who else knows this?"

"Some friends," Jordan offered reluctantly.

"Who, your new musician buddies?" Karlson asked with a sarcastic edge. "Thanks, thanks a lot! You've all dug me into quite a hole here, Jordan."

"Forgive my cheesy comebacks, mother, but I'm not the one holding the fucking shovel."

"Enough," Karlson barked. "I never would have expected the next generation of spies would be drafted from a bar band."

"Nobody spied on you," Jordan replied defensively. "In fact, it was alarming how easy it was to access the files. And the guy that manages your security?"

"What about him?"

"He's the one you should be angry at. If he'd been better at his job then —"

"Then what? Then none of this would have ever come to light? Jordan, exactly how many others have seen this?"

Jordan shook her head. "I'm not going there. This isn't about asking a few people to keep their mouths shut. This is national security. Who knows what other missions or secrets have been compromised by what you've done. We have to inform the military at the very least."

"All right, fine, we'll find a solution with them. I would expect that the military would be willing to work with me, with us. Would you and your friends be agreeable to something like that?"

"I guess that makes sense, yes. Please, tell them before any more damage is done or lives are lost."

Karlson grinned as though she'd scored points in the conversation. "See? There are ways to find a compromise. You just have to be willing to work toward an acceptable solution."

Jordan nodded thoughtfully, hopefully.

Karlson began processing her next six moves. She needed time and reinforcements. First and foremost, she needed to get word to Gene. Get him over here. She could not let Jordan leave before then. At least while she was here, the lid stayed on the pot.

"You and I have a lot to talk about," she said, her voice warm and hopeful. "I need a cappuccino. Would you like one?"

"I really should go," Jordan went to stand. "I have a lot to do."

"No, please, don't come and drop a bomb like that and then leave. You owe it to me to talk this through. Honey, I'm asking you to stay awhile. You can help me figure out the next steps."

Jordan looked into her mother's pleading eyes and knew she had to stay. At least for one cup. "Sure," she said, "sounds good."

Karlson went into the kitchen and fumbled one-handed, pulling the coffee mugs from a cabinet while dialing Gene Lawton on her cell. All color in her face drained away, along with her remaining composure. Her hands shook as she panted. The call connected, and Lawton answered.

"My daughter knows everything!" she hissed in a loud whisper. "She just told me she watched the security video from my office. You know, the one that was supposed to be destroyed and nobody would ever see?" She slammed the kitchen cabinet shut, her anger roiling.

"Everything all right in there?" Jordan called from the next room.

Karlson held the phone away and said, "Just bumped into the door. I'll have this ready in a jiffy." She pulled the phone back tightly against her mouth and growled, "She also told me if I don't come clean about this in public, right now, she'll do it for me. Hello! Are you listening?"

A tense silence hung in the air before Lawton summoned the words to respond, his voice quivering unsteadily. "How the hell. . .is that even possible?"

"She said some friends downloaded the file, and they watched it together." Karlson struggled to keep her own voice to a harsh whisper. "The only record of your perfect plan, the only proof of what really happened, was on that security computer. You swore to me that security asshole of yours had destroyed every trace and scrubbed the hard drives. Goddamnit, Gene!"

Karlson wanted to strangle him through the phone as she envisioned the full implications of this ticking time bomb. Her knees wobbled, and she gripped the countertop for balance.

"That's what he told me," Lawton said defensively. "All traces of those files were destroyed."

"Well, then the fat fucker lied, didn't he?"

"Who the hell are these people, Katherine? How did they access this information, anyway?"

"You mean the ones that played her the video that doesn't exist? I think it's her little musician friends. I'm not sure yet who else is involved. What I do know is this, this idiot who masquerades as a security professional failed at his job. This is all his fault! Meanwhile, Jordan is here, and I don't know how long I can keep her from leaking this."

The phone line went quiet for a moment as Lawton thought hard. "I have a suggestion," he finally said, "but you're not going to like it."

"Try me. We're so far up shit creek now that I'll listen to anything."

"Do you still have some of those industrial-strength sleeping pills?"

"I think I still. . .wait, you're not going to suggest that I drug my own daughter."

"I don't see as we have a lot of choices. If we can reason with her later, then she might understand what we've done and why. Break open three capsules and dump them in a drink. Make sure it's strong enough to cover that taste."

Lawton's solution was so far beyond repulsive that it hit like a punch below the belt, stealing Karlson's breath away. She gasped, dropping the phone to her side. She stared forward in disbelief, sucking in short puffs of air as panic tore at her like tiny daggers. The unconscionable ugliness of his words felt all the more vile as she repeated them to herself. She pressed the phone up hard against her cheek. "Goddamn it, Gene, NO! We're not doing this. There has to be another way."

"Katherine, you need to give me time to find out what's going on here. I need at least a day or two to get the facts and then figure out a plan of action. Either that or you let her go tell the world. I guaran-damn-tee it will be the end of your campaign."

She thumbed the end call button and pocketed the phone. It was all crumbling away. Her lower lip quivered as she shook with rage. Everything she had worked so hard for would soon be gone. And it all came down to having trusted this man at his word. It was all Gene's fault! It was his brilliant hair brained scheme to release the details of that damned military mission in the first place. That one misstep was now going to derail the most perfectly executed presidential campaign in American history. It was over, and there was no way out. She squeezed her eyes shut in disbelief. How could Jordan be so willing to destroy her own mother? The woman who gave her life, nurtured and coddled her, supported every childhood project and aspiration the kid had ever pursued. She did it all and more with a smile and a reassuring word. And this was her payback for being an exemplary mother? "I never failed you," she hissed through gritted teeth. "But you have failed me. It's not fair! It's not fucking fair! It's all too much. Way, way, way too much! I can't do this," she whimpered, shaking her head in disbelief.

"Stop sniveling," a stern reprimand replayed from the folds of her memory. Her eyes shot wide open with shock as she recognized the harsh tone of a long silent voice. Blanche Karlson. A mother who was long on criticism and short on affection. That was the advice she would offer right now. Not, 'You can do this,' or 'you'll find a way,' but a message more harsh and unsympathetic; 'Stop sniveling, you always were a whiner.'

Such were the chastising pep talks Karlson endured from a Hollywood mom more intent on marketing her child than wasting time and energy with unnecessary coddling. Her mother's image appeared as a vaporous apparition, still wearing the same black dress and sweater over a plain white blouse, old and worn, but always immaculately clean. Her jet black hair was just as she'd remembered, pulled back in a severely tight bun without a single strand out of place. She peered through the mist with that same disapproving scowl that would have sent a young Katherine Karlson cowering into a corner. She'd grown to hate the sound of her mother's voice and swore an oath that her own daughter would never go wanting for things she yearned for but never received. And yet, here was her own child, satiated to the point of being spoiled, threatening to take from her everything she accomplished. All because Jordan couldn't live with what her mother had done. Her conscience bothered her, and her friends were upset by what they witnessed on the security video.

'Boo Hoo! Toughen up, child.' That's what her own mother would have said. Strangely, it now seemed like the best advice in the world. The campaign was speeding ahead like a bullet train. Stopping now for any reason was unthinkable.

She thought of the influential, manipulative people that crept in the shadows behind the scenes. They invested millions in her quest for the White House. Every contribution to her campaign, every check offered at a fundraiser, every closed-door meeting with some holier than thou money manager offering support, they all came with strings attached. Strings, hell! Chains, cables, tentacles! These were political manipulators who would never accept a zero return on their massive investments just because a family spat upended her campaign.

Karlson didn't like to admit it, but it was a moment that demanded brutal honesty. These people controlled her, and they would set her presidential agenda more than she would herself. She'd always considered that a moot point since they supported the same issues. But the bottom line was she had ridden into town on a borrowed horse. Karlson needed to consider the backlash from these power brokers if her campaign abruptly ended so close to the election. It wasn't even her decision to make. She owed them. And Jordan owed her…She redialed Gene and said, "Three capsules, right?"

Karlson jammed the phone back into her pocket and loaded the cappuccino machine. While it brewed, she ran upstairs and grabbed the sleeping capsules, then hurried back panting. She drew a deep breath and poked her head out of the kitchen. "Almost done. Just another few minutes. Two sugars, right?"

"Yes, please," Jordan answered.

As the strong brew trickled down, she broke open three capsules and sprinkled their contents into the cup. A bubbly, yellowish foam formed at the top but began dissolving as she stirred. When she finished, it was indistinguishable from the natural froth of the milk. Karlson quickly prepared another cup for herself without bothering to refill the machine with a fresh coffee pod. She didn't plan on drinking much anyway.

Karlson came out of the kitchen carrying a silver serving tray and two steaming mugs of cappuccino. "This one is yours with the sugar," she said, setting the tray down and passing the big mug to Jordan. They both took several sips in silence before Karlson spoke in a cajoling tone. "I know it seems like a terrible thing that's happened, but in the end, it could save lives by helping to end this war sooner."

"Mother, can we start by being honest? You know that turning over those secrets to the enemy had the opposite effect."

"First of all," the senator held up her hand and began her rebuttal, "Al Jazeera is not considered an enemy. I have zero reservations about granting that interview. It was an unfortunate breach of trust if they somehow obtained any information from my office that I wasn't aware of."

"Seriously? That's how you're going to play this? That you didn't know what they were up to?" Jordan shook her head, disappointed. “Please, I saw you watching everything from the security room in your office. You set them up. Each of you thought you were pulling a fast one on the other. Spy versus spy. Honestly, mother, you’re going to have to do much better than that if you hope to fix what you’ve broken.”

Karlson was in no mood to discuss the point any further, though she was rather impressed by her daughter’s observations. She took a sip from her drink, hoping the action might persuade Jordan to do the same. It worked. She tried to remember how quickly she felt the effects of this medication in the past, taking solace in the fact that she had no recollection. That was evidence enough the pills worked very well, very fast. Still, Jordan showed no signs so far. Keep her talking, she thought. She took another long sip from her own mug and said, “I don’t understand how you saw a video that was removed from our security system.”

Jordan gave her a matter-of-fact glance. “Your security man didn’t erase the drives very well. They were pretty easy to restore.”

Karlson felt herself tensing. This was confirmation of the incompetence of her own security professional. “I’m impressed,” she said, struggling to appear calm. “But how did you gain access into that system? It’s supposed to be firewalled and all those other technical terms. Tell me, did your friend work for the security company?”

Jordan locked eyes and paused, her lips pursed. “You know, mother, I think we’ve discussed this enough. If you tell me you’re going to make an announcement and try to fix this, then I’ll wait until you do. You have no idea how sickened, how disappointed I am by what you’ve done. But I don’t want to hurt you. Please, don’t force me to go public. Do the right thing, mom, and do it now!”

Jordan pushed her chair out and stood to leave but fell

back. She put her hands to her head as though attempting to keep it from spinning. Her eyes flickered, struggling to focus. She looked up at her mother with an expression of bewilderment.

"Are you all right, dear?" Karlson asked in a concerned tone.

"All of a sudden I'm…I can't…mother, what did you…"

"I'm so sorry about this, baby. You didn't leave me much choice, did you? You'll be fine, I promise. You're just going to sleep awhile."

There was a knock at the front door. Karlson left the room to answer it, returning with Gene Lawton. "I put three in the coffee, and she drank more than half," she explained. "That should be enough for her to see stars for about eight hours."

Jordan slumped in her chair. It was all she could do to lift her head. She couldn't work out any words. Her eyes wandered, refusing to focus. Thoughts came out fragmented and nonsensical. She struggled to understand what was happening, wishing for once she would have had a secret service agent following her. Then again, who would have guessed the greatest threat to her personal security would come from her own mother?

30

Cody knocked twice on Ethan's apartment door, then let himself in. He found his friend sitting cross-legged on an old brown hand-me-down couch, staring out the window at the adjacent building. There was little to see through the streaky glass except for the chipped and fading bricks of another wall mere yards away. A thin sliver of sunshine found its way between the structures and sliced across Ethan's face. He seemed oblivious to it or anything else.

"She was supposed to call three hours ago," he said without turning his head or altering his pained expression.

"Hey, maybe her mother threw a couple of new assignments her way, and she couldn't say no."

Ethan eyed Cody, then stared down at a worn rug. "You honestly think Kat Karlson is going to ask for help from a daughter that just threatened to shut down her entire campaign?"

"No, not really. I'm just trying harder than you to stay positive. But dude, I can't imagine anything nasty going down. This is her mother we're talking about. Sure, she's gonna be pissed, but do you think she would hurt her own kid over this?"

"I hope not, but the stakes couldn't be higher. Who knows what someone is capable of in a situation like this. That's a lot of power to surrender without a fight."

Cody's cell phone began blaring out the old Deep Purple rocker, 'Space Truckin'. Glancing at the display, he announced, "It's Murray." As soon as he brought it to his ear, his face turned ashen. He didn't blink for the entire length of the one-sided conversation. A loud bang cut through the phone that made him flinch, and Murray abruptly disconnected.

"Now we worry," Cody said as he began pacing. "Murray is getting raided by feds. He saw them grouping in the parking lot and began dumping files. He managed to copy the video to a thumb drive and hide it. He wouldn't say where in case our phones were tapped but told me we would figure it out. They were beating on the door when he cut off. Dude, if they tracked him down so easily, we might be next. We should go into hiding for a while."

"What the hell have we done wrong?" Ethan asked incredulously. "That makes no sense at all."

"Hold that thought and go pack a bag. If Murray's right, then Jordan is in deep shit, and we won't be any good to her if we're detained by a bunch of black suits."

Ethan stared motionless, still not registering the urgency.

"Dude," Cody yelled, "move your ass!"

Ethan snapped out of his 'deer in the headlights' moment, got up, and ran to his bedroom closet. He pulled out a duffel and began stuffing it with clothes. They would not have time to run back to Cody's house, so he packed enough for both of them. Ethan was three inches taller and twenty pounds lighter than Cody, but that didn't matter much right now. He ran into the bathroom, grabbed a pre-loaded toiletry bag, then to the kitchen nook, where he unplugged and stowed his laptop. "I'm ready," he said, breathing heavy. "Any idea where to go?"

"I was thinking about Theresa and Joe's place. It's secluded enough that my car won't be seen."

"We're going to leave mine?"

"Think about it," Cody said. "They find my car at your apartment, and yours is missing. Even a government brain could figure out that means we're traveling together. Let's be a little less obvious and take my car."

Ethan nodded. "Thanks for being the one that's able to think this through. I'm still in a daze."

"I know. Most drummers are mentally challenged anyway." He gave Ethan a sly wink and a push as they headed for the stairwell.

31

Joe Fillmore liked his coffee strong, and that's how he made it for everyone. Although accustomed to the full-bodied brews from their favorite coffee shop, Ethan and Cody were jolted to a new level of consciousness from just half a cup. 'Costa Rican Rocket Fuel,' as Joe liked to call it, was pungent, powerful, and damned good.

Joe knew the guys through their band. He and his wife, Theresa, always filled them with a big meal when they played in the area. Their house was simple, secluded, and he lived off the radar, running a cash business as an electronic repairman, taking in anything from vintage guitar amplifiers to microwave ovens. The work didn't make him wealthy, but he was comfortable and doing what he enjoyed.

Theresa brought over a tray of cheese and crackers and joined the three men at the dining table.

"Any information yet?" she asked, watching as Joe, Ethan, and Cody tapped away at their laptops.

Ethan looked up as he reached for a cube of cheddar. "I've called everyone I know. Nobody has seen or heard anything."

Cody finished a call and set his phone down. "That was Jordan's friend, Amy, and she was scared to death. She told me two men forced their way into her apartment and went through her stuff. They wouldn't identify themselves and then drove off in an unmarked car."

"How long ago did you speak with her?" asked Joe.

"Just now, why?"

"Turn off your phones, now," Joe demanded. "They could be monitoring Amy's calls, and then they can triangulate your position through the cell towers. For that matter, log off your laptops, too. I can set you up with new secure names and passwords."

Ethan and Cody killed their computers and were powering their phones off when 'Space Truckin' cut through the silence.

"It's Murray," Cody announced, surprised.

"Who's Murray?" asked Joe.

"He's my cousin. He's the one that tapped us into the security system at Senator Karlson's office and downloaded the videotape of her giving away military secrets."

"Stop! Just stop for a second. Guys, this situation is getting uglier by the minute. I don't mind telling you I'm plenty scared already."

"Look, Joe, I'm sorry I dumped all this on you," Cody offered. "I didn't have anyone else to turn to that I could trust. We can leave. This isn't fair to pull you and Therese into this mess."

"Cody, listen to me, and do exactly what I'm telling you, okay? First of all, do not answer that right now. I need both of you to turn your phones off and give them to me."

They gave him a questioning look but complied. Joe then took the phones and put them in the microwave oven. "Microwaves have a faraday cage which blocks any electromagnetic signal from getting out," he said. He stopped a moment and snapped his fingers. "Wait here a second."

He ran into the garage and returned with what looked like a thick, heavy blue blanket. He pulled his car keys off a kitchen hook and set them, along with the phones and the blanket, on the table. "I have a better idea. This is a lead apron. Techs wear them when taking X-rays. Cody, wrap both of your phones inside. I want you to drive my car up to Gateway and then turn your phone on long enough to call Murray. Try to find out if they're holding him and forcing him to call you. If it sounds safe, then tell him to meet us here at about eleven tonight. Tell him to leave his phone at home. Then make another call to Ethan's phone. Don't turn his on, but leave a message. Drive another ten miles or so and then turn his on and check his voicemail."

"Wow, okay, but why Gateway?" Cody asked, trying to figure the logic behind such strange directions.

"We're going to assume that sooner or later, someone will come looking for you. The easiest way for them to find you is by monitoring your phone usage. Phones transmit your location, even when powered down. We're just going to lead them away and make them think you're leaving town. Making the call between the two phones establishes that you're both traveling out of the area, but you're not together. Got it? Call at Gateway, turn them off, drive ten miles, turn on Ethan's phone, and check voicemail. Head northwest another half hour and do it again. Keep the phones wrapped in the apron in between, then come back here when you're done."

He looked to Ethan and said, "There's a Value gas station on the main drag up near the outskirts of DC that sells prepaid burner cell phones. I want you to buy six. . .no, seven of the cheapest burners and put twenty bucks on each. Pick the phones out of order from off the rack, making sure the serial numbers are not sequential. Pay cash. They don't like to process paperwork there, so this transaction should be difficult to track. We'll give you the cash now, and you can write us a check later. Neither of you can use a credit card or an ATM machine. We'll figure out the rest after you get rolling."

Ethan stood looking at his friends, still unsure if he should be burdening them with such a terrible situation. Before he could ponder the point further, Joe said, "I know you would do the same for me. So get the hell out of here and get those phones, would ya?"

Ethan cracked an appreciative smile and headed for the door.

THE GUYS LEFT to complete their assignments, and the house returned to silence. Joe used the time to search for additional information on the internet while Theresa turned on the television for a little background noise. She was washing the cups when she heard Katherine Karlson's name being mentioned by a news reporter. Her hands went limp in the dishwater, turning her attention to the report. She noticed Joe heard it too and now stared at the TV, frozen in mid-step.

"An unidentified source said that Karlson's daughter, Jordan West, worked tirelessly on her mother's presidential campaign and pushed herself past the point of exhaustion."

The reporter stood outside the capitol building beneath a large, dark umbrella that shielded her from a steady stream of rain. She was surrounded by a swarming sea of other news teams doing the same. The sound of large droplets beating against the tightly stretched fabric played like an abstract rhythm in the background of every news report being taped.

All of them echoed the same statements with slight alterations.

"Another source, this one with close ties to campaign director Gene Lawton, sounded a more distressing alarm, saying Jordan West had indeed suffered a complete emotional breakdown. Details of West's hospitalization were not immediately forthcoming from Karlson or anyone who spoke for the senator. Credible sources who wish not to be named said West was taken to a reclusive private hospital outside Bethesda. That facility, we're told, functions mainly as a retreat for alcoholism and drug rehabilitation for the elite."

"Joey, doesn't that sound like the Haven Hospital? Mark still does temp work there as a Physician Assistant. Remember some of the stories he told us about the wealthy drunks and prescription addicts that go there to dry out."

"That's right, and Senator Toddick's wife was there the last time. God, she sounded like a piece of work! Do you remember how he said she had to be drugged constantly just to keep her from screaming and running around naked? What a perfect place to keep this poor kid locked up and quiet."

Theresa grimaced at the thought of Jordan being sedated and tethered down to ensure her silence for the sake of Senator Karlson's campaign. "I'll call Mark and see what he knows about this," she said, then keyed in her brother's number.

Joe wasted no time in finding related issues on the internet. The web was already awash in long-winded blogs and fabricated yarns. One source purported that this was a conspiracy and kidnapping by North Korea, while another insisted Jordan's disappearance was an alien abduction. There was so much bullshit being flung about that Joe half expected to see flies coming out of his computer's USB port. The internet had given a voice to so many with nothing intelligent to say.

Among the lines of garbage he sifted through on the net was a small snippet that set off his internal alarms. A government watchdog group posted a breach in security. Two persons of interest were being sought for questioning in connection with stolen government documents.

"This can't be good," he said aloud, knowing Ethan and Cody were the most likely subjects of the search. He hoped the assignments he'd sent them on would buy some time. Soon enough, he thought, his friend's likenesses would be part of these news reports. He also comprehended for the first time that he and his wife were now accessories to a crime by offering them shelter. Like it or not, he was already very much involved.

So what was the correct response? Trick question, he thought. Helping his friends was clearly the right thing to do. The real issue was more legal than moral. Do you take the safe route and kick these guys out? Turn your back to avoid the backlash that had the potential of destroying everything he and Theresa worked so hard to build? Or do you commit to do right by your friends and go further down the rabbit hole? There would be no straddling the fence. No chance to deny your involvement regardless of how innocent it seemed. That was the catch, wasn't it? If he stepped back now and let the situation play out, his friends would have no chance. They would be identified and apprehended, facing serious jail time on trumped-up charges from high treason to domestic terrorism. They might even be blamed for the leak of classified government documents.

Karlson's involvement would be played down, denied. Joe could envision the gag orders imposed by pre-selected judges to keep the truth from ever seeing the light of day. The fate of Jordan West would then lie entirely in the hands of her mother, who would be free to do anything she pleased to cover her tracks. The woman had already shown the terrible extremes she would go to if it ensured her political victory.

Joe feared all the more for Jordan's safety, imagining the experimental procedures they would perform to erase this event from the young woman's mind. To manipulate her into complete and everlasting submission. Joe envisioned a Jordan from the future, a neuro numbed mental vegetable. He shuddered at the thought and struggled to dislodge it from his head. It wasn't moving.

A few short hours ago, he was oblivious to this entire fiasco. Now it consumed him and represented the most significant decision of his life. He reminded himself that he could end it all right now with a simple phone call. 1-800-RAT-FINK.

Everyone could go find their own way out of this mess that he and his wife had nothing to do with. Entertaining that thought, however, even for a fraction of a second, felt vile and repulsive. No, doing nothing would never be a path he could walk and still face himself every morning. Then what? Call the press with an anonymous tip explaining what actually transpired between Karlson and the Al Jazeera news crew? Really? He almost laughed out loud at the absurdity. The press loved this woman. They would go out of their way to suppress and dismiss the story. No, revealing the truth was not an option. Then what? How could there ever be a happy ending to this nightmare? He scoured his mind, searching for another scenario, an alternative direction that would absolve his friends, aid Jordan West, and keep his comfortable lifestyle intact. His usually creative gray matter was not yielding any nuggets of wisdom. He stared down at the large kitchen table, refusing to believe there was not a better outcome.

Theresa grew tired of the same headlines being repeated by the overpainted talking heads. She tuned the tv to a seventies classic rock music channel. A golden oldie faded away as a memorable guitar riff cut through the air. He watched his wife swaying to the rhythm as she unloaded the dishwasher. Every motion was as smooth and flowing as the music that propelled her. He enjoyed the pleasant distraction, thinking that stacking dishes had never looked so sexy. The effect was hypnotic, clearing his mind as she performed the everyday household function against a new soundtrack.

The last song faded into silence, and a temporary stillness fell over the house. Quiet. Quiet.

A powerful guitar chord exploded out of the speakers. Joe jerked in his chair, electrified, every hair standing on end. He turned to face the television as a snare drum sounded out a tight flam, and the driving rhythm of a timeless rocker filled the room. Theresa grabbed the remote and cranked up the volume, head nodding along to the beat. He stared at first, mouth agape. A look of wonder giving way to a bright smile as he comprehended the gift he had been given.

That was it! The only way out of this mess. It seemed impossible, yet so flawless in its simplicity. He paused to question his own sanity for even generating such a fantastical idea. Really? Yes, really! Such outlandish thoughts seemed so foreign to him. And yet…

Joe eked out a quiet, unassuming existence with his high school sweetheart, Theresa. Together, they built a comfortable life with their individual unique skills. She freelanced as a makeup artist for local plays, weddings, even a few television commercials. He learned electronics early on and built upon those skills. He played it safe, kept his head down, aspiring only to goals that served a very immediate purpose. That was his extent of taking chances in life. He didn't gamble, didn't dabble in the stock market, even drove the speed limit. But this new thought entered his brain like the start of a grand life-changing phenomenon that he was pre-programmed to follow.

He questioned the end value of most tasks before beginning them, but not this. This concept, this quest, had emerged from the gray folds of his brain with all the necessary authorizations and approvals. Joe felt so compelled and moved by it that he knew with absolute certainty this was what he needed to do; and that it would work. He just needed to prepare and believe.

There was much to be done, like explaining this to Theresa and making sure she understood and agreed. Not yet, though, he cautioned himself. There were many details to work out before expecting her to take him seriously. This was a life-altering moment and decision, and he knew what side she would come out on if she understood how perfectly the thought was conceived.

There were so many moving parts of this incredible vision. It swirled and dangled in his mind's eye like a seemingly unmanageable tangle of loose ends. All good, he reminded himself. A head bursting with ideas was infinitely preferable to an infertile and empty cranium. Joe pulled the laptop closer, opened a blank document, and began typing the thoughts as they came, noting each step, the necessary actions, and the supplies and support needed.

It was the only solution that made sense. After all, the best way to prove his friends' innocence would be to seek the truth directly from the source, from Jordan West herself.

His head bobbed to the powerful pulse of the song, still filling his senses with everything he needed. Perfect timing, he thought, smiling as he read the artist's name and song title displayed on the flat screen; Thin Lizzie, Jailbreak.

32

"Katherine, what in God's name has happened to Jordan?"

Every news outlet was leading with the story of the Jordan West breakdown. Karlson had yet to inform her husband personally. The situation was nowhere near stabilized, and she feared his expected barrage of questions. Clifford West was, after all, a skilled attorney.

The storyline she and Lawton concocted still lacked vital elements and faced the risk of crumbling under cross-examination. Remaining purposefully vague was her best and only defense. She silently cursed his timing and slipped into character.

"Oh, Cliff, it's terrible," she mourned. "I'm so sorry for not calling sooner, but I've been overloaded since her breakdown."

"What are you talking about? She was fine when we talked last."

"I know," Karlson agreed, "I didn't see this coming either. She must have been holding it all in until it completely overwhelmed her."

West exhaled an exasperated sigh. "Tell me what happened."

"We were having breakfast and watching some clips on the news. At first, Jordan made comments about the story being reported. But then, she became more and more agitated." Karlson's voice rose and cracked, increasing with each painful detail. "The next thing I know, she's going on about conspiracies, drugging the water supply, government takeovers, and God knows what else. She kept working herself up until she was babbling, crying, yelling at me, at the television, at the world." Karlson paused, timing the release of tears. "Clifford," she sobbed, "it was like. . .like she didn't see or hear me. Something unwound inside of her. I watched the look in her eyes. I watched her fading away from me." Karlson paused, holding the phone away, allowing the full intensity of her rehearsed sorrow to engulf her. "I'm so sorry, I didn't realize I was working her that hard. She had so much responsibility with the campaign and school."

"That poor kid," West muttered. "Where is she now?"

"I wanted her in a facility where she could rest with no distractions, and especially no reporters. I found a private hospital. They're keeping her there for observation for a few days."

"All right, I can clear my schedule and be there in the morning. Give me the details of this place."

"Not yet," Karlson countered, "the doctors recommend we give her time to stabilize and then start with therapy. You should stay right where you are until they tell us otherwise."

She hoped that would be enough, for now, to keep her husband away from Jordan. There was much work to be done to change her daughter's mind. Karlson still struggled with repairing the damage. How do you convince an intelligent and articulate young woman that everything she had seen, everything she was trying to do, was wrong? She needed at least a few more days with Clifford West far removed from the situation.

"Katherine, my daughter is in a hospital," he protested. "I should be there with her."

"She's our daughter, dear, and I trust the doctors to know more about these things than I do. You should do the same. I'll keep you posted, I promise. But we have to give her what she needs. Right now, that's peace and quiet."

Karlson could almost hear his mind working, mulling her words over. She knew what she was up against and how difficult it would be to keep him away. West was a loving and attentive father. Not being at his daughter's side in her time of need would be nearly unbearable. He would never forgive himself if Jordan got worse and slipped further away. Every fatherly instinct must be screaming at him to come and offer support. She silently cursed at being forced to play the villain's role with the task of pounding a wedge between them. Although there were no other options, this was still the part of Lawton's royal shit storm that she regretted the most. His ineptness now forced her to stoop to subterranean levels, manipulating her own family to save the campaign.

"Are you talking with her? Is she being treated well?"

"I tried to speak with her right after she was admitted, but she was still very agitated. They've given her something to calm her down."

"So she's drugged up? Christ, Kathy! I'm coming out there. She needs to—"

"Clifford, no! She needs rest and quiet. Please respect the doctor's orders! And for God's sake, have some faith in me. Do you know how terrible I feel about this? I will make sure she gets everything she needs. Right now, that's going to come from the hospital staff and not either of us."

She listened to his labored breaths, knowing the internal struggle he fought to suppress all paternal compassion and reason. She hated putting him in such a position, but her plan had no nope of success any other way. She silently willed him to accept her explanation, promising herself to make it up to both of them as soon as possible.

"I'll wait a day or two," he finally relented, "but please, stay on top of this and keep me posted."

"You know, I will. I love you, Cliff."

"I love you too. Call me soon."

Karlson breathed a sigh of relief as she ended the call. There was much more damage control to be done if she was to stay ahead of this. She needed to prepare a formal press statement about Jordan's condition. Then she would track down the bastards that gave her the information that caused all of this trouble. Her sources pointed to Jordan's new group of friends. Damned musicians! Since when were they capable of putting more than five cohesive words together to form an intelligent sentence, let alone hack into a government installation and steal confidential files? Speaking of which, Gene still had a lot of explaining to do. How could these geeks have gotten their hands on information that should have been destroyed? She had trusted him implicitly, and for that, she now found herself in the fight of her life.

She and Lawton faced a monumental task before they regained control. Thankfully, that was his forte. No one was better. She thought a moment that sleeping together may have allowed him to take to his eyes off the prize. Was he taking too much for granted, thinking that command in the bedroom equated to more power? Karlson shook her head. Not now, not ever! Their sexual pleasures should not have compromised the professional relationship. He should have understood the rules before going down that road. Did he assume everything changed once he had a few of her orgasms under his belt? She would make it a point to discuss boundaries and expectations. Right now, though, she needed him to do what he did best. Well, maybe what he did second-best, she thought, smiling. After all, the son of a bitch was good in bed.

Gene's immediate task was to fix what he had broken, then carry the campaign over the finish line. They were so close that she could taste her first breakfast served in the White House master bedroom. It was time to get him working on a solution. Then, after this storm passes, it might be time to consider a new campaign manager. Gene Lawton may have already outlived his usefulness.

33

Ethan arrived back at Joe and Theresa's home after ten, wired from driving, and that last cup of Joe's nuclear coffee. He laid the bag of phones he'd purchased on the kitchen table and dropped into a chair, letting out a sigh that could be felt as well as heard. He stared at the brown plastic bag, still disbelieving his life was taking such a radical detour. One that he had no control over.

The past few days' events unfolded before him, like tuning into a movie halfway through and attempting to figure out the plot line and all of the characters. Nothing felt right. No internal voice of reason whispering it would all turn out well. His ears rang with the frequency of a swarm of Cicadas, stifling any logical thought. He tried to jump-start his brain, but it remained stuck in neutral. Like he was waiting for some grand plan to come and lift him, make him feel useful. He likened it to writing a song, which he preferred to do with a partner. When his own creative well ran dry, it only took a few chords or lyrics from another musician to make his mind explode with new ideas. That's all it would take, he told himself. A little input. Just a couple of chords.

Joe looked up from hours of staring at his computer. The lines of information still burned a phosphoric green in his retinas. He blinked a few times to clear the image away and looked over the top of his glasses at Ethan, who seemed miles away in thought.

"Let's open these up and get them charging," he told his friend. "We'll need at least four for tomorrow."

"What happens tomorrow?"

"We try to find Jordan."

Ethan sat bolt upright. "Wait, say that again."

Joe smiled. "I thought that would get your attention. We think she's being held at a rehab hospital in Bethesda. It's more of an asylum, really. My brother-in-law is a temp worker there and already made arrangements to cover a friend's shift tomorrow morning. He's going to ask around and try to find out if she's being held there."

"And what if we find her, what then?"

"Maybe we can get word to her that we're trying to help. That she's not alone."

Ethan nodded, his mind drifting to Jordan in the last moments they were together. He imagined them in another time, another place. Holding hands across a small table at a sidewalk café. She smiled back with an expression as warm as the morning sunrise. She squeezed his fingers tightly as a gentle breeze brushed a lock of dark hair across her forehead. Her green eyes sparkled with serene happiness. Ethan blinked, and the image transformed to a dimly lit cell with dirty white padded walls. Jordan stood before him, her face pale and drawn, eyes dark and sunken. Her blissful expression was replaced with one so empty that it chilled him to the core. Her fingers clamped around his hands as if clinging to a lifeline. He stared helplessly at her tear-streaked face and watched as she mouthed the words, help me!

He jerked back from the ghastly vision, shuddering. Those desperate, pleading eyes haunted him, begging him to come and find her. He thought of Jordan's mother, the cause of all this anguish. His sadness gave way to a simmering anger that stoked ever hotter. He hadn't expected the senator to take Jordan's ultimatum well, but her reaction was right off the charts. Light years beyond anything he could have imagined.

"Karlson locks up her own daughter to keep the campaign alive," he said, shaking his head. "Jordan trusted her. She told me that she owed her mother the benefit of the doubt. This is how she's rewarded." He closed his eyes, teeth clenched, still disbelieving anyone could do this to their own flesh and blood, regardless of the motive. "President Karlson," he said with disgust. "What a terrifying thought! She's no more worthy of that job than the lowest bottom feeders in this sick town."

Joe nodded in agreement as he tore open a cell phone pack. The noise of the crumpling packaging brought Ethan from his dark visions, and he followed suit.

"Jot down the numbers of each phone on this paper," Joe directed him. "We'll assign the names of who will carry each. Then write down the last two digits on the back of each phone with a sharpie so we can keep track of them. Once we have all seven identified, I'll take a ride to Mark's house and give him one."

"I don't know, Joe. It doesn't seem right dragging others into this mess."

"I didn't drag anyone. He volunteered. We had a long conversation while you were gone. He's not doing anything dangerous or illegal by confirming Jordan's whereabouts. He also happens to believe it's the right thing to do."

Ethan, at a loss for words, nodded gratefully.

Joe pulled the remaining phones from the packaging and plugged them into their chargers as Ethan labeled and documented each.

"You and Cody will each take two, and I'll take one for myself. We'll keep another for Cody's cousin, Murray, when he gets here tonight. All of you guys have to fly under the radar. Once we get a better handle on all of this, we can formulate a game plan."

Ethan shook his head. "Cody and I should be thinking about another place to stay until this blows over. I can't ask you guys to get any more involved in this."

"No, dude," Joe answered, "you're staying here. This is the safest place for you right now. It's also a lot easier to coordinate our next steps if we're all together."

"Joe, this isn't your fight."

"Says you. I happen to believe it is, and not just because of you and Cody. This woman is dangerous, and she's on her way to the White House. Look, we all see what she's done. And if she can do this to her own kid, then she is capable of far worse."

"You don't have to do this. Cody and I will find a way."

"See, I don't think you will. This is far bigger than the two of you, and you'll probably end up getting caught sooner than later. But with a few more people working with us, we might find a way to help Jordan. Hell, we might even figure a way to stop her mother."

Ethan set the last phone down. "You must have something in mind."

"Way too early to say, but we have to try. Karlson made it my fight, and that bitch will not see us coming."

"I wouldn't know the first thing about trying to bring her down," Ethan admitted. "Look at us. We're just regular people. We wouldn't stand a chance against her."

Joe smiled. "Trust me, Ethan. I wouldn't show up at a gunfight with a jackknife. You get me?"

"No, not really."

"Let's just say that when the time comes, we will all know what we need to do."

"I can't believe it could be that simple."

"I didn't say it would be simple. I say it doesn't matter. Because when a fight like this comes at you, there are few right choices. Doing nothing is not one of them. This isn't the time to wallow in fear, buddy. You have to have some faith in what can be done if we use our heads. For all intents and purposes, Karlson is waging a secret little war against everyone connected to this. She probably believes she can win just by intimidating the hell out of us. Well, we are not undefended." Joe tapped his finger to his temple. "These are *our* weapons. And I most definitely believe we are capable of out-thinking her. There are chinks in every suit of armor. We just have to be the smartest soldiers on the battlefield and exploit their weaknesses. That, my friend, I believe we can do."

Ethan stared back. It made sense. There were still more questions than answers, but Joe was right. There had to be a way. This battle was brought to them, and the only option was to return fire. Karlson would never expect it. A grin spread across his face as he began picking up on Joe's enthusiasm. "Thank you," he finally said.

"For what?"

Ethan got up and wrapped his friend in a bear hug, slapping his back. "For being the right guy in the right place at the right time."

"My friend, you're welcome."

34

Bethesda, Maryland

Mark Vistan heard the news he'd been waiting for early the next morning in the hospital cafeteria. While making small talk with two nurses, one of them began offering details of a mystery patient on the third floor. The RN's, friends for years, had softened their distant, professional demeanor and now practically clawed over each other for Mark's attention. His gray-green eyes and hard chiseled features made them behave like giddy teenagers. Mark was a seasoned flirt and used the effect he had on women like a power tool.

"So, Ernie, the night supervisor, he says an uncooperative government witness is being held in 3808," said Marcy, a striking brunette with high cheekbones and drawn-in eyebrows. She emphasized the word 'uncooperative' with finger quote marks, her Long Island accent further punctuating her point. Marcy had clumsily pocketed her wedding ring moments earlier.

Suzanne, a pretty, petite blonde, asked, "Can they do that?"

"That's what I wanted to know," Marcy answered. "Ernie says they do it all the time here."

"But why keep a witness here?" Mark asked. "Why not get them in some protection program?"

Suzanne nodded attentively, watching him from the corner of her eye.

"Ernie says that she's a material witness in some high-profile drug case." She again used air quote marks to emphasize 'high profile.' "He says they have to keep her sedated because she's an addict going through cold turkey. The only way they can use her on a witness stand is to clean her up first."

Suzanne shook her head. "Does that sound right to you?" she asked.

"Not really, so I talked to Rita. You know Rita in the kitchen? She spoke with one of the girls who run the meals up there." Marcy leaned in closer and lowered her voice. "She says," she paused to look around the room. "She thought it might be that senator's daughter on the news."

"Karlson? Katherine Karlson's kid?" Suzanne blurted out a little too loud for Marcy.

"SHHH! We're not supposed to know this stuff, let alone talk about it. Keep it down!"

Mark was amused that Marcy's already high-pitched voice rose a few notes higher.

Marcy scanned the room to see if anyone had noticed. It didn't appear so.

"Yes, Katherine Karlson's kid," she continued. "But nobody else is talking, so we'll just have to wait and see."

"That kind of stuff gives me the creeps," Suzanne added.

"I think Brittany does the meds dispensing on that floor. You should ask her."

"Pregnant Brittany that just went on medical leave?" Marcy asked.

"That's her," Suzanne nodded.

"Poor girl was huge!" Marcy imitated an inflating abdomen with her hands. "She looked like she swallowed a school bus."

"I thought she would have left a month sooner. She was so big. That's a lot of extra weight to carry around. I say twins or triplets."

"More like a basketball team. There's a girl that's going to have some premature varicose veins."

Mark tuned out of their small talk, concentrating on directing the conversation back to the patient in 3808 without sounding too inquisitive. He needed answers but could not afford to draw suspicion. He needed to move cautiously, ask the right questions. A simple solution popped into his mind, and he asked, "Excuse me, but do you know where the central pharmacy is located?"

Both nurses turned to Mark, realizing they had neglected him in their conversation.

"It's on the first floor of the Grace wing," Marcy answered. "Why?"

"I'm considering a Master's degree in Pharmacology. I need to have logged hours in the field before I can even apply. Do you know anyone in the department?"

Suzanne smiled. "Marcy does, right?"

"Oh yeah, Anthony is the pharmacist," Marcy said. "Would that help?"

Anthony would be precisely who Mark wanted to connect with. If he could get on the rotation doing patient meds dispensing, he could see if Jordan was here. Still, he could not afford to appear too anxious. Mark had to use the information without revealing his intentions.

"Yes, that would definitely help." He gave his sexiest bedroom grin. "Think you can hook me up?"

It worked. Marcy blushed with excitement, grinning as she found the courage to make a move on him.

"It's going to cost you!"

Mark sensed where this was going, but it was all right. He'd hoped his charm and good looks would unlock some doors, and now they had—time to play.

"Well, in that case, you need to tell me the price up front so I can make sure I can afford it."

"I think you can swing this one," she said slyly. "Drinks tonight at Baldwin's."

"Perfect," he answered. "Excellent restaurant and excellent company. Count me in."

"And Suzanne, you come along too," Marcy said, flashing a sly smile to her friend. "I think we'll have more fun as a threesome."

35

Mark Vistan exited the elevator and made his way to the first-floor pharmacy with the transfer documents he had picked up in the personnel office. Floaters and temporary workers were such a common sight that Anthony, the pharmacist, did not look twice at the new face presenting the forms. He glanced at Mark's identification card through coke bottle spectacles and pointed to a doorway next to the window. He buzzed the lock. Mark grabbed the handle and opened the thick, windowless steel door. Inside, he found a stainless steel cart pre-loaded with the medications he would be administering.

"Everything is documented on the check-off sheet on this clipboard," Anthony explained. He passed it over the barrier that separated them. "Take a moment to mark whether the patient received full meds or caused any problems, but do it after you've left the room and locked the door."

Mark scanned the form, then slipped the clipboard into a pocket on the side of the cart.

"We deliver the meds in two stages," Anthony said. "Start with cart one at room 1830 and work your way back to 1815.

I'll have the next cart loaded and ready when you return. You'll work up the next two floors the same way. When you've finished with all the carts, we'll review your check sheet and re-visit any patients that didn't get their full doses." He handed Mark a large key on a two-foot brass chain. "This opens all of the patient room doors. Attach it to your belt loop, and do not let it out of your possession for even a second. People get fired for less around here. You're filling in today because the guy before you made a simple mistake."

Mark nodded and backed the cart out the door.

THE FIRST RUN went smooth enough and was good practice to observe how things were done. Mark also took note of the overall security. He counted three orderlies performing various tasks on the third floor. All seemed easygoing and did not take much notice of him. That changed as he rounded the next corner. A lone security guard came lumbering toward him directly in his path. Mark tensed at the sight of this unforeseen obstacle and forced himself to keep walking at a measured pace to mask his nervousness. As the guard drew closer, Mark observed this wasn't some highly trained elite member of a ninja death squad. Just an average, out-of-shape rent a cop. Probably bored out of his wits and walking the halls to stay awake. There was a chair further down the hallway. Mark reasoned it was likely the guard's regular post. This was a new wrinkle that needed to be passed on to Joe.

The guard altered course and walked past without so much as a glance. A more disciplined security officer would not have let this interaction go by without making observations about a face he'd never seen before. Luck was on

Mark's side. He reasoned the hospital selected this security company more for their price than overall effectiveness.

He continued dispensing medications without incident until, at last, he found himself outside the room he had come for. The white metal door, with its small wired window, gave a sensation of foreboding not felt at any of the other identical rooms. He pushed the cart up against the wall and loaded a tray with a cup of water and the small plastic container of prescription pills marked '3808 Jane Doe'. He did a quick mental inventory of the meds so he could identify them later. Mark pulled the door open and stopped cold.

She sat on the bed with her head down, arms wrapped tightly around her folded legs, her thin frame clad in a wrinkled standard-issue green and white hospital smock. Her hair was a dark, tangled mess with thick strands draping her face and shoulders, completely concealing her eyes. Mark didn't know what he'd expected to find, but it wasn't this. He stumbled back a step.

Her anguish was palpable. Mark could sense the helplessness that consumed her, depleting what little energy there was left. He worked to get his breathing under control, then attempted to make out her hidden facial features. He was still not sure this was who he had come to find. She could be anyone. He set the tray on a countertop and took a moment to inspect the room, noticing the security camera located in the upper corner above the door, just as Joe expected. He would have to avoid doing anything that might arouse suspicion of whoever was monitoring that video signal. He picked up the water and med cup and called softly.

"Jordan?"

There was no response.

"Jordan, My name is Mark, and I'm a friend of Ethan's."

Her hands twitched as though she had received a slight

electrical shock. Slowly, she lifted her head toward him. Mark caught his first glimpse of her sad face through a curtain of unkempt hair and was hit with a wave of despair. Her tear-stained eyes appeared sunken, lost, and hopeless. It was the tortured face of innocence, betrayed by those she loved and trusted. It was Jordan West. Mark was sure of it immediately. He could feel her agony and struggled to retain his composure. His instinctive urge to reach out and shelter her in his arms was nearly overwhelming. He forced himself to remember that his every move was being observed. The wrong actions now could jeopardize what he'd been sent to do.

"Jordan, can you understand me?" he asked in a hushed voice. "Nod if you do, but remember, there is a camera watching us."

She was heavily medicated, that was clear, but Mark detected a faint spark in the depths of her dark eyes. She nodded once, without breaking her gaze. A shiver ran down his spine. She's doped up to high heaven, he thought, but she's still here.

"Listen closely," he said in a near whisper. "I am going to give you three pills. I want you to take them in your mouth and pretend to swallow. Then I want you to turn away from the camera and spit them out. I want you to do this from now on, okay?"

Jordan gave another weak nod.

"We are going to get help for you, but you need to keep acting drugged until I come back. Can you do that?"

This time she didn't nod. Her eyes blinked back tears as she managed a faint, weary smile.

"Here, take these," he said, holding the plastic cup of pills up to her mouth. She let him pour them in, then took a sip of water, seemingly washing them down. She turned away and lay down on the bed, shielding her face with her hand. He barely perceived her spitting out the pills and knew her actions had been concealed from the camera.

"Jordan, I'm going to let Ethan know you're all right. I promise you we are going to find a way to get you out of here as soon as possible."

She didn't stir, but Mark knew he was successful in delivering the message. She would be fully lucid within a few days. After that, this place would become even more hellish to cope with. They needed to act quickly, or the Haven would really make her crazy.

Mark locked the door, returned the med cart to the pharmacy, then headed toward the elevators. He stopped in a men's room along the way, bolting the door behind him and slipping out the cell phone that Joe gave him. He tapped the text button and fingered in a single word message: 'Verified.' He powered off and unlocked the door.

That was the easy part, he reminded himself. He reached the elevator and pushed the down button to take him back to the pharmacy. Now he would return the cart, then punch out and head over for cocktails. He still had to fulfill his commitment with Marcy and Suzanne for putting in the good word with the pharmacist. He didn't expect it to be a late night. He would do his best to feign a smile and act the part, but his thoughts were still in room 3808.

36

The sun was making a grand entrance in a cloudless, pale blue sky as it burned off the last breaths of morning dew. Slivers of brilliant light cut and danced through the branches of thick oaks that lined the blacktop road. Mark Vistan noticed none of it. He drove along, staring straight ahead, his mind racing miles beyond.

The first time into room 3808 was innocent enough. But returning the second day while wearing a hidden camera broke more than a few privacy laws. Not to mention breaching the terms of his employment agreement. It wouldn't take much more than a whispered rumor of his actions to ruin an otherwise spotless career. And yet, he was risking it all over a cause he wouldn't have bothered considering just a week ago. He moved forward on compulsion alone. Mark had no say or even a seat at the table where decisions like these are internally weighed, measured, and acted upon. The switches were thrown, and he was in motion, whether kicking and screaming or quietly complaint. It didn't matter. He was fighting only himself and his conscience on this one, and he was losing. The enlightened side of him, the usually subdued voice of reason and clarity, was at the controls. He was going to do the right thing whether he liked it or not.

Keeping his distance and doing his own thing had made for a comfortable way of life up until now. He wasn't searching for some noble, feel-good cause to supplement the emptiness left from childhood trauma or a broken heart. Life was good the way it was. So then why was he driving to his sister's house on this beautiful day instead of working on his golf swing? Why was he even thinking about getting involved with a bunch of strangers and their soap opera drama?

His mind replayed the image of those eyes again, drowning in a depth of despair he'd never seen before. That look changed everything. Sealed the deal. Now he was minutes from meeting a group of people that would become his co-conspirators. He slowed and turned into Theresa's driveway, resigned to do what was right. He crossed his fingers, hoping he wouldn't feel compelled to make it a habit.

"Ah, good, you're here!" Murray called from across the room as Mark let himself in. He walked through the bustling hive of activity in Joe's living room and shook Mark's hand. "You think you got a good image of her? Good enough to make a positive ID?"

Mark nodded as he handed Murray the video camera and recorder he wore on his rounds the day before.

"That was definitely a new experience," he said. "I felt like everyone knew what I was up to the whole time."

"It would have taken a very trained eye to notice this," Murray said, smiling as he held up the device. The camera lens was concealed in a flag pin that Mark wore on his lab coat. The recorder, not much larger than a typical USB stick, was taped to his chest.

"I'll get this downloaded," Murray said, heading back to a

folding table where he had assembled his equipment. "Showtime will be in about ten minutes."

Mark gave his sister a hug, then shook Joe's hand and accepted a steamy mug of coffee.

"You get it?" Joe asked anxiously.

"Yeah, I think so. We'll know soon enough either way." He nodded toward Murray. "So, he's like some super geek, huh?"

Joe laughed. "Just met the guy myself yesterday, but yeah, that's the impression I got. Hey, hold on a second." He turned and flagged Ethan to come to join them. "I want you to meet somebody. Mark, this is Ethan Ludwig. He plays drums for the band I told you about."

Mark held out his hand, grinning. "He doesn't shut up about you guys. Sorry I haven't seen you play yet. Maybe I can get your schedule and try to lock in on a night I have off."

"That sounds good," Ethan said, shaking Mark's hand. "Joe and Theresa have supported us from the get-go. They believed in us even when we didn't believe in ourselves."

"You're being modest," Theresa chimed in. "These guys have played to packed houses since they put this band together." She looked back to her brother and added, "They kick ass."

Mark nodded, then turned to Ethan. "So you're the one that knows Jordan West, right?"

A pained expression flashed in Ethan's eyes as he nodded. "Shitty trick of fate," he said in a sigh. "She didn't do anything wrong except to have been the daughter of a tyrant. Jordan has a strong moral compass, and her mother obviously doesn't. Talk about clashing philosophies."

"She understood me when I said your name," Mark offered. "She's pretty sedated, but she was definitely aware of what was going on." He struggled past his own emotions and added, "I saw a flicker in her eyes. It was like all she needed was to hear was that she wasn't alone, that people were thinking of her, trying to help. I told her she was being watched by the video camera, and she had to control her expressions." Mark paused, remembering the moment, the look in her eyes. "It was actually pretty amazing. One moment she's doped and distant, and then, it was like she cut through the haze of the drugs." He nodded, smiled. "It takes a strong-willed mind to pull that off."

Ethan's expression brightened. "Wow, I needed to hear that. I kept imagining her stoned out of her mind with that Jack Nicholson expression from One Flew Over The Cuck-oo's Nest."

Mark smiled. "She wasn't quite that bad, and now she knows not to take any more of the meds they're giving her. The only thing is," He hesitated, searching for the right words. "That place is going to be even harder for her to deal with now."

"There's gotta be a way to get her out of that place," Ethan said.

"That's why we're all here," Murray answered from across the room. "By the way, it's showtime."

The small group gathered around the monitor connected to Murray's laptop as he pressed start. The screen flickered and flashed and then began replaying the stark white hallways of the Haven hospital. The high-resolution, wide-angle image showed the med cart being pushed along as Mark made his rounds, stopping outside each of the secured doors, unlocking and stepping through them.

Everyone anxiously anticipated the appearance of 3808. There was a collective breath-hold as each room number plate came into view. When it finally appeared, the room went deathly still. Mark's hand was seen reaching out and unlocking the door. He stepped in, and everyone had their first disturbing glimpse of Jordan. She stared downward, hair streaming over her eyes, seemingly lost to the world. But then there was the slightest acknowledgment as Mark spoke to her, told her of the camera he was wearing. Her head tilted up, eyes making contact. From one frame to the next, it seemed as though that look of empty despair was replaced with a fragile glint of hope. There was that faintest of smiles as she held her gaze at the camera. And then she did something unexpected. Ever so subtly, she winked.

"Did you see that?" Theresa called out, pointing with wonder at the screen.

Mark took a double-take. "I didn't even notice at the time," he said.

Everyone let out a deep breath of relief as their conversations began buzzing with new hope over the small, positive sign. The topic soon turned to freeing Jordan from her prison. Each took turns offering suggestions while the others either built on their ideas or found holes in the plan.

Joe sat listening as the ideas flowed, and the enthusiasm grew stronger. By their passioned voices, he could tell that the mood had gone from wishful thinking to seeking a real solution to rescue their friend. It was the moment he was waiting for.

He always feared he wouldn't know when his moment of truth arrived, and the tides of fate would flow unnoticed over his feet. He needn't have worried. This was it, and he knew exactly what needed to be done. It was the most unusual and uplifting sensation of perfect clarity that life ever offered. His plan could work. He had the answers these people desperately sought. He would be successful. He knew this with absolute certainty, grinning as a momentary silence fell over the room.

With quiet confidence, Joe said, "I've got an idea."

MURRAY WORKED his way back through the video, capturing still photos of the various hallways and doors while graphing a floor plan. He added X marks for camera positions and noted when hospital personnel entered and exited the images. He conferred with Mark to add any additional details that the camera missed. They both agreed the final product was a very accurate representation of the hospital floor plan and staff movements.

"Okay, guys, here comes the fun part," Joe announced. "Mark, can you get Ethan into the hospital to help retrieve our package?"

Mark thought for a moment, envisioning the obstacles he might encounter. "That could be a challenge."

"You don't even have to get him all the way into that wing," Joe added. "Just close enough that he can assist you in getting her out as quickly as possible."

"Yeah," Mark replied, nodding. "I think I can do that. I'll have to make a few calls to the personnel department. You can be my cousin that will take any job available."

"Whatever it takes," Ethan offered.

"Wait, you can't risk going in there and being filmed by all those cameras," Theresa interjected. "There's already a BOLO for you. We'll need to alter your appearance," she said, setting a fresh carafe of coffee on the table.

"She's right," said Joe. "Mark, you're still safe. You haven't done anything illegal yet."

"YET!" Mark chuckled.

"Right," Joe continued, "and we can hide you here until this blows over. But Ethan, you need a new identity."

"I have a buddy with a back door into the DMV," said Murray. "We can borrow someone else's name and face for a few days."

"Excellent!" said Joe. "Theresa just happens to be an incredible makeup artist. Once you find an identity to borrow, she can give him the finishing touches." He looked to his wife and asked, "Babe, think you can do that?"

Theresa nodded. "Can do."

"Oh, and while we're at it," Joe added, "I meant to tell you the part I wanted you to play in our little show. You're going to love this!"

She beamed and gave him a thumbs up.

Murray ended a phone call and scribbled a few notes, then turned to Mark. "As soon as we have a new identity for Ethan, we'll send it over. Then you can call the personnel department and make a recommendation. Use your own cell to make the call, but wait until you get home. I will find the company that does security for the hospital and tap into their video feeds. Those cameras will be our eyes while you're in there. We'll be able to give you real-time information about what we see on the floor."

Murray pulled a burner phone from his jacket pocket and punched in a number from memory. "I could call every security company in Maryland and still not find the right group faster than getting a hold of. . ." He put the phone to his ear and said, "Roscoe? Hey buddy, it's Murray. I need to know who has the contract for the Haven hospital security and internet servers. . . yup, exactly right, time to expand my business. I got a pen. Go ahead."

37

Murray entered a string of passwords and tapped into the hospital security system. The first image to come up was a view of the stately mansion through a light fog, shot from camera number six at the old gatehouse. Even seen through the low-resolution black and white video, one immediately sensed the stately stature of the beautiful old building. It stood in silence, surrounded by manicured, sprawling lawns and landscaping.

The Haven Hospital, as it was now called, bore the weight of a hundred years of mysterious notoriety. Constructed in 1926 as a lavish estate, it was abruptly converted into a private psychiatric facility six years later. The decision for the change was borne from a personal tragedy. The owner's beloved wife, Grace, suffered a complete mental breakdown shortly after childbirth and required constant supervision. Over time, more patients were admitted. The reputation of the Haven grew, and the facility flourished.

The list of damaged actors kicking drug habits and alcoholic wives of powerful men brought in to dry out became the mainstay. Cliff McArthur, heartthrob actor of the fifties, came here for an experimental cure to his homosexuality. And a famous Hollywood bombshell resided here while on a suicide watch after enduring a movie studio mandated abortion.

The facility still maintained a tight veil of secrecy surrounding the identity of its patients coming for treatment. It was at the top of a short list of treatment options for those who sought anonymity. Confidentiality was the cornerstone of the Haven. For all these reasons, it was the perfect facility to make someone disappear.

MURRAY ADJUSTED his headset and rechecked the monitors. All camera feeds from the hospital were displayed on the massive video array he had constructed in the middle of the living room. He also mounted a GPS tracking device on the recovery vehicle and monitored its progress on his tablet. Murray smiled to himself. What a perfect time in time to be a geek.

"Okay, I'm punching in," Mark reported as he fed his card into the Haven time clock. "Ethan is headed to the shipping office."

"Remember not to touch your earpiece or talk unless you're alone," Murray reminded him through the nearly invisible device. "Ethan, snap your fingers twice when you're on the way to your post."

"Got it," Ethan replied quietly, rounding a corner and stepping into the shipping office. His new position at the hospital loading dock involved accepting shipments and delivering supplies to each department. He had hoped this would give him full access to the third floor. But on his first day, he realized it wouldn't be quite so easy. Supplies for the third floor were dropped off at a holding area.

Employees from each department would then come to get them. There was no direct access to the places where he would be needed to assist with the escape. Once the facility was mapped out, a spot was chosen where he could be best utilized.

Ethan checked in with the dock manager, then got to work.

"Cody, I see you stopped," Murray said. "What's up?"

"Putting a medical equipment repair logo on your van was a great idea ," Cody's voice crackled over the radio. "But we forgot to gas up ahead of time. I'm filling the tank now. I should be about three miles out."

"I show two point four miles, but who's counting," Murray answered, monitoring the progress of the van. "Remember, you're going to park in the reserved section for repair vendors in the back. Sit tight, and I'll tell you when to move into position."

"Got it," Cody replied as he paid with a gas gift card.

Mark worked his way back to the pharmacy and was given his med cart with no more than a fleeting glance from Anthony. Mark signed the clipboard and rolled out of the pharmacy toward the elevators and his first stop. The path seemed all the more familiar since he'd traced it out on paper with Murray the night before. He pushed the cart along, discreetly noting each of the cameras. His every move was being observed in Joe's living room.

"Nod twice if you hear me okay," Murray instructed.

Without looking up, Mark nodded two times and kept walking. To anyone else watching, the gesture would have gone unnoticed. That was all Murray needed to see. The high-frequency transmitter/receivers he had borrowed for the group were better than expected. He was also impressed with how Mark handled himself. The guy was definitely cool under pressure. They would never have gotten this far without his help.

Murray watched now as Mark pushed the med cart up to room 3808. He stopped and acted out a cough for the camera. "Ready?" Mark asked.

"Drop to tie your shoe, and stand by," Murray answered, then checked the monitors once more. "Ethan," he said, "you're between cameras. I can't see you. Are you ready?" Murray heard only a cough, which was their prearranged signal that he could not talk.

"Mark, go to the lavatory behind you," Murray instructed. He watched as Mark pushed the cart back the way he'd come to a staff restroom around the corner. He made sure to leave the cart in plain sight of the camera and went inside.

"What's up?" Mark asked, shutting the door behind him.

"I'm making the video loop while we wait for Ethan to check-in," Murray explained. "He's near his spot but isn't responding. It should be just a—"

"All set here," came the anticipated reply from Ethan. "I had to wait for a janitor to tell a bad joke. He's gone now. I'm grabbing a wheelchair and heading for the stairway."

"Excellent," Murray said as he processed the video loop. Once enabled, the hospital security team would only see a thirty-second repeating loop of the med cart stopped outside the staff lavatory. He rechecked the monitor to verify everything was ready to go.

"Mark, leave the bathroom and run toward the south emergency exit in three, two, one, now."

Murray pushed play on the video loop. Mark bolted out the door, then raced toward the exit as Ethan worked his way up the stairwell with the folded wheelchair. Mark pushed open the fire door, then watched below as Ethan ascended the steps toward him.

"Let's do this," Mark called down, holding the steel door open. Ethan scrambled up the remaining flight to the third level, breathing heavily. He unfolded the wheelchair and pushed it through. Being observed was no longer an issue, and the two men broke into a run toward Jordan's room.

The clock was now ticking. The chain of events needed to happen fast or not at all.

They reached 3808, and Mark unlocked and pulled open the door.

Ethan entered first. The sight that greeted him was a gut punch, sucking the air out of his lungs. He staggered and reached out to balance himself against the wall. Although he was cautioned about what to expect, nothing could have prepared him for this moment. The tiny room was no larger than a prison cell. The image of the woman lying curled up on the bed with arms wrapped tightly to her chest was like the ultimate display of submission and hopelessness. Jordan looked dreadful. Ethan froze in place, feeling ashamed to see her this way but unable to look away.

Jordan glanced up and blinked the pair of men into focus. Her eyes lit with the recognition of Mark but then gave a wary expression to Ethan. Had she lost her memory of him? His heart sank on the thought but then he recalled that he was in disguise. Right now, he was just some bushy-eyed geek in chunky glasses. More than likely, she didn't recognize him. Ethan watched her watching him as she scrutinized his features. Within seconds, her face brightened with wonderment as though catching a glimpse of the man within. There was the slightest upturn in the corners of her mouth. Her eyes revealed her recognition and welled with tears of hope.

Ethan felt a surge of energy and fought the urge to rush forward and take her in his arms. He stood waiting for instructions, his impatience clawing from within like a bad itch. He grinned back at her and winked. Nothing in this world could ever look as wonderful as the smile she returned.

"Are we good to go?" he asked, listening in his earpiece for Murray to respond.

"Hold up, I need to make a loop of Jordan sitting alone."

A long, tense moment passed as Ethan and Mark waited.

"Go," Murray finally yelled. "Get the hell out of there now!"

Ethan dashed to Jordan's side as she reached out and embraced him like he was a firefighter rescuing her from a blazing inferno.

"I thought you'd still be a medicated mess," Ethan whispered as he kissed her. "My God, it's so good to see you."

Jordan wiped away a joyful tear. "Mark told me not to swallow any more of the pills, to hold on a little longer." She looked to Mark and said, "Thank you."

"We don't have much time," Mark said anxiously. "Get in the wheelchair, and we'll get you out of here."

"I think I can walk."

"Not fast enough, you can't. Roll now, walk later."

She nodded as Ethan positioned the wheelchair next to the bed and dropped in. She didn't have near the strength she expected and now gladly accepted being pushed to safety.

"Murray, we have the package," Mark announced into his microphone. "We're ready to roll,"

"Copy that. Cody, power up and get into position. The package is on the way."

Out in the parking lot, Cody turned the ignition of the "Medical Specialties" van. He drove around to the loading dock and pulled up near the receiving door.

"Ethan and Mark, you need to be past the exit in forty-three seconds. Move it!"

Murray checked the clock on his video loop and scanned

for other movement on the hospital floor. His eyes locked on one of the camera feeds. "Oh shit," he said, "hold on. You have a security guard coming your way." Murray cursed again under his breath as he looked at his checklist. "This guy should have been by twenty minutes ago. Close your door and duck down. And get her back in bed!"

"We can't let that door latch shut," Ethan cautioned, "the guard might hear it."

Mark stepped over and worked the master key into the lock. He held the deadbolt open as he silently pulled the door closed, then turned the key back and allowed the lock to set.

"Good call," Ethan whispered as he helped Jordan back into bed. He rolled the wheelchair up against the door, out of sight from the rectangular window. They both crouched down and waited.

They could hear the guard coming from all the way down the hall. He had a habit of noisily clanking a nightstick on the patient's doors as he walked along. He moved slowly, oblivious to the reactions of his intrusion. He was very close now, the clicking of his hard soles echoing off the corridor ahead of him. His footfalls abruptly ceased as though he had left the area. Mark and Ethan listened, straining to hear some telltale rustle of clothing or the clank of that annoying billy club. There was nothing.

Without warning, he was right over them, peering through the window. His presence could be felt as his silhouette blocked out the light from the hallway. The guard stared in at Jordan, who laid on the bed, acting sedated. No one moved for what felt like nerve-wracking minutes. Finally, with a crack of his nightstick to the door, his shadow passed out of view of the window. The cool fluorescent light once again streamed in. Everyone anxiously held their places. The footfalls faded with each step, finally ceasing as the guard rounded a corner into the next hall.

The tense silence was broken when Murray's voice cut through their earpieces.

"Move now, right now!"

Ethan grabbed the wheelchair and pushed it back to the bed as Jordan worked herself in. Mark gave them a nod, and they slipped silently out of 3808 and ran toward freedom.

Murray watched the monitor as the security guard casually lumbered down the next hall, tapping his stick as he went, annoying another ward of patients. The next turn would bring him to the abandoned meds cart that Mark left by the restroom. The window of opportunity was closing fast. They needed to be clear of the area before the guard spotted it.

Ethan, Mark, and Jordan had covered half the distance to the stairwell when the guard came upon the cart.

"Anyone in here?" he called through the lavatory door. There was no response. Suspecting something amiss, he pulled out his radio. "Stan, this is Ray, over?"

"Go ahead, Ray. You staying awake today?"

"I Only fell asleep on the job that one time, and you know it."

"Yup. Just happened to be during an inspection. What's up?"

Ray's face reddened with embarrassed anger. That pencil-pushing desk prick was never going to let him live that down. "There is a cart filled with medications outside the can up here."

"Where, exactly?"

"East end."

"Stand by, please."

Stand by, Ray chuckled to himself. Pompous blowhard, probably thinks he's—

"Raymond, please state your exact location again." There was an urgency in Stan's voice.

"Restroom, third floor, east end."

"Listen to me, Ray! I don't see you there, just the med cart, so if this is some little game you're playing, it's not very…oh, shit!"

"I'm standing right here, man. What's your problem?"

"My, ah, my monitor for camera twelve just flashed. One minute you weren't there, and now you are. Something weird is going on. Take a quick walk around the whole floor, will you?"

"Copy that. Stand by."

Ethan, Mark, and Jordan were nearing the exit when a loud voice bellowed behind them.

"Hey, you there, stop! Stop right now!"

Mark turned and saw the pudgy guard trotting awkwardly toward them with a radio in one hand and that obnoxious billy club in the other. He muttered under his breath but took solace that the guy wasn't built like a marathon runner. Mark shot ahead and pulled open the exit door. Ethan and Jordan followed through seconds later.

"Stan! We have a situation on level three," the guard huffed into the radio as he ran, struggling to catch his breath. "Two orderlies. . .with a patient . . . just went into the south stairwell."

"Copy that, Ray. Stay on them."

"I think. . . I think it's the one. . .from 3808."

There was a pause.

"Goddamn it, Raymond, we're going to catch major shit for this. I'm sounding the alarm. We're going into lockdown. Do not let them get out!"

Mark glanced back as the guard narrowed the distance

between them. "Ethan," he yelled, "grab Jordan and get down the stairs. I need that wheelchair."

Ethan bent down in front of Jordan. "Piggyback, okay?"

She nodded and latched her arms around his neck, and hooked her legs around his waist. As soon as he felt her locked on, he sprinted down the stairs.

Mark took the wheelchair and positioned it to block the steps, then followed them down. They had descended one flight when the guard rushed through the door. He crashed into the chair and tumbled down the stairwell, flopping end over end until he slammed into the next landing, out cold.

Murray watched the flurry of activity on his monitors. The planned escape route was being choked off by an inrush of guards. Workers from every department scrambled out of the way. The entire hospital was now alerted to their presence. The trio had been thirty-seconds from freedom but was now trapped. He surveyed the images from all cameras, searching for an alternative path. There was one area that still appeared relatively calm.

"Change of plan, guys," he said, "head for the basement." He spotted another guard making his way toward the stairwell. "Be ready. You've got more company coming."

Mark descended the steps toward the basement, trying to think one step ahead of the pursuers. An idea came to him, and he stopped at the first-floor door. "I'll be right behind you," he called down to Ethan and Jordan.

They continued down the stairwell without asking questions.

Mark peered through the window, watching for anyone coming their way. He needed to buy some time by creating a distraction. He spied an IV pole across the hall and lunged through the door, and grabbed it, pulling it back inside. As he did, a voice boomed from down the corridor.

"Hey, you! Stay where you are!"

Mark slammed the door shut and jammed the IV pole down behind the release bar, wedging it in tightly. The angry face of a heavy breathing security guard filled the window. The guard tried opening the door and realized it was secured from inside.

"Open this now," he commanded, pulling on the handle.

Mark decided to send his pursuers in the wrong direction. As the guard glared angrily, he backed away and bolted up the stairs.

"All units," the guard growled into his radio, "suspects are headed back up the stairs. Repeat, they're headed up!"

Mark stopped outside the second-floor door and paused, listening. He heard the rapid, retreating footsteps of the first-floor guard. The subterfuge worked. He shot down to the basement, taking the steps four at a time, then peered through the window. No guards. He slipped out the door and caught sight of Ethan and Jordan walking arm in arm down the hallway. He caught up and grabbed Jordan's other arm, then scooted them along the empty corridor.

Outside the bustling kitchen, they came upon a row of lockers.

Ethan signaled them to stop and began flipping through each. He pulled out a lab coat for Jordan. "Put this on," he said, holding it as she slipped her arms through.

"Can you walk on your own?"

She turned to him and nodded.

"All right then, follow me toward that exit sign down the hall."

Jordan's balance and strength were still off, but she willed every ounce of energy to walk at a measured pace while Mark tried checking in on the headset. There was no response. The transmitters were not working in the basement. They were on their own for the time being and blended with the increasing stream of workers. Mark reached the back stairway exit and held it open. Once inside, the men lifted Jordan from either side and scrambled up the steps toward the main floor.

"The shipping dock is ahead to the right," Ethan said as they peered out the stairwell window. "I'll take the lead. You guys follow."

Ethan was about to open the door when Murray's voice crackled back into their earbuds.

"Package pickup, do you copy?"

"Package pickup, we read you," Mark answered, breathing a sigh of relief. "We're on the main floor, shipping department, rear stairwell."

"Good job, I see you now. Back away from the window and don't move. I'm going to record a video loop with the camera near you. Just about got it. . .and there, done! Head for the exit. Your ride is waiting."

The shipping department camera was taken offline, and another one of Murray's video loops played in its place, masking their movements. They were in the home stretch.

Ethan walked with controlled calm toward their final destination. Mark and Jordan followed closely behind, yearning to sprint the last few yards. They were so close.

The loading dock was directly ahead. Just to the right of that was the exit. Ethan was never so happy to see that red-lettered sign. He looked about and saw no one observing them. "We're clear," he said in a forced whisper, "let's go!"

Cody sat at the loading dock with engine running, watching through the rearview mirror. The exit door suddenly burst open in a flurry of motion. He scrambled out and ran to the side of the van, pulling open the sliding door as Mark, Ethan and Jordan ran toward him. As they jumped down the concrete steps, Jordan lost her footing and began falling forward. She was immediately grabbed from either side and whisked the rest of the way to the van. She and Ethan dove through the open side door while Mark ensured they landed safely. He pulled the door shut behind them and jumped into the passenger seat.

"We're set, Cody," Mark huffed, "get us out of here!"

Cody dropped the van into drive and floored the accelerator, making a hard turn out of the shipping bay and heading onto the circular hospital drive.

Jordan and Ethan were tossed around the back of the van like tennis shoes in a dryer. Jordan clung to him as though they were still running through the hospital halls, only now daring to believe she was free.

Ethan brushed the hair away from her eyes and stroked her cheek. "Sorry I didn't show up with a limo," he quipped, "but I'll make it up to you."

Jordan hugged him tighter. "This is the best ride of my life. I wouldn't change a thing."

The blissful moment was abruptly cut short.

"Save it, you two," Mark called out. "We're not in the clear yet." He tapped his earpiece. "Murray, can you hear me?"

"Five by five, go ahead."

"There's a security car with lights flashing coming from the other side of the hospital."

"We're on it," Murray responded. "Backup One, do you copy? Tell me what you see."

An aging Ford Explorer SUV sat idling on the side of the road near the hospital entrance, flanked by the old stone wall that encircled the property. The driver scanned the massive estate for any sign of activity. Through a copse of thick trees, she spied the flicker of flashing lights moving fast along the inner road. Seconds later, the cargo van, package delivery, burst into the clearing. Directly behind it, nearly kissing its back bumper, was the hospital security vehicle.

"Right in front of me," Backup One replied, "and coming fast."

"All you need to do is block the cop long enough to get the package past. Can you do that?"

There was a pause before she answered. "It's gonna be tight. He's right on their ass." She thought for a moment, imagining the scenario needed to make this work. "Package pickup," she finally responded, "make a left when you hit the main road, and don't slow down no matter what you see!"

"Copy that," Cody answered tensely. "Here we come!"

Backup One threw the Ford into gear, slammed the pedal to the floor, and headed directly for the two vehicles as they raced forward. The distance between them was no more than a car length as the van shot out directly in front of her, making a hard, sliding left turn onto the shoulder of the road. Her left front bumper kissed the left rear of the van as it swung around, struggled for traction in the loose gravel, then fishtailed as it sped away. She slammed both feet down on the brake just as the pursuit vehicle came flying through the intersection. It broadsided the Explorer with an ear-shattering concussion of crumpling metal. The forward momentum spun both vehicles around ninety degrees, screeching to an abrupt halt.

SECURITY OFFICER HENRY WISS opened his eyes, shifted his aching jaw from side to side, and blinked his vision into focus. He glanced out over the crumpled black and white hood of his security cruiser and watched as hissing steam rose from the crushed radiator. His ears stopped ringing as he took in the unnatural stillness. He looked down and saw what looked like his facial imprint in the now deflating airbag. Shit, that hurt!

He took a quick mental inventory of body aches and sensations. He was lucky and would walk away from this with little more than a massive headache and a very stiff neck. Then he thought of the other driver!

"Oh my God," he mumbled. He'd run the stop sign and plowed into the old SUV. "But I had my lights going," he tried to reason his way out of feeling blame. "They should have yielded."

His thoughts went to the occupants of the vehicle he creamed. Were they hurt? Were they dead? "Son of a bitch," he mumbled. "I just started this job! How much worse can it get?" As if washing out from the police academy wasn't bad enough. This second-rate security job was supposed to buy him time until he could reapply. But now this! This could ruin him! If he'd killed someone, then he was doubly screwed.

He unbuckled his seat belt and prepared to go check on the condition of the other driver. He froze as he caught motion in the corner of his eye. Coming around the back of the SUV, drenched in the taillight's red glow, was an old woman in a light-colored robe. She held her neck with her right hand. Her head, full of large pink rollers wound with silver hair, gyrated slowly back and forth. Fuzzy slippers scuffled on the pavement as she made her way toward him. He rolled his window down apprehensively as she approached, feeling equal parts of shock and nausea.

"Are you all right young man?" The old woman asked in a soft, concerned tone. Her weathered features were exaggerated by the flashing lights against the radiator steam. She looked and sounded like every grandmother he'd ever remembered.

"Yeah, I think so," he answered.

She appeared relatively unharmed. Thank God she wasn't a bloody mess. Just squeezing and rubbing her neck a lot. Maybe things weren't as bad as—

Her eyes suddenly narrowed, her entire face contorting into a mass of deep, scornful lines. In a raspy, paint-peeling voice, she yelled, "Happy to hear it, you stupid son of a bitch! You ran a stop sign and hit my husband's favorite Ford! What the hell is wrong with you! You think you're in a race? You think this is NASCAR?" She extended her left hand and tossed a business card through the open window. "My husband is Sid Brinkman, the attorney, kid. And you just destroyed his SUV. I'd advise you to find a better lawyer, but there aren't any. I'm gonna sue you for every penny you'll make from now until the day that empty head of yours starts going bald. You'd better pray my neck's not broken, 'cause it hurts like hell!"

Before he could comprehend what happened, the old hag was walking back toward her vehicle.

"Wait! Don't we need to...exchange insurance information? You need to stay until the cops get here."

She kept walking and climbed into her van. She backed up and turned hard right, ripping the smashed vehicles apart. The separating sheet metal squealed and screeched in protest. The front bumper of the patrol car ripped off and clanged onto the road. She rolled back until her passenger window was even with him.

"Call this in, Kojak," she yelled. "I'll be back in a bit. Shiela's having a heart attack, and I'm taking her to the vet."

"The Vet? Wait, you can't—"

"Can and will, you horse's ass. My cat is more important than you or this mess you made. Call it in, and tell them you hit Lolli Brinkman. Tell them I'm hurt, I'm mad as hell, and I'll be back!"

The tires chirped on the pavement as Backup One floored the van and headed back the way it had come.

Henry Wiss sat dumbfounded, still attempting to process all that happened. Slowly, his mind cleared, and he recalled the urgency of the situation. He pulled the radio microphone from its cradle. "Stan, this is mobile unit two."

"Henry, did you get them?"

"Negative. I, ah, was in an accident. I hit a civilian vehicle. The van got away." Henry went on to explain as many details as he could remember.

"Copy that," Stan said when he'd finished. "Ray, up on the third floor, reported that these people kidnapped a patient. They threw him down a flight of stairs after he gave chase. We're calling the state police in on this. There's nothing more you can do. Come on in, and we'll get you checked out."

"What about that old bag in the SUV that I hit?" he asked.

"Cross your fingers that she was bullshitting about her husband being Sid Brinkman. You don't want to put this hospital through a lawsuit with that ambulance chaser. I don't know why she left the scene, but I'm sure our legal department will be calling you soon for a full review. In fact, we might want to think about this before calling in the police. She left the scene of an accident. Even old Sid would have trouble defending that. Is the squad car drivable?"

"No, the front end is wiped out."

"Copy that. I'll make a call and get you towed. We'll write it up as a hit and run. Nothing else we can do. It's someone else's problem now."

38

"Package Delivery, please confirm your position." Murray's voice crackled through Cody's handheld radio.

"Coming up on Fulton Street," he replied, still shaking from the adrenalin-pumping chase and getaway.

"Very good, your GPS tracker quit working. Follow the plan, and we'll see you soon."

"Got it," Cody answered as he turned into the lot of an abandoned gas station. He drove around the building and pulled up next to Joe, who sat waiting in a minivan, then got out and slid open the side door. Jordan and Ethan scurried out and hopped into the next vehicle. Cody pulled the magnetic signs off the doors and heaved them into a dumpster, then jumped back into his van and drove off.

Mark climbed into the passenger seat of the minivan and looked back. "Are you guys okay?" he asked.

A moment of silence passed as they all began to comprehend everything that had happened over the last twenty minutes. Determined game faces gave way to elated smiles.

They did it! The security of the safe house was now just moments away.

Joe dropped the gearshift into drive and glanced back in the rearview mirror, a tear sparkling in his eye. "Let's get the hell out of here!" he said, pulling the minivan onto the main road. "One more stop to make, then back to base." He drove a few miles further up the road, then pulled up to a boarded-up convenience store.

A severely damaged Ford Explorer came rattling down the road and pulled behind the building. Moments later, a strange apparition appeared in a loose terrycloth robe, fuzzy bunny slippers, and a head full of curlers. The old woman strode up to the driver's side window, leaned in, and said, "How bout a ride, handsome?"

Joe smiled and kissed her, then turned to Mark. "Jump in the back and make room for your sister, please."

Mark stared at her a moment longer, then grinned and climbed out. Theresa walked around the front of the minivan doing a less than sexy shimmy that had Joe nearly in tears. "Is she good at makeup, or what?" he exclaimed.

Theresa climbed in, reached over, and planted a big kiss on Joe's lips. "Sorry, honey, but the Ford is toast. That rent a cop T-boned me pretty bad."

"So long as you're all right, nothing else matters. I got that thing in trade for a repair years ago. It served its purpose. And by the way, great job!"

"That was kinda fun," she mused, "but if that was a theme park ride, I would never do it twice."

"Anyone up for a cup of coffee at my place?" Joe offered as he pulled back to the main road.

"If it's all the same to you, I could really go for a beer and a pizza," answered Jordan. "And thank you all so much for what you've done. I would have rather died than stay in that terrible place for even one more day."

"We're not done, Jordan," Ethan said. "I think you know we have to find a way to make this right."

She nodded. "And we will. I will. Just give me a day to enjoy this moment, to be with the best friends anyone could ever ask for."

39

Washington, DC

"Governor and Mrs. Paylick, so good to see you, and thank you for coming. Tiffany, that dress is absolutely stunning!"

"Oh, well, thank you, Senator Karlson. Do you really think so? My daughter helped me pick this out."

"She has wonderful taste, and you wear it well." Karlson smiled, thinking she looked marginally better than a whale in a canvas tarp, but that was pushing it. She turned back to the governor. "John, I do hope we find more common ground after the election. I'm thinking you and I can force some positive changes into your next governor's summit."

"You know that you have our full support, Katherine. Let's get you into the White House, then we can really make things happen."

Karlson shook both of their hands and headed for the next group of guests. Gene Lawton intercepted her.

"Excuse me, senator, but there is a phone call that you need to take."

Karlson started to say something, but Gene cut her off. "Right now," he whispered, with no attempt to mask the urgency.

Karlson got the message. She excused herself from the two-thousand dollar per plate fundraiser and walked with him toward the ballroom entrance.

"Gene, I hope this is important. Every minute I'm not out here working this crowd is money lost." She chuckled to herself. "Did you get a load of that mail order housedress that Tiffany Paylick was wearing? God help her, she actually believed it looked good! Her daughter's taste in clothing is actually worse than her own."

Lawton wasn't listening. He directed Karlson down a wide hallway and into a nearby meeting room. Two of the seats at a long table were occupied by a pair of dark-suited men who rose to greet her as she entered.

Karlson paused, struck with the oddity of Gene bringing her back here for a private consultation. He knew damn well she needed to be working that ballroom right now. "Gentlemen, I'm sorry but—" she started to say.

"Senator," Gene put his hand on her arm and cut her off. "These men are with the FBI. They have something important to tell you."

Karlson felt him shaking through his touch. There was also a strange pallor that she hadn't caught in the dimmed glow of the ballroom. Here in the harsh lighting of the meeting room, it was so apparent that she wondered how she'd missed it. His entire demeanor was off. His expression, usually self-assured, was one of concern, even fear. She now noticed tiny beads of sweat on his forehead, typical enough for anyone else, but not this guy. Gene Lawton was unflappable. He would be the one keeping it together on a sinking ship, calmly loading the lifeboats. So what had shaken the unshakeable? She looked from Gene to the two men and realized this was going to be bad.

The taller of the two stepped forward and held out his hand." Senator Karlson, I'm Special Agent Masterson and this Special Agent Barnhart."

She shook both their hands, forcing a smile. "What can I do for you, gentlemen?"

"Please forgive the intrusion," SA Masterson said, "but I'm afraid I have some distressing news. Senator, early this morning, there was a security breach at the Haven Hospital in Bethesda. I'm sorry to inform you that your daughter, Jordan West, has been taken by a group of as yet unidentified persons."

"Taken?" She looked from his face to the other agent. "You mean kidnapped? Are you telling me my daughter… was kidnapped?"

"Regretfully, yes, Jordan has been kidnapped."

That word sounded so foreign, out of place. Kidnapped. As though it was never meant to be uttered in a sentence with Jordan's name. This could not be right, could it?

"No, there has to be some mistake," she said, waving her hands dismissively. "My daughter is being cared for in a secure location under the tightest security. What you're saying is not possible. There has to be some other explanation. Honestly, the FBI ought to know to get their facts straight before scaring the hell out of people. This could be a case of mistaken identity. Maybe, maybe one of those crazy patients strolled off the hospital grounds again. It's happened before, you know."

She tried thinking of other possible scenarios, but the truth was already taking hold. She just wasn't ready or willing to accept it. "Jesus Christ, no," she pleaded as the weight hit home. "This can't be right. Someone has made a mistake, and…oh God, give me a scrap of hope that this is wrong! Please!"

"I wish I could say that were possible," SA Masterson's consoling tone failed to soften the blunt impact of his words. "A headcount of all patients this afternoon confirmed that Jordan was indeed missing."

There it was then, the worst thing a mother could hear. Someone had abducted her daughter, her child! Karlson blinked hard, trying to wake up from this ghastly nightmare.

"No. . .my. . . don't you see that. . .oh, dear lord!"

She sank into the nearest chair, all color draining from her pained face. Jordan kidnapped! But why? Who would have any reason to take a simple college student who was assisting with her mother's election? A terrible new thought rose up. "Me, it's because of me!" her voice cracked with guilt. "God help me, I've brought this scourge down on my own sweet, innocent child!"

Karlson questioned the timing and the location. Why did it happen at that hospital? Had she set these wheels in motion by taking Jordan to that dreadful place? Did she personally deliver her own child into the hands of those who would use her as a gaming pawn to extract, what, money? Power or influence? Maybe force her to turn her head on an issue or vote differently on legislation? She couldn't think clearly.

"I, we. . ." she began, not quite knowing what it was she wanted to say, only what she didn't want to hear. She felt dizzy, sick, her stomach reacting as though she were dropping multiple floors on a runaway elevator. Nothing she'd ever felt or heard could be worse than this. Would she ever see her daughter again, alive? She tried to imagine who would do such a thing and why? Did she actually have enemies this powerful? Surely it could not be someone from across the aisle in the senate. There wasn't a spine to be found among them. Or a set of balls, for that matter. No, these must be people with more sinister intentions, with a much bigger payoff in mind than a few coerced senate votes.

Her mind flashed to the earliest memories of Jordan. The kick of a tiny foot as it pushed from inside her very pregnant belly. Holding her for the first time, that tightly bundled, black-haired, perfect little girl. A laughing face covered in baby food. Her giggles of excitement in her first Halloween costume. Chasing away the tears from a skinned knee with a cookie and a kiss. The trembling hands of a pimply faced kid attempting to pin a corsage on her dress for a middle school dance. Her belly laughs, her pouts, her infectious smile, her everything! This couldn't be happening, not to her, not to her daughter, her only child!

Karlson cleared a lump in her throat and wiped away a tear. "Please, tell me what you know. Was she injured when they. . ." She choked on the words that were so hard to imagine, even more difficult to say. "When they took her?"

"No, Ms. Karlson, Jordan was not harmed in the abduction. This we know."

"Thank God for that!" she said, finally taking a breath and straightening in her seat. New questions began filling her mind. "But, but how do you know this? Did someone see it happening and not try to intervene?"

"We know this because Special Agent Barnhart's team has viewed some of the surveillance videos and confirmed what we are telling you."

Karlson nodded in silence. Okay, Jordan was alive and unharmed. But how long would she stay that way? Would these people hurt her? Not if they intended to follow through with a ransom exchange. She prayed silently that these weren't the kind of barbarians who would send one of her fingers or some other appendage in a box as a warning that they were not to be crossed. But what if they were? What if they tortured her for information about her mother. For state secrets, forced political favors, blackmail? Shit, she thought, blackmail! What if Jordan told these people of her discovery of the military mission leak? That she had seen proof of her mother's involvement? Even if they got her daughter back, that secret could be used as a devastating tool against her. Karlson could be forced into any number of compromising situations, and there would be no end. She would be as powerless as a dog on a long leash.

Karlson could never share any of this with the FBI. She hoped this was a typical kidnapping that would simply require a hefty ransom. Are you kidding? A typical kidnapping? The appetizers she'd nibbled on earlier began churning in her gut as she was repulsed by her own inner dialogue. What terrible thoughts to have concerning the fate of your own child! But as awful as these thoughts seemed, she could not help but have them and forgave herself.

She had reached this pinnacle in life because of her ability to see things from all sides. This might be as bad as it could ever get, she reasoned, but it was still necessary, no, make that absolutely critical, that she consider even the most morbid and painful of scenarios. She had no control over this nightmare being thrust upon her. Still, she weighed every word for the subtle tells that revealed when even accepted facts concealed something more sinister. Small details that would catch most anyone else off guard. For these reasons, she remained constantly vigilant, seldom lowering her defenses. With her analytical side now fully engaged, she grew hungry for more answers.

"How is this even possible? To kidnap a patient from a hospital, I mean."

"We are in the preliminary stages of the investigation,"

said SA Masterson. "But I can tell you from what we've seen so far this appears to be a highly coordinated effort involving multiple personnel with a long list of resources at their disposal."

"Have you heard anything from them?" she asked.

"No, nothing yet, but we anticipate her abductors will attempt to make contact with you. For this reason, I think it imperative—"

"Please, please tell me how something like this happens at such a secure facility?"

"Agent Barnhart has been the go-to for this case. I'll let him tell you what we have so far."

SA Barnhart pulled out a black notebook and flipped through the pages. "As Special Agent Masterson stated, this appears to be the act of a very well-coordinated group."

"How coordinated, exactly?" she asked.

"Excuse me, Ma'am?"

"How-coordinated-were-they? How did they pull this off?"

Barnhart turned to another page. "We believe it would have required information on the schedules of the floor staff and security, as well as a thorough knowledge of the layout of the building itself."

Mental gears turned, ground, and meshed. Karlson tried to envision it happening, to enter the minds of those who took her child to see how it was done. But she could not. Large pieces of the puzzle were missing. The math was all wrong. There would have been far too much to learn and plan in such a limited amount of time. Jordan was only there a few days. These people would have had to bring an elaborate plan together in the blink of an eye, then execute it flawlessly. NO, NO, NO! Even a rank amateur screenplay writer would come up with a more believable script than this. She needed to know more, far more, before allowing these two to leave. SA Masterson, the tall, silver-haired agent with the western accent, pulled her back from her thoughts.

"Senator, I'm here to coordinate the setup of a headquarters for working through this case. We need to be ready to communicate with these kidnappers if and when they contact you with their ransom demands."

"Do you believe that will happen?" she asked.

"In most of these cases, yes, the underlying motivation for abduction is usually monetary. Our plan is to ascertain enough information from them that we can thwart their plans and bring Jordan safely back home."

"How often is that successful?"

"Excuse me?"

"How often does it work out that you get the victim back unharmed?"

"I don't have the information to answer that."

"Oh, come now, Agent Masterson! Straight answer for a straight question. How likely is it these people have any intention of returning my daughter alive?"

The agent looked away a moment, then returned her gaze. "I will tell you this. The clock is ticking, and we must do everything correctly and promptly to ensure Jordan's safe release."

"So you're saying you don't know, that there's no way of knowing, is that right?"

"Senator, I am saying we have a protocol to follow that has been proven to increase our chances of success exponentially. That's what we're trying to do here. Part of that protocol is setting up a base to monitor any contact between you and the kidnappers. Now, with all due respect, and for the sake of your daughter, we must move to that end. Would this be a good place to establish our command center, or do you prefer another location?"

Karlson thought a moment. This office space near the hotel ballroom would not do. It was too far from her home and could pose a potential security nightmare. Then again, if she chose her condominium, all privacy would be lost. Everyone and his brother would know where she lived and would hound her until after the election when she moved into the White House. Her downtown election headquarters would be a lousy location. She would be stuck there with no way to pull back from a relentless press corps that would be all over this story at any moment. At least she would be relatively comfortable by allowing them to set up shop in her home. "All right then," she decided, "let's do this at my condominium."

SA Barnhart pulled out his cell phone and began making the arrangements.

"Agent Masterson," she said, "I'm still perplexed. How could this group have brought such an enormous plan together so quickly? After all, Jordan has only been there for five days. Please tell me how big this operation was? Twenty armed men? A getaway helicopter?"

"Agent Barnhart knows more of the finite details of the abduction. But to answer that specific question, initial reports indicate two men were directly involved inside with the extraction. At least one other individual assisted on the outside by driving the getaway vehicle."

"Two men," she said, mulling that one over. God, it didn't sit right. No, that was way too hard to swallow. "Two men," she repeated. "Are you shitting me?"

"I'm sorry?"

"You heard me! Two men? You're telling me that two guys stroll into a mental hospital that is world-renowned for its discretion and security and casually kidnap the daughter of a sitting United States Senator! Does that sound about right to you, Special Agent? And where the hell was the extra security that I was promised?" Her voice cracked with anger, indignation, along with a strong belt of sarcasm.

"Senator," Masterson finally managed to slip in, "I know nothing of the security arrangements you made with this institution. As to how the perpetrators gained access, my understanding is these two individuals may have been hospital employees. We're reviewing all of the personnel files now and will know more very soon."

"Jesus Christ, doesn't anyone do background checks anymore? How do you—"

"It would be best if we continued this conversation once we've set up our headquarters. By then, we should have more facts to keep us all from drawing incorrect conclusions."

"Then tell me this," Karlson still pressed, "how do two men, employees no less, manage to get this sedated adult woman out of her locked room, down the elevator, and out the damn door without somebody at least saying, 'Hey look! There's two employees dragging a patient out of here against her will?'"

"Actually, the security video shows they did not use the elevators. They made their way down the stairwells."

"Wait, that makes even less sense, don't you think? Jordan could not have been making it easy for them. So why wouldn't they take an elevator? Were they armed? Did you see weapons in the video? And how the hell did they manage to force her down multiple flights of stairs while keeping her from screaming the entire time?"

"Senator, these are all issues we're struggling with. It seems your daughter did not offer any resistance. Kitchen personnel on the basement level say they saw a woman matching Jordan's description walking along unescorted, wearing a lab coat."

Karlson's eyes widened. Red flag, her mind screamed. Bright, beaming huge fucking RED FLAG! One of many so far, all signaling the same thing; nothing here is as it seems. The whole situation was already stinking to high heaven. None of the answers were adding up and she now wondered if there was a completely different explanation. She had to keep asking questions. Only then would she get anywhere near the truth.

"Wouldn't that mean that Jordan was. . .helping them? Is this some sort of Patti Hearst thing, like Stockholm Syndrome?"

"That is a very real possibility. Whether out of fear or whether your daughter trusted these men, we don't know exactly. Until we do, her abductors are considered armed and dangerous. Senator, please, there is much more to do. We have people waiting to set up recording equipment to tap your phone for intercepting ransom demands. We are wasting time with questions that can be answered after the more pressing issues have been addressed. Now, I strongly suggest we all go do what needs to be done to get Jordan back safely. Is that acceptable?"

"Yes, of course," she agreed, as though it were stupid to even ask.

"Very good," said Masterson. "Until then, none of this can be released to the general public. We would like to control the quantity of information so as not to push the kidnappers into reacting erratically."

"I understand," Karlson said, nodding. "I'll go excuse myself from the function I'm attending here and meet you at my home. Thank you, Special Agent Masterson. I hope you'll forgive the anger and frustration I'm heaping on you."

The agent nodded his understanding.

"One more quick question. I promise it will be the last."

"Ma'am."

"You told me these people knew the schedules of staff and security, as well as the floor plans of the hospital, right?"

"Yes, that much is certain."

"Agent Masterson, how does someone acquire that much information about a seemingly secure medical facility in such a short amount of time?"

Agent Barnhart finished his phone conversation and chimed in. "That's an excellent question, senator. Although we don't have all the details, we did discover from the security video technician that they experienced some unusual glitches in the system this morning."

"What sort of glitches?"

SA Barnhart flipped to another page of his notebook. "He believes someone hacked in and installed a video loop."

"I don't know what that is."

"The security camera is temporarily taken offline, and a repeating image, a video loop, plays in its place. It appears the kidnappers used a number of these loops to mask their escape."

"How did they know to do that? How did they get in?"

"We have our people working on that right now. To breach the hospital's security measures would be technically challenging, to say the least. It would be even harder to hide your footprints once you've been inside. That may be what leads us to Jordan's captors. It also sheds some light on another question you posed; how do you get so familiar with this facility in such a short time?"

"Yes, how would one do that?"

SA Barnhart lowered his notebook and locked eyes with Karlson. "They were watching. They tapped into the hospital video grid and were watching everything, observing it all in real-time. They would then relay that information to their people on the inside."

An arctic chill gripped Karlson. Icy fingers cascaded down her spine as adrenalin flooded her heart. She staggered back and swallowed hard. They were watching. What an ironic choice of words. She could hear the echoes of Jordan's voice. *'I saw the security video. I watched you watching them!'*

"Well, I'll be damned," she said quietly. This was no coincidence. She didn't believe in them. There was so much more here than the abduction of her daughter. Every feeling of sorrow and fear for Jordan's safety drained away and was replaced with cold, hard anger with a newfound determination.

40

The FBI agents had barely left the room before Karlson grabbed Lawton's arm and spun him around.

"I need you to arrange an immediate press conference from the stage right here. We have an opportunity to pull in some sympathy votes, and the rest of the country needs to believe that my poor, overworked, broke down daughter has been kidnapped."

"Katherine, what the hell is wrong with you?" Lawton nearly yelled. "Your daughter *has* been kidnapped! That was the goddamned FBI!"

"Jesus Christ, Gene! Don't you see what's really happening here? She hasn't been kidnapped. She's been rescued by her fucking little geek friends!"

Lawton started to answer, but her reaction shocked him into silence. He stared back, wondering what was going on behind those fiery eyes. Maybe she was cracking under the strain and strayed off into her own little private reality. How else could she come up with such a convoluted conclusion? Was this the beginning of the end? The final meltdown of his candidate and the end of a near-perfect campaign? A more distant, nearly inconceivable thought sprang forward. His expression changed from one of fear to astonishment. What if she was right?

"Think about it," Karlson said. "These guys had five days to conceive and implement a kidnapping from a secure medical facility. The preliminary planning alone should have taken weeks all by itself. Then it's pulled off flawlessly by two, count 'em, two employees that casually walk her out the back door against her will in a stolen lab coat. Oh, and here's the clincher, they accomplish this with the aid of a super hacker genius who taps into the security system. Then he miraculously guides them past a small platoon of guards. Does any of this sound wrong to you? Does any of it sound familiar?"

Karlson paced the room like a caged animal. "Who the hell could pull off something like this? I'll tell you who. A bunch of local nerds that knew Jordan, knew the inner workings of that hospital and could hack into the security system. Just like they'd done in my office. Does that about cover it, Gene?"

The words struck Lawton like a lightning bolt. "Oh my God," he muttered, staggering back in near disbelief. Karlson had nailed it. What a brilliant plan! And perfectly executed by a bunch of rank amateurs who came together to help a friend! He chastised himself for missing the clues before Karlson had put them together. He was better than this. "Let's hope the FBI doesn't think the way we do and figure out what's really going on here," he said.

Karlson nodded as her mind raced forward, processing stray fragments of information and attempting to plug them into the remaining questions. "You can practically read their game strategy," she said with a look of amazement. "No wonder it seemed so easy. A bunch of super nerds crack a system maintained by overconfident, overpaid blowhards." She put her hand to her mouth to stifle a laugh. "They waltzed right in and took over like they owned the place."

She turned to Lawton as her demeanor changed, her jowls tightening as her nostrils flared. "Find out who the ass hole is that runs the security at that hospital. I want answers, Gene, and I want them now." She thought another moment, then said, "No, we'll wait on that one. Set up a press conference right here, right now, to milk this moment for all it's worth. We need to appear distraught. Start throwing some blame around. Make them think the president had a hand in this to kill the momentum of our campaign. Create some doubt in people's minds. Control the moment."

The look of extreme confidence reappeared as she pointed at Lawton. "Arrange our announcement, then start making calls. We can use the FBI to our advantage in tracking her down, but we should also have our own people working it. Some rules may need to be bent. I'm not going to wait for some judge to get his ass out of bed to sign a search warrant. You know what to do. We've dealt with similar situations before."

Lawton watched in awe as Katherine Karlson transformed. On cue, she summoned the biggest sobs and tears he'd ever seen. He couldn't remember a movie moment that could top this.

"Gene," she cried with the sorrow of a woman whose heart had just been ripped from her chest. "Get those cameras turned on. We have a statement to make!"

Lawton was mesmerized. What a performance! Say what you would about Karlson being a manipulative bitch, which he often thought privately. This performance was nothing less than brilliant! He loved a woman who could kick off her pumps and tread through the mud, especially now.

This could all get very dirty, very fast. He could also envision this becoming a potential threat to his own career. Maybe it was time to establish a discreet distance from his boss. He would do whatever was necessary to bring her plans to fruition. But he would now build a buffer between them. Give himself room to claim plausible deniability. Make sure he wasn't privy to all the facts. That way, he could swear she kept him in the dark. It could be done, but cautiously, or she would see right through.

It was time to cover his ass and think of his own future. If her ship was going down, then he didn't want to be caught up in the swirling eddies pulling everyone else to the bottom. He would watch for the right moment to abandon the ship, which now seemed close at hand. It was time to double down and take care of Numero Uno.

GENE LAWTON STEPPED up to the podium of a hastily arranged press conference and opened the notes he drafted only moments earlier. He tapped one of the many clustered microphones before him and began his introduction.

"At approximately eight thirty-five this morning, members of an extremist group stormed into the Haven rehabilitation hospital in Bethesda Maryland and overpowered security forces. They made their way up to the third floor and abducted Jordan West, the daughter of Senator Katherine Karlson and California Governor Clifford West. Ms. West was recuperating at the facility from physical and emotional exhaustion suffered as a result of working tirelessly on her mother's presidential campaign. She was taken against her will and forced into an awaiting vehicle. As yet, we have not received any ransom demands but expect them at any time. It is difficult to ignore the suspicious nature and timing of such an egregious act. There is a strong suspicion that the perpetrators are attempting to usurp the American voting process.

"The FBI and local law enforcement are working together diligently and are making progress in identifying the group responsible for this crime. At this time, however, they cannot rule out the involvement of foreign or political elements. Further statements will be made as additional information becomes available. Right now, senator Karlson would like to make a brief statement."

Lawton stepped back as an emotionally distraught Katherine Karlson made her way to the podium.

"Someone has taken my daughter, my baby," she began. "I am asking that group of terrorists, if they are listening, to please let me talk to Jordan. This is not about politics. This is not about money. This is about the life of Jordan West, and she is not a pawn to be used for your twisted purposes. You can still release her and walk away from this before it's too late. You have my word that no one will come after you. But if you don't," Karlson paused a moment, sniffling back a sob and looking straight at the camera. "If you don't, then I will find you. Jordan, baby, if you're watching this, I want you to know… that I'm coming for you. Please," her eyes filled again, "Please let my daughter go," she begged, "Please…"

Karlson finished her short plea with an Oscar-winning breakdown, televised live around the world. Her performance would stand the test of time as one of the pinnacle moments in American politics. The tears continued to stream as she maintained her breakdown. Inwardly, she felt as though she'd just thrown the winning pass in the super bowl.

Lawton took Karlson's arm and guided her through the throngs of microphones, cameras, and bright floodlights. "We have nothing further to add at this time," he announced.

"Now please, make room and allow a mother to grieve for her missing child."

Karlson made a show of hiding her face in her hands while occasionally peering out. Each time she did, the multiple flashes of cameras captured the moment—every one of them perfect—a made-to-order closeup to accompany the front-page headlines. Absolutely heart-wrenching, absolutely soul-searing, absolutely superb, she commended herself.

They made their way to the curb, where Lawton opened the rear door to an awaiting limousine. As she climbed in, Lawton turned to face the cluster of cameras. "You can all help by giving this woman some time and some privacy. We will let you know when there is any news to report. In the meantime, please, say a prayer for Jordan."

He followed her in and pulled the door closed. The limo pulled from the curb, rolling slowly through the unrelenting throes of photographers, all hoping to catch that one in a million photo and sell it to the highest bidder.

"That was catchy, what you said back there," Karlson said, checking her makeup in a handheld mirror. "Say a prayer for Jordan. Nice touch."

Lawton flashed a grin.

She added, "You should include that every time we make a statement."

He nodded and wrote the memo in his phone notes.

"Let's stay on top of this, Gene. We need to be one step ahead of the FBI in tracking her down, now that we know what's really going on."

"Agreed. I can bring in the same private security group we used last fall. I'll call and get them up to speed with what we know. I've already brought in another company to pose as secret service agents. They questioned all of Jordan's known friends. That's how we found out about the connection between this computer hacker and the guys in the band."

"Very good," she answered, "just make sure your fake agents don't cross paths with the real cowboys. I don't want to be backtracking with questions about every little thing we're doing."

He nodded. "I'll pass that on now."

"Give me a minute before you do. There's a call I need to make right now." Karlson pulled out her phone, pressed the first name in memory, and put it to her ear. She locked eyes with Gene. He watched the transformation all over again. The tears, the pout, the grief on command. "Clifford!" she cried, "Oh Clifford, our baby's been taken!"

41

Joe and Theresa froze in the middle of preparing food and stared at the television and the breaking news bulletin. The room fell silent as Gene Lawton strode to a podium. He made a brief announcement and then introduced Senator Karlson.

Jordan's face turned an ashen hue as she walked over and stood next to the image of her tearful mother. Ethan came up behind, putting his hands on her shoulders. She took little notice.

"Jordan baby, if you're watching this, I want you to know. . . I'm coming for you."

The words landed on her like a pallet of bricks. She could see through those manufactured tears, could see mommy's mind working, hear it whirring, manipulating, right through the manufactured veil of deception. She felt pity for everyone else watching who could not. They were being sold a bill of goods that did not exist. Her mother was using this moment for all it was worth. Jordan shook her head, wondering why she had expected anything different.

She remembered this woman serving her drugged coffee, then watching the false expression of concern on her face. Jordan was rendered powerless to resist, unable to speak or even hold her head up. She recalled the conversation between Gene and her mother as she lay sprawled out on the back seat of Lawton's car. Karlson spoke of her initial reluctance to slip her own kid a mickey. She had obviously gotten over it. They discussed Jordan's fate. Karlson clung to the hope that her daughter would come around to seeing things differently sooner than later.

Gene posed the question; what if she didn't? Karlson did not respond. Jordan took her mother's silence as an answer in itself. She would be given a choice, either go along with the plan or kiss any hope of a normal existence goodbye. It was as simple as that. In this theatrical performance from hell, Jordan was the new villain. Nothing more than a hindrance, a dead weight. An immovable object blocking the path of the great Katherine Karlson, the future president.

The words rang in Jordan's head again; *I'm coming for you.* God, her mother figured it out fast. How did she know? Was this some motherly premonition that her daughter was safe and the entire kidnapping story was a ruse? Or was it possible that she was actually agonizing over locking her daughter up, believing Jordan was indeed in mortal danger? No, she knew. There was no doubt in Jordan's mind that she had received much more than a message of hope from a mother pleading for her daughter's safe return.

"That was a threat," she said, pointing at the screen. "She's coming. She knows what really happened, and she's coming."

"How could she possibly know?" Theresa asked, staring back, perplexed.

"I don't have an answer for that," Jordan said, shaking her head, "but you have to trust me on this. She knows. She was talking to all of us when she said, 'I will find you.' Murray, you said earlier that your home was raided by the Secret Service."

Murray nodded.

"The Secret Service does not participate in such activities. Were you aware of that?"

"No, but they looked pretty official to me," he said.

"Did they show any identification before they entered your home?"

"Come to think of it, they didn't even offer. They just stormed in and did an extensive search."

"My mother uses private companies for different projects. I'll bet that's who came to your place. That's how she stays ahead of the curve. She is adept at extracting information. She always knows who is plotting against her before they can ever make a move."

Jordan lowered herself into a chair with the motions of a wilting flower.

"It would have been nice to see my mother act like I mattered. Like she was truly concerned about me. Just to be a plain old mom for a few minutes. That would have meant so much to me."

Her voice trailed off, cracking. So much to think about, she thought. Solutions would come. She was sure of that. Right now, though, she was so tired. Maybe she would sleep, though she doubted it. It was worth a try anyway. She stood and put her hand on Ethan's, kissing him on the cheek. "I'm gonna lie down for a while," she said in a voice drained of all energy. A thin streak of a tear glistened on her cheek, her eyes dimmed by exhaustion. She turned and walked down the hall to Theresa's spare bedroom and pulled the door closed behind her.

The room fell silent except for the muffled voice of a news anchor recapping the senator's impassioned plea. The small group sat at the kitchen table, shocked and saddened by all they had witnessed. Karlson had skillfully manipulated the crowd with a contrived breakdown while her adoring daughter watched in pained stillness, dying a little more inside with every word. There seemed to be no end to the despicable acts of this woman. And yet, she found a way of lowering the bar even further.

"I hope Jordan's able to sleep," Theresa said, breaking their silence. "God knows she needs it."

Ethan nodded. "I've seen some cold things in my life, but nothing near what Karlson the ice queen just laid down." He paused to sip from a soda can, then pointed at Cody. "This is such a wake-up call. Everything happening here will be spun and flipped around so many times that the truth won't even be part of the story. But at the end of the day, this little group, right here, will be the only ones who know the facts. It'll be interesting to see if anyone ever bothers to ask what really happened."

"Thank you very much, Walter Cronkite," Cody ribbed his friend. "The revolution will not be televised."

"You mean the truth will not be televised," Joe added, "the spin is in."

"I wouldn't have believed this if I wasn't watching it all from the inside," Mark said.

Everyone nodded, voicing their agreement.

"Well, I don't mind telling you guys that I'm scared shitless," Ethan said. "I just hope we can make this right, and we're still around to tell the story to our grandkids."

"Not shouting it from behind bars would be preferable, I think," Cody chuckled.

Ethan attempted a smile. "That one hit home, buddy. I can almost imagine the view from the bottom bunk of a federal prison. Not pretty. It really could come down to that, you know. If the FBI walked through the door right now, everyone in this room would be charged with kidnapping. Jordan would be taken back to that hospital, filled full of drugs, and kept there until she agreed to do things mommy's way. Even then, they would keep her out of the public eye just in case she had a relapse of conscience."

Ethan shook his head, attempting to erase the images. He knew that pondering over negative scenarios would only give them life and help them come to pass. He rocked in his chair as inactivity began burning holes in him. "We should be doing something right now. Not sitting around and waiting for Karlson's next move. But what? There's so much yet to figure out. So much more to come before this is anywhere near over." He looked around the table. "But I promise all of you, I'll do whatever it takes to get Jordan to the other side of this shit storm."

"Well said, my brother," Cody said, nodding.

"Here, here," Joe added, raising his cup in a toast. Everyone acknowledged with a clank of soda cans and mugs.

"She's going to need a lot of support to get through this," Theresa added. "I can't imagine the pain and betrayal she feels right now. Poor kid's world was run over by a truck."

"More like a steam roller!" Cody exclaimed. "Tell you what, if this girl had nine lives, she went through three of them tonight. I feel like an idiot because I bought into all of her mother's lies. I would have voted for Karlson!"

"Don't beat yourself up too hard," Murray consoled. "The woman is a great actress, and that's exactly what we saw tonight." He looked to the rest of the group and said, "I agree with Cody. I really thought she was bringing something new to the table for this country. I believed in her, and most of the people watching her did, too."

Mark nodded and said, "Sort of makes you wonder if any of these politicians tell the truth. Or do they say whatever will keep them in a job?"

Ethan listened, his eyes absently tracing the wood grain of the table. "It means those types of people are always out there," he said. "Working only for themselves, but insisting that everything they do is all for us. We can't allow ourselves to keep getting fooled over and over."

"I'm disappointed we're so gullible," Theresa said. "It feels like we're all a bunch of kids playing with matches, wondering why our fingers keep getting burned."

"It's because we want to believe them," Ethan added. "We want all of those promises to be true. They're not. I think the moral of this story is to think for yourself. Use your head, develop a good bullshit detector. Oh, and only trust people who have proven themselves worthy of trust."

"Well, that eliminates better than half of them, doesn't it," Cody chuckled. "I think that I..." He stopped mid-sentence and stared. Jordan had quietly returned and now stood listening to their conversation.

"Oh honey, you should be trying to get some rest," Theresa said, getting up and walking over.

Jordan looked as though the last ten minutes of lying down only served to energize her. "I need to speak to my dad." Her voice was forceful yet calm. "Now, please."

Murray stood, ready to discourage her from making the call. Doing so could reveal her actual situation and location. Just as quickly, he realized it would be futile. The look in her eyes said she would not be talked out of this request. It wasn't even a request, he thought. It was a politely stated demand, and he could not argue the point. Jordan West was the victim. Arranging to speak with her father seemed the very least he could do. Logic, however, still dictated a cautious, methodical approach. Murray began constructing and then explaining a plan of action to accomplish the task.

Jordan listened intently until he finished speaking, then nodded. “Thank you,” she said.

42

Senator Karlson sat at her desk basking in the warm glow of a bright new morning. The non-stop ringing of the phone played like a symphony of her success. She fielded call after call from television news, talk radio, and tabloid shows. Each of them requested, make that begged, to be selected to host her next interview.

The latest spike in ratings was rocketing her lead into double digits. It was expected to continue growing through election day. The media now believed the incumbent president could be beaten and wanted to share in the jubilation and march in the parade. Karlson was only too willing to oblige. She ended a call, took a satisfying sip of tea, and penciled in her next appearance in one of the few remaining open spots of the calendar.

No sooner had she set her cup down than the secretary buzzed to announce the next caller waiting patiently on one of the many flashing phone lines. What an appropriate change in attitude, she mused.

The days of struggling for a few precious seconds of air time were a thing of the past. Talk show hosts were not leaving it to their secretaries to book a few golden moments with the new maverick candidate. Instead, they were sending the show producers, or in some cases, making the calls themselves. Karlson savored the irony by making them wait, even when she could have taken the call right away. Prominent media celebrities sat parked on hold as she poured hot water over a fresh tea bag, took notes, or gazed out the window at the city that now bowed at her feet.

This was the reception she expected from the beginning. All of Washington, DC, was finally realizing she was not just a brilliant and beautiful political powerhouse. She was a hidden jewel unearthed at precisely the perfect time to carry a weary nation onto its greatest glory. Her country needed her more desperately than it would ever acknowledge. And she had the vision, the intellect, and the ovaries to succeed where every POTUS before her failed.

Karlson expected backlash over some of the policies she would champion. There would be disagreement across the aisle, even dissension within her party. It didn't matter. She had the momentum and the ability to institute these visions into what she called her 'New Olympus.'

An unexpected caveat to her heartbreaking story was that it now graced the front page of every paper and internet posting worldwide. Getting her message to the people was not costing a cent.

Karlson pursed her lips, restraining a grin as she remembered the words of a cunning presidential advisor who once said, 'never let a crisis go to waste.'

The moment was no longer lost on unnecessary emotions over her daughter's fate. She now assumed that Jordan was safe, even complicit in her own escape. If the kid was smart, like Karlson knew she was, she would do her best to maintain a low profile. Jordan would not want to be found any more than Karlson wanted her dancing in the spotlight. Keeping silent about the details of her hospitalization and dramatic rescue was the smartest thing her kid could do.

Jordan's friends dug themselves into a bottomless pit with their noble but stupid actions. No one would take the word of a bunch of zero credibility nobodies over a grieving mother. Even better, the story they told was beyond belief.' Yes, we kidnapped the senator's daughter, but…' But nothing! Guilty as charged.

That can of worms would only be opened if they were arrested by the local authorities. This was not in Karlson's best interest. Eliminating the nuisances altogether was much more preferable.

That's where Karlson's private security firm came in. They monitored police radio frequencies. Once Jordan was spotted, they would sweep in before law enforcement could arrive. The former military mercenaries were disciplined, tough, well-compensated, and therefore very dedicated to their employer. Karlson even had a mole within the FBI, keeping her apprised of every new lead. It cost a small fortune to deal with the situation in this way. But she could ill afford to be distracted from the more important job of running the campaign.

In the end, Jordan would be the only one remaining who could corroborate the details of this debacle. Karlson had already set a plan in motion to assure her silence. With all the bases covered, she was free to return to the most crucial task at hand; taking the oval office.

43

The next afternoon, Ethan and Jordan drove toward the destination chosen by Murray. He had studied cell tower maps and determined the optimum location to call Jordan's father. Murray agreed to make the phone call happen as soon as possible but persuaded Jordan to be patient. He needed time to arrange the details. If she were caught now, everything they had gone through would be in vain. They needed to develop a plan and carry it out as though it were a military exercise. As anxious as she was to just dial the damned phone and call her father, Jordan acknowledged that Murray was right. She stepped back and waited for him to organize the specifics of their next steps. It seemed like a lot to go through. But the more she listened to his plan, the more she agreed and trusted in him. He was actually turning out to be very good at this. She was also glad that he talked her into getting some rest before they set off to make the call. She was exhausted, and once the plan had begun taking shape, she was able to doze right off.

Theresa did a brilliant job of transforming the two of them into likenesses of herself and Joe. Nothing thus far could link either of them to the breakout, so their identities were borrowed for the task. Today, Jordan had a new face with a new name. She now carried Theresa's purse and identity. She was a redhead and made up so that her eyes appeared large and alluring. Her nose looked thinned, and her cheekbones were more prominent. The result was stunning, and Jordan, already an attractive young woman, couldn't believe the transformation. The skin tones and eye colors had the effect of masking Jordan's lighter, softer features. It would take a trained eye to see through the facial camouflage. But that was not all it accomplished. When you caught a glimpse of this woman now, your mind wouldn't be on anything except her dazzling beauty.

Ethan carried Joe's entire wallet, including driver's license, credit cards, and car registration. He could have passed for Joe's identical twin, right down to shorter, lighter hairstyle and goatee.

The short trip from McLean, Virginia, to Gainesville took a little over thirty minutes. They pulled into the parking lot of the Grafton Street Pub at 1:40 pm.

Ethan handed his burner phone to Jordan. "Remember, keep it under three minutes," he reminded her. "And here's the list of points you need to cover. Are you ready?"

Jordan took the phone and the list, then leaned in and kissed him. "Yes, I'm ready," she said, pulling away slowly. "And if I haven't said it before, thank you. Words cannot express my gratitude. And I want you to know something else."

"Okay," he smiled, "what's that?"

"This is the weirdest second date I've ever been on." She winked and tapped in her father's cell number. She listened as the phone rang three times before he picked up.

"Yes?" The voice on the other end sounded annoyed with

the call. This was the governor's personal cell phone, and very few people had the number. Clifford West was in no mood to be gracious or hospitable to an unknown caller ringing in. Especially now that his daughter had been kidnapped.

"It's me!" Jordan managed to say, struggling to hold back a flood of tears. "Please don't say my name in case they have word recognition software running on this line."

Shock, elation, and alarm jolted Clifford West upright in his seat. It was his daughter's voice, without a doubt. But it came in on an unknown number, with the most baffling words he could imagine. A thousand questions flooded in at once. He found himself overwhelmed and unable to respond. Finally, the initial impact subsided. "Is it. . .is it really you? Where are you?" His voice sounded high pitched and cracking, betraying his otherwise stoic demeanor. His throat was suddenly so dry that he struggled to speak. He caught himself before doing exactly what she had instructed him against. He glanced up at the limo driver, then over to his assistant to see if either were paying attention to his conversation. He held the phone closer and whispered, "Are you all right? Where are they holding you? Can you talk?"

"Daddy, I'm fine," Jordan sniffled. "I wasn't kidnapped. I'm with friends—"

"What sort of friends force you from a hospital against your will?" he said, agitated. "Tell me where you are. I'll come and get you. I just arrived in DC."

"Daddy, please listen to me. I was drugged and held against my will at that hospital."

"What…what are you saying?"

"I'm saying this isn't what it seems. My friends came and rescued me from that place. They're helping me now."

"If these are real friends, then tell them to bring you to me now. Right now."

"It's not that simple."

"What do you mean, it's not that simple? Of course, it is. All you have to do is—"

"Dad, stop! Please trust me on this. I will explain everything very soon. For now, just know that I need your help. My friends are not the bad guys."

"This makes no sense at all."

"It will. I need you to write something down for me."

"Wait," He said, grabbing his notepad and pen from a valise. "All set, go ahead."

"Buy a disposable phone. Please be sure no one else knows the number, so the line can't be traced. I'm going to text you a coded number. The code will contain my own cell number mixed in the string. You need to remove my number and read the remaining digits from back to front. At 4:00 pm I want you to dial that number from the new phone. Did you get all that?"

"Yes, I understand, but," He caught himself again before saying her name. "If you are truly safe, then why are we doing this?"

Jordan paused before answering. She knew how difficult this was to comprehend and hoped her father would indulge her long enough to explain what was really happening. "Because I'm not safe yet. Call at 4:00. I'll tell you everything you need to know."

Jordan hit the end button on her phone, looked at the time display, and held it up for Ethan to see. "Two minutes, forty-seconds," she said.

"Very good! Have you done this before?"

"No, smartass, and I promise to never do it again after we

get through this." She gave him a sly grin and pulled the battery out of the phone. "Okay, next stop, sir?"

Ethan threw Joe's Chrysler into gear and pulled back onto the road. The plan was to be twenty miles away from here when she sent the code. They would destroy the phone and power up another burner to be ready to receive the incoming call. Ethan drove north on I-485 until he had traveled the distance worked out by Murray. He looked over to Jordan and said, "Go ahead with the code."

She reloaded the battery pack, powered up and texted the code to her father, then powered down again. Ethan veered into a rest area, where Jordan yanked out the Sim card and battery, then dropped all the parts into a trash barrel.

"One more stop," he said, taking the first exit and looping back onto the freeway in the opposite direction. "Are you ready for this?"

"Ethan, I have been dying to tell my dad what was really happening ever since all of this started. He's got to be worried sick and thinking the worst. I don't know how he will handle it once he knows what my mother did. It's going to hurt him so bad. I do know," she paused a moment, remembering the words and deeds of a good father, "I do know that I can trust him, no matter what. He's always been there for me. Even as governor, he's always tried to do the right thing and stay above the muck."

Ethan laughed. "Sometimes you know you did the right thing when you've pissed off both sides."

They rolled on, momentarily oblivious to the storm that swirled around them, enjoying a brief but fleeting taste of normalcy. Ethan glanced away from the road, and their eyes met. His hand reached out and found hers and their fingers wove together. A thousand words passed between them, with none needing to be spoken. They held tight until an internal alarm went off in both of them at the same time. Jordan looked at the dashboard clock. 3:56 pm. They would arrive at their destination a few minutes before the next call was due to come in. She reached in her purse and pulled out the new phone, and powered it up.

Ethan spotted the sign for the rest area and breathed a sigh of relief. He wanted to be off the road and stationary when Jordan spoke to her father. With seconds to spare, they pulled into a spot at the back of the rest area. Both got out and walked up a path that led to a cluster of picnic tables, then crested a hill and into a meadow-like clearing.

The signal strength read one bar on the phone. Murray had spent an hour looking over the maps of cell tower locations before picking this spot for their conversation. It was nearly a dead zone. Even if someone attempted to trace the origin of this call, it would take longer than usual. The results would be vague at best, with no way to pinpoint Jordan's phone location down to less than a half-mile. Anyone pursuing them would likely approach from one of the rural roads they now looked down upon from their vantage point. They would see the other guys long before being observed themselves. This offered a few precious minutes to make their escape, though neither believed it would be necessary. Jordan trusted her father, and Ethan trusted Jordan.

At 4:01 pm, the phone chirped in her hand. Jordan flinched and looked to Ethan, who nodded his approval. She held it to her ear and said, "Operator."

"Oh, thank God," she heard her father's voice exhaling with relief. Her eyes welled. Even under the duress of their plight, his familiar tone gave a reassurance that warmed and revitalized her.

Clifford West served the public for most of Jordan's childhood, but she always felt like the most important person in his life. He was there for all the big moments and events. Ever the proud daddy with a video camera at school plays and talent shows. No matter how small the part, Jordan West was the star in her father's eyes. He was always there to help pick up the pieces when she stumbled, and she needed him now more than ever. If she couldn't trust this man, then nothing else in life mattered. Jordan glanced back to Ethan, who seemed to sense all she was feeling, and nodded. They were going to be okay.

"Yes, daddy, it's me. I'm so sorry for the secrecy and for making you worry. It's been… It's been the worst time of my life."

The governor took a moment and composed himself. "Are you all right?"

"Yes, I'm fine. I'm with a group of people that rescued me. Daddy, they risked everything and arranged for me to call you."

West was immediately suspicious, as he should have been. None of this made sense. Maybe his daughter was actually under duress. "Tell me where you are. Tell me, and I'll come to you. Let's bring an end to all of this right now."

"Like I said, it's not that simple."

"Are they listening? Do you have to choose your words? Do they have ransom demands?"

"No, I told you, they're not a threat to me."

"Then who is? Come on, Jordan, cut to the chase and tell me—"

"It was mom."

There was a long silence. "Come again?"

"The security leak that exposed the military mission to track Abu Dahl in the Middle East… it was mom. I saw the video from her office. She planted that information for Al Jazeera to find during her interview with them. She wanted the mission to fail, needed it to fail. She said she could lose the election if it succeeded, and we caught Sirhan Abbas. I confronted her about it, and she said she would explain later. Daddy, she drugged my drink! The next thing I knew, I was in that cell. That tiny little…" She caught herself before going too far off message. "I don't know how they did it, but my friends got me out. They're hiding me until we can figure out a plan to set this right. Mother has people looking for me. That's who I'm hiding from. If I'm caught, they'll lock me up again!"

"Your…your mother did this?" West stammered, unprepared for such devastating news. It wasn't possible, was it? How could anyone turn on their own daughter, allowing political aspirations to eclipse their love of family? West never could. And he could not fathom his own wife sinking so low so fast. He cursed himself for ignoring the signs and encouraging her when she had first shown interest.

West grounded his own calling into public life with a strong sense of morality and ethics. He recalled those early days of Katherine's rapid political ascent. It suddenly struck him that those critical virtues were missing even back then.

Katherine was always interested in hearing about his day in government at the dinner table. It was much more than simple interest, he now admitted. Her inquisitiveness danced on the edge of hunger. Still, he viewed her as selfless and warm-hearted, willing to give up a life of glamour to be a wife and mother. But he also recalled the cunning, methodical, and driven person who slowly took the place of the one he loved. He watched the progression, starting with that first conversation about running for office, any office.

"With what I've learned from you, Cliff, I could be a damn good stateswoman."

That was the start of her unprecedented ascent into politics. It also marked the beginning of the end. West saw the cracks in their relationship long ago and subconsciously ignored them. He'd clung instead to the memories of a life that brought such happiness. His mind replayed images of a woman pulling away bit by bit, leaving her small family to flounder in her wake and her absence. Regardless, these were terrible accusations against the woman he still chose to love. Denial, he admitted, was a natural defense mechanism.

"Are you absolutely sure of your facts?" he asked, hoping for a different response. When Jordan answered in the affirmative, he did not question her again.

"I want you to talk to someone who will explain what's happening," Jordan told him, "and what we're trying to do. I trust him, and you should too." Jordan handed the phone to Ethan.

"Governor West, my name is Ethan Ludwig."

"Mr. Ludwig, how about you bring my daughter to me now and stop this cloak and dagger bullshit right here!"

"Sir, it is my intention to bring Jordan to you myself. But I need to explain the situation we're in. And I need to ask for your help."

"Answer me a few questions first, if you don't mind. How did you come to know my daughter?"

Ethan smiled at Jordan as he recalled their first meeting. "I was talking with some friends at a coffee shop. She interjected herself into the conversation."

"Go on," West prodded.

"She made excellent points, and It's hard to argue with facts and logic. I'm sure you know that your daughter has a lot of both."

West was adept at sizing up a man's character from a brief conversation. What he was hearing came as a great relief. Jordan approached him, not the other way around. It was less likely that she had been stalked and tricked. Still, it was possible their first meeting was orchestrated by a skilled manipulator. West pressed on.

"May I ask your political persuasion?"

What a confusing question. "Governor, why would that matter right now?"

"Humor me, son," he replied.

Ethan thought before answering. "Okay, but I don't think you'll find this very humorous. As a rule, I vote for the other side."

Interesting, West thought. A good bullshit artist would have jumped on the opportunity to butter him up about being of like minds. This guy didn't take the bait.

"I see," he answered. "And how is it you still find middle ground with Jordan?"

Ethan looked to Jordan again and smiled. "Because your daughter thinks with her mind and her heart. I happen to believe you need both to make good decisions."

A little sappy, West thought. But this was definitely not someone in the business of lying. He'd seen many of them in action and knew the tells that could give away the best of them. He was now confident Ethan was truthful. So far, at least. Their story still sounded incredibly far-fetched, but now he had a reason to trust the man.

"Proceed, Mr. Ludwig. You have my undivided attention."

"Thank you, sir. Now what we have in mind is…"

Jordan noticed a swirling cloud of dust out of the corner of her eye. She looked down the hill as two police cars traveled fast in their direction. She spied a third approaching from the other road. She grabbed the phone from Ethan. "Daddy, did you buy that phone yourself, or did someone buy it for you?"

"I sent Riley Comstock to pick it up for me. You know she's worked in my office for quite a while. Why?"

"She may have given that number to someone, and the police are coming. We have to go. Where are you staying in DC?"

"Your favorite, I'll be in room 825."

"I'll be in touch." She ended the call and pulled the battery from the phone.

Ethan kept watching the progress of the police cruisers. "Walk with me nice and slow toward those trees," he said, putting his arm around her. From any vantage point, they looked like two love-struck travelers taking a break from driving. Once the thicket of branches concealed them from the roads below, he pulled her into a run.

"Cross your fingers that they're not looking for us on the freeway yet," he said.

Jordan snuck a glance back. The speeding police cars were now a few hundred yards from the cross street that lay at the bottom of the hill. From there, the road stopped at a T-intersection with no access road leading up to their location.

Murray's plan was working exactly as he said it would, but they shouldn't have needed the plan at all. Her father's assistant had compromised this meeting. It came as little surprise that it would be Riley Comstock. She was one of the governor's two aides. Jordan long suspected that Ms. Comstock secretly held aspirations of serving on her mother's presidential staff. She must have seen this as a way to curry favor and passed the phone info onto Karlson, who then traced the call. Jordan didn't worry as much about the contents of their conversation. Listening in would have been nearly impossible, even for her well-connected mother. But obtaining triangulation data with the company's cell towers could be done simply enough by slipping the right person the right bribe.

As they crested the hill, Ethan glanced over his shoulder and noticed the police cars split up at the divide. One now headed north, another west, while the third officer stopped and got out. Ethan watched as he surveyed the landscape, then fixed his gaze on their location up the hill.

"I think that cop just figured this out," he said. "Things are about to get hot. Come on, move faster."

Once back over the hill and out of the cop's sight, the pair darted for the car. Ethan slid in and turned the key, eased out of the lot, and merged into southbound traffic. He traveled to the first exit, looped around, then headed back north. After a few miles, he looked to Jordan and breathed a sigh of relief. "No cops yet. We might be all right..." He stopped mid-sentence as two state police cruisers shot past over on the southbound side.

He thought the change in direction had given them the slip when a third cruiser came up fast from behind with no lights or siren. Ethan maintained his speed as it approached in the left lane. The cruiser neared and dropped its pace to match his. This was not a good sign. A stone-faced trooper in the passenger seat gave Ethan a thorough once over. Ethan returned the look with a courteous nod. The cruiser continued to match their speed.

"God, please don't pull us over," Jordan whispered under her breath.

Ethan could tell she was frozen with fear as she stared forward. If they were caught now, they would have to act the parts of their false identities. He doubted she could pull that off.

A single thought came to mind, and he said, "Turn on the radio and crank it."

She gave him a questioning look but followed his instruction. The radio was already tuned to a good rock station, and she turned it louder. Ethan began nodding his head to the beat. Jordan followed suit with a bit more flair. A grin crept across her face as her rigid muscles began relaxing. Now they looked like two people who couldn't care less about being scrutinized by a pair of Maryland troopers.

It didn't work.

The cruiser slowed, and its red and blue lights began strobing brightly as it dropped back. The radio continued blaring out a driving rock anthem, but their hearts pounded louder than the rumbling bass. A lifetime passed in a matter of seconds. Ethan wondered how well he and Jordan could act out a scenario they hadn't talked much about. He glanced back in the mirror. The cruiser had tucked in tight on his tail. He signaled and let off the accelerator, pulling to the shoulder. It was going to take a miracle to fight through their fear and stay on script.

That's what they got.

The cruiser abruptly shot to the left shoulder and wheeled into an emergency turnaround. It fishtailed as it turned and accelerated, tires smoking as it zoomed off in the opposite direction.

Ethan watched as his heart pulsated in his throat. He finally forced himself to take a breath. *It didn't get much closer than that.*

The momentary relief vanished as he realized the cruiser was headed to the rest area where they just made their phone call.

No words were exchanged as Ethan pulled back onto the freeway. He took the next exit and traveled east. He made a turn, then another, driving a circuitous route back to Joe and Theresa's house. The tension was all-consuming. He maintained the speed limit, passing two more police cars parked on the shoulder along the way. Each time he went by one, he would add a few additional loops to his route, ensuring he was not followed. He glanced over and noticed Jordan's pallor and fearful expression. Poor kid, he thought as he reached over and took her hand. She barely acknowledged his touch, staring forward at nothing, her thoughts miles beyond.

They drove the rest of the way in silence. Ethan finally pulled the car up the long, tree obscured drive and into the pole barn. He killed the engine and sat for a moment, decompressing.

Jordan squeezed his hand and locked eyes with fixed determination. "We end this," she said. "We end this now."

44

Katherine Karlson and Gene Lawton sat across from each other on the twin leather sofas in her office. Seated between them in the tall armchair usually reserved for Karlson was Riley Comstock, assistant to Governor West. Her manner and expression exuded confidence.

Comstock knew early on that her position with Governor West would not carry her career to the heights she aspired. For that, she needed to aligned herself with Karlson. West was content to remain as governor for at least another term, and a presidential bid would never be in the cards. And although Comstock admired his conviction, Senator Karlson was her ticket forward. 'Presidential Advisor' had such a distinctive ring. It sure beat the hell out of 'Governor's Assistant.'

Comstock kept the senator updated on all incoming news concerning Jordan. She also watched for any activity that seemed out of the ordinary. Being asked by the governor to buy a disposable phone seemed like an odd request. She passed the information on to Lawton in case it turned out to be valuable. It was.

She smiled as she eyed Karlson, envisioning the fires that burned beneath the surface. This was a driven woman who would stop at nothing short of her goal. Both of them shared that trait. The young assistant could sense the energy emanating from this meeting. The same auras of dynamism must have existed when the most influential world leaders assembled together. How the air must have crackled with electricity when Franklin Roosevelt, Winston Churchill, and Joseph Stalin met in the same room. That's what Comstock felt right now; a plasmid field of energy connecting them. She was confident the senator could feel it too.

She wondered if Gene Lawton was even remotely aware of the sparks that flew between her and Karlson just beyond the visual horizon. Or was it something that could only be perceived by those who possessed such power? It was a question she pondered throughout her young life; did anyone comprehend who the hell she was, or more importantly, who she would become?

Senator Karlson offered a pained smile. "I wanted to personally thank you for contacting me, Riley. These last few days have been the worst of my life. Any information on my daughter's whereabouts," she paused for effect, "is greatly appreciated. Please, tell us everything you've heard."

Comstock returned the gesture with an expression of rehearsed sympathy. "Senator Karlson, I can only imagine the pain you must be going through. If there is anything I can do to help bring Jordan home safely, you can count on me."

She paused, waiting for a reaction from Karlson. When none came, she continued. "Governor West received a call shortly after we landed in DC. He didn't offer details of the conversation, but I could hear the concern in his voice. He instructed me to pick up a disposable phone and bring it to the hotel—an odd request. My first thought was the governor was being contacted by the kidnappers. So I jotted down the number from the package and immediately called you. Did it prove useful?" she asked, knowing the answer.

True to form, Karlson thought, very predictable. She wondered what would her husband think if he knew this beautiful Judas was offering knowledge of his private calls in exchange for a spot on her campaign team? She, on the other hand, knew Riley's type and expected nothing less.

Karlson began sizing up Riley Comstock the day she was hired as an intern on her husband's staff. There was a hunger, an unbridled determination in the articulate young woman. Karlson knew of dozens just like her. The type that would stop at nothing for a taste of success. Rather than treat her like an enemy combatant, however, she accepted Comstock as a known commodity. A dazzling mare who would steal the Queen's jewels if given the opportunity. Nonetheless, she was a valuable asset within her husband's inner circle. Karlson vowed to use that unbounded energy to her advantage.

She entertained the thought of her husband taking advantage of the striking young blonde. There wasn't a doubt in her mind that Comstock would oblige only too willingly if she believed it expedient to her career. It didn't matter. Even if she moved in for the kill, Governor West would never reciprocate. He operated on a higher ethic level, a quality that endeared him to Karlson when they first met. Now she wondered if that was a stoic character strength or a personality flaw. Some men weren't wired to deal with the guilt and possible backlash of maintaining an extramarital affair. She wondered if her husband stayed true to her merely because it would demand so much effort to lead a double life. In any case, men with a strong sense of conscience were more predictable. And controlled. Definitely not an attribute in politics, she thought. In this business, even morals could be an exploited weakness.

"Yes, I believe it will prove useful, and we'll know soon enough," Karlson said. "For now, rest assured that you did the right thing. The FBI was adamant in their instructions concerning future communications with the kidnappers. I'm sure my husband would have passed this information on eventually. He likely failed to realize how time-sensitive it could have been. We will be discussing this tonight." Karlson reached over and put a hand on Comstock's black stockinged knee. "Thank you again, and please contact us with anything you see that might help us in locating Jordan." Her throat tightened around the words, driving home the performance of a mother's pained plea to find her child.

Karlson rose, signaling the meeting was over. "Oh, by the way, might you happen to know the governor's schedule for the next few days?"

"Yes, of course," Comstock answered crisply as she stood and straightened her gray pencil skirt. "I can email that over if you like."

"That would be very helpful, thank you."

Karlson ushered Comstock to the door and closed it behind her, then turned to Lawton.

"What did you learn about the line trace?"

"At least eight police cars converged on the cell signal and found nothing. An analyst from the phone company said they were in an area not well covered by towers. That can greatly decrease the accuracy of triangulation. But now we know Jordan is communicating with her father. That adds another major obstacle to your success."

"You mean our success, don't you, Gene?" Karlson tested him. She needed his complete devotion and undivided attention for at least a little longer. There was too much riding on his involvement to even think of changing horses anytime soon.

"Of course, Kat," he answered, not showing the least bit of wavering. "I had the team trace the license plates of the vehicle used in the hospital escape. They were expired, registered to a car in a junkyard. We have people staking out some of Jordan's hangouts and her friend's houses. If she shows up, we'll get her. Oh, and everything is on track for your speech Friday night. The caterers and all of the special arrangements are locked in."

She nodded, sauntering up to him, getting close enough that her lips touched his. "Well, then," she cooed softly, "it sounds like we have the situation covered for the time being, doesn't it?" She slid her hand down the front of his slacks and held it there, feeling his excitement build and pulsate. She nibbled at his lower lip while undoing his belt. "Maybe it's time we took care of a little business of our own..."

45

"I was sweating bullets when that trooper checked us out," Jordan told the anxious and worried group upon their return. "I thought it was all over."

"Same here," added Ethan, relaxing into a chair and accepting a tall cool one. "I still don't get why they would have even looked twice at us. We were going in the opposite direction, and our disguises were pretty damn good."

"They wouldn't have been looking at all if my dad's assistant hadn't ratted us out," Jordan added. "She nearly got us caught."

"Then consider yourselves lucky," said Joe. "Picking that location to make the call may have been the only thing that saved you."

Mark nodded. "Could have been the descriptions they were given were so vague that they didn't know exactly who they were looking for."

"Very possible," Murray agreed, as he ended a phone call and rejoined the group. "The only two faces they know for sure are Jordan's and Mark's. They must have pulled the personnel records at the Haven by now and come up with a name to go with Mark's face from the security video. They won't be getting to Ethan anytime soon since he went in under an assumed name and disguise. Anyway, this was all anticipated, and Mark stays here until we get through the rest of this." He turned to Mark and added, "We have plenty for you to do while we figure out our next moves. We'll keep your car in Joe's garage, and you can be the central coordinator on all of our movements via phone."

Mark gave a thumb's up. "Whatever you need me to do."

Murray turned to Jordan. "Were you able to find out where your father will be staying?"

Jordan remembered the last thing her father said in their brief conversation. It made her smile. "He's staying at my favorite hotel, the Watergate, room 825."

"There's a little bit of twisted history in that one, don't you think?" Murray asked, grinning.

"Yup, there is," she said. "I always had a curiosity about the place because of the Nixon wiretapping that went down there. So my dad took me for a tour shortly before it closed. I fell in love with the place. There's something about it that makes it so unique. Then once they rebuilt, it became my father's favorite, too. The decor now is so opulent, done in modern art deco. Whenever he's in DC, that's where he'll stay."

Murray stepped around the table and said, "I think we all understand how hard this has been for Jordan and everything that's at stake here." He gently squeezed her shoulders. "I have to believe the last thing you want on your conscience is knowing you were the one who took this election away from your mother. That you personally destroyed her chance to be president."

"Slippery slope, Murray," she said, nodding, then paused, searching for the right words. "I wish…"

"What?"

"I wish that…she could do it to herself. That she would get so tangled in her own lies that she would trip and fall for everyone to see. So that at the end of the day, she would have to admit this was all her own fault. Then maybe there would come a time when she would forgive me for my part in this."

Murray smiled warmly. "Well said, and I'm sure we all agree. This burden should never have been yours to carry."

She turned to him silently, their eyes meeting, and he saw a kid pleading for help. At that moment, he wanted nothing more than to offer precisely that. He scratched his chin as he walked around the table. Trying to attack the problem logically, methodically, like formulating a new mathematical equation. "There has to be a way to get her to bring this all down on herself," he thought aloud. "Think about this, you guys. All we have to do is find a way to use her own words against her. The rest should take care of itself."

"Yes," Jordan answered, "I don't know how you would pull something like that off, but yes. That's how I would like to see this end."

Murray nodded, looking around at the determined faces assembled before him. "Any one of us could have the solution floating around up there in their head right now. Maybe you have an idea you think is so far-fetched that it would never work. And you're probably right." He leaned in and whispered, "But what if?" He grinned and pointed at each of them. "What if your crazy idea was just what we needed to end this nightmare once and for all? Come on, guys, let's hear it. Give me anything you got."

Theresa spoke up. "What if we could get Jordan out of the country? Get her across the border to Canada?"

"Yeah, yeah," Murray nodded, "but that would only address half the issue, right? She would be safe, but none of us would."

"Well, I'm trying," Theresa said defensively.

"And it was a good thought," Joe assured her. "You've shown how difficult the solution will be. We have to ensure Jordan's safety, but we also have to stop her mother from tracking the rest of us down."

"That is exactly right!" Murray added. "How do we get Katherine Karlson to knock down her own house of cards while keeping Jordan and the rest of us safe?"

"What if I turned myself in to the FBI?"

The group went silent and stared at Jordan.

"No," Ethan said, shaking his head, "there's no guarantee that you or the rest of us would be safe."

"Now hold on, buddy," Cody said. "She's got something there. If we could plead our case to the FBI, they might protect us all from the senator."

Mark spoke up. "It would be our word against hers, a bunch of nobodies against a presidential candidate. Who do you think they would believe?"

Joe drummed his fingers on the table with eyes closed. "It's actually a good piece of a plan," he finally said, "but it only accomplishes half of what we're after." He looked to Jordan. "We have to make sure your mom admits what she's done. Otherwise, all of this has been for nothing."

"We can help her a little with that," Murray said.

"What do you mean?" Theresa asked, leaning in closer.

"We still have the video from the Al Jazeera interview. That's practically a signed confession. All we have to do to take it the rest of the way would be—" His expression darkened, and he turned away.

"Wait, what's the rest of it?" Jordan prodded, "Finish your thought."

Murray stared off a moment, then turned to Jordan. "You would have to let your mother retake you."

46

"Are you out of your fucking mind?" Ethan nearly screamed at Murray. "Do not discount what that place did to her or what it took to get her out."

"Calm down, Ethan. We got her out together, remember?"

"No, you sat comfortably at your computer while Mark, Jordan, and I ran for our lives with everybody and his brother in hot pursuit." Ethan shook his head, lips pursed, jaw muscles locked. "No, man, a thousand times no. You can't expect her to go through that again!"

Jordan put her hand on Ethan's. He looked into her eyes and took the hint. "Sorry, Murray," he said, backing down. "I didn't mean to discount your part in all of this."

Murray nodded. "It's all good. Everyone here is feeling the strain."

Theresa would have none of it. "For God's sake, no! You can't ask her to do this. It is dangerous and foolhardy. Murray, please, there has to be a better way."

Jordan listened as Theresa argued on her behalf, grateful for their effort yet terrified of what Murray was asking. Her legs tingled with an overwhelming urge to run. Run anywhere. This was the worst thing he could have possibly asked of her. She was free now only because of the selfless efforts of everyone at this table. Other than that, nothing had changed. Her fate was sealed the moment she was back in her mother's grip. Her only salvation would be to plead forgiveness, repent, then fall in lockstep behind her. There was no other alternative, was there? She couldn't keep running. And cowering in the shadows would be nearly as confining as being locked away again. A life spent living in fear was its own prison. She held out hope that someone would offer a better solution.

Still, Murray's suggestion rattled around in her mind, producing more questions than answers.

"Why?" she asked him. "Why would I give my mother the chance to lock me away forever?"

"Because she is hosting her biggest fundraiser next Friday, right here in town. The eyes of the world will be upon her. There will never be a better place and time to expose what she has done."

"And how do we keep Jordan safe?" Theresa demanded. "How do we stop her mother from repeating this entire nightmare?"

Murray nodded. "That's where we use Jordan's idea. She turns herself in. To her father, actually. This won't work without him. And forgive my asking, Jordan, but do you trust him to come to your aid, even if it means destroying your mother?"

"I would bet my life on it, on him," she answered.

"In effect, you will be."

Jordan looked to Murray. "There are few absolutes in life, but he is one of them. I know my father. I know his heart. He would protect me to his last breath."

"Good," he said, "that's what I expected, but I wanted to

hear you say it. Governor West will be the one who keeps your mother from taking you. He will be the cavalry. Does that give you enough confidence to go forward?"

"Yes," she answered without hesitating. She reached out and took Ethan's hand in her left, Theresa's in her right. "Yes," she said even more firmly. "Tell me what we need to do."

"Okay," Murray said, flashing a grin, "this is what I'm thinking. We start by arranging a meeting between you and your father. He needs to see you, to know you are safe. To do that, our first task will be to establish communication with the governor without leaving a trail. That means no phone calls. We need a creative solution to getting him a message. Any ideas?"

"Package delivery?" Joe suggested.

"No," Jordan said, "he would never open an unsolicited box. Too many wackos out there."

"That makes sense," Cody chimed in. "But would he open a pizza?"

Jordan mulled it over, then grinned. "Yeah, I think he would if he knew who sent it."

Murray clapped his hands together. "Excellent idea, you guys! Jordan, I'm assuming he likes pizza?"

Jordan remembered a simpler time that seemed like a thousand years ago. Her father helping with late-night homework, laughing together while munching pizza. The memory brought a broad smile. Maybe Murray's optimism was contagious. "Yes, he does. Pepperoni, green olives, and onions," she answered.

"Let's start there," he said. "Cody, the idea was yours, so you can be our delivery man. Theresa, can you create a disguise for Jordan so we can get her in and out without being noticed?"

Theresa nodded. "Come on, Jordan, let's go try on some wigs."

THE NEXT TWO days were like riding out a Texas twister, except that everyone in Joe's house flew about in a ballet of coordinated mayhem. Murray had laid out a plan for the events to come, and the group performed flawlessly under his direction.

'Cody, check-in please,' Mark texted on his phone. A moment later, he received the response, 'walking in now.'

Cody entered the Watergate hotel's front door like he owned the place, carrying a stack of pizza boxes. No one interfered. No one questioned him as he headed for the elevators and the eighth floor. He turned to the right as he exited the elevator, found the suite number, and knocked briskly. A moment later, a voice behind the door responded.

"Who is it?"

"Checkers pizza."

West cracked open the door and eyed the tall, long-haired delivery man in a red and black checked hat. "I didn't order any pizza," he said, annoyed, and pushed the door shut.

"Deep dish pepperoni, green olives, onions, the bill says JW to CW."

West flung the door open and stared at the man.

"I would try the second pie, sir. It's probably the warmest," Cody said. He passed the stack of boxes with a wink, then turned and walked back toward the elevators.

Governor West accepted the offering and glanced down both ends of the hallway, then stepped back into the room, still unsure of what was going on. He set the boxes on a table and stared down, wondering how to proceed. 'JW to CW.'

Okay, he thought, it's from Jordan. Now, what did that guy say?" Try the second pie."

West set the top box aside and opened the other, smiling as he found his favorite pizza inside. He pulled on a large piece, grabbing the long strings of hot cheese hanging over the edge. There was something written on the bottom of the box where the pizza slice had been removed. Now equally hungry and curious, he took a bite as he cleared the rest of the pieces away, revealing a message written beneath; World Brew Coffee Shop, Thursday 10:30 am.

He ate as he pulled out his phone and did a map search of the coffee shop. It was just a few blocks down the street. He could use the garage exit and walk there unseen. The governor sat down and enjoyed a second slice, grinning at the simplicity of his daughter's message. Even the security detail in the lobby hadn't picked up on this delivery guy. Not bad, he thought, not bad at all.

GOVERNOR WEST ENTERED the coffee shop promptly at 10:30, wearing a dark blue sport coat, jeans, and a denim shirt. He fit right in with the other patrons. Scanning the room, he noticed a young man sitting at a table near the window, subtly signaling him. He grabbed a large coffee and a newspaper, then walked over and sat down facing him.

"Hello, Mr. West, I'm Ethan Ludwig. We spoke on the phone."

West nodded his acknowledgment.

"Give me one moment, please," Ethan requested as he texted a message on his phone; 'He's here.'

He waited, then said, "Governor, please look out the window over my shoulder across the street."

As he did, he noticed a young blonde woman standing outside of a drug store.

"Is that?" The words nearly caught in his throat.

Ethan nodded. "Yes, sir, she wanted you to see that she's all right, but we have to keep her identity hidden until we finish this. In fact, if you look a little further down the street, you'll see one of the guys from senator Karlson's private security detail."

West glanced less than twenty yards to Jordan's left and picked the guy out quickly. He looked back to Jordan, who remained long enough to ensure he had seen her. She tugged on her earlobe, a little sign they gave to each other when leaving for school or business trips. He'd already seen through her disguise, but now he also knew she was under no duress and was here of her own volition. He watched as she then turned and walked down the sidewalk. She paused to look back as if pleading to her father to make all this madness stop and take her in a secure and loving hug.

West could feel the distance widening between them as she ambled away. Frustration and pain clouded his face. He made no effort to conceal the emotions. He watched long enough to ensure no one was following her, then turned to Ethan.

"Young man, you realize if she comes with me right now, then this entire ordeal is over, and we can all go home."

"That's not exactly true, sir. There will be kidnapping charges against us. Add that to any other laws they will say we broke by getting her out of that hospital. I'm pretty sure that even you couldn't make this mess go away just by saying, 'it's all been a big misunderstanding.' Think about it. I know you were careful in watching for people following you on your way here, but they found you anyway. They will find all of us eventually. And let's face it, the easiest way to deal with us is to make us disappear. "

"Then why didn't you ask for help earlier," he said, frustrated. "Back before this small hole became a bottomless pit."

"It was never a small hole, governor. Senator Karlson deliberately revealed military secrets to the enemy. When Jordan confronted her, she was drugged and locked away. The senator has been working to track us all down and cover her tracks ever since."

West made a face like he'd received an electrical shock.

"We saw her do it," Ethan continued. "Jordan was heartbroken. But she couldn't live with herself if she didn't confront her mother and allow her the opportunity to fix what she'd done. Well, she tried and look where it got her. Locked in a padded cell and medicated out of her mind. At that moment, we didn't know who we could trust, you included, sir. As her friends, we saw ourselves as her only option. So we broke a lot of laws and took on forces we had no business competing against. And there she is, safe and sound, at least for now. We know that if we don't do this right, then it's a simple case of our word against the senator's. Jordan is adamant that we close this chapter once and for all. For the sake of everyone involved, she is asking for your help because you're the only one she can trust. The only one that can make this right."

"Treason," West repeated. He closed his eyes and the word was still there, etched into his mind. His wife actually committed treason, then locked up their daughter to cover her trail. No amount of political backpedaling could ever undo these egregious acts. The consequences would follow them both for the rest of their days. The life they built together was over, and he mourned its loss.

The confrontation with Katherine would come later. Right

now, his first responsibility was guaranteeing the safety of the most precious player on the field; Jordan.

"I need to know that she is protected," he finally said. "Tell me what assurances I have that no harm will come to her?"

"She will be safe because we're no longer in a defensive position, sir. We're proactive. We control a bit of the battlefield now, and we know things they don't. With your help, we can catch them in the act. That is the only way this ends well for all of us."

"From my perspective, this seems like a long way around what should be a straight line. You realize that, don't you?"

"I'm sure it appears that way. But if we don't follow our plan, then everything your wife has done will remain nothing more than unproven allegations. Speculation and conjecture in the eyes of the law, and therefore plausibly deniable. The only way this story stops here and now is for the senator to be caught in her own lie."

The governor's eyebrows raised in surprise. "That was a very compelling argument. I don't make a habit of judging a book by its cover, but that's not what I would have expected to hear from a musician."

Ethan smiled slyly, as though one of his life secrets had been revealed. "My father was an attorney. And though I had no interest in that direction myself, I always listened when he spoke. He was. . . a knowledgeable and articulate man." Then he added, "And greatly missed."

Ethan's words were having a disarming effect on West. Each bit of information garnered from the young man further proved he was someone of high intellect and strong moral value. West probably wouldn't have chosen him as his daughter's love interest and protector, but here he was. He was also satisfied that Jordan was in good company.

"So, how do you propose we move forward?"

"That involves a rather big favor we have to ask of you. If you can set the wheels in motion, we can take care of the rest."

For the next ten minutes, Ethan laid out the plan and what they needed. West made notes in his phone as he listened, nodding from time to time, never interrupting.

When Ethan finished, West pocketed his phone. "You've covered this well," he said. "It's a good plan. An excellent plan, actually. I do believe, however, that we need to stay in close communication until this is over. I would suggest. . ."

Ethan nodded before he could finish. "There's a burner phone taped under the table with my number in memory. This one is secure and untraced."

"I should have figured you have that covered as well. I think you've missed your calling, Ethan. You could have a future with Central Intelligence, maybe the FBI." He subtly pulled the phone loose from under the table and slipped it into his jacket pocket. He rose from his seat and said, "You have my full support. And tell my daughter… tell her that I love her." He smiled and added, "But she already knows that." He reached over and shook Ethan's hand, then headed out the front door.

Ethan remained seated, tapping away at his phone. After a few more minutes, he headed to the restroom and locked the door. He peeled off his jacket and reversed it, pulled on a brown beret and black-rimmed glasses, then adhered a false mustache to his lip. He opened the door a crack and peered through cautiously. Seeing it was clear, he slipped out the employee entrance and took a circuitous route to Joe's house.

Governor West strolled down the street, stopping at a few stores as instructed. He then climbed into a town car that awaited him at the end of the block. Once inside, he pushed the button to raise the divider between himself and the driver. He dialed one of the numbers from his phone book and waited. When a receptionist answered, he said, “Special Agent Masterson, please.” A moment later, he was connected. “Agent Masterson, this is Governor Clifford West. I have some information to share with you at your earliest convenience. It concerns my daughter, Jordan.”

47

Katherine Karlson spent most of Friday afternoon in the Presidential Suite of the DC Kingston hotel. On another day, she would have enjoyed the sprawling patio with its breathtaking view of the Washington monument. From her vantage point, the flow of people and vehicles below appeared as living cells, each carrying essential nutrients to a ravenous, monolithic organism.

Karlson took no notice. Instead, she concentrated on the steady stream of wealthy donors as they filed in to greet her, shaking hands and offering sizable checks for future favors. Karlson moved about the two-thousand square foot suite shaking hand after hand while rehearsing her speech between visits.

Gene Lawton worked in an adjoining office, struggling to regain control of the Jordan West situation. The public sentiment still played in their favor. But what Karlson saw as light at the end of the tunnel, Lawton envisioned as the headlight of a freight train rumbling toward them.

Despite Lawton's pessimistic view, Karlson maintained the belief that Jordan could eventually be coaxed back under her wing. She was also confident that the rest of the situation could be ignored until the inquiries quit coming. The news media often treated their chosen candidate with that courtesy. They stopped asking difficult questions if they sensed Karlson was becoming frustrated. Or that she might struggle with an authentic and newsworthy query that had not been pre-screened.

Karlson broke away from her speech notes, stretched, and let out a long yawn. "Have you heard any more from the FBI about possible Jordan sightings?"

"Nothing from them or the state police," said Lawton. "All they're offering are theories. Our own agents believe Jordan and her accomplices are lying low. She'll contact you when she feels the time is right."

"She wants me to quit the campaign and step aside. I doubt she'll be changing her mind until we can get her away from that brainwashing band she's shacking up with."

"Probably not, but it might buy us some time if you tell her you're considering it. At least let her know that you're looking into a way to correct what's been done."

"That's a tall order, Gene. I wouldn't know who to trust if we wanted to find another way out. All we can do now is play dumb about the whole damn thing. Speaking of which, do we know for certain that the security video of the interview has been destroyed?"

"Yes, the job was done. This time, the hard drives were physically destroyed."

Karlson chuckled disdainfully. "I'll believe it when I see it. I have zero faith in that fat fuck. I wouldn't doubt he left the drives in the trunk of his car and forgot about them. I want you to bring in someone new, Gene. Verify those drives are gone for good, and then fire that piece of shit."

Lawton nodded. "Let's just get past tonight, and then we

can start looking for a replacement. Smart people are plentiful, Katherine. Finding someone you can trust, now that takes time."

"Loyalty can be bought, remember that." She spoke with a smugness that warned Gene not to challenge her.

"Speaking of which," she continued, "maybe we approach this situation with a new spin. Let's throw out a news line that Jordan is suffering from exhaustion and depression. Say that she is in critical need of medical attention. That could bump the sympathy vote and get people watching for her. Let the country know that we fear for the safety of my daughter. We'll need a few key people to start repeating that line."

"I'll plant the seed tonight."

Gene was packing away his computer when he heard a rap on the door. A tall, dark-suited secret service agent let himself into the room. "Excuse me, senator, but we need to move you to the stage dressing room now."

Karlson nodded without looking up.

"Time to bring home the labor vote," Lawton said as he walked over and held the door open.

Karlson smiled as she tucked her speech notes into a leather binder. "Let's be honest," she said, "the labor vote was mine by virtue of who I am not." She let out a short, sly laugh. "They're going to vote for me because I am not Davis Tenor!"

Karlson's cell phone chirped on their way to the dressing room. She dug it from her purse and caught it on the fourth ring. The caller ID displayed 'anonymous.' Typically, she did not answer unrecognizable numbers but then had a thought. What if…

"Yes?" she answered cooly.

"Mother, it's me."

Karlson stopped dead in her tracks. Lawton, who was

walking beside her, continued on a few more steps before realizing she had halted. He turned and read from her face that it was Jordan.

"My God, baby, where have you been? I've been worried sick! Are you all right? What are those terrible people doing to you?"

Lawton noted how the woman's words did not synchronize with her face. He heard the concerned tone of voice but saw no change of expression as her eyes stared forward, revealing nothing. It was like watching a movie with bad overdubs. This was an aspect of the woman that Lawton feared. She was proving him right for not fully trusting her no matter what that buttery smooth voice said.

Karlson gestured with a finger for Lawton to wait as she listened to her daughter.

"I'm in the building, and I have to speak with you," Jordan continued. "You and I need to have an understanding. There is an empty meeting room called the Sierra Hall. Please come alone, mother. I'll be waiting."

The call ended, and Karlson whispered into Lawton's ear. "She's here, now. She wants to meet with me alone in the Sierra Hall. Get our people to cover the exits in case this doesn't go well."

Gene nodded and hurried back the way they came. He pulled a two-way radio from his pocket and gave instructions to the private security team. The trap was now set.

Karlson excused herself from the secret service escort and found one of the wait staff to direct her to the new destination. She located it quickly enough and let herself in.

The lighting was low in the immense, empty hall, but she recognized the outline of Jordan sitting at a table near the back wall. Karlson sauntered toward her, observing everything around, watching for movement in the shadows. She could make out Jordan's face now and was relieved to see her daughter safe. Her maternal instincts being quenched, Karlson immediately began formulating her next steps. Constructing the conversation that would take place. She had to convince Jordan that her actions were for the sake of the country. If she could just get in a few words edge-wise, then she might still make this all work out. If not, she hoped her security team would not hurt her only child. She moved closer. Jordan made no effort to stand and greet her.

"Hello, mother." Jordan's tone was flat, simmering with undercurrents of anger.

For a moment, Karlson felt a slip in the balance of power, a strange tingle of uncertainty. It was not a welcome sensation, and she pushed it out of her mind.

Her daughter regarded her blankly. "Have a seat," she said, pointing to an empty chair.

"Is this how you greet your mother? After being kidnapped and disappearing off the face of the earth for days?" Karlson's voice was brimming with indignation.

"This is how I greet the woman who drugged me. This is how I greet the woman that sent me to that terrible place like a prisoner. Christ, mom, your own daughter! How the hell do you think you could ever justify yourself to me? Or to my father, let alone the rest of the country? Did you really believe you could talk your way out of everything you've done?"

Karlson expected some anger, but Jordan was standing up to her more than she'd expected. Although annoyed with this newfound attitude, she still admired the girl for showing some backbone.

"Honey, you left me little choice. If you just tried to be a little more reasonable we—"

"Reasonable? You revealed military secrets to the enemy. Why? Why would you betray your own country like that?"

Karlson waved off the comment like brushing away a pesky fly. "Because that's how things get done in this town. Give and take. I gave up the details of a mission that had the potential of destroying all that I've worked for."

"It would have shortened the war," Jordan said. "Maybe even ended it."

"Oh, there's so much more at stake here than just that." Karlson looked down, shaking her head. "That mission would have jeopardized everything."

Jordan laughed out loud. "Bullshit! How could ending the war sooner possibly be a bad thing?"

"We couldn't allow anything like that to happen until after the election. Only then could we use diplomacy to end it on our terms."

"Diplomacy? Mother, let's be honest, you don't know a fucking thing about diplomacy. That's why you pay people like Gene to negotiate for you."

Karlson had heard enough. Her buttons weren't merely pushed, they'd been smashed in. Nobody questioned her motives or intentions like this. And certainly not an ungrateful daughter who was incapable of grasping the fine art of politics. She stood outraged and pointed a trembling finger down at Jordan.

"I am a United States Senator, little girl! I am weeks away from winning the presidency. Make no mistake that I am a diplomat, first and foremost. You are way out of your league here and so very out of line! As usual, you learn a little and think you comprehend the entire situation. So let me explain once and for all how this really works. If that mission had been allowed to go forward, then yes, it could have ended the war before the election. But do you have any idea what that would have meant? Hell no, you don't. It would mean the current president could take credit for it happening on his watch. His poll numbers would have shot through the roof. That would have been the end of my campaign, right then and there. Now, we can wait until I've been elected. I'll send in my diplomats to broker a peace treaty. We will end this war on my watch, on my terms. History will reflect that I accomplished what five presidents failed to do before me. My legacy will be carved in stone, and a second term is all but guaranteed."

"But those people want nuclear weapons! They're less than a year away from becoming the most dangerous threat in the Middle East!"

"Too goddamn bad! They're going to figure a way to get them regardless. At least this way, I will have a treaty with support from the rest of the world. If OASIS attacks their neighbors with a nuclear bomb, then we would retaliate by blowing them off the face of the earth. And we would have the blessing of nearly every other country."

"All except the one that OASIS destroyed with that first nuke. They would all be dead."

"Collateral damage, darling! World peace would grow from the ashes."

Jordan stared in disbelief. This was far beyond anything she thought her mother was even capable of conceiving. The words slammed her back into her seat. She gripped tightly to the table edge and struggled to maintain her composure.

"I can't believe you actually said that," she finally managed to answer. "Allowing two countries to destroy each other because it would be better for your election? My God, mother, what have you become?"

"I've become a politician—a damned good one. Now you need to accept how things are done and stand by my side. This is not a game. This is for control of the most powerful nation in the world, and it is within my grasp." She paused, clearly for effect.

Jordan expected a shallow show of sincerity to finish the argument. She was not disappointed.

"Please, honey," her mother asked with rehearsed kindness and concern. "Trust me on this. In the end, it really does work better for everyone."

Jordan was through. The two tasks she had come to accomplish were now complete. She knew that attempting to change her mother's mind would be an exercise in futility. But the meeting also answered the question; what if? What if her mother was wavering? Not sure she wanted to go forward with her plan. Willing to consider another way out. Well, now she knew. Nothing could deter the senator from her collision course with destiny.

What frightened her to the core was that she knew many people would blindly follow this woman and her fractured logic. They would enable a horrible nightmare to play out simply because Senator Katherine Karlson looked them square in the eye and swore it was the right thing to do.

The piper played, the mice fell into step.

Jordan had a brief vision of the country under her mother's leadership, and it sent a shiver of dread down her spine.

"I was hoping you would come to see reason," Jordan said sadly. "I know now that you won't, that you can't. I'm sorry, mother, but I'm not going to stand by and watch you do this. And I will not allow you to imprison me again—your own flesh and blood—just so you can dance in the light of the grandest lie ever told. Goodbye."

Jordan stood and stared across the table at her mother. One final glimpse of the woman who had been the sun of her universe. She paused, memorizing every detail of this moment, then turned and walked toward a back exit.

"It can't end this way, Jordan," Karlson called to her. "You can't walk away like this."

Jordan reached the exit and turned back to her mother. "Watch me," she said defiantly.

She pushed open the door and walked out. . .into the waiting arms of two of the senator's agents.

KARLSON SAT ALONE in the cavernous room, stunned into silence. Raw anger raged, screaming at her core, drowning out any rational thoughts. Her gut churned, head pulsating in a fog-shrouded pain. It was like the worst Sunday morning hangover she'd ever endured. She willed herself to rise, but her muscles did not respond. The conversation looped back in her mind's eye. She squeezed her temples, straining to block it out. She had failed. Jordan was forcing her to now take actions she truly detested. It wasn't her fault. The kid should have seen reason by now. Instead, she mucked up things even further by walking away, defiant and oblivious as ever.

This night was to be her defining moment that would put the lock on the election. It should have been a slam dunk success story. Only now, through no fault of her own, she was being relegated to nursemaid running cleanup. Karlson swore she would never let the kid forget what she put her mother through.

There would still be the issue of those meddlesome geek friends of hers. The potential backlash from any one of them opening their mouths was too dangerous to ignore. There was far too much on the line to second guess how to deal with the problem. Her security detail only needed to track down one of them. A little forceful persuasion would make them reveal the location of the rest. The remaining problems would be identified, located, and eliminated. She doubted such urchins of society would be greatly missed.

A sharp rap on the door brought her thoughts back to the moment. One of Karlson's personal security detail entered the room and walked swiftly toward her.

"Senator, Mr. Lawton is looking for you. Everything is ready in the main ballroom."

All thoughts of self-doubt were discarded as she rose from her seat. "What is the status of my daughter?" she asked, walking with the broad-shouldered agent toward the exit.

"I have confirmation she is in our custody. She's being taken to the location that Mr. Lawton specified."

Such cold words to describe the handling of her one and only child, she thought. She promised herself to check on Jordan's condition after giving her speech. Tonight would solidify her position and guarantee success. Karlson could afford to relax a little once she had the unconditional support of the unions. This election was already won before a single vote had been cast. And it was showtime.

48

Ethan, Murray, and Mark sat in a hotel room a short distance from the main ballroom. Under normal circumstances, it would have been the least desirable and last room to be sold when the massive convention center was utilized. It was noisy, with nearly non-stop foot traffic. But for Murray's purposes, it was the room of choice.

The three of them had spent the afternoon rolling in audio and video interfaces. It was easy blending in with the chaotic stream of workers as they prepared the main ballroom for the Katherine Karlson dinner. All were so busy setting up the rented PA, lighting, and stage equipment that no one paid any attention to them. With over twelve hundred guests in attendance, this would be the biggest show ever hosted by the facility. This made it very easy for Murray to deliver and set up his array of equipment completely unnoticed.

They worked efficiently, each with their own list of tasks to complete.

Mark sat in a corner donning a large headset as he monitored a radio transmission. His face was illuminated by the pulsing green volume indicators of a digital recorder.

Murray read off a list of cable inputs and network IP addresses. Ethan located each corresponding plug and connected them.

Mark suddenly stepped away from his table and slid off his headphones. "They have her," he said solemnly.

Ethan froze while Murray hurried into a seat at the audio console. "Did we get what we need?" he asked, adjusting sound level inputs.

Mark nodded. "Yeah, yeah, we got everything."

"Good, cross your fingers, guys. Now the clock is ticking. Ethan, have you finished making those connections back there?"

Ethan broke out of a momentary stupor and rechecked all the inputs of the routers, hubs, and audio cables. "Yes, everything is good to go. Did you ever make contact with the company running the sound?"

"Yeah, but it didn't pan out like I wanted. I was hoping to work with them and tap into their system. The guy in charge is a bit of a prick. He won't let me anywhere near the controls. We'll just have to work around him. That won't be too much of an issue since I tracked down one of his former employees. I found out the equipment he's using, along with their network addresses."

"What else do you need me to do?" Ethan asked, trying to remain useful.

"You could help Mark do the editing we talked about. You know what we need."

Ethan nodded, then went to Mark's console and donned a pair of headphones. He booted an audio software editing program and began playing back the captured audio files. The recorded sound waves danced on the video monitor. He labeled each of the clips and started cutting and pasting them together.

Murray ran down his list of connections, pinging each address to ensure all systems were active on the network. He stopped abruptly at the one that would hack him to the convention hall soundboard. There was no reply.

It was too early to panic, but nonetheless, it caused a stab of self-doubt. Everything being attempting tonight depended on this one connection. He grabbed his notepad and reviewed the instructions, verifying he'd followed them to the letter. Yes, all done correctly and in the proper sequence. Then what was the hangup? He looked at his watch as a nauseating wave of anxiety swept over. This was cutting it way too close. The system was supposed to have been ready for final checks ten minutes ago.

He powered the entire console down and back up, hoping the minor glitch would correct itself. Still no change. He cringed and re-entered all of the network addresses. Maybe a single digit was off somewhere. He tried to ping again. Nothing happened. Now he was in trouble. The entire plan teetered on the brink of failure. A bead of sweat coursed down his temple. He had just sent Jordan into the hands of her mother. Getting her back and vindicating everyone depended on this connection. Depended on him!

"Damnit," he mumbled aloud, staring at the tangle of cables as he searched for the source of the problem. The full weight of the entire project bore down on him, making every breath harder to inhale. Memories of past mistakes suddenly filled his mind and obscured his view, making it even harder to formulate a solution. He was now suffering a full-on panic attack. His judgment was impaired all the more. Wave after wave of self-doubt and insecurity slammed him further down a dark chute. He felt like a drowning man, knowing the end was upon him but refusing to inhale that fatal lungful of water and get it over with. He heard the rumble of applause and cheering through the walls from the main ballroom. The show was beginning.

He was failing! He looked over and watched Mark and Ethan working diligently on the audio editing program. Their part of the master plan would soon be complete. His piece of the puzzle, meanwhile, the keystone of the entire project, sat idle. Dead in the water. Dead, as in no connection, as in. . .shit! He rushed to the back of the console and re-checked all of the wired connections that Ethan made. He manually traced the cat five cables from output to input. Holding each one and following its course, he verified it was plugged in and terminated in the proper receptacle. He didn't find anything wrong. Nothing stood out that could cause the problem. He was down to the last few cables when he saw it. Two jumpers connecting the mixing console into the wireless hub were reversed.

"Oh my God," he exhaled, praying now that the simple mixup in Ethan's connecting job was the only issue. He stood over the laptop and attempted to ping the connection again… nothing! Not a goddamned thing! He was sure that should have been it. A depressing message displayed over and over; NO RESPONSE.

"Wait," he yelled out loud, remembering the system would not initialize without the proper connections at startup. He closed out of the program and rebooted the computer. His hands clenched and unclenched as the laptop took its sweet time restarting. Finally, the welcome screen appeared. Slowly, carefully, he entered the ping command and the address of the house console he wished to connect into. This time he was rewarded with a new message; 'reply from remote server successful.'

Murray closed his eyes and blew out a sigh of relief. He dropped into the seat and entered the instruction sequence to seize control of the house system, drumming his fingers impatiently while waiting for the acknowledgment message. Such a simple problem that caused such anguish. He knew that Ethan was not to blame for the mistake. In his haste, he hadn't gone back and verified all the work himself. My fault, not his, Murray admitted.

The computer beeped as the new program screen opened. A broad smile of relief spread across Murray's face as he pressed the enter key one more time. Done!

His console was now live and connected to the main controls of the convention room. It was also invisible to the users sitting at that other console. Murray had done it! He glanced over at Ethan, who looked up, made momentary eye contact with a nod, then returned to his screen. Murray thought how close he'd come to a full crash and burn on the entire project. This was one small detail that didn't need to be shared with the rest of the group. He pushed one of the audio channel sliders forward and announced, "Here we go."

49

Karlson was led around the back of the massive convention hall via a service walkway. She entered a sizeable curtained-off staging area that served as a dressing room and found the refreshment table. Gene Lawton caught sight of her and hurried over as she popped the top of a diet soda.

"Katherine, I've been looking everywhere for you! We're behind schedule and need to get you on stage." Lawton's expression was once again a few degrees south of his usually unflappable demeanor. Although he was doing his best to appear in total control, Karlson could see that the ordeal was taking its toll. She was confident that she could get both their heads back in the game with a little horizontal interlude. The thought aroused her. She imagined throwing him down on a table and taking all that she needed to satisfy her unexpected craving. All in good time, she reassured herself, all in good time.

Karlson pulled out her speech notes as an audio tech clipped a lapel microphone to her gray herringbone Armani jacket. She eyed Lawton slyly as she flipped through the pages, verifying they were in order. They would be utilized more as props. Karlson always memorized her speeches like a movie script. She could also read from the teleprompters if necessary. Technology had forever changed the political landscape, and these were the tools of a convincing statesman. The speaking and literary skills of the founding fathers themselves were Jurassic by comparison. Very few, if any, would ever have survived their first televised debate.

The audience of over twelve hundred were pleasantly stuffed and tipsy after being treated to an evening fit for royalty. Union representatives, business owners, and political contributors were indulged with some of the finest food and drink that money could buy. Though this evening's fare might be a typical meal for the wealthiest attendees, most of the union delegation and the smattering of blue-collar guests could never afford such amenities on their simple working man's wages. These people were here only because the union needed to show a united front to its candidate. The lucky recipients were only too happy to oblige.

Karlson catered the event with the very best culinary cuisine from her favorite suppliers. It was a masterpiece of a meal, and it cost the senator nearly $200 per person to wine and dine them. But the $5k per plate charge more than covered the luxuries being enjoyed by her supporters.

GENE LAWTON WATCHED in awe as Karlson prepared for the speech. It seemed that the woman could walk through the screaming winds of a hurricane and exit the other side with hardly a hair out of place. He was also wary of such controlled callousness. She had shown her claws on enough occasions for him to expect the unexpected. Lately, he'd been devoting more and more time to a backup plan of self-preservation. His personal assistant was currently holding a resignation letter drafted by Lawton over the last two days. In it, he wrote of learning about the Jordan West situation only recently and was personally outraged. 'In clear conscience, I cannot continue in my position as campaign manager,' the letter read. With a phone call, Lawton would instruct her to put the envelope on the senator's desk. More of the blame for this entire affair could be shifted to others, including Governor West's assistant, Riley Comstock. If that wannabe wanted to see action, then she'd get it, and a lot more than she bargained for.

The stage producer positioned Karlson at the base of the stairs. Lawton came and stood next to her, offering a nod and a thumb's up. Pulling off their modified plan would be a tremendous accomplishment. The odds were stacking up against them, but he was now prepared for whatever came. He accompanied her up the steps and slid behind the curtains.

The owner of a medical equipment company was finishing his speech on the future of socialized medicine in America when he caught sight of the senator. He nodded at the cue, then began his introduction.

"LADIES AND GENTLEMEN, since her explosive entry into the political arena, the people of this nation have borne witness to the rise of a natural leader. Her first term as a California senator signaled the start of an amazing career that would bring us to this day, this place, and this next great challenge. There is one and only one candidate who has shown the intellect, creativity, resourcefulness, compassion, dedication, and determination to guide us through the dark days ahead. Our country now calls on every one of us to follow her lead. It is time to take America back from the elite billionaires who have manipulated our flawed system to serve only themselves. It is time to put a leader in the oval office who believes in sharing the fruits of our collective labors. One that reaches out to other nations with a promise to end world hunger and poverty. One who believes that all countries should become one united world community. She knows what needs to be done and stands ready to lead us down that bold new road. She is here with us tonight and is asking for your support. Please welcome the brilliant statesman, the courageous fighter, the bright shining beacon of hope that now lights our way. I give you the next president of the United States. Senator. . .Katherine. . .Karlson!"

The room erupted in thunderous applause. Cheers and whistles echoed shrilly as Karlson stepped out into the bright lights of the stage. With hands held high, she waved to the clamoring crowd. A pair of twelve-foot video monitors on either side of the stage had been displaying photographs of Karlson hugging destitute children as she toured the slums of the world. They now flashed and filled with her live image. At this moment, Katherine Karlson was bigger than any rock star. She was in her element and made the most of every second, allowing their adulation to continue unabated for all of three minutes.

Karlson smiled brightly, affectionately, pointing to key supporters in the audience and returning their applause. She walked back and forth, blowing kisses, bowing her head, and mouthing her thanks. Then, as the sounds of the enthusiastic audience began to wane, she took her place behind the podium.

She gazed out over the smiling faces of working stiffs and wealthy supporters, savoring the moment as the last of the applause slowly died away. This was the pivotal milestone of her career, her life, and for the country as well. Few others would ever know such power and distinction. She stood at the pulpit, ready to receive the scepter. Ready to be the catalyst of change for a nation that so fiercely guarded its freedom yet so freely empowered others to make the critical decisions that could take it away.

Among this audience were a few of the elite who would strongly influence her decisions and dictate her policies. Operating from the shadows, they would essentially write her marching orders. Right now, that didn't matter. Right now, it was all about Katherine Karlson, and she loved it. Her smile beamed brightly with the warmth that thousands of movie fans had fallen in love with. The teleprompters flashed and queued up to the first line of her speech.

"Ladies and gentlemen, distinguished and courageous members of the labor organizations, the backbone, the muscle that propels this great nation, good evening! Thank you from the bottom of my heart for your support and your attendance here tonight. Make no mistake, this is the turning point and the time to re-write the script for our country's future. It starts here, it starts now, with you and me and the promises I will make to all of you. And with God as my witness, I swear that I keep my promises!"

The room exploded with a fresh round of applause and cheers with nearly every attendee on their feet. Karlson felt a sense of control that she had only dared to imagine. Here were her loyal followers. The ones she needed to fall into step so that millions more would follow suit and join the parade. She hosted many fundraisers in the past few months. This one, however, signaled the actual beginning of the slow, steady walk down Pennsylvania Avenue to that seat of power, and that grand monument of all past presidents. To her new home. At this moment she felt as though she were being handed the front door keys. Every problem of the past would now be a minor formality.

50

"You can't do this to me!"

Jordan struggled against the vice-like grip of the private security agent. A second dark-suited mass of muscle stepped in and grabbed her other arm, nearly lifting her off her feet. They directed her down a short hallway toward a nearby exit.

"I refuse to go with you," she yelled, hoping someone would hear her pleas. "You have no authority to do this!" She dug in her feet and resisted. It had a negligible effect. They moved her as though she presented no opposition at all.

The first agent used his elbow to push through the exit door. He directed them out into the back parking lot toward an awaiting black van. Jordan stared at it as the last of her confidence drained away. She half expected to be confronted by her mother's guards but not taken by them.

Murray promised she would be safe. No harm would come to her while she collected the needed evidence. But the vision before her exceeded her worst fears. They were going to take her, and she would disappear. This time, no one would ever find her.

"Daddy, where are you!" Jordan pleaded under her breath. "I need you now."

She desperately scanned the parking lot and rooftops of adjacent buildings, searching for her rescuers. They were nowhere to be found. Despair tightened around her chest, and she found it difficult to breathe. An angry tear formed in her eye as she grit her teeth in defiance. Every step closer to that van diminished her hopes of ever seeing freedom again. *No!* She told herself, fighting through the fear. *I am not going in there. No! These bastards are not getting away with this a second time!* Adrenalin surged through her pounding heart as Jordan summoned every bit of strength. Core survival instincts took over. In one swift move, she shot her arms up and then rolled them out while throwing her weight backward. It was a simple self-defense maneuver taught to her by a school friend. It worked perfectly, taking her captors by surprise. She broke free, then turned and ran across the parking lot. Jordan had put ten feet between them before they recovered from their shock and gave chase. Their footsteps echoed off the walls. The sound willed her to go faster, faster than she'd ever run before. She searched for a path of escape, caught sight of a bustling intersection ahead, and ran toward it.

Suddenly, from behind the building, from behind parked cars, from every direction, agents came running toward her with weapons drawn. An overwhelming dread consumed her as she realized her momentary escape had been for nothing. It was over. Her legs stopped pumping and she came to a halt, still disbelieving this was how it would end. Her eyelids fluttered as though working to expel the terrible images from sight.

Murray hadn't lied, but he'd been so wrong. "They won't take you again," he promised. "You'll be safe, but you have to let them try." She closed her eyes and awaited the inevitable. What a foolish daydream, she thought. Who were they to believe they ever stood a snowball's chance in hell to beat her mother at her own game? Still in all, it was better to try than to accept the fate being imposed. A noble and worthwhile effort at that, she had to admit. Even though his plan ultimately failed, she loved Murray for trying. She loved them all for what they attempted. It had been the most amazing experience of her life and the most precious gift she'd ever received.

The squeal of tires tore away the thought. Jordan opened her eyes as another black van skidded to a halt directly before her. The side and rear doors burst open as more agents clamored out and poured into the parking lot. . .then ran right past her.

Jordan turned to watch in astonishment, only now noticing the large, yellow FBI letters emblazoned on the backs of their jackets. The passenger door of this new van flew open. A man in a gray suit leaped out and ran toward her with a look of dogged determination. It was her father. He grabbed her in his arms and pulled her down between two parked cars.

The sound of a bull horn cut through the surrealistic backdrop of the charging onslaught. "Drop your weapons. Drop 'em now! You are completely surrounded!"

Jordan peered out from between the cars to see the two agents who had dragged her from the auditorium unholstering their sidearms and tossing them to the ground. Their hands went in the air. A small army of FBI agents swarmed in from every direction and laid them face down on the black asphalt, cuffing their hands behind them. Another group surrounded the first van and ordered the occupants out. Two men opened the doors, climbed out, and got on their knees with hands on their heads. FBI agents rushed in, and within seconds, they, too, were cuffed and down.

Jordan looked at her father. His suit was a mess from shielding her when they dove for cover. She wrapped her arms around him and held tight, finally feeling safe again. Knowing now that the terrible nightmare was really over.

"You did it!" she exclaimed, sobs of joy catching in her throat. "You came for me!"

He looked through misty eyes, unable and unwilling to fight back his own tears as he finally held his daughter again. He brushed a lock of hair from her face and kissed her forehead. "Little girl, I will always be there for you."

51

"Friends," Karlson spoke into the microphone, then paused until the room fell whisper silent. "We have been told by an elitist president that many of the benefits we propose are impossible to fulfill. He would tell you the costs are unsustainable. That such changes would challenge our constitution. That a nation built on capitalism cannot demand its wealthiest to shoulder the weight of redistribution, ensuring all Americans the essentials for a prosperous life. To that, I say, 'just because you haven't found a way does not mean it cannot be done.' It most certainly can be accomplished. And it must be. I will find the answers. I will level the playing field to ensure that everyone among us has what they need. And that everyone with the ability to help make that happen will become part of the solution.

We will all share in the wealth of this great nation, and we will all be equal very, very soon. The answers are more straightforward than you would think. It is the commitment to implement change that is the greatest challenge. Well, I stand before you as the agent of change. I am here to make those difficult decisions. I am here to accomplish what those who came before me have failed to do. I stand before you and make this promise; trust and fight with me for all that is rightfully yours, and today's dream of an equal America can and will come to pass. Then, when your friends ask why you choose to join me, tell them of these dreams we share. Tell them that with their support, we will have the power. Tell them that together we will change the world. Tell them, 'Yes. . .Kat. . .Can!'"

From overhead, a thousand gold and silver balloons were released and floated down into the crowd. Each was emblazoned with the new campaign slogan, 'Yes Kat Can!' The sound system boomed out the Star-Spangled Banner.

The audience reacted in kind. They jumped to their feet, catching and swatting the balloons while roaring their approval. Karlson watched over the assembly of influential labor leaders as they played like children with a new toy. Her smile remained fixed as her eyebrows dipped maniacally. She scanned the exuberant audience, then looked backstage to Gene Lawton. How this excited her so! Her thoughts filled with having him inside of her tonight. The vision abruptly dissolved in the wash of stage lights. Standing beside Gene was her husband, Clifford West. His expression was unreadable. But she felt his eyes laser locked with hers, scanning her internally. Examining her every thought. A stab of disquiet tore at her confidence, and she grit her teeth behind the smile that never faltered. She was, after all, an excellent actress.

MURRAY LISTENED to the live feed of the senator's speech through headphones. Karlson reached her crescendo, and he watched on a monitor as the balloons were released from overhead and dropped into the cheering crowd. "Here we go," he called to Ethan and Mark as he pressed a key on his laptop, sending the override command to the house system. The result was near-instantaneous.

TWO FLOORS above in the A/V control room, Duane Hershey pushed a master slider of his audio console, increasing the volume of the national anthem. He watched out the large window overlooking the controlled chaos. Below him, the formally dressed crowd romped and jumped at balloons like brainless idiots. Hershey chuckled at the frightful thought that these were the people who would be running the country. He rolled his eyes and spoke into his headset microphone. "Tommy, Queue video clip B in three, two. . .wait, what just happened?"

Hershey watched the signal lights flicker on his console. His mouth fell open as the motorized audio sliders began moving to new levels by themselves.

"What the hell is this?" He yelled, pulling the controllers back to the original positions, only to watch them return to the new values as soon as he let go.

"Tommy, I lost control of this board. Find the user manual, fast!"

He and Tommy began digging through empty road cases for the manuals on the new equipment he had used only twice before. He had no clue how this was even possible. His only hope was to call the manufacturer for emergency support. He prayed there would be someone standing by.

A SINGLE LINE of computer code containing a new IP

address was all it took. Murray was successfully hacked into the house system and wrested control of all audio and video from his competitor. He knew that Duane would be unable to figure his way out of this until long after the night was over.

"We're in, guys," he said, grinning at Ethan and Mark, who stood ready to replay their edited audio and video clips. Murray readied the pirate master controller. "Stand by. The real show starts now."

KARLSON ALLOWED the moment to play out as the audience remained immersed in frolic, giddily cheering and laughing. But then, something changed. Slowly, one by one, the crowd's attention was drawn to the side monitors. The right screen displayed a shot of a large desk with people sitting before it, their backs to the camera. The left screen was filled with video noise, flashing like colorful snow. An attractive Middle Eastern woman stepped into view on the right monitor. She picked up a file from the credenza and held it up for the others to see. Even from the bad angle and marginal video quality, it was easy to read the bold red header. 'TOP SECRET EYES ONLY.'

A collective gasp resonated through the audience as all other activities ceased. An unnatural silence rolled through the room, leaving only scattered conversations and the occasional clink of silverware. In time, even that dissipated to nothing. The entire stunned audience watched as the woman flipped through the classified file pages as a cameraman filmed the contents.

The left screen suddenly flashed, then resolved into the image of a woman and two men with their backs to the camera. They were watching a monitor as it displayed the people in the next room rifling through the top-secret document.

"They're watching it happen!" someone yelled from the back of the room. The missing audio signal now crackled to life through the forty-thousand-watt sound system. A familiar voice commented, "Christ, she's good! Tell me she hasn't pulled that one before."

One of the men said, "I think we have what we need here. Let's finish this up."

All three abruptly left the room.

Seconds later, Katherine Karlson reappeared on the right screen. By that time, the secret folder had been returned to its original position. The film crew now sat patiently, waiting for the return of their host, unaware that their act of espionage was both planned and captured on video.

The audience remained deathly still, watching in disbelief as the likeness of Karlson ambled behind the desk, sat, and faced the group, wearing a deceptive smile. No one dared move or utter a syllable in the palpable silence.

Oblivious to the images revealed to her audience, Karlson stood perplexed behind the podium. What had stifled their mood? She found out soon enough as a recording of her own voice began playing back through the massive sound system. Her jaw dropped, mouth agape, nails clawing into the sides of the podium. This could not be happening!

The audience paid no attention to her and stared instead at the images on the large monitors. Her beaming Oscar-nominated smile replayed as she apologized for her brief absence to the people who had just photographed state secrets.

"Now, where were we?" She asked. Her demeanor did nothing to cloak the undeniable truth that she had betrayed her country. Everyone in the auditorium now knew it as well.

News reporters broke out their cell phones to call in the story while their cameramen filmed the video.

Karlson listened to the audio track, aware now that it was the security footage from her office. She glanced nervously to the side of the stage for Lawton. He was nowhere to be found. One of her security team was talking into his wrist microphone. Karlson moved out from behind the podium and waved to get his attention. She pointed up at the audio-video control room four levels above the auditorium floor.

"Stop them!" she screamed.

She fought to regain her composure, searching for the words to convince this crowd that what they were viewing was not at all as it appeared.

She looked over once more to the place where Gene last stood and saw her husband instead, staring back with an odd expression. This hadn't surprised him at all. Did he know this was going to happen? That outside forces would seize control of her speech? "No, damn it," she growled, refusing to accept that this was where and how her story would end.

She stepped back behind the podium to console the shocked audience. "My friends, I don't know who is playing this terrible prank on us, but I assure you it is not what it seems. If we can get the perpetrators of this hoax out of the control room and stop this horrid lie from playing any longer, then I'm sure that—"

"Reasonable? You revealed military secrets to the enemy. Why? Why would you betray your own country like that?"

A new audio track reverberated loudly through the sound system. It took Karlson a moment to make the connection. It was Jordan's voice, but where did this conversation emanate?

"Because that's how things get done in this town. Give

and take. I gave up the details of a mission that had the potential of destroying everything I've worked for."

A collective loud murmur went up from the room.

"It would have probably shortened the war," the other voice replied.

"Oh, there's so much more at stake here than just that."

Karlson pounded her fist on the podium, shaking her head as she listened.

"That mission would have jeopardized everything we've been working for."

"Oh, dear God," Karlson choked out. A jolt of panic tore up her spine as she began to comprehend the full gravity of the situation. Her diaphragm muscles convulsed, emptying her of breath. She swooned but remained on her feet, clinging to the podium for balance. "Not this," she mumbled, realizing the origin of this conversation. Hot, acidic bile burned up the back of her throat. "Jordan," she whispered, "Jordan wore a wire and recorded our conversation! This can't be happening! This can't be…" She looked up at the control room and noticed the expression of helpless frustration in the face of the sound engineer. He threw his hands up in resignation. He had no control over anything being broadcast. Karlson stared in disbelief, her hands held up and out as if pleading to a higher power for intervention.

"Bullshit! How could ending the war sooner possibly be a bad thing?"

Few in the audience recognized the other voice as Karlson's daughter, Jordan.

"We couldn't allow that to happen until after the election. Only then could we use diplomacy to end it on our terms."

"Diplomacy? Mother, let's be honest, you don't know a fucking thing about diplomacy. That's why you pay people like Gene to negotiate for you."

A small cheer erupted from the audience. Now everyone knew the identity of the other voice.

"If that mission had been allowed to go forward, then yes, it could have ended the war before the election. But do you have any idea what that would have meant? Hell no, you don't. It would have meant that the current president would take credit for the victory on his watch. His poll numbers would have shot through the roof. That would have been the end of my campaign right then and there. But now we can wait until I'm in office. I'll send in my diplomats and broker a peace treaty. We will end this war on my watch, on my terms. History will reflect that I accomplished what five presidents failed to do before me. My legacy will be carved in stone, with a second term all but guaranteed."

"But they want nuclear weapons! They're less than a year away from becoming the most dangerous threat in the Middle East!"

"Too goddamn bad! They're going to figure a way to get them regardless. At least this way, I will have a treaty with support from the rest of the world. If OASIS attacked their neighbors with a nuclear bomb, we would retaliate by blowing them off the face of the earth. And we would do it with the blessing of nearly every other country."

"All of them except the one that OASIS would have destroyed with that first nuke. They would all be dead."

"Collateral damage, darling. World peace would grow from the ashes."

FOR ONCE IN HER LIFE, Katherine Karlson was speechless. It was over. There was no conceivable way to shift the blame for this one. She had been exposed, and she felt naked, humiliated, defeated. This was the end of her campaign and likely the end of her senate seat. There would be hearings, demand for her resignation, and then censure. The world would rip her apart for months to come. Finding sanctuary, a place to simply exist hidden from the public eye would be next to impossible. The life she once knew was over and would never return. A tear formed in her eye as she looked to her husband again with a look of innocent bewilderment. She had probably lost him, too. It couldn't get any worse.

The auditorium of now indignant supporters glared coldly at the stage. Their former candidate now stood exposed in the full light of day for the first time. Nothing more than a flawed charlatan looking down from her high pedestal. More and more eyes turned away from the side monitors and focused center stage at the face of a living lie. The boos began, first one, then several in unison. Within moments the entire room was reverberating with that low, disparaging rumble.

Karlson scooped up her notes and began the shameful short walk off stage and out of this terrible place. "Just get to the car," she told herself. "Just get to the car, and…no, not now. Please, not now!"

Two figures stood together in the shadows of the side curtains blocking her way. Their faces were illuminated in short bursts by the pulsating stage lights and camera strobes. Even from here, she could see the anger, the hurt, the disappointment.

Karlson stopped dead in her tracks, nearly tripping over her own feet. She could not move around them. This was a battleground that she was being forced to confront with no hope of victory. She stared back like a defeated general, wishing only for a hasty retreat. She struggled for words, but none came. She could not confront them now, maybe not ever, but no choice was being offered. She felt herself further deflating, stripped bare before the eyes of these two that were no longer fooled by the false image she created of herself. She had no viable excuse, no explanations for why she drifted so far from moral ground.

A strange thought crept through her mind. Her entire political career could be likened to an incredible carnival ride. It had brought years of heart-pounding swoops and exhilarating ascents. She'd been tossed and lofted skyward by that magnificent machine that propelled her tantalizingly closer to the goal of absolute power.

The ride was over now, and she could see it for what it was; an ancient contrivance, rusted and caked with congealed grease. A rickety old contraption that so many others still stood in line to ride. She imagined the behind-the-scenes manipulators of the political system as throngs of shadowy repairmen rushing about below to ensure its continued function or attempt to alter its purpose. It had all been the grandest of illusions.

Karlson felt small, defenseless, human. No longer protected by the belief that rules of mortals do not apply to gods and emperors. She stood unveiled for the first time in years. The last remaining bricks of her impenetrable fortress fell away, exposing the words and deeds of a defeated woman.

It was all too much. Far more than she could ever attempt to explain, to atone for, to live with. She looked up into the eyes of her husband and daughter as they stood together in the glittering light. There were far too many conversations she needed to have with herself before confronting them. She was suddenly aware that she had turned and started walking toward the opposite side of the stage. She glanced over her shoulder at the expressions of surprise and resentment while revealing no reaction of her own. She reached the back exit door and stood motionless, fingers wrapped around the door handlebar. She had no clue of what lay beyond, no idea where to go or what to do. All she knew was she could not remain here. She managed to stifle the taunts and boos in her mind. But now, the sounds returned as a single monolithic voice, repeating a chant over and over: LIAR! LIAR! LIAR!

It grew louder and more articulated, like a torturous one-worded song being sung by a demonic choir. She listened a moment longer until it propelled her into motion. Katherine Karlson closed her eyes, pushed the handle, and stepped out into the mottled sunset.

EPILOGUE

November 5

The melodic morning call to prayer echoed off the walls of the ancient city. Sirhan Abbas set his espresso down and turned to face the glowing new dawn. He silently sang along with the lyrics, feeling every note flowing within him. "Hasten to real success. Hasten to real success." As always, it was the line of the call that stayed with him throughout the day.

He listened until it finished, then powered up his laptop and opened a news site. There was much to be done this morning, but he never began his workday without reviewing world events.

The United States celebrated the re-election of its incumbent president. Davis Tenor rode to an unexpected landslide victory following a shocking scandal that shook the pillars of American democracy. His rival, Katherine Karlson, had leaked confidential military documents to a reporter from Al Jazeera. Once the shocking revelation was made public, her campaign was destroyed.

The document in question detailed a covert mission utilizing a former Guantanamo detainee to locate and eliminate Abbas himself. That mission was scuttled in the process, but would likely have succeeded if not for the concerted efforts of Ms. Karlson and Miss Gohar. And although thankful for its failure, he was nonetheless troubled by the misguided ambitions of the two power-hungry women.

Abbas silently cursed the naive reporter. Deeba Gohar had predictably taken the bait and been played like a pawn, broadcasting the contents of the document. She should have known that even the most ignorant of fools would never allow military secrets to fall into enemy hands so easily. Unless, of course, it fulfilled an agenda. Common sense should have made her suspect something was amiss. Abbas contemplated a few strategically placed knife cuts across Gohar's pretty face to ensure she would never again be so foolish. The cost of her folly was unacceptably high. He lost one of his most valued lieutenants, Abu Dahl, in the process. True enough, exposing the plan undoubtedly saved his life, but it was their underlying motivation that bothered him. They shared a lust for personal gain, power, and self-adulation. It was always the same with such narrow-minded, self-centered people. None of their actions were done in the name of the greater good.

Karlson, he could understand. She was American, after all, behaving as he would expect any other from that decadent country. Deeba Gohar, on the other hand, knew better. Despite being a Middle Eastern woman raised with proper traditional values, she rejected them in favor of the filthy western ways. Perhaps butchering her pretty face was a bit extreme, but she must be reminded who she served. He made a mental note to send a subtle warning.

His mind returned to Katherine Karlson and the military mission she helped to thwart. He would have been in her debt until she'd opened her big mouth and revealed her true intentions. A secretly recorded conversation between herself and her daughter was broadcast to a roomful of admiring supporters. So disturbing were her comments that they derailed her presidential campaign. She spoke of the battle that raged in the Middle East as though it were a trivial annoyance. Of blowing nations off the face of the earth if their interests belied her own.

His hands clenched into tight fists. Few could evoke his anger, and he chided himself for the momentary loss of control. Karlson was an extremely dangerous woman and would have been a formidable opponent. Now that she had been scorned and pushed from the spotlight, she would be a much simpler problem to eliminate.

Abbas opened a secure portal on his laptop and typed an encoded message; 'Crico, please report.' He waited a short moment before receiving a reply.

'Preparing for the Rapture, my general.'

Sirhan Abbas smiled. The use of the Christian term, 'the rapture,' still amused him. So many people in this world were so easily led. The Parousia, or second coming, was imminent. However, these sheep being led to the slaughter would never suspect that the gates of heaven they dreamt of were actually the portal to the kingdom of Allah. And they would be denied entry.

He typed another question.' What is the status on the Sword of Salazan?'

'Proceeding exactly as planned. Manufacturers awaiting to fulfill our requests. Original timeline still within range.'

'What of the secondary activities?'

'Awaiting your orders, my general.'

Multiple attacks on multiple fronts always had the effect of confounding an opponent. He would use that logic and strike at many targets at once, sending the message that more of the same would follow. The enemy would drop their flanks in preparation for the next wave. That is when he would swing the mighty blade of the most formidable weapon the earth had ever seen. The blood would flow like rivers. Mankind would tremble and drop to its knees—world domination in three easy steps.

'Give the signal,' he typed.

He remembered Katherine Karlson and decided her story needed a fitting end. His fingers danced spritely on the keyboard once again. 'I have one more small detail that requires your attention. . .'

ACKNOWLEDGMENTS

Penning the words to a novel is only the first step of a long journey. The input and support received along the way helps shape and redirect the story, and the end product would not be nearly as complete or polished without it. I thank everyone who was part of the reviewing process.

My wife, Johanne, is a constant sounding board, reading draft after draft. Forgive me for bombarding you with ideas before you've had your morning coffee.

The Grand Blanc writers group offered insightful and invaluable feedback all along the way.

My first readers, Margie, Tim, Cindy, Doug, Mark, and Scott, thank you for investing the time to ensure the final product was as glitch free as possible.

And thanks to all of you readers who were willing to sample the wares of an otherwise unknown author. You are why this process is so fulfilling. If I've managed to entertain you for a few hours then it was all worthwhile. Please feel free to use the provided links to contact me and share your thoughts. Until next time, I wish you all the best. . .

Richard

ABOUT THE AUTHOR

RICHARD DRUMMER is an emerging author of action and suspense thrillers. He grew up in Rochester, Michigan and now resides in Bonita Springs, Florida with his wife and first reader, Johanne, as well as his assistant, Caticus Maximus.

ENEMY WITHIN THE GATES is Richard's second book to be published, and he is currently working on the next: THE SECOND LIFE OF ARTHUR BLADE.

Made in the USA
Middletown, DE
31 May 2021